BORN

OF

SHADOW

AN EMPIRE OF BLADES NOVEL

BOOK ONE

NICOLE CONWAY

BROADFEATHER
BOOKS

For anyone seeing the parallels: just know, *my* Violet (and dragonrider world) was created in 2013-2025.

Cover illustration by Lulybot

Interior illustration by Covered by Nicole

For Sam & Ashley

PANTHEON of REATIA

FOREGODS
Itanus
Enais
Milontos
Vescor*

OLD GODS
Giaus
Astaris
Avgior*

LESSER GODS
Paligno
Clysiros
Undae
Proleus

GODLINGS
Ishaleon
Adiana
Tykeron
Iksoli

* deceased or banished

ONE

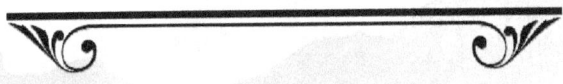

I didn't mean to kill him.

I just wanted to get away. Hide. Be somewhere safe.

But there was no escaping. Not then ... or now.

Crouched in a tiny metal cage, I licked my dry, swollen lips and stared out into the gloom. Through the salt-rusted, criss-crossed iron bars, I could only see the dark hallway that led out through the open cell block of Sol'Karr's city jail. Finest and most secure in all the kingdom.

Which is why I hadn't made it very far down that hall after I'd slipped out of my first cell.

Now, things were looking significantly more complicated. Fantastic.

I couldn't hear any noise from the city far above—no shouts of street merchants, screeching seagulls, or chatter of sailors and dockhands. No armored guards with swords and iron-tipped flails clunking around with a racket like wobbly stacks of pots and pans.

This far underground, there was only darkness and silence.

It should have comforted me. I should have felt right at home.

I didn't.

There were no windows to let in daylight. No food or water. The reek of stagnant ocean water hung thick in the air, burning my eyes and throat with every breath. The wavering light of torches danced in rusting sconces along the rough stone walls.

All of the cells lining the right side of the room were empty. The city guards, with all their fine armor and polished weapons, would never make the mistake of putting me back in one of those again. Not after last time.

Beyond the cells, somewhere out of sight, a door lock clunked. Rusted hinges groaned. Then came heavy footsteps, thumping over the stone. Two people. Big. Most likely men.

More guards?

Or the executioner?

I swallowed, my body shuddering as my senses came alive in an instant. My breathing slowed. I drank in the putrid scents of the room, hidden under the briny ocean musk.

Old vomit. Blood. Urine.

The vibrations of those slow, casual strides made the cold floor beneath my bare feet pulse faintly. They were coming this way. My heartbeat kicked fiercely in my chest, so hard it made my eyes water.

I curled back into the farthest reaches of my cage—as far as I could get from the door—and cradled my left arm close against my chest. It still throbbed, no matter how I held it. My hand and fingers tingled whenever I clenched my fist. But I could still move it.

I could still fight.

"You told me to send word if I came across anything else out of the ordinary. Well, this brat certainly fits the bill," the Guard Captain of Sol'Karr rambled, his voice booming down the corridor.

The footsteps grew closer.

Almost here.

Cold sweat prickled on my skin.

"Don't get my hopes up, Evrol," another male voice replied. "Last time it was just a Damarian pickpocket with an extra finger—which didn't serve him any better at his craft, by the way."

"Aye, but this one has *red eyes*," Captain Evrol added, his tone practically humming with pride.

The footsteps paused. "You're certain?"

"See for yourself," the Captain huffed.

The door leading into my cell block gave a shuddering clank, unlocking before it swung inward with a low groan of rusty hinges. Silvery starlight spilled in from the passage beyond, outlining the silhouettes of two men in the doorway.

Captain Evrol, short and stocky, stood beside a lean, broad-shouldered man in a weathered brown overcoat. For a moment, neither of them moved.

I held perfectly still, not even daring to breathe.

"You put her in a dog kennel?" the second man asked, his rugged features creasing with a tense, disapproving frown.

Guard Captain Evrol bristled and stood a little straighter. "You might've done worse if you knew what these creatures are capable of. She slipped from a regular cell the second I turned my back. It took five men to get her back under control. Had to send one to the healer. She nearly bit off two of his fingers."

"I see." The strange man in the coat tilted his head to one side, still staring at me.

My breath caught. His demeanor stayed calm, even as he held a hand out and took something from the Guard Captain.

The man strode forward, approaching my makeshift cell and finally dropping down into a squat before it. Even from a few feet away, I caught a musky, almost animal-like scent wafting off him. Strange. Not unpleasant, though. Earthy, like dark, sun-warmed soil.

"Hello there," he said, his tone oddly soft and warm. Inviting.

No. *NO*.

My body trembled as every nerve drew as taut as bowstrings. Ready to snap. Ready to do whatever it took to survive this, too. Just like before. Just like *always*.

"Not having the best go of it, are you?" He let his elbows rest on his knees. "What's your name, girl?"

I flinched and turned my body away, trying to hide my injured arm against the back of the cage.

Gods, why couldn't I just disappear?

"You the one who broke her arm?" the man in the coat demanded suddenly.

I dared peek back over my shoulder and found him glaring at Captain Evrol.

Evrol crossed his thick, hairy arms over his breastplate, his jaw working from one side to the other. "*I* didn't put a finger on her. Can't say the same for my men. They only did what they had to."

I pressed myself further into the iron bars and tried not to listen. To force my mind to be somewhere, anywhere, else.

It didn't work.

"She probably got that from the blacksmith. My men said he tried fending her off with a pair of smithing tongs. He must've gotten a lucky hit before she gutted him," Evrol said.

My hands curled into shaking fists.

Evrol shook his head and looked down at the toes of his worn leather boots. "Poor fool likely had no idea what he was up against; he just knew he found a Pitathi squatting in his attic, stealing whatever she could get her slimy little hands on."

My jaw clenched, but I fought back the urge to snarl. Wrong—all wrong. *Lies.*

The man turned back to face me, his gaze catching mine before I could turn away. Every muscle seemed to lock up solid, as though that one look had frozen me in an instant.

He gave a calm, easy smile that made his eyes crinkle in the corners.

"There you are," he murmured.

I jerked back again, wanting to turn away. But I couldn't. Something in those light brown eyes still held me captive.

"Does she talk?" The strange man's wide shoulders fell some, his expression softening.

"Not that I've heard." Evrol's beady little eyes glittered with malice. "She screams loud enough, though."

The man shifted to take a knee right in front of my cage. He combed some of his lengthy, dark brown hair away from his face and studied me more closely.

"You're in a bad spot, you know that?" he said. "You understand what they do to murderers here?"

My throat constricted, making it nearly impossible to breathe. Of course, I did.

I'd seen the executioner in the prison yard square, and the bloodied stone block. I had spotted the enormous axe, and the crows waiting eagerly on the eaves for the feast. I'd heard the prison guards casting bets for their prisoners' clothes and wares before that axe ever fell.

But no one threw bets for stolen rags stained with blacksmith's blood.

"What if I could offer you something else? A different path," he continued, holding my gaze with an intensity that made my heartbeat stammer.

What? What did he mean by—?

He pulled something from his pocket and held it out toward me.

My body shuddered with a sudden rush of skittering cold that surged up my spine.

A silver coin rested in his outstretched palm, glittering in the torchlight. Its surface shone as flawlessly as a mirror, save for the marking etched right in the center. A symbol I had seen only a few times before.

A slender crescent moon with a sword through the middle.

The mark of the Zenith's Call.

Even street urchins knew that symbol.

I stared up at him, chest heaving in desperate, frantic breaths. Gods, this man ... Did that mean he was an *assassin?*

"Listen, girl, I won't dance around the truth. I came here because I need an apprentice. My last three failed to pass the tests necessary to become a member of the Order." He rubbed at his stubble-flecked chin. "And quite honestly, I don't know if you can, either."

I barely realized I was moving, turning to face him as he pocketed the coin without ever breaking eye contact.

"Unfortunately, we're both short on time. And the way I see it, you have two choices now. Either you face the consequences for the life you took, or you take me at my word when I say this is your best chance at ever walking free in this kingdom again."

My mouth opened, feeling the weight of each word like the tightening of a noose around my neck. He wanted *me* to join the Zenith's Call? To become his apprentice?

Gods, what did that even mean?

His expression darkened, long features set in a grim frown as he bowed his head and lowered his voice. "Make no mistake, this will not be easy. You ought to know well enough by now that life guarantees nothing but pain, struggle, and death for us all. The Order is no different."

He pulled something else from his pocket, holding it up so I could see a small brass key. The one that would unlock my cage. That must have been what the Guard Captain had given to him earlier.

"The Order will try to break you, body and spirit. They push all new prospects beyond their limits in ways you cannot even fathom. It will be worse for you because of what you are," he warned.

He didn't say it. He didn't have to.

Viperi. Pitathi.

"But I can promise you one thing: be honest with me, and I will stand by you. That will be my oath to you. Trust for trust."

"Why?" The word scraped past my cracked, swollen lips before I could stop it.

But I *needed* to know.

The smile that spread over his thin lips never quite reached his eyes. "Some were born to forge chains. Some were born to break them. I'd like to see which one you are."

I hesitated. No. He was lying. He had to be.

But why?

He held the key out right in front of the cage door where I could easily slip my fingers through to take it.

Everything else in the room seemed to slip away as I watched the torchlight dance and gleam off the surface of that single brass key. The only solution. The final answer.

My very last chance.

My hand shook as I reached for it. I could do this. I could play along until we were out in the open. Then I would escape.

He drew it back slightly. "Is that a yes?"

I hesitated, daring to meet his gaze once more. I nodded slowly.

"Your name?"

I scowled at the key, now just a few inches out of reach.

Trust for trust.

"Violet," I whispered, my voice broken and hoarse.

His eyes narrowed, chin tilting up a little as his mouth pressed into a dissatisfied line.

Fine. Violet was not a Viperi name. But some things had to be left behind.

I met his stare, trying to match that firmness and determination as I repeated, "My name *is* Violet."

"I'm Roxus." He grinned again, wider this time, and moved the key a little closer.

Still too far away to reach.

"How old are you, Violet?"

I licked my lips. Desperation shuddered in my chest. My vision tunneled, focused squarely on that key. "I don't know."

Not a lie.

Roxus didn't seem shocked by that. "Not even a guess?"

"Older than nine." That was the last time it had mattered to anyone.

He moved the key a little closer.

Just enough.

I swiped it and scooted to the front of the kennel.

Keeping a careful watch out of the corner of my eye, I scrambled to unlock the door. My trembling hands were clumsy and desperate. My injured arm throbbed with fresh agony. But I did it.

The door gave a rusty screech as it swung open. Then there was nothing between Roxus and me except his outstretched hand, offering to help me out.

I eyed it, noting how large and callused his palms were. Big enough to crush my neck if he wanted.

Hmmm. Nope. No touching.

I stood without taking it, and my face flushed hot. Keeping my body angled away and my throbbing arm clutched at my chest, I glanced all around the row of cells.

Curse it—only that one doorway with the Guard Captain still blocking it.

"You want a collar for her? Gods know she'll bolt the second you get outside." Evrol stood as tense as a hound pointing a fox, his eyes never leaving me.

I leaned sideways around Roxus just enough that I could shoot that hairy old man a glare with my teeth bared. He would not put another shackle on me, not if he wanted to keep all his fingers.

Evrol had one hand already on the hilt of his sword. "Might want a muzzle, too. Look at those teeth—fangs like a cursed snake! Are you sure about this?"

Roxus stood with a grunt and leaned back, giving his back a stretch until it popped a few times. "I'm touched by your concern, but that won't be necessary."

On his feet now, I had to look way up to meet his gaze. Tall and lean, something about how that shabby old coat draped over his wide shoulders reminded me of a scarecrow. He wasn't even carrying a blade that I could see.

What sort of assassin didn't carry a weapon?

Evrol's glare practically scorched the back of my head as he followed us out of the prison's sublevels. Waiting for me to make a wrong move. Wanting it so that he had a good excuse to ram that sword through my back, probably.

I wasn't *that* stupid.

We stopped at an office where Evrol must have kept a stockpile of gear for his men. He grumbled bitterly when Roxus insisted on having a cloak for me to wrap up in. I guess my clothes, or what was left of them, weren't fit for a walk through the open streets.

I scowled, wrinkling my nose when Evrol shoved a threadbare black cloak in my direction. From a few paces away, I could see the blood heat rising in his head. Anger was always the easiest to read, and he was white-hot.

But I stayed silent. Just a bit longer, and then none of this would matter anyway.

Then we shuffled onward, following behind Evrol as he led us toward the prison's back exit. My blood went cold in my veins as we crossed the empty courtyard. There, bathed in the last bit of starlight, the executioner's block stood in the center of the square. Layers of old blood had stained the ground around it darker than the rest.

Just the sight of it made my heart feel small and cold, as though it had been crushed inside an icy fist.

I looked away, speeding up to keep pace right behind Roxus. At least he seemed set on keeping me alive. Better to stick close to him.

For now, anyway.

Evrol led us to the back of the prison complex, which wasn't all that large since most of it was underground. He stopped before a narrow door forged of reinforced iron and locked with a huge bolting mechanism connected to a single padlock.

He muttered in Damarian as he produced a ring of keys from his belt and opened it. I made sure to note which key he chose to slip into that lock. A black one with three teeth.

I'd remember that.

The door groaned mournfully, swinging ajar. The open streets of Rienka stretched out before me, barely lit by the first touch of soft purple twilight. Roxus and Evrol exchanged hushed words and a handful of gold coins before the Guard Captain finally waved us off.

My heartbeat thrashed like a fish in a net, wild and reckless. Desperate for the freedom that was only inches away.

Roxus swaggered past me, his hands now deep in his pockets and his face tilted into the cool morning breeze. It rustled in his hair, blowing shaggy locks over his long nose, brow, and stubbled jaw.

I staggered after him a few steps. But as soon as my feet struck the cobblestone road outside the prison's small back door, my mind went completely silent. My chest seized on my first breath of the cool, salty night wind. Buzzing, frantic energy welled up inside me like a crashing wave as I stared up at the canopy of a million tiny burning points of heat-light.

I should run. I could do it.

I could bolt into the night and never look back.

This guy—Roxus—would never catch me. Not when thousands of other urchins were running the tangled streets of every island in Rienka. I'd be gone like a phantom in a second.

But staring at Roxus's tall, lanky figure standing before me, I couldn't get my feet to move. My thoughts whirled like sand in a dust devil. All I could do was watch the lengths of that long, ragged brown coat blow around his legs.

This man claimed to be offering me something else. Something better than a few more nights of freedom until I got caught again. *A different path.*

One that didn't end at that executioner's block.

It could still be a trap. People didn't help Viperi, no matter how kind they seemed. There was always a razor edge hidden somewhere under that veneer.

I just hadn't found him yet.

Roxus turned back, glancing down at me. One of his dark eyebrows arched upward, as though silently asking if I'd made up my mind yet.

I didn't move.

My eyes welled in the stingy, salty breeze. My stomach ached. My arm throbbed.

He might be lying about absolutely everything. There were plenty of things far worse than death. Worse starving in the city streets, or having my neck under the end of an axe.

This might be a mistake. It could be my doom.

But just this once, I wanted to hope.

I wanted to be wrong about him. I wanted to be something more—even if that meant making my worst mistake yet: trusting an assassin to keep his word.

Trust for trust.

He was obviously giving me his. That didn't mean I owed him mine, though. I didn't owe him anything. I just couldn't stop thinking of the alternative.

Getting caught again. Surrounded by big men in armor, swinging swords and snapping whips and flails. More chains. More bars.

Execution.

I drew in another long, slow breath of the briny night air, dipping my head and letting all the whispers in my mind go quiet. Warnings. Fears.

Things that had always kept me alive.

I pulled the cloak tighter around me and raked some of my tangled hair behind my ears before pulling the hood down low. Then I took a step after him.

And another.

I followed Roxus into the fading starlight, my sweaty hands shaking in fists at my sides. Onward into the dawn, knowing this might be my first real chance to be something more.

Or a march straight to my doom.

Two

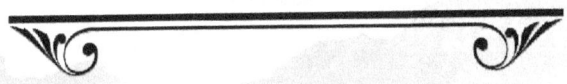

This was a huge mistake.

I didn't belong here. I had never even dared to get close to a place like this before.

But here I was—a filthy, murdering Viperi urchin—standing on the doorstep of an assassin's house.

No, wait, not just a house. It was so much more than that.

It wasn't a shack on the beach. Not an abandoned ship left to rot in the harbor. Not even a grimy apartment above one of the grungy taverns down by the docks, which was honestly what I'd been expecting from an assassin of the Zenith's Call.

I mean, the man looked like he had never even bothered to wash that coat.

But, no. Roxus ambled casually up to the front door of a nice, proper-looking place at the end of a narrow street in the Nassiterna Terrace district.

A *real* home.

Spirits divine, who was this guy? And what did he really want with me?

I stopped, keeping well back while he opened the front door, stamped the mud off his boots, and made his way inside.

The soft fragrance of incense drifted out through the open door. Cedar, jasmine, and something else. Something tinged with cinnamon and clove.

Food.

The aroma of freshly baked bread hit me like a punch to the jaw. My stomach clenched hard, making my vision swim. My mouth watered and my knees shook, ready to buckle beneath me at any second.

"Come on, then. We've got to get you cleaned up so the healer can have a look at that arm." Roxus turned, casting me another cryptic smile. He tipped his head in a gesture for me to come inside.

I pursed my lips, my stomach still writhing around like I'd swallowed a live eel.

Roxus didn't wait around. He shrugged out of his coat and hung it by the door, then trudged off into the house without looking back.

I shivered, the inviting smells of the house wrapping around my neck like a chokehold, dragging me slowly inward. My heart pounded so fast it made my head go foggy.

I couldn't resist.

My bare feet touched the cool, worn wooden floors inside, feeling them give and creak faintly. The sound made me cringe as I shuttled forward, stopping only to take off my cloak and hang it right next to his coat.

My injured arm throbbed in protest as I wandered farther in, and I set my jaw to keep from trembling as the pain flared with every tiny movement. Now wasn't the time to show weakness.

Stopping just inside the entryway hall, I stared around the dimly lit space.

Directly ahead, the wide-open sitting room was arranged with low furniture and velvet floor cushions. Dark wood shelves spanned many of the walls to the ceiling, crammed full of books and artifacts. Wool rugs woven in intense, deep colors stretched across the floors, depicting scenes of animals and beautiful landscapes.

A fire pit in the center of the main room still smoldered, the deep red coals glowing like brilliant red eggs in a nest of white ash. That, and candles flickering in colorful glass lamps all around the room, made for a cozy dimness and heavy shadows.

Beautiful. Peaceful. But somehow ... lonely.

Sad, even.

"At this hour? Merciful goddess, man!" An older woman's voice huffed in dismay, coming closer down a hallway off to the right.

Footsteps approached, and I whirled around. My pulse boomed in my ears. I drew back, edging toward the still-open door, cradling my wounded arm against my chest.

I wasn't supposed to be here.

Run. I had to—

Roxus strode into the room with that lazy grin playing on his lips. He ambled alongside a stoutly built human woman with a long mane of golden brown hair that fell in gentle waves down her back, and deeply tanned skin dusted in fine freckles. She fussed, muttering under her breath as she tied an apron over what looked a lot like her nightgown.

Had he pulled her straight out of bed?

The woman froze as soon as she spotted me, eyes wide and expression slack in shock.

Or maybe that was just horror.

Probably both.

"Sweet Fates," the woman gasped. "She's so tiny. Is there even a speck of a girl under all that dirt?"

Heat crept up my neck to my cheeks. My shoulders drew up, and I quickly looked away.

"More than a speck, I'd wager. She gave five city guards

quite a tussle tonight. Even Evrol was worried for my safety."
Roxus smirked proudly, and I could have sworn there was
fondness in his eyes.

The woman shot him a hard look. "They had her locked
up in the prison? A *child?*"

Roxus shrugged. "A *Viperi* child. In truth, she's lucky they
didn't just butcher her on the spot. Just do what you can with
her, and I'll fetch the healer."

"You're bothering Leruna? She won't answer—not at this
hour," the woman warned. "Not if she has any sense."

"Don't underestimate the depth of my charm." Roxus
flapped a hand at her dismissively.

Her eyes narrowed dangerously. "You best be reserved
with all that *charm* around the young priestesses."

Roxus just laughed and went to grab his coat again, but his
hand halted. His gaze lingered on where my cloak hung right
next to his, and the lines around his eyes and mouth seemed to
deepen. Was that disapproval?

I couldn't tell.

"Violet, this is my housekeeper. Her name is Delthene," he
added without ever looking my way. "Do as she says. I'll be
back shortly."

I nodded.

He left in a flurry, shutting that heavy front door behind
him and sealing me inside his place. His home.

Or was it a new cage?

Delthene puffed an exasperated breath and shook her
head, her warm golden eyes looking me over from head to toe
like a sculptor eyeing a slab of untouched stone, silently
deciding whether or not it had any real potential.

I doubted it.

"This way, dear," she said. "It seems we've got a lot of
work to do."

I followed from a cautious distance as Delthene led the

way deeper into the house. Down a narrow hall and up a wide, dark wood staircase, she finally stopped on the second floor. She opened a door that led into a spacious washroom and began rushing around inside, lighting lamps and drawing hot water into a large white marble tub.

As the tub slowly filled, she poured in fragrant bath oils and salts mixed with dried herbs. I stood in the doorway, watching as she tied all her slightly graying curls up into a ponytail and began digging through drawers and cabinets for fresh towels.

The air quickly filled with fragrant steam, and Delthene laid out an array of brushes, combs, and sponges next to a chair at the tub's edge. She sat down there, rolling up her sleeves and testing the water with her hand. My heart gave a twist of dread when she finally beckoned me over.

No turning back now, though.

I couldn't bring myself to even look her way as I skulked to the edge of the tub and slid off my tattered, patched-together clothes. What little of me lay underneath those rancid rags was emaciated, ghostly pale, mottled in bruises, and flecked in a thousand scars. Not beautiful at all.

Sickly, more like it.

I didn't need a mirror to know how the bones of my hips and ribs showed, pressing far too tight against my skin, like thin, damp parchment. Or that my hair was so tangled it had clumped and matted like an animal's. I might as well have been one, I guess.

Roxus's new pet apprentice.

"Goddess, girl. No wonder he sent for the healer," Delthene whispered. Her expression had gone dim with pity as she helped me into the tub, holding on to my good arm to steady me.

I hissed and cringed as the hot water hit my skin. Every sore place, old wound, and gnarled scar screamed in protest as

I slowly sank in and sat with the water right at my neck. Tears filled my eyes.

But I still didn't look at Delthene—not even when she began working combs and brushes through my hair.

I sat shoulder-deep in the water, my head resting back on a rolled-up towel, while she worked for hours. After what felt like an eternity of her picking, combing, and trimming, she finally sank back into her chair. "I'm sorry, darling. There's just too much matting. I'll have to cut it."

I fidgeted with one of the long locks she had managed to free. It floated in the water, so pale it looked silvery white like cornsilk. Just like my mother's.

"Okay," I agreed.

Delthene scrubbed all the places I couldn't reach with a soft sponge, then helped me out of the tub. She wrapped me in a clean towel and sat me down in her chair in front of a dressing mirror. Her hands worked quickly, snipping and cutting away the knotted clumps of my hair inch by inch. They fell in a filthy ring all around my chair.

I watched each lock tumble down in silence, my heart sitting like a cold stone deep in my chest, and wondering what —if anything—would be left when she finished. Would I be bald? Would people mistake me for a boy?

I should have stolen a brush. Or tried learning to braid. Or ...

"There we are." She gently grasped the sides of my head and lifted it so my gaze fell on the mirror before me. "Much better, isn't it?"

I didn't know. I didn't even recognize the girl in the reflection.

She was young, although not quite a woman yet. Her ruby-red eyes were wide and haunted, and her skin was ashen and sunken at her porcelain-pale cheeks. Her frosty-colored hair was bobbed off at her jawline, and her bottom lip was split and swollen. Her collarbones stuck out too far, and her thin neck was mottled in dark purple bruises in the shapes of fingers.

City guards' fingers.

My stomach turned and my throat burned. I looked down into my lap again.

Thankfully, Delthene didn't seem to notice my reaction. She rushed out of the room long enough to search for something I could wear, muttering under her breath about how Roxus could do this to her without a word of warning or chance to prepare.

I waited, tugging at the ends of my now much shorter hair. It was strange to feel the tickle of every breeze on my neck. But I didn't look boyish. If anything, I looked even more childlike.

Eyeing the array of brushes still sitting out, I dared to run my fingertips over the ornate silver and ivory handle of a comb. I'd never seen anything so beautiful. It had to be worth a fortune.

What was I doing here, in this place, touching these fine things? Being treated like something ... valuable?

I bit down hard, fighting the way my mouth wanted to screw up and quiver.

I sat in the chair until Delthene returned with a thin, white cotton chemise several sizes too big. It nearly dragged the floor and hung off my shoulders as I followed her out of the washroom and back downstairs.

"Now, Miss Violet, you mustn't be shy with me," Delthene said as she walked ahead of me. "I look after this house and everyone in it. Roxus apparently has no idea what it means to keep a girl around, so if there's something you need, you be sure to ask me. I'll see to it that we have a proper wardrobe prepared for you as soon as possible."

"Shoes?" I dared to ask. I couldn't remember the last time I'd worn them.

She smiled, her cheeks dimpling beautifully. "Of course. You'll need a variety for different occasions."

I pressed my lips together tightly, suppressing a smile.

By the time we returned downstairs, Roxus was already sitting at the low table in the main downstairs room. A beautiful young elven woman sat across from him, speaking in a hushed voice. She wore the flowing, sky-blue robes of a healer and had her long, dark hair braided down to the base of her back so that her pointed ears peeked out.

I tensed, bringing my injured arm in closer to my side.

She was a Rienkan elf.

Our people—the Rienkan elves and the Viperi—had despised one another practically since the dawn of time. Didn't Roxus know that?

Well, to be fair, most other races felt that way about Viperi. We'd never win a popularity contest among the many peoples of the Southern Kingdoms.

But should I even trust her to touch me at all?

The elven healer stood when she spotted me, her turquoise eyes glittering in the lamplight. She smiled and bowed to us, then stepped closer to peer down at me curiously. Her gaze halted on my arm, brow knitting ever so slightly.

"Hello, Violet. My name is Leruna. I serve as a healer at the Temple of Undae. Roxus has asked me to take a look at you, if that's all right."

It wasn't.

I didn't answer and just stared past her to Roxus, who had turned all his attention to a small stack of papers on the table before him. He was scribbling away with a quill, not paying attention to me or anyone else in the room.

Great. So he really expected me to just go along with everything?

No.

I squared my shoulders and finally met Leruna's gaze. No cowering. No weakness. "I'm fine."

Her eyebrows drew up, her whole demeanor seeming to soften slightly. "You're probably right, but let's just be sure. Your arm is causing you quite a lot of pain, isn't it? Roxus is concerned it might be broken, and it would give him some peace of mind just to check before he takes you to meet the other agents he works with."

I narrowed my eyes.

Oh, she was clever. Her tone was so soft and sweet, she probably didn't think I noticed that critical way those turquoise eyes were soaking in every detail of my body, evaluating everything about me.

But she was right.

My arm trembled in agony, and what I'd hoped was just dirt hadn't scrubbed off in the tub. Deep bruising now bloomed across my forearm, and it was getting more swollen by the hour. I couldn't go on like this.

One glance past her and I found Roxus staring straight at me, quill in hand, and a forbidding frown on his lips.

I didn't have a choice.

If I started refusing this stuff, he could just march me straight back to that prison cell, or kick me right out onto his doorstep. I had to play this game by *his* rules.

Curse it all.

I bobbed my head and stood, teeth clenched and heart hammering as Delthene chased Roxus out of the room so Leruna could examine me.

After shrugging out of that too-big chemise, I stood in numb silence while the elven healer looked me over. She inspected my scalp, my eyes, ears, teeth, and joints. She asked me a thousand questions about every embarrassing detail you could imagine–whether I had ever broken any bones, had trouble going to the bathroom, or had ever had a cycle.

Delthene looked on, her brow furrowed as though she were measuring every answer I gave.

Embarrassing.

"It's almost certainly broken." Leruna handled my arm carefully, applying pressure and testing the feel of the bone through my skin.

I squirmed, my face twitching as pain flared up from my arm all the way to my neck. It made my vision swim until she finally let my arm go.

"Fortunately, the bone still seems to be in alignment," she said. "Given your physical state, your body might not heal as quickly as it should. I'll be prescribing a strong healing remedy, but you'll need to allow it to heal for at least three weeks."

My shoulders dropped. *Three weeks?* Gods, would Roxus even allow me to stay here that long? Surely not.

"I'll put together a list of tonics to help ease the discomfort while her body adjusts to having more food," she decided and nodded to Delthene. "You'll have to be careful with her eating for a while, too. Bland foods only in small amounts to start. That means rice, oat porridge, or broth. She could probably handle some bread, as well."

I frowned, unable to hide my disappointment as I pulled the chemise back up onto my bony shoulders. So much for all those delicious smells.

Leruna wasted no time fitting me to a wooden splint from my elbow to my wrist. She wrapped it tightly in lengths of gauze and a clean strip of satin so my arm was fixed and protected. Too bad it didn't hurt any less.

I choked and gagged on a tablespoon of a thick, foul green paste she claimed would help to jumpstart my healing process. She allowed me to wash it down with a waterskin filled with a strong ginger tea she said I could keep and drink as needed—just in case my stomach gave me issues.

"Other than the arm, she's in fairly good shape. I can't see any more lingering injuries that would be any reason for worry," Leruna continued as she began packing up her medical wares. "The malnutrition is the biggest concern, and that will just take some time to remedy."

"How old is she?" Roxus's deep voice filled the room, making us all turn.

He stepped into the doorway, his arms crossed and his expression tight and grim.

Concerned, even.

My insides fluttered, making every muscle tense up like I was about to leap from somewhere too high.

Leruna had begun scribbling notes on a piece of parchment. Writing out that list of potions, I guess. "It's difficult to say when she's been emaciated for so long, but I would guess around fourteen. Plenty old enough for your trials, if that's what you're worried about."

"But she's so tiny," Delthene protested, her brow crinkling in concern.

Leruna didn't look up from her work. "*Petite* is a kinder word, but yes. Viperi are known to be more slight in build. And since she's spent most of her life living on scraps, it's likely her growth was stunted, as well."

I swallowed back a growl. The way she said it—with such arrogant assurance—made that wretched fire kindle in my gut.

The urge to crush, to intimidate, to dominate.

I'd show her how *stunted* I was ...

"However, she is the first living Viperi I've examined, so these are only my educated guesses," Leruna added. "We know very little about them beyond myths and rumors, and to my knowledge, there's never been a Viperi child raised outside of their subterranean cities. It's possible changes to her diet and environment might have other effects on her growth. Time will tell."

"Is it true they can see in the dark?" Delthene's tone was a hushed, awed whisper, as though she were almost afraid to ask.

I frowned harder. Why were they talking about me like I wasn't here? Or like I couldn't understand what they were saying?

"No. We can see heat, if we choose," I snapped. "There's a difference."

Now everyone was staring at me.

Fantastic.

I turned away, but I could still hear the grin in Roxus's voice. "A valuable skill for an aspiring prospect to the Zenith's Call."

My mouth twisted to one side, but I didn't reply. My insides clenched, trying to wrap around that word and make sense of it.

Valuable.

"Let me know if there's any issues. And remember to take it easy on the food. I mean it. You don't want her to start throwing up because you overdid it too soon. Her body can't handle rich foods yet," Leruna warned.

She folded her list of potions and handed it to Delthene, then flicked Roxus a heated look—a silent warning.

Then she turned to me with another one of those gentle, all-seeing smiles that made her turquoise eyes sparkle in the lamplight. "Best of luck to you, Violet."

I watched her, unable to muster up a reply. Every move she made, every step and turn, was effortlessly graceful. She flowed through the rooms and out the front door like a cool evening breeze.

And the house immediately felt emptier somehow.

Delthene wasted no time herding me into the kitchen. She offered me a small bowl of rice and a cup of pork broth. It wasn't much, but the smell made me queasy and I gripped my spoon so hard my knuckles turned white.

I tried to eat slowly. But the instant that warm broth touched my tongue, I couldn't help it. I downed it all in one gulp and stared mournfully at the bottom of the empty mug. Gods, I would have given anything for more. Delthene probably would have given it to me.

I didn't want to spend the night puking my guts up, though. I had seen that happen before, whenever another urchin managed to score a decent meal—usually from an empathetic tavern cook.

Begging for scraps and leftovers had never worked well for me, though. People didn't feel that kind of sympathy for Viperi. Not in my experience, anyway.

Roxus was nowhere to be found when we emerged from the kitchen. The quill and papers on the low table were gone, and most of the lamps were doused. There was still no sign of him as Delthene led me up the stairs again.

Had he already gone to bed? Or just left the house? He seemed to come and go like the wind—unpredictable and wholly unchecked.

On the third floor, Delthene opened a door at the end of the hall and stood aside, a strange, almost sad smile on her lips as she motioned for me to go in.

I only made a few steps into the room before my feet dragged to a halt.

My eyes roamed the spacious bedroom, lingering on the big canopy bed, claw-footed armoire, and dressing table next to a framed floor mirror. The broad screen doors on the far wall opened to a balcony, letting in the soft rumble and roar of the ocean and the salty wind.

"I know it's a new place, so things are still going to feel a bit strange, but try to get some rest," Delthene said as she turned back the blankets and helped me into bed.

Strange?

No. More like utterly foreign. Even in my homeland,

living among my kin, I'd never had a room like this. Not to myself.

Delthene helped put a small pillow under my bandaged arm before she went around putting out the oil lamps hanging around the room. "Now then, see that you stay put unless it's to use the toilet, hmm? Roxus doesn't want you out roaming —not when you're on the mend. Understood?"

I nodded.

Delthene gave me one last, almost worried smile before she doused the last lamp and wished me goodnight.

And I was alone in that beautiful space.

The mattress was so soft it practically devoured me, and I ran my fingers along the cool silk sheets. Long drapes of light, sheer fabric swayed gently in the wind that ebbed in from the balcony. The sterling moonlight cast faint shadows along the floor.

It was so quiet. So peaceful. Clean. Still.

And utterly wrong.

My toes curled up tightly. I shivered.

It would end badly. It always did.

I shut my eyes tightly, drawing myself down deeper into all that soft, downy coziness like a rat nestling into a hay loft.

A foolish, naïve little rat who didn't belong here at all.

I just had to bide my time. I had to be prepared. To always be the one who swung last, no matter what.

If I had to, I could still run. I could flee back to the bitter shadows of the city's underbelly where all the other monsters were still waiting for me to return.

THREE

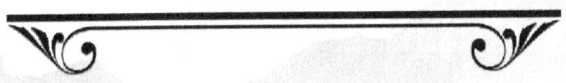

"*YOU DARE DEFY THE BROOD FATHER?*"

My whole body shuddered with a pang of terror as a voice like thunder cracked through the darkness. It ripped through me, piercing my chest and immediately snatching the breath from my lungs.

Run. Oh, gods, I had to run.

My heart pounded. I pumped my legs faster than they'd ever gone, pouring every ounce of strength into each step. I had to go faster. Faster—but careful.

Before me, the twisting tunnel seemed to stretch on forever, turning and veering, winding up staircases and along corridors.

My lungs ached as my mind whirled with confused horror. I-I didn't know where I was. None of this was right.

Where was she?

I whipped around a sharp corner and slammed into a strong arm. It squeezed around me, dragging me back into the shadows and holding me firmly.

Soft breaths panted against my ear and the faintest hint of perfume tickled at my nose.

Mother.

Footsteps ran past us. Shouts echoed down the corridors, seeming to come from every direction at once. I shut my eyes tightly, fighting to control my frantic breaths. Silent. I had to be silent. If they found us ...

"Visha," she whispered into my ear. "Ist cursuindui. Noqum cursu prohi."

My throat constricted, squeezing around every tiny, hitching breath as tears filled my eyes. I gripped her arm as tightly as I could.

"You must run. Never stop running."

But, gods, I was so tired. I couldn't do this. Not for much longer.

My legs throbbed. My feet hummed with a heavy numbness. Her heartbeat thrummed against my back, so real and alive.

"GO!"

My eyes flew open. The arm around me vanished, exploding into black mist.

Gone—she was gone.

I couldn't hold back a frantic scream.

CRAAACK!

The stone flinched and split beneath my feet, crumbling away into an endless dark void.

The voices grew louder, shouting curses and spewing orders to kill on sight. The scrape of blades leaving their sheaths mingled with the low whine of bowstrings pulling taut. The acrid smell of poisonous smoke filled the air.

I stumbled, pitching and screaming as I plummeted backward into that yawning void.

It swallowed me over, stifling my cries and sucking me down into frigid chaos. I clawed at the empty air. Something —I needed anything to grab onto!

But there was nothing.

No one.

Just the dark that filled the crushing, reckless fall.

* * *

My whole body flinched as my eyes flew open. I bit back a yell, drawing into a tight ball with my knees and arms in close. Every part of me trembled, drenched in cold sweat, as I struggled to breathe.

It wasn't real. None of it. Just a dream. A nightmare.

Again.

I stared around in a daze, trying to make sense of where I was. The wooden floor was warm beneath me, and I was wrapped up in a silken bedsheet. I was underneath something. Not a filthy alley or a blacksmith's cluttered attic. A bed?

A very large bed.

The memories came flooding back, dousing all the crackling fires in my mind. Roxus, the prison, cutting my hair, the healer ... I'd crawled under the bed because I couldn't stand to sleep on it. It was far *too* soft, and I didn't like feeling so exposed.

You didn't survive as an urchin in Rienka by daring to snooze where anyone might find you. Not for long, anyway.

I let out a long, shaking breath, willing my body to relax.

Calm. I had to stay calm. Push it down. Make the whispers shut up.

I was safe here.

Right?

Gods, I still didn't know. I wanted to believe that Roxus had good intentions. But I didn't know him. I didn't know any of these people.

What I did know was that Roxus had plans for me that involved the Zenith's Call. Just thinking about it still put a cold pang of dread through my gut. I had to prove myself. I had to make sure he never had a reason to turn me back out onto the street.

I'd do whatever it took.

I just needed to know why.

Why had he chosen me? What trials was he going to put me through?

I couldn't stop thinking about it. My mind spun in circles like a miller's wheel, grinding through everything that had happened over and over. None of it made sense. These people were treating me like ... like something other than what I was.

Viperi.

Gods, what was I doing here?

Trust for trust.

I bit down hard, resisting the urge to snarl into the dark at the thought of those words. He'd brought me here and hardly given me any reason why—other than some vague idea of being his apprentice. I needed more than that.

I needed real answers.

Crawling out from under the bed, I held my arm close to my chest as I crept across the room. The door gave a low, creaking groan as I pushed it open and peered out into the hall. My heartbeat throbbed in my throat as I stared out into the gloom. I blinked hard, opening up the secondary lenses in my eyes that allowed me to see the full spectrum of heat.

Nothing. No faint traces of yellow leftover from footprints. No dull glow under any of the doors from fires burning within. No brilliant red spots from the lamps that all hung dark on their gilded chains down the hallway.

No one in sight.

Hmmm.

I moved on the balls of my feet, careful not to make a single sound as I slipped down the hall. With my back to the wall and all my senses on high alert, I roamed the house like a ghost. I peered in each room, finding mostly empty bedrooms.

Delthene's room was closest to the stairs, and she was already sound asleep when I peeked inside. Her whole body glowed red with heat-light I could pick out easily even in the total dark—but something else glowed, too.

A much smaller body lay right next to hers, shining brightly with warmth. I could pick out its short, pointed ears, round body, and big eyes staring right at me like two moons.

A huge cat.

It growled at me faintly, swishing its poofy tail.

I growled back as I slowly shut the door. We could settle that dominance dispute later.

I prowled silently down the stairs, making my way to the second floor and exploring the rooms one by one. Behind a tall wooden door engraved with the figures of trees and mountains, an office stood still and empty, lit by only one of those hanging glass lanterns. Cinders burned brightly in a more northern-styled fireplace with an intricate black stone mantle around it.

The heat-light washed out my vision somewhat with hues of ambient yellow, and I gave another hard blink to close my secondary lenses. All the fine details came into view then, bathed in the gentle light of the flickering flames.

My mouth opened as my gaze roamed the walls covered in oil paintings, framed maps, shelves packed with scrolls, books, and hunks of strange stone. Pieces of sculptures? I edged further in, carried away by the collections of odd weapon fragments, ceremonial masks, and jars of animal teeth, claws, and brilliantly colored feathers. A patchwork museum of everything odd and archaic.

But every inch of it smelled strongly of a strange, earthy musk—Roxus.

The broad wood desk in the middle of the room was stacked high with more books, pieces of parchment, stoppered glass vials, and an empty wine glass with purple stains at the bottom. Used. The bottle beside it was empty, too.

Two long, slightly curved daggers hung over that foreign-styled mantle on a wooden display plaque. Each one had been crafted into the shape of a bird's wing with feather engravings that flowed from the hilt and faded off at the sloping blades. Beautiful. Lethal.

But not the sort of weapon I pictured Roxus using.

Strange ...

I stopped before the window, studying the huge embroidered drapery that covered it. The vividly colored stitching depicted the scene of a historic battle. A beautiful woman with six black-feathered wings held a long silver dagger and hovered over an entangled hoard of armored men, war beasts, and licking flames.

With her face twisted in a look of savagely beautiful anguish, she drove the point of the blade into the breast of a man with flowing white hair. His huge, powerful form stood above the armies, arms splayed, as though trying to shield them from her. A halo of light streamed from his brow, and a pair of leathery, draconic white wings hung limp at his back.

It was a story I knew well. The Viperi told it often.

It was a scene from the War of the Stones. The fall of the god Avgior at the hands of Clysiros, Goddess of Death. Something about seeing it this way, painted in glimmering threads of brilliant color, made my breath catch.

It made me feel impossibly small.

I turned away ... and then I saw the book.

Sitting at the top of the center pile on the desktop, a massive book bound in old, black leather lay open, like he had been thumbing through it recently. The yellowed pages were curled with age at the corners, and the lines of ink were faded and tinted red from where the iron in the ink had rusted long ago.

Hmmm.

The ancient pages crinkled as I ran my fingertips over them, and I frowned as I carefully turned one after another. I couldn't make sense of any of the tiny markings etched into the parchment.

I couldn't read at all, honestly. I might be able to pick out a few letters written in Viperi. But this was some other tongue, one I didn't even recognize. In fact, nothing in the book looked familiar—

—Until I saw the image etched into the center of the very next page.

A drawing of a single red eye surrounded by two arching, opposing swirls seemed to stare back at me from the depths of my memory. My stomach dropped. My heartbeat skipped.

The Eye of the Foul Father. The Dire King Zarexius.

The father of all Viperi.

My lips pulled back as I bared my teeth, tongue tracing my pointed incisors. Teeth like an animal—that's what the common folk here said. I wondered if saying things like that made them feel better about kicking me to the deepest pits of the gutter when I'd first come here. Back when I tried begging for food instead of stealing it.

Somehow, it felt like that eye knew all of that. As though it could see straight through to the darkest depths of my soul. It knew all my secrets. All my fears.

All my vicious, angry urges.

Just like my father had.

Gods, what was this book? Why did it have Viperi symbols in it? And why was Roxus reading it?

My blood rushed like icy sludge in my veins and my hand shook as I seized the cover and hefted it closed. It shut with a heavy *thunk*. Another symbol stared back at me, leafed into the black leather of the cover in chipping, shimmering silver.

The sword and the crescent moon.

The symbol of the Zenith's Call.

The flurry of memories whipped through my mind like flying shards of black glass, cutting and slicing with ruthless chaos. None of them fit together. None of them made sense.

And every cut snatched me right back to that moment.

Back to the first time I saw the sky.

I could still smell the blood in the air. I could hear the echoes of shouts and cries of the switchbeasts. I could feel the whizzing breeze of arrows flying past us and the grip of my mother's hand clinging desperately to mine.

BANG!

The office door whipped open suddenly, smacking off the wall.

I whirled around, my heart already in my throat, as light from the hallway poured in. It outlined the tall silhouette of a man gripping a sword in one hand.

Roxus.

He'd found me.

FOUR

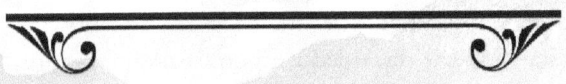

I had already broken a rule.

Not daring to move or even breathe, I watched his every move. Ready to fight or flee–whichever I could manage.

Would I be cast out? Sent back to that cage in the city prison?

Or worse?

The image of that executioner's block, stained with layers of old blood, flashed through my mind. I stiffened. My throat went dry.

Oh, gods, what had I done?

"I *distinctly* remember locking that door." Roxus's tone was ominous and flat, his gaze holding mine for a few seconds that might as well have been an eternity.

I froze, caught like a fawn in an open road. My heart pounded in my throat as every one of my senses seemed to come alive at once, noticing every subtle movement and gesture.

He never looked away, even as he strode into the room with that sword still in his hand. The old floorboards creaked and groaned under his footsteps. A small noise to human ears, but a startling screech to my far more sensitive ones.

Was he about to lunge? Would he swing with the sword? Or the pommel? He was much larger, but I was faster, so I could—

Roxus tossed the sword, sheath and all, onto his desk with a clatter and sighed.

"It's late. You should be asleep. Care to explain?"

I stared at the discarded weapon, sparkling beautifully in the weak light, and then slowly back up at him.

My mind went utterly blank.

Roxus shuffled around me, breathing hard and stinking of sweat, and finally threw himself down into a big wingback chair next to the desk. He grabbed the wine bottle and put it to his lips, only to frown sadly down into it when he turned it up and didn't get a single drop.

"Were you training?" I dared to ask.

He sank back into the chair and finally returned his gaze to me. "I have a sparring room down the hall. You'll be able to use it, as well, once that arm heals."

I cradled it against my chest, biting back a defensive growl.

"Does it hurt?" he asked.

"No."

"Are you feeling sick to your stomach?"

"No."

"Planning on running off into the night with my valuables?"

I bristled. "No."

He crossed his arms, light brown eyes catching the weak firelight like amber glass. "Then I ask again, why aren't you in bed?"

I licked my teeth behind my lips. Every word I wanted to hiss and bite at him tasted so delicious, but I fought to keep myself in check. If he turned me out, I had nowhere else to go.

Except for a prison cell, of course.

"The bed is too soft," I deflected. "It hurts my back."

"You've been sleeping rough for a long while. It'll take some time to adjust," he reasoned.

Fair enough.

"And?" He arched an eyebrow, almost like he knew I was just fishing for excuses.

Ugggh.

I moved away, putting a little more distance between us and hedging for the door before I dared to say another word. A sudden pop from one of the embers in the hearth made me flinch.

Curse it—I was a total wreck.

"I have nightmares sometimes," I muttered, half hoping he wouldn't hear me.

Roxus looked off toward the hearth, his expression softening to something far away with that small, stern little crease right in the middle of his brow.

It was hard to place his age. Maybe somewhere in his mid-thirties. But at that moment, something about him felt timeless and strangely powerful.

My heartbeat skipped at the thought that he might be something far worse than a mere assassin for a secret organization.

Something even a Viperi should fear.

"You're not my prisoner here, Violet. That room is yours, along with everything in it. I realize that is probably a foreign idea for you, but I didn't bring you here to be my slave or pet," he said softly.

"Then why did you bring me here?" I finally asked, unable to keep the accusing bite from my tone. "You said you were going to make me your apprentice—what does that mean?"

His smile was cryptic. It only lasted a fraction of a second before he panned his gaze back to meet mine. "Think of me more as a guide. Someone offering you the one thing you need most and can't get anywhere else."

I drew back a step and narrowed my eyes. "What is that?"

"A purpose."

My heartbeat skipped.

Silence hung between us like a lead curtain, heavy and stifling, until he looked away again. Only then did I feel the tension in my body begin to ease. All my aching muscles relaxed slightly.

"I know what that must sound like coming from someone like me. A stranger. But I've stood where you're standing now. I know what you're capable of." He traced a fingertip around the rim of the empty wine glass, making the crystal sing faintly.

"Because you've been reading about Viperi?" I pressed, tipping my chin toward that book on his desk.

He tilted his head to the side slightly, eyeing the old tome with his mouth pinched to one side. His fingers drummed on the desk in a restless rhythm, as though he were considering his next words more carefully.

"It's difficult to find much written about your people in detail," he said. "But considering how long you've been separated from them, I doubt anything I've found in this book will be of help to me now."

"How do you know how long I've been separated from my kin?" I challenged.

He shrugged. "For starters, you've adopted a Damarian accent—so you must have been away from them long enough to learn to speak the common language here without a Viperi one. That usually takes a few years."

I sank into my heels, working my jaw from one side to the other. Curse it, he was more clever than I'd thought.

"You told me before you knew that you were older than nine. Does that mean you were nine years old when you left the Viperi?" His rugged features turned solemn and his gaze sharpened, as though watching every tiny hint of expression that crossed my face. Seeing me.

Reading me as easily as that book.

I had to look away.

"Yes."

"That's quite young to be on your own," he said. "Did you come immediately here to Rienka?"

I bobbed my head once.

"On your own?"

My eyes stung. My throat was stiff and wrong as I answered, "Yes."

Roxus didn't need to know *everything*.

"Look at me, Violet."

I tensed. My injured arm throbbed. My chin trembled. But I lifted my head and stared straight back into his eyes.

"I know things must have been difficult for you. And surely you realize by now that it won't get any easier for you out there—not unless you find a new path." His chair creaked as he sat forward and rested his elbows on his knees while he considered me. "Within these walls—*my* walls—you are safe. That is my promise to you."

I glared at him, not wanting to believe a single word of it. These people, humans and elves, were so full of trickery and lies. They hated anyone who wasn't exactly like them. They hated what they didn't know or understand. Gods, they even hated each other some of the time.

Most of the time.

So why should I trust him? Why should I trust any of this?

The answer rose from the dark, twisted depths of my heart like a raw black pearl: Because I had no other choice if I wanted to survive.

"What does it mean?" I asked, my voice trembling and

broken. "What does it mean to be a member of the Zenith's Call?"

A smile spread over his lips.

"Everything," he whispered.

A tingling chill climbed my spine, shuddering out to every part of me.

It wasn't a real answer. But I felt the weight of it on my chest like a block of solid ice. It left me shivering and helpless, gaping back at him with no idea what to say.

"Go back to bed, Violet. Rest, eat, let your arm heal, and humor Delthene as much as you can. She's already lectured me thoroughly for not having proper clothes ready for you," Roxus said and nodded toward the doorway behind me. "Enjoy these next few weeks and get your strength back. What comes next is going to demand all of it you can muster."

"Combat?" I guessed, glancing at the sword tossed lazily across his desk.

His smile widened. "At times."

I pursed my lips. "I am already proficient at that."

"I'm sure you are." His tone was serious—no hint of teasing or patronizing anywhere. "I've read that Viperi train their younglings to fight practically from birth. Even at nine years old, I have no doubt you were perfectly lethal when you arrived here."

Once again, he wasn't teasing me. Not that I could tell, anyway.

I snorted, whirling on a heel and starting for the door.

What did he know about my kin? That book might have a few truths scribbled there, but Viperi didn't keep a record of their histories and laws in any book an outsider would be able to read. They guarded their secrets carefully, and outsiders were not tolerated.

Anything in that book was bound to be hearsay at best.

Although he was right about our combat training. I'd chalk that up to dumb luck.

"Goodnight, Violet," Roxus called after me. "I'll see you at breakfast."

Oh, he most certainly would. No way would I be missing a single one of my daily rations. If that was going to be his method of bribery, well, I guess he would win.

For now.

I made my way back up the stairs to the third floor. Peering down the hall, I hesitated when I spotted a big shape crouched right outside my bedroom door. Two big eyes stared back at me, reflecting the moonlight and seeming to glow.

The cat.

I moved closer, stopping right in front of the furry creature and waiting for him to make the first move. He was much bigger up close, with a wide head and long hair of deep, striped orange that stuck out in every direction. His big green eyes tracked my every move as he swished his long tail.

We stared one another down until he yawned widely and gave a scratchy, hoarse mew.

Approval?

I squatted down, and he stood and swaggered toward me on three pudgy-looking legs, flicking that bushy tail. I held still as he rubbed against my knees, making two passes before he went to give my bedroom door the same treatment.

Ah, so that's what he wanted.

"I guess we're both down one limb," I muttered as I opened the door and let him in. "Granted, yours is a little more permanent."

The cat gave another croaking cry and trotted off toward my bed. He was busy kneading one of the pillows, turning in circles like he was searching for the perfect spot.

He purred and settled down with his tail wrapped around him when I climbed into the bed, too. The downy blankets and pillows swallowed me up again, and I flopped around. Tossing and turning, I couldn't figure out how to lie there without my back, hips, or neck hurting.

Gods, how did anyone get used to this?

Sighing, I stared up at the velveteen canopy overhead while Roxus's words ran through my head over and over.

Did he even understand what it would mean for me to have a real purpose? To be able to pick a path for myself that didn't hinge on pure survival? To be a part of something by choice instead of desperation.

I still didn't know.

But immediately, I was swept back across the barren, salt-crusted wastes, golden dunes, and blackened Pitch Graves to a sandstone canyon where my mother's bones probably still lay. Unburied. Unmourned.

Her last words probably still echoed through that arid landscape.

I couldn't give up. Not yet. Not when this might be the only chance I ever got to do something with my life other than fight to survive it.

I had to try the hardest I ever had, do whatever it took, to stay here and prove myself worthy.

I just prayed I could ... before Roxus figured out what I truly was and this all came crashing down. What he knew about the Viperi—what was scribbled in those old books— couldn't be the whole truth.

And when he did find all that out, I had to be ready.

I had to be prepared to run for my life again.

FIVE

Everything had changed.

I still didn't know what game Roxus was really playing, but my life was now unrecognizable. It probably looked blissfully perfect to everyone else. Too bad I wasn't sold on the idea of charity. Roxus had a motive.

Everyone did.

Beneath the veneer of all his so-called compassion, I couldn't shake the suspicion that had taken root and was growing wild through my mind.

He was preparing me for something dangerous—but what?

Somehow, I had a feeling I'd be figuring that out very soon.

Standing on a dressing pedestal in a cramped tailor's shop, I stared into the long mirror before me and saw the proof plain as day.

A doublet of black leather with fine silver embroidery hugged my frame, matching the thick leggings that fit perfectly into my calf-high boots. All were riddled with hidden pockets and places where I would be able to hide weapons and tools.

An outfit made for an assassin.

Er, an *aspiring* one, anyway.

I flexed my freshly healed arm. It had only been out of the cast for a few days now, but renewed strength already bloomed through every muscle as I curled my fingers and twisted my wrist.

Perfect.

My entire body felt that way now—reborn into something much closer to what it should have been. I'd gained a little weight. My skin no longer looked ashen and corpse-like, although I was still frightfully pale. Even some of the scars on my body had begun to fade thanks to Delthene's many lotions and oils.

Now I was ready to hold up my end of this bargain.

Ready to prove myself to the Zenith's Call.

Roxus lurked behind me, his expression intense and lips pressed into a thin, scrutinizing line, as the tailor moved around me. I stood still with my arms out while the older man adjusted the details of my new ensemble.

I couldn't hold back my smirk as I admired the way those shining silver threads made swirling patterns against the dark leather, contouring my hips, waist, and arms. Even the purple silk of the sleeves was so deep it was nearly black. The matching knee-high boots were padded on the bottom and allowed my feet to flex and move freely.

"Well, she'll certainly cause a stir tomorrow, I'll grant you that," the tailor huffed as he stood back, giving me that same examining look from every angle. "I've never made a prospect's set this small."

I snarled a little, showing him one of my pointed incisors. I'd show him small.

Roxus cleared his throat and shot me a glare of warning.

Ugh. Right. No growling at people who were supposedly helping me.

The tailor didn't seem surprised or even put off by it, though. He made a few more adjustments to the lacing on the back of my fitted leather doublet. It wore more like a corset and made it depressingly obvious that I was still lacking in feminine curves. Maybe that would come with more time and good food.

"Can you move in it?" Roxus asked as he rubbed his chin thoughtfully.

I did a few twists at the waist, flexing my arms and shoulders. I bent over to touch my toes. Easy enough.

So I bent the other way, easily dropping into a full back-bend off the pedestal and flipping into a crouch on the floor before him in one fluid motion. The fresh leather squeaked some, but that would stop once I'd broken it in properly.

"Sweet Fates," the tailor marveled.

Roxus just grinned wolfishly. "I told you it had to be maneuverable. Apparently, Viperi are born with a hyper-flexibility far beyond most other races."

I snorted. "You say it like it's an accomplishment."

"It is—take it from someone who nearly threw out his back this morning trying to hang up the washing." The tailor chuckled and hobbled away to start cleaning up his tools.

I watched him grunt and shuffle along, rubbing at the base of his back as he straightened. His salt-and-pepper gray hair was long and pulled back into a ponytail that revealed his slightly pointed ears.

"Now then, I'll set to work on this secondary set. It'll take a bit longer to get the steel plates sewn into the right places, but you'll be glad for the extra protection if you should find yourself in a scrap," the tailor said.

"With her, it's more a matter of *when*, not *if*," Roxus

muttered. He shook his head, slipping me another one of those teasing little smirks as he crossed the shop.

I tried not to stare when he counted out ten shiny gold bars into the tailor's hand. *Bars*—not coins. More money than I'd ever seen in my life.

Holy. Gods. Was he wealthy? Or was that blood money paid from an assassination?

I didn't know, and now didn't seem like a good time to ask.

"Come back in two months, and I'll have the rest done," the old tailor promised.

Roxus agreed, shook on it, and thanked the man before leading the way back outside.

I followed right on his heels and squinted into the glare of the midday sun. The heat and rich smell of brine washed over me, seeming to soak through right down to my soul. Even from a few streets over, I could feel the rumble of the ocean through the leather soles of my new boots, as though the heartbeat of the earth itself were pounding right beneath me.

"Delthene will have a fit if we don't come back with fish." Roxus sighed as he lit his pipe.

"She wants flatfish," I reminded him. "And scallops."

He grunted in approval and gave a few deep puffs on his pipe before he ambled off down the sidewalk. I'd been around him long enough now that it didn't bother me that he never looked back to see if I was following or not. Roxus drifted, wandering like an untethered boat wherever the winds of thought took him. Or that's how it seemed to me, anyway.

I wondered if that's how he had ended up at the prison the day he'd found me. Maybe someday I'd ask.

But not today.

We took the avenue down toward the docks, following the flow of foot traffic along the sidewalks that sloped and moved with the steep countryside.

Gulls floated on the strong winds that gusted in from the massive, crescent-shaped bay before us. Dockhands shouted back and forth as they worked the decks of the massive merchant vessels that groaned and bobbed at their moorings around the bay.

I'd never wandered on these white cobblestone streets without needing to hide in the shadows—or without feeling dread like an iron collar around my neck whenever a patrol of city guards passed.

But standing next to Roxus while he went on puffing at his long wooden pipe, the guards minding the dockside shops didn't even give me a second glance.

Some of them even nodded a greeting to him.

Roxus seemed to be the kind of man who had friends everywhere. Or, at least, people who liked him well enough that they would entertain a favor. Like an old tailor willing to take an alarming amount of gold for special, would-be assassin outfitting.

Was this normal for members of the Zenith's Call to be so well connected? Or was this just Roxus?

I hadn't figured out how to ask that just yet. Somehow, all that shmoozing and forming useful connections didn't seem like it would come as easily for me. Hopefully, that wasn't a requirement.

As we drew closer to the dockside, the crowds thickened and filled the streets with noise. I stuck as close to Roxus as I could manage as he wound a crooked path through all the shoppers, dockhands, and sailors to where the fishermen had stalls selling their day's catch. Of course, Roxus knew one in particular who was willing to give him a bargain.

My gaze wandered while they chatted, spotting a group of people who didn't quite blend in with the rest of the market's crowds.

They weren't a family. None of them looked even

remotely similar, with hair and skin in a variety of different hues. But the group of around fifteen men, women, and children all shuffled along close together, moving like a herd of scared goats down a gangplank into the dockside market.

The only thing they seemed to share—besides a pasty look of terror—was a large T-shaped symbol that had been branded into the sides of their necks.

As soon as they were all off the boat, one of the older men fell to his knees and began sobbing and kissing the ground. A few of the others from their group gathered around him, hauling him back to his feet.

"Tibran slaves," Roxus murmured.

I flinched away on reflex. Good gods, I hadn't realized he'd finished his shopping and was standing so close beside me.

"You mean they're from the Tibran Empire?" My understanding of the world beyond the Southern Kingdoms was limited. I'd never needed to know about the lands and realms beyond the sea—a great wide world scholars called Reatia.

But even I had heard of Tibrus.

It was supposed to be a long way from here, far north over the Elondran Ocean, where white-crowned mountains ruled every horizon.

A world far different than where these poor souls stood now.

"What are they doing in Rienka?" I asked.

"Fleeing, no doubt," he said, his tone somber. "Rumor has it that their emperor, Argonox, has eyes for conquest and an appetite for bloodshed. He's already invaded four neighboring kingdoms: Braskol, Nothlam, Ethalan, and the Forran Plains. Word is he's also fond of taking slaves from the lands he's seized and forcing them to fight under his banner."

Hmm. Well, that explained the desperation on their faces as they stared all around at the sprawling dockside markets, almost like they had no idea where to go or what to do next.

A feeling I remembered all too well.

"What will happen to them?" I whispered, barely feeling the words leave my lips.

Roxus put a strong hand on my shoulder and squeezed it. "They'll find their way. Gods know what they had to do to make it this far. But at least now they're well outside of Argonox's reach. That's something."

He was probably right. Rienka was a busy place with lots of opportunities for those who were willing to work.

Unless you were a Viperi, of course.

Then the rules were completely different.

"Come on." Roxus gave my shoulder a small shake before he let go. "Let's go home."

That word—*home*—hit my heart like the bite of a whip.

It made my toes curl up inside my new boots and my heartbeat skip. I didn't know why. It wasn't something I could wrap my head around, let alone put into words.

I turned to follow him back through the market, watching the way that long brown coat billowed at his boot heels and his shaggy hair blew in the sea breeze. I still didn't know what to think of him.

He was too young to be like a father, and I'd already had one too many of those in my life. I didn't want or need another.

What was left, then? A brother?

No, that didn't feel right, either.

He was just ... Roxus—a man who, for whatever reason, cared about what happened to me. A guardian. Maybe soon, a mentor, if my most recent run of luck held out.

My mind ran in circles like a dog chasing its tail, replaying that image of the Tibran refugee weeping in the streets, as we left the dockside district behind. We walked side-by-side along the quieter, more residential streets that wound up the steep sides of the island's white stone cliffs. Away from the crowds and chaos.

But that piece of it still stuck in my brain like a thorn.

Even through dinner, I couldn't stop hearing that man's cries or seeing the faces of all those people looking around as though they expected to see their former captors suddenly appear and drag them all back to Tibrus.

Cold chills shivered over my skin even as I sat in the bath late that night. I watched steam curl from the water's surface, listening to Delthene hum a merry tune while she came and went through the house. It had all become so normal in such a short amount of time.

But how long would it last?

Would I cry like that if Roxus turned me out into the street? If I failed to prove myself to the Zenith's Call?

I could *not* allow that to happen.

Whatever it took, whatever I had to do, I would make myself worthy.

Tomorrow was my chance. No turning back. No room for hesitation or weakness. I had endured the very worst this cursed world could do. I'd been crushed to nothing, beaten and starved, betrayed, and left for dead.

I would not let it all be for nothing.

I waited until the house grew quiet and everyone else had gone to bed before I slipped from my blankets. I crept to the balcony's screen doors and pushed them open. The sea wind roared in, snagging on my thin nightgown and whipping through my hair.

Far off across the dark ocean, tongues of blue lightning crackled through a big evening storm like veins of light. Each flash illuminated the towering shape of a huge, limestone sculpture of the sea goddess, Undae, that stood in the middle of the bay.

With a fishing spear in one hand, she held a conch shell to

her lips with the other and stared fearlessly into the coming storm.

It took almost a minute for the low boom of the thunder to reach me, but I could feel it all the way down to the marrow of my bones. A raw and ancient power that made every tiny hair on my body prickle.

"Do your worst," I dared in a low growl, baring my teeth to the lashing of the wind.

And I meant it.

The old gods had cursed my kin ages ago, and they had obviously made no exception for me. I had been born in darkness, bred to kill, and doomed to wander as a shadow in a world that knew only hatred for my kind. But I had endured.

Whatever happened next, whatever the Zenith's Call demanded, would not break me, either.

I had to pass their every test ... no matter what it cost me.

SIX

Weeks—I had waited three agonizing weeks for this moment.

Standing next to Roxus, I stared up at the entryway with my lips pursed, trying to decide if this was his idea of a joke or not.

Nope.

Arx Eburna, the fabled stronghold of the mysterious and powerful Zenith's Call assassins for more than six thousand years, was in … a garden.

No, worse than that.

It was in a *temple* garden.

I was expecting a fortress. Or maybe a castle. Something tall, grim, and majestic that oozed with mysterious deadly energy.

Not an open, airy acropolis with manicured courtyards. Nothing about the place seemed daunting at all. The white limestone buildings clung to the side of the steep, volcanic mountainside like barnacles, offering staggering views of the many islands that made up Rienka.

I'd never been all that good at hiding my emotions, but I guess my disappointment was painfully obvious because Roxus patted my head and chuckled.

"Don't make that face. I promise it's a bit more impressive inside."

I seriously doubted that.

I'd spent the last three weeks doing exactly as I was told—within reason. I'd eaten what the healer, Leruna, had insisted upon. I'd taken all those potions and tonics. I'd bathed every day, and even gotten used to putting on refined clothes and shoes. I'd even adjusted to sleeping in the bed, rather than under it.

Now, I felt powerfully capable with every step I took at Roxus's side. I could move in the dark like a soundless wisp of shadow. I could pass any physical test. I could kill without hesitation or remorse.

What other skill could an assassin possibly need?

All *I* needed was a blade in my hand and a target.

Somehow, I doubted I'd find either in a temple, though.

We climbed the steep switchback stairways that led up into the temple grounds, passing broad terraced courtyards where dozens of statues cut from milky white stone stood bathed in the morning sun. Some of the deities I recognized easily enough from stories I'd heard. Others were just more lovely faces that stared at me with empty expressions as we passed. Some had wings. Others held weapons or items.

None of them mattered much to me.

Viperi had no use for the gods, and neither did street urchins.

I wondered if any of the priests and priestesses gawking at me when we passed knew that. Had they never seen a Viperi before? Or maybe just not one trotting into the temple alongside a Zenith's Call assassin?

I couldn't hold back a grin as we climbed the steps to the final terrace where a beautiful, dome-roofed structure stood. It looked something like a grand, enormous gazebo with pillars made of that same white stone holding up the golden, bowl-shaped roof. A cool breeze blew through, teasing at my hair and tickling the back of my neck.

The soft leather soles of my new boots didn't make a single sound as we crossed through the rotunda, and I couldn't pry my eyes off the floor. Every square inch of it was covered in a sprawling mosaic made of thousands of tiny chips of colorful glass, stone, and precious gems.

An image of gods and goddesses, wreathed in clouds of sapphire and mother of pearl, was framed with glittering quartz stars in a dark onyx sky. Every step changed the angle and seemed to change the image, too, making different portions of it sparkle as though it were moving.

"What are we doing here? Isn't it supposed to be a holy place? Why are there assassins meeting in it?" I asked, not even realizing until that instant that I'd stopped walking altogether as I gawked.

I stood in the center of the mosaic, staring all around at the ethereal figures that spiraled out from the center in every direction. Somehow, seeing it this way made me feel so much smaller.

Insignificant.

Roxus stopped and stared down at the mosaic, too.

"Try to be patient," he answered at last, his expression strangely distant. "You have a lot to learn."

I blinked up at him, squinting into the glare of the rising sun. Something about the way it cast hard shadows across his rugged features reminded me of those statues in the terrace courtyards. Like he could suddenly freeze up, turn to stone, and join them.

It sent a shiver of unease through the pit of my stomach. I

couldn't shake the feeling that he knew something was coming —something bad or dangerous.

Then it was gone. That look vanished like smoke in the wind, and he flashed his roguish smirk again.

"We'll be late." He tipped his head back some, gesturing for me to follow.

"For what?" I jogged a little to catch up and fell in step beside him again.

"She likes to meet with each new prospect individually before the trials begin."

"Who is she?"

"You'll see."

I scowled and wrinkled my nose at him. "Do you ever give a straight answer?"

His grin widened. "Depends."

Ugggh.

I let my head loll back as I groaned. Gods, trying to get any sort of hint about what was about to happen was like trying to wring water from a stone. Exhausting and impossible.

We crossed the rotunda and made our way through another courtyard with a large marble fountain in the center. Three large, rectangular buildings stood around the courtyard, mostly hidden by the looming tropical plant life—like the jungle itself was trying to swallow them whole.

The front of each building was open and lined with more large, supporting white pillars that arced together at the top. Each one was covered in intricate engravings and more chips of colorful precious stones. Ornate bronze and silver braziers burned on tall stands between each pillar, filling the air with the sweet fragrance of smoldering incense.

"What is this place?" I asked as we entered the middle structure, passing through those huge arched columns into the cool interior.

"It used to be a building for political meetings when the

Avoran elves lived here long before the War of the Stones," he said. "Now, it serves as a sacred religious site, one of the largest shared temples in the Southern Kingdoms. It's called Nai'Pol —the Temple of Many."

We stopped before an open doorway flanked on each side by crouching winged, masculine figures holding long golden halberds. Their fine, elven features and heavy plate armor had been cut from the same milky stone as the rest of the building, but with so much detail, it looked like they might have been alive. Or simply frozen in time.

Each one was roughly eight feet tall, and I had to wonder if Avoran elves were that tall in real life. Rumor was that they never left what remained of their long-fallen kingdom—a city of glass and cloud that floated on magical breezes far to the north.

A little chill rippled up my spine, and I quickly looked away.

Roxus didn't slow his pace as he led me into a long, cavernous hall flanked with more of those sorts of statues. More doorways led off into near-darkness, filled with the thick aroma of incense and something like old parchment. I caught a glimpse into several rooms that were lined with shelves that spanned from floor to ceiling, each one crammed tight with scrolls.

Was this ... a library?

"Have you ever seen one?" I whispered.

"Seen what?"

"An Avoran elf," I clarified.

His broad shoulders tensed slightly. "Once, a long time ago."

I gaped at him. "Here? In the Southern Kingdoms?"

He nodded.

The questions poured past my lips before I could stop

them. "What was he like? Is it true they live for centuries? Do they really use magic?"

Roxus stopped with his back to me, his stance rigidly straight but his head bowed. Before us, another yawning archway led deeper into this labyrinth of halls and scroll-filled rooms. But this wasn't like the others.

This one had a door—a door of solid black wood. No knob. No handle. Only a symbol engraved right in the center and painted silver.

The sword and crescent moon.

"No more questions," he murmured. "Mouth closed, eyes open."

I swallowed, feeling the pressure between us steadily rise like the heat from a teakettle as he put a hand on the center of the door.

Roxus muttered something, a word in a language I didn't recognize, and his palm began to glow. His jaw clenched hard, brow furrowed as eerie silver-blue light spread from his hand out across the door, igniting every chiseled marking as though it had been painted there with pure starlight.

The door shuddered, and I flinched back, ready to bolt in an instant.

He let out an exhale as the door slowly swung inward, revealing a corridor lined with sconces that glowed with strange blue flames. At the far end, light streamed down from somewhere overhead and the rush of water filled the air.

A cave?

Roxus prowled in, his jawline staying tense as his gaze cooled to cold steel. His movements were sharp and direct as he pushed the door closed behind us. He didn't even glance my way as he forged onward, purpose in every step.

I followed, breathing in the scent of minerals and not daring to speak as I stayed close on his heels. My heart pounded in my throat as we emerged from the entryway hall into a vast, open chamber. Sunlight poured down from a domed ceiling roughly forty feet overhead, revealing a wide staircase that sloped down into a huge spiral.

Or, at least, I thought it was sunlight.

My steps dragged to a halt as I gaped up at the ceiling where an impossibly intricate replication of the night sky was adorned with thousands of glittering pinpricks. Right in the center, a big crescent moon showered the room with a radiant beam of bluish-silver light.

It wasn't real. It couldn't be. We had just come from outside, where it was most definitely early morning.

Was this ... magic?

Roxus didn't stop to explain, and I had to run to catch up with him as he descended the stairs. The farther down we went, the weaker the faux moonlight became until it gave way to a dim, somber darkness. The sounds of the rushing water grew louder, and that mineral smell grew thicker.

The stairs poured like a sloping waterfall into another large room—but this one was lit by two rows of ten-foot-tall bronze braziers. Each one stood before an even larger sculpture of a deity, bathing it in flickering firelight. Sixteen in all, with a matching altar adorned in bowls of sweet incense, candles, and offerings.

In the very center, a huge fountain gurgled, crystalline water spilling over the entwined images of two dragons. One was made of pearly white stone, but the other seemed to be cut straight from black volcanic glass. Their eyes were flawless rubies, and their fangs and horns were jagged crystals.

The Viepol ... two draconic beings that supposedly guarded the boundary between the mortal and the divine realm. I'd heard a few stories about them long ago.

More mosaics covered the floor, telling stories of divine lore. Huge hallways branched off in every direction with a large golden plaque over them depicting a letter or symbol—I couldn't tell which. Labels maybe?

I stiffened at the sight of tall figures dressed from head to foot in black leather armor flanking each hallway entry point. Their keen eyes watched us pass, tracking our every move with their faces half-covered by fine silver shawls. Something about the way they didn't move or even seem to breathe made every primal instinct in my brain scream in alarm.

I shouldn't be here. I didn't belong. I was a threat.

My lip twitched as I fought back a snarl.

Control—I had to stay in control.

"Vindexori," Roxus muttered quietly as he led me toward one of the hallways.

"What?" I whispered back.

He nodded toward the nearest pair of black-armored figures. "There are many specialized jobs among the agents of the Zenith's Call. Vindexori are guardians of the stronghold. Mind yourself around them. They don't suffer fools or troublemakers."

I hesitated, unable to hold back a dubious frown. Something about this felt so ... off.

Why would an order of assassins need security like that? Weren't they all supposed to be deadly warriors? Why would they put their stronghold here, in an ancient temple? Why would they keep honoring all those statues of the gods?

What wasn't Roxus telling me?

I waited until we had gone a few yards down the next hall to finally ask, "The Zenith's Call aren't assassins, are you?"

Roxus stopped so suddenly I nearly crashed into his back.

He turned to face me, that cold, calculating expression focused down on me like the heat of the midday sun. "Who told you that we were assassins?"

I choked and sputtered while I tried to remember. "I-I don't remember. Everyone says it."

"But who actually *knows?*"

I pursed my lips and racked my brain, trying to find some way around the only answer I knew to be true—the thing he must have wanted me to say.

"No one," I admitted at last.

One corner of his mouth quirked up in a smug grin. "Exactly."

"If you're not assassins, what are you, then?" I pressed.

"I guess you'll just have to find out." Roxus tossed me another one of those cryptic smirks and kept on walking.

I crossed my arms and stalked after him, glaring daggers at his back.

Curse him, I hated these little mind games. Part of me hoped he could somehow feel me seething with every step. Or maybe if I glared at him hard enough, his hair might spontaneously catch on fire.

I could dream, right?

Roxus didn't slow his pace until we stopped at last at the far end of a hall before another grand door covered in spiraling silver designs. This one, however, was made of dark wood and had a crystal knob. Two of those Vindexori guards stood on either side of it, not even blinking as Roxus rapped his knuckles on the door.

I stood as close as possible to Roxus's side while we waited, and finally, a voice called out from the other side.

"Come in."

Roxus's hand halted, hesitating for an instant, hovering over the knob.

He took in a slow, deep breath, holding my gaze for a second as he murmured, "The woman in this room decides your fate now, Violet. She commands all the Zenith's Call west of the Pitch Graves. Remember what I said."

I bobbed my head once. *Mouth shut, eyes open.* I could handle that.

Probably.

Roxus squeezed his eyes shut, taking another long breath as though he were mentally preparing himself. Then he opened the door and motioned for me to go in first.

I squared my shoulders, hands clenched in tight fists at my side, and strode into a beautifully ornate office. The rich, sweetly spiced fragrance of incense hung thick in the air. Every inch of it smacked of luxury—from the velvet sofas in the sitting area, to the large oil paintings and silken tapestries on the walls.

At the far end of the room, an older human woman stood behind a broad desk of dark wood and onyx stone. Stiff and poised, she glowered at us with eyes of deep, burnished gold catching in the soft light from the silver chandelier overhead.

Her black hair was pulled into a neat, plaited braid and had begun to gray around her temples, and her clothes reminded me of the fine silken robes the high priestesses wore.

Only hers were all black with details of silver and purple.

The woman's gaze followed me like an owl observing a mouse as Roxus shut the door and followed me over to stand before her desk.

"Cutting it a bit close this time, aren't you, Roxus?" the woman quipped, her ruthless stare shifting to him. "Why have you waited so long to bring her before me? Did you think I would not hear about the young ward you've been housing? Or did you hope I would be so shocked that I would not even consider refusing her?"

Roxus dipped his head with a forced apologetic smile that never reached his eyes. "I know better than to think anything I do will shock you, Mistress Orvana."

"And yet you've nearly accomplished it today." The woman's tone dripped with distaste as she flicked me another disapproving scowl. "Out of all the urchins you could have scraped from the gutter, *this* is what you choose to bring before me? Why in the world should I accept a *pitathi* whelp into the trials? Let alone in the order itself!"

I had to look down to keep from baring my teeth. Pitathi was the Rienkan word for Viperi. Or rather, it was the name they preferred for us ... mostly because it was also a curse in their language.

A curse that meant *"dirty snake."*

"I didn't realize the order had begun discriminating *again*. Shall I see myself out, as well?" Roxus growled softly.

"Take care and mind your accusations," she warned, her tone sharp.

Whoever this woman was, she clearly had some authority over Roxus. He'd told me she held my fate in her hands, but the way she talked down made me wonder if she held his, too.

Regardless, I couldn't afford to lose it, no matter what filthy name she called me.

"She's more than five years removed from her kin," Roxus replied. "I found her nearly dead from starvation in the pit of the city prison. She's been living in the streets and has no ties back to her people."

"You think I fear her as a spy?" Mistress Orvana balked. "Don't play me for a fool, we've known each other far too long for that. I know what she's capable of all on her own. It's not something you can simply nurture out of them. They are what they were born to be—an enduring curse upon this world."

I bristled as she came striding around the desk and circled behind us. Her every step was smooth and calculated, like a leopard circling its prey.

Just waiting for me to make the smallest wrong move.

"She has potential," Roxus said, matching the bite in her tone.

"She is a walking threat to everything our Order stands for," Mistress Orvana snapped. "I already have enough to worry over. I won't tolerate infighting and dissent among my agents because I let this creature walk among us."

"There will be no infighting unless someone else starts it," he snarled back. "She knows what's at stake, and she knows how to follow orders. I wonder how many of the other prospects have their lives hanging in the balance of their success at the trials?"

Orvana stopped in front of me, her gaze locking with mine for nearly a minute.

I didn't move a single muscle.

That frigid, unblinking stare might have startled other children her agents dragged in here as prospects to join their ranks, but if Mistress Orvana thought she could rattle me that easily—oh boy, was she in for a shock.

I did not rattle. I did not quake or tremble.

You are steel pulled fresh from the fire, Visha. You bend. You sharpen. But you do not break. My mother's voice was molten in my mind. It made my breathing and heartbeat begin to slow.

"You may have this man's trust, pitathi, but you will have none of mine. Make no mistake, I will be watching you *closely*. If I even suspect you are a danger to any of my agents here, I will have your rotting corpse tossed back to whatever reeking pit Roxus found you in. Am I clear?"

My tongue writhed in my mouth, tasting nothing but poison and all the hateful words I wanted to snarl back. My vision swerved some, threatening to go red as my heartbeat thundered in my ears like cannon fire.

But I couldn't afford to slip now. Not when this woman wanted me to so badly.

I would not bend. I would not break.

I squared my shoulders and met her gaze. "I understand."

Mistress Orvana's eyes narrowed, her frown tightening as

she studied me from head to foot, taking her time to evaluate every single detail.

Then she turned sharply away.

"I cannot stop you from choosing whatever prospect you believe will be a valuable asset to our ranks. But know this, Roxus, she is *your* burden."

I licked my teeth behind my lips. *Burden?* Gods, I hated that.

I was no one's burden.

"Her failures are yours. Her mistakes are your messes to clean up," Orvana warned as she swept across the room and sat back down at her desk. "You will be held accountable when she proves to be no different from the rest of her ruthless kin."

Roxus made no expression and bowed his head in acknowledgment. "Understood, Mistress. Now, by your leave, I will have her presented at the Eternal Hall."

Mistress Orvana met my gaze again, her expression still touched with that faintly simmering wrath. An unspoken warning.

"Go," she hissed.

So we did—quickly.

Roxus practically scruffed me like a puppy and dragged me out of the chamber with his hand on the back of my neck.

I shrugged away as soon as we were outside and shot him a venomous glare. "Definitely not assassins," I fumed.

He didn't reply. That ferocity in his hard, road-worn features burned low and hot like a smoldering bed of coals as he glanced me up and down, then started away back down the corridor.

I gave him a few paces of space before I followed. I needed enough room to let my thoughts whip and whirl like debris in a hurricane. The Zenith's Call weren't assassins, but I still had no idea what they really were.

They clearly knew a lot about my people, though. Somehow, that wasn't comforting in the slightest.

I'd have to watch my back, or Mistress Orvana might see to it that I didn't pass these so-called trials. A woman like that, powerful and clever, was a force I'd dealt with many times.

It was what had destroyed my entire life once already.

I shook my head, clearing those thoughts. Focused—I had to stay focused.

I didn't know why Roxus had brought me to these people. But I would have to walk a fine line here or my fate could be something far worse than death.

SEVEN

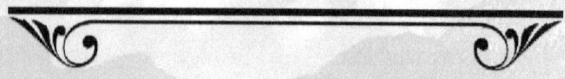

Roxus would pay for this.

Somehow, someday, I'd make sure of it.

I kept my head down, muttering under my breath as he led me back through the winding halls like a baby goat. He might as well have strung a bell around my neck. I'd done everything just the way he wanted, kept my mouth shut, and resisted the urge to lunge at that Mistress Orvana woman while she treated me like a dirty little beast.

And he *still* wouldn't give me even one real answer about what all this was for.

What did he want from me? Who were the Zenith's Call? Why did Roxus think I had a place here?

I spat and seethed, glaring at his back as we returned to the huge chamber with the draconic fountain in the center. Only there were far more people standing around it now.

A crowd of around twenty other young prospects stood with their patrons, talking quietly and staring as we made our way over to join them.

I was the smallest—curse it all. Sure, they all appeared to

be somewhere around my age, but out of the thirteen assembled, I was the shortest by at least a foot.

Ugh. Great.

The other prospects must have noticed it, too, because I could feel their confused, wary stares following me as Roxus and I made our way to the front of the group.

Most of them were humans with the tale-tell hard features and golden eyes you only found in people from Damaria. I spotted a few Rienkan elves with their strange turquoise eyes and long pointed ears standing among the prospects, too.

I guess the Zenith's Call looked everywhere in the Southern Kingdoms for potential members.

Of course, none of them were Viperi, but I wasn't the only oddity.

Another girl stood out a little more from the crowd, too.

At first glance, nothing about her seemed all that remarkable. Her long coppery-colored hair hung in a braid down to her waist, and she had a slim, willowy build. Just an average human. Nothing to worry about.

But the more I studied her, the more I noticed how the many freckles on her face nearly disguised dozens of small scars that dappled her fair skin. Her eyes darted around, taking in everything, but she didn't move a muscle—as though she were used to standing at attention for long periods of time.

Interesting.

My body tensed when she flicked a glance in my direction. Our gazes locked, and immediately an alarm in the back of my mind tolled like a tower bell. She had that familiar cold focus in her eyes—the look of someone who had seen the world's ugly, brutal heart and survived it.

Hmmm. She might be a problem. I'd have to watch carefully to see if—

"*Pitathi,*" someone whispered at my back, spitting every

word as though it were something vile. *"What are they think-ing? Why would they bring one of those murdering snakes in here?"*

I stiffened, clenching my teeth. It took every ounce of self-control not to growl back at them. No—I couldn't do that. Not here.

Roxus had warned me that I had to stay calm.

The Mistress had threatened what would happen if I lost control.

I shut my eyes tightly, feeling the swell of those instincts coming alive inside me like scorching flames.

My hands slowly curled into fists. My ears rang, hearing every sound like cymbals clashing in my head. Every subtle breath, rustle of fabric, and heartbeat was so loud.

Too loud.

The pungent stench of adrenaline and fear hung like smog around me, wafting off every prospect standing nearby. They were afraid of me?

Good.

I would assert dominance quickly and with a crushing force they'd never forget. I might be the smallest, but I was the strongest of them. I'd prove that soon enough.

I would be the best or nothing at all.

Because that was the Viperi way.

The gurgle of the towering fountain filled the tense silence until Mistress Orvana appeared, followed by the two Vindexori guards who had been lurking outside her office. She wore the same sour, forbidding frown as she strolled to the front of our group and faced us.

For a few long, grueling seconds, she didn't say anything. Her gaze moved over our group, examining each of the prospects who stood alongside an older individual—the Zenith's Call member who had brought them here. Our patrons, I guess.

Then Mistress Orvana's gaze focused squarely on me again.

Heat rose in my chest, and every muscle in my body clenched.

"It is either by fate or fortune that you have all found yourselves here," she said, finally glancing away. "Regardless, you now stand in Arx Eburna, and on the precipice of great change. Some of you will come to know this place as your refuge and home. Some of you will not. What we do, and have done for six thousand years, is not a task to be taken lightly."

I shuddered, feeling that number sink into my bones like a dagger point. Gods, who were these people?

"You must be wondering what it is we do, who we truly are, but that information is one of many carefully guarded secrets," she went on. "Only when you have begun to prove yourselves will such things even be mentioned. I have no doubt that what you do learn of our purpose will ensure that you never breathe a word of what you witness here—regardless of whether or not you are invited to join us."

Mistress Orvana began to slowly pace back and forth, every movement smooth and fluid like a lioness pacing in a cage.

"You have *four months* to earn your place as a bladesworn to the Zenith's Call; four months to prove your merit on several fronts. Once that time is up, failure to meet our standards in any of the trials will be cause enough to dismiss you. The patrons who chose you will be your guides, responsible for every breath you take within these walls."

She glared at me, her lips pressing into a tight, dissatisfied line.

I didn't dare take a breath until she finally looked away. Not when I could feel that pressure growing like a vibration rumbling under my feet, rattling me right to the top of my head.

"Over the next few weeks, we will perform initial assessments of your skills to determine whether or not you may prove useful, or if your abilities are worthy of further refinement. Follow me," she commanded.

And we did.

Our entire group of prospects and patrons shuffled along, following Mistress Orvana down another long corridor lit by those odd blue torches like a line of ducklings.

This one was much wider, and it ended at another grand, open chamber with many rooms on each side. More Videxori lurked in the shadowed corners and blended in with the obsidian statues of angelic, armored beings along three of the four walls.

Mistress Orvana motioned to the farthest wall—the only one without statues. There, on a narrow dais, three golden frames stood like massive dressing mirrors with no glass panes inside.

My heartbeat skipped as I stared up at those empty, intricate gold structures. Each one was around eight feet tall and covered in beautifully engraved runes like spirals and whorls.

Beautiful. Timeless.

Undoubtedly something made by the ancient Avoran elves.

But what were they?

"This is the Eternal Hall." Orvana motioned around to all the doorways, elegant statues, and those towering golden frames. "It has endured throughout the ages, and countless agents of the Zenith's Call have stood where you do now. You may report *only* to this chamber and the rooms connected to it. If you are found elsewhere without permission, you will be dismissed."

Whispers and mutters rushed through our group like wind through leaves.

"Consider this hall your proving ground. Each room contains a trial you must pass." She turned to face us, clasping her hands and panning another formidable stare over our group. "Combat, stealth, deception, sleight of hand, language, divine lore, history, and most of all—unrivaled charisma. All of these are tools of our trade, and your proficiency in them may very well seal your fate ... and the fate of the world as you know it."

I frowned and stole a sideways glance up at Roxus. *The fate of the world?* What did that even mean? All of Reatia could suffer if we failed?

He didn't react and kept his gaze fixed on those empty frames with a look of solemn concentration.

Well, at least I knew for certain now that whatever the Zenith's Call was, they weren't assassins. From the sound of it, spies seemed far more likely now. Or maybe mercenaries.

Regardless, my position hadn't changed. Whatever they were, whatever they required, I would not back down.

Not when the alternative was death in a prison cell.

"We will begin with an assessment of combat ability. Every member must know at least the basics of self-defense, but those who will go on to be active agents carrying out missions abroad in the Southern Kingdoms and beyond will be required to show a much higher level of skill," Orvana said. "Your final performance in this trial will determine which role, if any, you are best suited for. For now, we will assess you for potential."

Gods, yes. Finally.

Now I'd shove all those condemning words right back down her throat.

I was *not* a burden.

One glance around at my competition and I couldn't fight back a smirk. None of the other prospects seemed even remotely challenging. That ginger-haired girl might have some

fierceness in her eyes, but I doubted she would pose a challenge with a blade.

Not when I'd been taught to handle one since I could
walk.

I *would* be the dominant prospect. I'd cut them all down
one by one.

Not even Mistress Orvana would be able to refute my
value then.

"Patrons, you may take a moment to prepare your
prospects. We will begin shortly." Mistress Orvana made a
gesture, and all the patrons began moving at once.

Roxus put a hand on my shoulder and began steering me
alongside the others toward one of the adjacent rooms.

"Are you ready?" he murmured low, like he didn't want
anyone else to overhear.

I snorted. "It's just combat."

"No," he corrected. "For you, it's control."

My jaw tightened. Right.

I took a steadying breath as we stepped into what must
have been their sparring room. Inside, the smell of sweat hung
thick in the air like a stale, salty breeze. The wide open space
was lit by sconces that crackled with more bluish flames and
filled with all manner of combat training equipment.

Wooden and straw dummies were lined across the far wall,
and five big stands displaying practice weapons stood in the
center. Targets for throwing knives, daggers, or darts hung on
the left wall, with markings on the floor to measure out the
distance. All were things I had used before countless times.

This was the sort of place that had been my personal
crucible as a kid.

Surveying it all, I finally dared to swallow. My body
relaxed. My heartbeat began to slow as all my senses came alive.
I slipped into that comfortable numbness that had been my
refuge for so long.

The quiet eye of the storm that would once again decide my fate.

"Bring forth the prospects." Mistress Orvana's voice rang out through the room. She stood, coiling a long braided leather whip around her forearm, and stared at me with malice oozing from her toothy smile.

"Let us begin."

Eight

Time was up. No more waiting and wondering. This was it—*my* moment.

Time to show up, or shut up.

Everyone in the room snapped into motion at once.

The elder agents ushered all the prospects to one side of the room, urging us to form a line so we could be evaluated on our combat abilities.

In all the pushing and shoving, I wound up at the very back.

Anxious energy shivered through my body, buzzing under my skin as I watched some of the elder patrons still setting up the challenges. I paced a few steps as I waited in line, unable to keep my weight from shifting and my toes from curling up in my boots as each obstacle, weapon, and target was set into place.

The first was a series of dueling circles—three, in total—and each one smaller than the one before. The second was an archery course, which apparently we would have to complete while moving. The third was some sort of hand-to-hand sparring ordeal, which I could only guess meant they would be pitting us against more experienced agents.

The only thing I didn't see was what, or where, the actual challenge of this was meant to be. This was all basic, wasn't it? Would we be doing it blindfolded? Or one-handed? Or with poison coursing through us?

The idea made a wicked grin spread over my face. Perhaps it would be all three.

Now that would be a *true* test.

Several Vindexori in their all-black ensemble were marched in and stationed at the sparring and armed combat circles. With most of their faces covered by black shawls, and their eyes nothing but steely, relentless focus, they stood eerily still and waited for their first round of victims.

My heartbeat thrilled, adrenaline already singing its dark melody through my veins and making every one of my senses come alive. Gods, why did I have to be last? Maybe I should just shove my way to the front and—

One look from Mistress Orvana as she prowled to the center of the room made every muscle in my body lock up solid. My lip twitched. My skin burned as heat thrummed through my veins.

Control. I had to stay in control.

With that whip coiled around her arm like a black leather python, Mistress Orvana finally looked back across the rest of the prospects. The air crackled with tension, all eyes glued to every smooth, fluid move she made. My heartbeat was thunder in my chest, and I licked my teeth behind my lips.

Any second now.

Mistress Orvana raised her hand, signaling to the Vindexori.

The order to start.

Disappointment made my shoulders drop as I watched the

first prospect begin. She staggered forward, faltering at the weapons table before choosing a dulled practice blade and stepping into the first sparring ring with one of the Vindexori.

No blindfolds. No poison. Nothing but a bland run-through of all those obstacles. Even the Vindexori seemed to be holding back when they sparred with each of the prospects ahead of me in line.

Ridiculous.

I couldn't decide what was more frustrating—that they believed this would challenge me, or that the other prospects actually seemed to be struggling with it.

This was their way of assessing whether or not any of us had potential? Disgraceful.

I crossed my arms and waited, watching one prospect right after another flounder through all the obstacles. Every now and then, one of them would manage to shoot the bow decently or could handle a blade with passable finesse. But not a single one of them made a clean pass.

One boy did come relatively close. He was taller and a bit older than the rest of us, but his balance and reflexes were pathetic.

I sighed and rolled my eyes when he tripped during his final sparring challenge with the Vindexori. A second's hesitation allowed the much larger man to get him into a headlock and pin him to the floor.

So much for that.

I guess the boy noticed my critique of his mediocre performance because as soon as he got to his feet, he stormed straight toward me. His hands shook in clenched fists and his sweaty face burned deep red, nostrils flared like an angry bull.

"You think this is easy, pitathi runt? Let's see you do better!" he shouted in my face.

I froze.

Every instinct raged like hellfire, making my hands curl

into fists and my teeth grind. I could break him. I could rip his tongue right out of his throat.

And, gods, I *wanted* to.

No one made a sound.

Out of the corner of my eye, I spotted Roxus standing with a group of other patrons. His jaw worked from one side to the other, like he was thinking it over. Finally, he gave me a small nod.

I grinned.

"Fine." I glared up at the older boy, noting all the angry veins that stood out against his neck and forehead.

One of his eyes twitched.

None of the other prospects protested as I made my way up to the front of the line, taking my place right in front of the coppery-haired girl. I rolled my shoulders and flexed my fingers, bouncing up onto the balls of my feet to get the blood moving to all my toes.

Then Mistress Orvana gave the order to begin.

Adrenaline burned in my veins as I charged from the starting line, bolting toward a table where an array of practice weapon options were laid out. I seized a dagger and stepped into the largest sparring circle, nodding to the Vindexori agent. I was ready.

His eyes narrowed. Then he surged for me with a short-sword clenched in his hands.

I bared my pointed incisors and growled, dipping and spinning out of his reach as he swung wide with that blade. He moved like a lethal blur, diving toward me in a basic series of strikes as though he were testing me.

We dipped and feinted, whirling through combat maneuvers and then springing apart to pace like two circling wolves. Every inch of my body thrummed with energy. My pulse boomed. My lungs stretched for each breath of the cool, sweat-tinged air.

I couldn't hold back a grin.

Prowling slowly, I watched his every move as the Vindexori spun his blade over his hand, taking a few more test swings—likely as a distraction or a flourish to try and intimidate me.

I narrowed my eyes, measuring his every step. He was slow on the left defense. I'd have to exploit that.

I moved like a striking viper, stepping wide in a feinting strike. The air sang off my dagger's edge. His eyes went wide and he made a frantic swipe with his sword, giving me more than enough room to duck in close and slip my dagger to the base of his back where a slice into a large artery would have ended the fight.

One of the patrons watching held up a hand. "Victor—the pitathi girl. Move to the next circle."

I did.

My muscles thrummed with delight, clenching hard with every step, like the first good stretch after years of being asleep. Gods, it felt *so good*. Like I was finally awake after years of restless slumber.

I smirked as I stepped into the second, smaller sparring area and locked gazes with the next Vindexori agent. This one seemed more womanly in shape, although she was taller and leaner than the first one I had dueled. Her mismatched eyes of intense gold and sea blue peered over the shawl that covered her nose and mouth with frosty determination.

Mistress Orvana gave the signal, and she immediately dove at me. Her swing was much faster but far more obvious. I dispatched her even faster than the first one, not bothering with a feint and going straight for an abdominal strike that made her cough and wheeze.

The Vindexori in the third, smallest circle didn't do much better. He was stockier and stronger, but so slow I didn't even have to plan my movements as he came for me with a pair of handaxes. I hooked a heel around his and tripped him as he barreled for me, using his bulk and momentum against him.

I was already waiting with a blade at his throat by the time he hit the floor with a weighty *thud*.

He blinked up at me in surprise, as though he were still trying to figure out what had just happened.

Too easy. He wouldn't have lasted a day in a Viperi nursery.

Tossing my dagger down next to him, I gave a disapproving snort and moved on to the next challenge. Archery had never been my strong suit, but I couldn't possibly be any worse than the rest of these idiots.

Nothing like low standards to make mediocrity shine like a diamond.

I seized a light crossbow and started moving through the obstacles. They wanted me to be able to hit the targets while I walked along thin beams, balanced on a series of vertical poles barely six inches wide, and ran up and down a series of steep ramps pitched like the rooftops of buildings. The crossbow flinched in my grip every time I pulled the trigger, the string snapping and sending a bolt howling across the room.

Five targets—five bull's-eyes. Not all of them were dead-center hits, but then again, I hadn't handled a bow at all in quite a while. Street urchins didn't exactly stumble across those tossed in the alleyway trash.

I didn't stick around to revel in my victory, though, and prowled to the final obstacle.

This sparring circle was somewhat wider than the first I'd dueled in, but there was no table of weapons waiting. This would be a test of hand-to-hand skill. Wrestling maneuvers, flexibility, strength, and stamina.

Any other time, I might have felt a twinge of unease since I was so much smaller than all my would-be opponents. But now, after everything I'd seen from the other prospects so far? Hah!

Someone must have given these Vindexori the order to go easy on us. That—or the ranks of the Zenith's Call weren't nearly as fierce as I'd heard.

Standing on the edge of the sparring circle, I watched my opponent enter the ring with her gaze already fixed on me. She was also more petite in build, but there was a quiet ferocity in her eyes that sent a little thrill of excitement through my chest. Perhaps she would be more of a challenge.

I worked my neck from one side to the other, loosening my shoulders and arching my back to limber up. It might take three seconds. Two, if I pushed it. I mean, after how the basic weapon sparring had gone, I didn't expect her to—

"Are you really going to stand by and allow this to happen?" an older, male voice barked suddenly.

I turned just in time to see one of the other Vindexori pushing his way through the group of gathered patrons. He had a pair of golden pauldrons and aiguillettes built into his black leather armor, which must have marked him as some sort of commanding officer over the others. None of the other Vindexori I had dueled had those on their armor.

Maybe he was unhappy that I'd beaten them so easily?

He stormed toward me, then thrust an accusing finger in Mistress Orvana's direction. "You're going to just stand there and allow this thing to shame us?"

Mistress Orvana didn't even blink. She stared back at him silently, her expression as cool and stoic as the statues guarding every doorway of this place.

When she didn't respond, the Vindexori officer whirled on me, his brow twitching with wrath. His much taller frame loomed over me, like a tidal wave of dark armor and blind fury.

My blood boiled like streams of molten rock in my veins,

building pressure with each passing second. Not good. I bit down hard, steeling every shred of nerve I had.

I didn't want to erupt. Roxus was counting on me. My entire life depended on it.

Snapping his hands back, he drew two longswords from the cross-sheath on his back. Not dulled practice weapons.

His personal tools of war.

"You think you know how to fight? Choose your weapon, pitathi. Let's see what you do with a real opponent," he taunted.

I licked my teeth behind my lips, tracing the points of my long incisors.

So he wanted a *real* fight? Well, then.

By all means.

A wide smile curled up my lips, and that fire in my veins smoldered with dark delight as I walked calmly toward Mistress Orvana and held my hand out.

She finally blinked, glancing between me and the fuming Vindexori officer a few times.

I waggled my fingers a little and nodded.

If she didn't want this to happen, all she had to do was refuse. I would relent. After all, I was on *her* orders to behave, right?

But if she handed me that whip coiled around her arm, then that was essentially permission.

Permission to do what I had been born to do.

"Mistress!" Roxus shouted. "You can't seriously be considering this! This is completely outside of protocol for new prospects!"

Mistress Orvana's mouth pinched tight. Her eyes narrowed upon me. With a final, uncertain scowl, she dropped that long, braided leather whip into my hand.

I held it by the sturdy, black ivory handle, giving it a gentle wave to test the weight as I made my way to the other side of the sparring mat.

I rolled my shoulders with every step, flexing each burning muscle. My senses sang a dark melody. The fear and anticipation filled my nose like a fragrant wine.

Delicious.

And now I would feast.

NINE

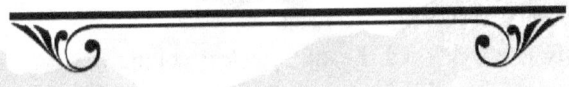

No one dared to move.

No one made a sound. Not a cough. Not a sniffle. Just that blissful silence like the last gasp before a steep drop.

I drank it in like the sweetest honey, hoping it would keep those writhing demons in my soul quiet and calm.

The instincts that had kept me alive so far.

My Viperi instincts.

Standing on the edge of the final sparring circle, my heart pounded low and steady in my chest. Each pulse made my fingers throb. My toes curled and stretched, flexing and testing the balance of these new boots. I felt everything—every vibration, every sound, every breath.

My whole being came alive like lightning sizzling in a glass bottle, ready to explode.

My gaze fixed on my opponent, standing before me on the other side of the sparring circle. His broad chest heaved with each manic breath as his eyes twitched, the dark silken shawl over his nose rippling as he blasted snorts from his nose like a furious stallion.

He was easily twice my size. Probably more than twice my age. Most bets would have been that he sliced me in half like a freshly picked cucumber with one strike of those fancy matching longswords.

But he was not Viperi.

And I was not afraid.

"You are steel pulled fresh from the fire, Visha." My mother's voice rang through my head.

My jaw tightened. I sank low, legs coiling beneath me. I gripped the handle of the whip in one hand and touched two fingers to the ground before me with the other. I was a serpent poised for the strike.

Everything seemed to slow. My breath. My mind. My heartbeat.

It all faded away until I felt nothing but the fire in my blood.

"You bend. You sharpen. But you do not break."

The Vindexori lunged first.

I waited, focusing on the thunder of his steps under my feet. The rhythm.

One second. Two.

Three.

I sprang skyward, drawing my legs to my chest and leaping over his head. I fell into a roll and kicked up, landing behind him. I snapped the whip, making the length of black braided leather ripple and howl through the air until it wrapped around one of his arms.

He was too heavy. If I tried to pull him down, I'd just be dragged along by the overwhelming force of his momentum.

So I ran, using the length of the whip like a rope to swing through the air, gathering speed and force, and curling my legs in. I swung past his head and kicked both feet out at once, landing a hit across his jaw.

Bone gave way beneath my heels with a *crunch*. His head snapped back. His gait faltered.

I landed in a crouch, still gripping the end of my whip as the Vindexori dropped his blades, yanked off his shawl, and clutched at his face.

The smell of blood wafted past my nose. Coppery and sickly sweet.

My adrenaline rushed like a mudslide, burying everything else in the chaos. Reason. Logic.

He let out a string of curses, eyes wild as he spun on me.

I grinned.

"You will show no fear. No hesitation. No mercy."

He lunged again—armed only with his bare fists this time. Grabbing the end of the whip still wrapped around his arm, he tried to drag me toward him.

I rushed him, surging in with all my speed and dropping into a slide straight through his legs, taking my end of the whip with me.

Risky. In that close, if he managed to get ahold of me, I would be at a terrifying disadvantage. He could crush the life out of me with his bare hands.

But he'd have to catch me first.

The Vindexori swung, his big fists pounding the ground right next to my head. With only a few feet of free whip to work with, I danced just out of his reach. Bending and whirling through his space, I twisted what I could of the whip around his other leg.

He tripped, hitting the ground on his knees with another bellowing curse.

Perfect.

Taking up one of his dropped longswords, I sprang for him. I'd finish this quick and clean. There would be no question. I was worthy of the Zenith's Call.

More worthy than anyone else in this—

BAM!

A fist bashed me upside the head.

I staggered back, nearly dropping the sword as the world flashed white. My ears rang and bright spots winked in my vision. Something warm drizzled from my nose down onto my lips and chin. Blood.

My blood.

My chest heaved deeply. Every muscle clamped down as my lips curled back into a snarl. All my mental fortifications seemed to groan like a chain barely tethering a bear.

Control. I had to stay in control. I could not afford to lose it.

This was just a sparring match—not real combat. I wasn't in danger. He wouldn't actually kill me.

Right?

Ripping free of the whip, he rushed me in an instant, moving a lot faster than before.

His gaze locked with mine, possessed with bulging fury. His mouth twisted and twitched with hatred as he pulled a long dagger from the side of his boot.

He lunged at me like before, but faster this time. I ducked out of reach, my heels brushing the perimeter of the sparring circle as I brought up the sword just in time to deflect his strike.

Close one.

He swung over and over, going faster and forcing me to the defensive. Each blow was stronger than the one before, rattling my teeth as my much smaller arms struggled to hold him off.

I couldn't. Not forever. He was bigger—a grown man. I had to change tactics *now*.

"You wretched little monster," he snarled, baring teeth stained pink with blood.

I saw it written in every throbbing vein that stood out

against his forehead and neck: he didn't just want to win. This wasn't about proving a point anymore.

He wanted revenge.

My heartbeat hammered through my body, vibrating me down to my very core. I dipped low, bracing as another mighty blow clanged against my blade. My arm faltered slightly, nearly buckling under the weight of his strike.

Just enough to let the point of his dagger nick my cheek.

"You must have no mercy, Visha... because this world will have none for you."

A scream tore past my lips, erupting from that place in my soul where my mother's voice still lived. Where it whispered and kindled the coals of my own fury.

"You are Viperi. You will kill or be killed."

Something deep in my chest snapped. The last tether. All my control.

My body moved without my permission as flashes filled my mind. A blacksmith's dying gurgle. The roaring and screaming of guards. The splatter of blood. The flash of steel in the night.

The gasp of a dying man's final breath.

The Vindexori screamed Damarian curses, swinging that dagger and stepping through complex strikes. But I might as well have been made of smoke. I was untouchable, ducking and whirling around every feral strike the Vindexori made.

His blade howled through the empty air as I dropped into a back flip, spinning and landing on the balls of my feet—only to spring straight at him. Fast and lethal. A tongue of lightning splitting the night. We danced that deadly waltz, testing and probing for any point of weakness.

The longsword was heavy. It didn't suit me. But I'd done more with worse.

He was delirious with rage. It made his swings wilder with

each passing second. Frantic and floundering, like a child wailing at the wall with a toy.

A chorus of shouts went up around the room as I bashed his face again with the hilt of his sword in a blurring pass. Bone crunched, giving way beneath the impact. He staggered, eyes wide in shock, but I gave him no time to recover.

I went in for a killing strike, bringing that long, lethal blade around to swipe at his throat. The end of the dance. His blood would be all the proof I needed that I belonged here. They could not refuse me—not if I was the victor.

My head snapped back suddenly, as though someone had grabbed my hair and jerked me off balance. I tripped, barely catching myself and blundering the strike.

Curse it! Who would dare?!

I whirled around with a scream, looking for who had interfered so I could exact some revenge.

But there was no one.

I blinked.

What the ... ? I-I hadn't imagined it. Someone had yanked me off balance. I—

CRACK!

Everything swerved out of focus as the Vindexori bashed me over the back of the head with the pommel of his dagger. My ears rang. My vision swam and my legs buckled.

I dropped the longsword.

I hit the ground with a wheeze, my legs and arms tingling strangely. Every movement felt delayed, sluggish, like I was trying to wrench my way through deep mud. Gods curse it, why wouldn't my arms move? Why couldn't I stand?

BAM!

The Vindexori hit me again, this time with his fist.

All the wind rushed out of me at once as a heavy weight crushed down on my chest—almost like someone was sitting on me.

He was.

The Vindexori pinned me down, his knees on my shoulders, and pounded my face with his fist.

More shouts went up around me, seeming to come from every direction at once. I could have sworn I heard Roxus's voice shouting my name.

But I couldn't see him. I couldn't see anything but smears and flashes of color as my head whipped from one side to the other, taking hit after hit as the enraged man wailed on me.

Terror seized my heart like an icy fist. Every instinct fired at once. *Kill or be killed.*

I drove a knee up into his groin with all my strength.

The Vindexori let out a hoarse howl of pain and reeled forward, off balance just long enough. With my vision still swerving and blurry, I twisted my body around his.

In less than a second, I had his neck between my thighs, clamped into a brutal chokehold. He writhed and fought, but I didn't let go. I squeezed harder.

My whole body shook with force as I squeezed his neck with all my strength.

His face turned red. Then purple. Then blue.

Suddenly, everything went dark.

I tried to scream. To flail. But my body—gods, it felt like I didn't have one. There was nothing but strange numbness.

Then a hint of light. A faint glow that grew. I could barely make out motion and hazy colors moving within it. Was that ... people? I couldn't tell.

Then, out of nowhere, the world swerved back into view.

I let out a garbled scream as the room snapped back into focus. The shouts were too loud. The lights were too bright.

Away! Oh gods, I had to get away!

I lashed out wildly, screaming and fighting—until a face appeared over me.

It wasn't the Vindexori. It wasn't Roxus, or even Mistress Orvana.

A man I didn't recognize sneered, his dark eyes flickering with malicious delight. The instant our eyes met, every muscle in my body locked up solid, frozen in place like a stiff corpse.

What was happening? Why couldn't I move?

His features twisted and contorted, seeming to ripple the more I tried to focus on him.

My vision tunneled, going gray and dark around the edges until all I could see was a strange, faint halo of soft bluish light around him.

Was he *glowing?*

I-I couldn't tell. The outline of his form seemed to radiate that eerie light. It shone brighter as everything else grew darker.

What did that mean?

I couldn't think or even move, paralyzed as I stared at him with my mouth open. Someone roughly rolled me over onto my stomach. My cheek met the smooth stone floor. Then I felt it—the cold steel of a blade pressing against the back of my neck.

A feeling I knew well.

It was the pause before the final strike.

Before they cut me down.

TEN

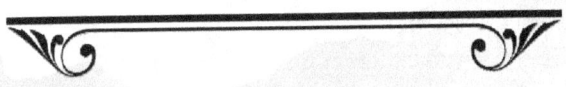

I couldn't be dead—not yet, anyway.

Not with my head pounding like a war drum. I doubted mortal pain like this stretched beyond into the afterlife. Er, well, unless you were condemned to the prison of stars for mortal wrongs. And I probably was.

Ugh. Great. Maybe I really was dead, after all.

Sharp pain throbbed in the back of my skull, as though it might just explode at any second. My pulse, hard and heavy, pounded away in my temples so hard it made my teeth ache. My tongue writhed in my mouth, tasting a faint, sharp, metallic flavor like one of Leruna's healing tonics.

I groaned and tried to force my eyes open, but that only made the pain sharpen until it felt like my eyes might pop right out of their sockets.

One glance was all I needed, though.

I was back at Roxus's home. Back in my room, lying stretched out on my bed's silken, downy-stuffed blankets and pillows.

Soft morning sunlight ebbed through the drapes on my room's balcony doorway. I hissed through my teeth, shutting my eyes again and trying to roll over onto my side away from it.

"Leruna says you have a concussion," Roxus's gruff voice spoke up suddenly. "Not to mention your face looks like ground meat. Try not to move around too much."

I cracked one eye open just long enough to see him sitting there, sprawled lazily in a chair right at my bedside with that smoking pipe between his teeth.

The heavy circles under his eyes seemed darker than usual, and he still wore the same clothes. A stack of plates and an empty wine bottle sat on the dressing table beside him.

Gods, how long had I been out? Days?

And had he been sitting there the whole time just waiting for me to wake up?

No, surely not.

I lay still, trying not to focus too much on the constant throbbing in my face. My skin felt stretched and hot. Everything was probably puffy and hugely swollen. That Vindexori man hadn't held back, after all.

I was lucky he hadn't beaten me to death.

Did I have Roxus to thank for that, too?

Ugh. Probably.

But still ... that strange man's face had appeared over me, wreathed in bluish light right at the end. Had he been the one to stop the fight? To save me?

Or something else?

I didn't know how to ask, or even if I should. The silence hung thick, cold, and heavy. It crushed all the breath from my lungs like a block of steel on my chest. My eyes watered, and I didn't dare look back at Roxus.

It was all over now, wasn't it? I'd broken the most important rule—the one boundary both he and Mistress Orvana had set before me.

I'd let those instincts take over. I'd lost my head to the

same urges that had left me in that prison cell. Now... I was doomed to be sent back there. Executed. Thrown away.

Because I had failed.

"I'm sorry," I whispered hoarsely.

His chair groaned as he shifted. "For what?"

"I lost control."

He gave a bemused snort. "Only after Carsus did first. In your case, I'd call that an improvement. You were protecting yourself."

My throat went dry, seizing on the words that hung in my throat like a fistful of rusty nails. I didn't want to tell him. It was too easy just to stay silent and accept that excuse.

But the truth was impossible to swallow.

Of course it had looked like self-defense. That Vindexori man—Carsus—had been furious. He'd come at me with intent to harm.

But *I* had been the first to make a killing strike.

Only someone pulling my hair at the last second had stopped me from landing that blow.

I swallowed hard and winced against the flare of pain in my neck and chest. It made my eyes sting and my mouth screw up. I couldn't say it. I couldn't admit what had really happened.

If I did, he might reconsider letting me lie here, recovering in this bed, and just toss me to the curb right away.

"Is that how it was before? With the blacksmith?" Roxus asked, his tone softer and oddly gentle.

I bit down hard, shutting my eyes tightly.

"What did he do to you, Violet?"

My lip twitched, wanting to snarl. But it hurt too much. Inside and out, it hurt so much.

"I didn't mean to kill him," I snapped brokenly, knowing full well he wouldn't believe me.

No one else did.

"Tell me what happened."

My body started to tremble, visions of that night coming alive in my frazzled, aching brain. My hands clenched at the bedsheets. My chest shuddered as I gulped in a shaking breath.

And all the words spilled out like water from a cracked bucket.

"I just wanted to sleep somewhere out of the rain," I whispered. "Somewhere safe. Somewhere quiet. I'd never seen anyone go in that attic. But the window was always propped open."

Roxus didn't make a sound or even move, his gaze fixed on me as he puffed slowly on his pipe.

"I found some old blankets behind crates of old weapons and tools. I spread a few out in a corner and fell asleep," I said. "I wasn't going to stay long. Just a few hours. Just to sleep a little. But he found me there."

"Did he say anything to you?" Roxus asked. "Tell you to leave?"

I tried to think. To remember. It had all happened so fast, and I was bleary-eyed and barely awake at first.

"N-no, I ... I woke up and he was already crouched over me. I don't know why. But when he saw what I was—when he saw my eyes—he started yelling. He pulled a pair of old tongs from one of the crates and swung at me. I tried to run, but he'd already shut and locked the window. He kept yelling. Kept coming for me with the tongs. I saw an old dagger on the floor. It was rusty, but I ... "

The words hung in my throat, tangling around each ragged breath as I tried to keep them in. The fear still felt so fresh and close. It simmered right beneath the surface, making my throat feel stiff and my chest ache.

"When did the guards turn up?" Roxus pressed, his tone much more stern and cold.

"Not long after. There was so much blood. I was looking

for another way out when they came through the hatch door. So many of them. Maybe they heard him yelling from the street. I don't know," I finished.

He could figure out what had happened after that. It was pretty obvious, wasn't it? I could hold my own fairly well. But weak with starvation and exhaustion, and cornered with nothing but a rusty dagger, I eventually slipped up.

They took me to the prison.

And Roxus had wound up being the only thing standing between me and the executioner's block.

For now, anyway.

"That happens to you a lot, doesn't it?" He made a strange chuckling sound and blew a few smoke rings into the air.

"What?"

"You finding yourself in situations where you have no choice but to fight like your life depends on it."

I frowned. "Because it usually does."

"Fair enough. And I can't help but suspect that this isn't a recent trend."

My mouth scrunched up and I turned my head away, ignoring that sudden throb of pain as my cheek brushed my pillow.

I could hear the disapproving frown in his voice. "Do the Viperi men handle women that way?"

"Only if they believe they can get away with it," I muttered, too embarrassed to look at him.

"What do you mean?"

"Male or female—it does not matter so much among the Viperi. It is always a struggle for place. For distinction. For dominance. If things come to violence, it almost always ends in death, regardless of whether or not it's a man or woman fighting. Men are clan leaders or high guard. Women are warriors or oracles. You do what you must to secure your place within the clan."

"Even among the children?"

I hesitated, not liking the odd softness in his tone when he asked that question. Was that pity?

Ugh. Whatever it was, it left me feeling dirty and pathetic.

Gritting my teeth, all I managed was a grumble of affirmation. Weakness in any form was not tolerated among the Viperi—and being a child wasn't an excuse.

For what felt like a miserable eternity, Roxus just sat there smoking that pipe and not saying a word. I could almost feel his gaze boring into the back of my head, watching my every move as though trying to read my thoughts.

Maybe he could. For what little he knew about me, I knew even less about who he really was.

It bothered me.

Why did he care so much what happened to me? It couldn't just be because he wanted an apprentice. Not when there were thousands of other urchins squatting in the filth of this city who would have done far worse than butcher a blacksmith to be where I was now.

No, he had a motive. A reason. A secret.

And I had no right to ask what it was—not when I now owed him my very life.

It made my stomach burn and my heart wrench in my chest. A cold pang of dread burrowed deep in my gut, twisting and wrenching until it made my whole body shudder.

I didn't like it. I didn't want to be used for some unknown plot.

But I didn't have a choice.

Or, I hadn't, at least. After what happened with the Vindexori, though ... No way were they going to let me darken the door of any Zenith's Call building ever again.

I scowled up at the ceiling, trying to decide what that might mean for me now. What would I become? Where would I go? Would Roxus turn me out as soon as I was back on my feet? Or would he even wait that long?

He must have been able to read my thoughts, or at least guess them by the look on my face as I gaped at him, because Roxus stirred in his seat again. Reaching into his coat, he pulled out an all-too-familiar black leather whip and laid it on the bed beside me.

Mistress Orvana's whip.

I stared at it, now better able to appreciate the fine craftsmanship of that weapon.

The black ivory handle was about seven inches long and tipped with a pointed, silver diamond shape that could be used as a bashing weapon. The handle was also engraved with beautiful geometric patterns that were inlaid with silver, and the whip itself was made from many strands of oiled black leather all woven together.

A beautiful prize by any warrior's standards.

So why was he giving it to me?

"You're being given a week to recover, then you'll return to Arx Eburna to continue your trials and assessments," he announced.

My heart gave a frantic twist, and I almost bolted upright in bed.

What? Really? They weren't kicking me out?

Gods, why not?

Roxus just shrugged and gave a sly smirk as he blew another perfect smoke ring.

"Don't look so excited," he snickered. "It took me two days of bickering with Orvana to allow you to stay, and she has set firm boundaries. You're banned from any further combat assessments, even from practicing with any of the other prospects. I suspect they are all now thoroughly convinced of your *talent* in that regard. No further lessons needed. I doubt they will even require you to do the final trial."

I let out a slow, halting breath as every muscle in my body relaxed. I was still allowed to be there. To walk among the Zenith's Call. To be Roxus's prospect.

I still had a chance to become one of them.

"I can't promise it will be easier for you now, though. You were well on your way to besting one of the highest-ranking Vindexori guards in the compound. Quite the introduction, and not one to be quickly forgotten. The other prospects might fear you now, but make no mistake, the rest of the Zenith's Call is going to be scrutinizing every single move you make."

"As if they weren't doing that already," I snorted.

His grin widened. "True, but now you've gone and made yourself a credible threat, not just a potential one."

I pursed my lips. "They're never going to accept me, are they? Even if I pass all their trials?"

Roxus chuckled softly. "I don't know, Violet. But what I can promise is that, so long as I'm around, they will treat you fairly. Fair is all I can guarantee."

I finally looked up to meet his gaze. Fair was more than enough. It was more than I'd ever had before.

For whatever reason, that thought made my eyes well. My mouth twisted and my chin trembled. I turned my face away again.

The bed lurched as he sat down on the edge of it. One of his big hands came to rest on my shoulder.

"Violet? What's wrong?"

I tensed, ignoring the swell of pain in my head as I buried my face in my pillow.

"Talk to me, girl," he said. "Nothing changes unless you talk to me."

Gods, I wanted to.

I wanted to yell. Scream. To curse at him.

The words writhed in my mouth, sharp and jagged like a

ball of thorns. I tried to swallow them down, to push it all far away. But they just came roaring back.

Louder. Stronger.

Questions I didn't even know how to ask.

If I failed him like last time, what would happen? When something else went wrong—because it always did—what if I couldn't keep my instincts under control? Would he stand by and let them kill me next time? Would he even have a choice?

Or would he send me back to jail so I could slowly starve or finally make that final trek to the executioner's block?

I didn't know.

And worse, I couldn't even ask. Not without letting him see everything.

Every fear and shred of weakness that festered inside me like a putrid disease. Everything that made me unworthy and inferior.

I couldn't show him any of that. It was unacceptable. Things like that had to be crushed and eliminated.

And I had to do everything I could—whatever it took—to stay here. To survive.

Even if that meant risking his trust in me, too.

ELEVEN

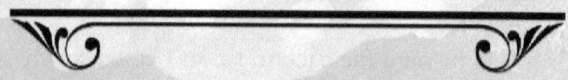

No one made a single sound as I stepped into the sparring room.

All training stopped. The other prospects froze, gaping at me.

I could practically hear the dust settling.

The Vindexori posted along the exterior perimeter of the room tensed up, hands drifting toward their weapons. Even the elder agents working with the prospects at various stations stared at me like they'd spotted a phantom. With their eyes wide and haunted, it seemed like they hadn't expected me to come back at all.

Well, neither had I.

But here I was, back like a bad case of foot fungus.

It had taken just under a week for Leruna to announce she was satisfied enough with my healing progress that I could return to Arx Eburna. Her many potions and tonics had sped up the recovery process quite a bit, and now all I had left to show for my sort-of victory were some dusky bruises on my cheeks and forehead.

Okay. Fine. So I probably still looked pretty grotesque.

The swelling was gone, though, and Leruna had reminded me daily how lucky I was that I didn't have a broken nose or facial fractures.

My *"lovely"* face was still intact.

I doubted anyone else in this place would consider me beautiful. Certainly not any of the other prospects. Not that I cared.

Beauty didn't mean much amongst the Viperi.

Their gazes followed my every move as I walked past the weapon racks and sat down alone against the far wall, dropping onto my rear end with a sigh.

Nearly a minute passed in the most uncomfortable silence I'd ever been a part of until, finally, a few pairs of the prospects began to resume their sword practice.

Mediocre sword practice, of course. Meh.

I stared around the sparring room, watching each group of prospects and their respective agent patrons move through combat maneuvers, basics of archery, and hand-to-hand combat fundamentals. They floundered. Flailed. Stumbled.

And all I could do was watch and try not to laugh.

Roxus had lectured me all the way here about not allowing myself to be baited into anything, even by another patron. He'd left me alone just long enough to speak with Mistress Orvana, but wasted no time ordering me to go in, sit down, and keep my mouth shut. No fighting. No sparring. No touching weapons of any kind until I had passed all my other trials and could be formally accepted as a member of the Zenith's Call.

Ridiculous.

I sighed and let my chin rest on my palm, watching the coppery-haired girl I'd spotted on my first day execute a truly pathetic excuse for a cross parry. She'd definitely get killed in a real fight, especially if the patron she was sparring with kept going easy on her.

Roxus had suggested that I could practice on my own at his home if I wanted. He had a decent sparring area. But wailing on wooden practice dummies was nothing like a real fight. It wouldn't help me keep my edge.

And he hadn't volunteered to spar with me, either.

Part of me wondered if that was because he didn't trust me. Not that I blamed him. But still ...

He was the whole reason I was here in the first place. If he didn't trust me, then what was the point?

My thoughts circled and twisted around that notion, tangling in my head like ivy through a lattice until a sharp whistle from one of the elder patrons, one they called a magister, made everyone stop.

"That will conclude formal practice time for today. You're welcome to come back in your own time, but for now, we will move on to other studies. This way, please." He waved everyone toward the door.

I stood, waiting until the rest of the crowd had moved out into the Eternal Hall before I followed. Keeping my distance was safer, even with Roxus lurking out there.

His gaze locked with mine as soon as I stepped through the doorway. His wide shoulders sagged, as though in relief. I'd managed to be alone for an hour or two without it devolving into a complete disaster.

Hooray for me.

The magister led the way into another room directly across the broad, grimly shadowed hall. This one was far smaller but angled sharply down to form a rounded, sloped auditorium lined with seats and writing desks. The air smelled strongly of parchment and the heavy metallic odor of fresh ink.

Down at the center, another elder agent stood behind a broad stone lectern, this time draped in robes of dark purple and emerald green silk.

In build and appearance, he was the epitome of average—a

middle-aged human man with long black hair swept back in a smooth ponytail and a sharp, deeply creased brow. His quick golden eyes perused an open tome before him as he stroked his chin, not seeming to pay any attention to the rest of us filing in like a herd of spring lambs.

But just the sight of him made me lurch to a halt, as though my feet had been frozen straight to the floor.

His whole body seemed to glow faintly, as though he were wreathed in a weak, flickering blue light.

What by all the gods was that? Was this the same man from before? The one who'd nearly killed me?

He was going to be some sort of instructor?

His gaze suddenly darted up, locking squarely onto me. His eyes narrowed, lip curling at one corner.

My jaw clenched hard. A growl rumbled in my throat, and my stomach sank in a fluttering, swirling panic.

Then a heavy hand fell on my shoulder and gave it a gentle, reassuring pat.

"That's Domitri," Roxus murmured. "He's a master of divine lore. He'll be giving this assessment. It's all right, Violet. It's just ink and parchment. Nothing to be tense about."

Tense? Don't be *tense?*

Had he completely lost his mind?!

"You can't control how people react to you," he said quietly. "Only how you react to them. In your case, I realize that's more difficult. But you have to try."

I gaped up at Roxus and I *almost* asked him. Maybe he'd suffered some sort of head injury when I wasn't paying attention.

I was trying. I'd been trying since he had handed me that key in the prison. Couldn't he see that?

But this ... Gods, I needed to know if I was the only one who saw that strange blue light around that man—Domitri. I tried, and instantly the words hung in my throat, tangling up around that spinning vortex of panic that made me feel like I might vomit.

Before I could force out any sound, Roxus steered me to an open seat right next to the main aisle and stepped away to the back of the room to join the rest of the patrons.

I sat alone, staring at Domitri down in the center of the room. Thankfully, his focus had shifted elsewhere now. He muttered to one of the prospects—the same ginger-haired girl I had spotted on my very first day here, before waving her off.

But I still couldn't breathe.

My heartbeat thundered as I sat behind the fine wooden desk, stiff and nearly delirious as I wheezed for air. I stared down at the piece of blank white parchment spread out in front of me. A small ink bottle and feather quill were placed at the front of each desk.

Immediately my heart took a nosedive straight to the soles of my new boots.

We had to *write* something?

Oh no.

I whipped around in my seat, searching the lurking crowd of patrons for Roxus. But he was nowhere to be seen. Curse it! Where would he go now?

The seat next to mine scraped on the marble floor, and I turned back to see the girl Domitri had been speaking to settling into it. One by one, all the other prospects chose their seats, and the murmuring in the room died to silence.

Too late.

"Today, you will all be assessed on your knowledge of divine lore. That is to say, how much you know about the history and divine rites of the gods. This is a fundamental and crucial element of your training. A basic understanding will not suffice. You must be *experts* in such things," he began in a thick Damarian accent.

His gaze panned the room, searching every face until he settled onto me again. His thin mouth split with a cruel smirk.

"I expect some of you already have a vast knowledge of *certain* aspects of the divine realm. Particularly the ... dark and unsavory parts."

I swallowed, not daring to move an inch until his frosty gaze panned away.

"Now then, take up your quills and prepare. You'll be writing out each of the gods by name, what they govern, and their role in the War of the Stones. You will also list any and all artifacts attributed to them, and if you should happen to know where they are believed to be located," Domitri continued.

Rushes of whispers echoed through the room until he cleared his throat with a scowl. He motioned to a large bronze hourglass on the corner of his lectern.

"You will have until the sands run out. If I should suspect you are sharing answers, you will be immediately dismissed," he warned. "Begin."

The second he turned that large hourglass over, releasing the black sand to spill down from one egg-shaped glass vial down into the other, all the other prospects snatched up their quills and got to work. The silence was filled with the scratching of the nibs on the parchment.

I stared at my quill.

I'd never used one before.

But that wasn't the biggest problem.

"Do not let them see any weakness in you, Visha. Weakness will be crushed. Destroyed. It will suffer a long and painful death."

My mother's voice rose from the inky depths of my soul again. My body went cold. My pulse thumped in slow, desperate beats, battering at the inside of my ribs like a blacksmith's hammer.

Try. I had to try.

I glanced sideways at the girl sitting at the desk beside mine. She was already busy scribbling little lines of symbols onto her parchment. Her brow was crinkled with focus, and she stopped every so often to re-wet the quill tip in her ink bottle.

Mimicking her movements, my hand trembled some as I took up my quill and stroked at the long, blue feather. It slid between my fingers like silk. I tried dabbing it in the ink and watched as little droplets of black hit the parchment and spread.

The sand was a third of the way empty now.

I tried making a few straight lines and managed to smear some of the ink on my hands. Great. This wasn't working. Even if I could somehow figure out how to use this thing, I still couldn't—

"Pitathi girl," Domitri snapped suddenly.

I flinched and slowly looked up.

He was glaring at me again, his golden eyes narrowed into vicious little slits.

"Is there a reason you aren't writing anything?" he demanded.

My heartbeat skipped. I squeezed the quill harder.

A few of the other prospects had stopped to stare at me, too.

Run, Visha.

"Do you have nothing to share about the gods? Or is it that your knowledge is so singular in only certain deities?" Every word he spoke had a venomous edge.

I could feel their eyes on me. Watching. Waiting. Holding their breath.

"Speak up," he shouted. "Or else I'll be forced to dismiss you and perhaps spare the order from wasting any more of its time on you."

Sweat rolled down the back of my neck. My vision swerved and my hand shook. I could barely keep a grip on my quill.

But I had to try. I couldn't give in. I knew of the gods—their names and what they oversaw. I could answer out loud, at least. Surely that would suffice.

Right?

"I'm waiting," Domitri bellowed again.

"I-I ... I can't do this," I murmured.

Domitri's brows rose, as though he were genuinely surprised I'd said anything at all.

"Can't do what? Remember the names of the gods? Not even the one who created your vile kin? Surely the Pitathi love to tell that story," he taunted.

I bit down hard, focusing my glare on the splotches of black ink that dotted the parchment in front of me. Mistakes.

Like me.

Run. Get away. Don't let them see any weakness.

They'll kill you for it.

My face burned. My eyes welled.

They were all watching. Expecting me to lash out. To explode.

Gods, what was I doing here? I didn't belong with these people. I'd never be one of them.

Not when I couldn't even read or write. Not in their language.

Only in the Viperi one.

"Just kick her out already. It's disgusting that she's even here at all," an older boy chimed in. The same one who'd gotten in my face during the combat assessment.

A murmur of agreement went up around the room.

Domitri grinned, like he could tell I was hanging by a thread.

"That's enough," Roxus's booming voice filled the auditorium. "Domitri, you walk a dangerous line."

"Do I? Perhaps you should check your own footing, then, friend," Domitri hissed. "I'm not the one dragging god-cursed vipers into this sacred place. To even dream she could be one of us is a joke I refuse to laugh at. She will *never* be one of us!"

Too late, I felt the spark light and the flame catch in my chest. In an instant, it was a wildfire, and all I could taste were cinders.

Run, Visha. It's all you can do. Run or fight. Run ... or die.

"STOP IT!" I screamed and threw down my quill.

A few other prospects gasped and yelped in alarm.

Roxus stared at me, his eyes wide and expression fractured with something like pity.

Or maybe shame.

I couldn't tell. And it didn't matter. I only had one choice left now.

Slinging all my parchment and ink bottle aside, I bolted out of my seat and ran for the door. It slammed behind me with a *bang*.

I ran, pumping my legs as fast as they would go, and seeing nothing but the blur of the dim temple rooms. I couldn't stop. I couldn't look back.

All I could do now was find somewhere safe ... and pray I hadn't just ruined everything.

TWELVE

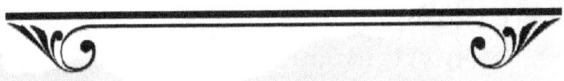

It was all over.

I would be dismissed from the Zenith's Call.

I knew it with every fiber of my useless being. How could I ever pass any sort of assessment about theology and divine lore without being able to do the simplest things—read and write?

I couldn't. And certainly not quickly enough to still be considered as a member of their guild of whatever-they-actually-were.

Definitely *not* assassins—I was more than sure of that now.

Curled up inside a poofy blanket under my bed, there wasn't a single part of me that didn't feel numb and queasy. I couldn't stop shaking. I could barely remember the long run back to Roxus's house. I must have been down here for hours, hiding like a complete coward.

Gods, what a disgusting creature I'd become.

I was a little surprised Delthene hadn't come into my room to try to fish me out. She cracked the door open long enough to peer inside, but didn't say a word.

Even her big orange cat, Gibb, had only strolled by long enough to peer at me for a few minutes and then swagger away with his tail in the air.

Then again, maybe Delthene was just busy doing the day's errands. She probably had no idea I was here—not when I was supposed to be away at Arx Eburna.

Roxus hadn't come in, either. I couldn't decide if that was a relief ... or a very bad sign.

Either way, it didn't matter.

I wouldn't be able to stay here for much longer. My presence had always been conditional to becoming a member of the Zenith's Call. Now that was impossible. It was only a matter of time before Roxus dumped me back in the gutter.

I needed a plan. Somewhere else to go.

But where?

The creak and thud of the front door downstairs made my pulse skip. I drew my legs in close to my chest, burrowing deeper into the blanket like a turtle into a shell. Maybe, if I were perfectly still, no one would find me.

Heavy footfalls climbed the stairs, and I bit down hard against the thick knot of emotion that lodged in my throat. That awful feeling—like trying to swallow a fistful of cotton. It made my eyes well up.

The footsteps stopped right outside my bedroom door. I heard someone let out a heavy sigh. The door creaked as it opened wider.

I knew it was Roxus just by the sight of his road-beaten brown boots and the frayed bottom of his coat.

For a few uncomfortable seconds, he just stood there in the doorway. Then he trudged over to the bed. It lurched and groaned some as he sat down on it.

More heavy silence.

"You gonna come out so we can have this talk face-to-face?" he asked. His tone was hoarse and weary, like he'd just spent the last few hours yelling at someone.

Domitri? Mistress Orvana?

Both?

I didn't dare venture a guess.

When I didn't answer, the bed shifted again over my head. Then a hand appeared ... holding what looked suspiciously like a strawberry tart wrapped in a piece of wax-coated paper.

Really? *Bribery?*

My stomach gave a desperate gurgle that he could probably hear.

But no. I could not be bought. Not even by sugary deliciousness.

Even if I hadn't had anything to eat all day.

And even though he must have stopped by that fantastic little bakery on the street corner on his way back home.

Curse him. And curse the rich, buttery fragrance that wafted past my nose and made my stomach clench and growl.

Roxus sighed noisily. "Guess I'll just have to eat this myself since you—"

I sprang forward and seized the pastry. I was already stuffing all that flaky, melty goodness in my mouth as I wriggled out from under the bed. Sitting on the floor in front of him, I refused to look him in the eye as I chewed.

I didn't have to, though. I could hear the relieved smile in his tone as he murmured, "Glad to see that appetite's still firmly intact."

I wiped the crumbs from my cheeks and finally stole a glance up at his face. Tired lines were set in the corners of his soft brown eyes. They deepened as his smile widened some. "There you are."

My mouth twisted to one side as that awful stiffness returned in my throat, making my eyes start to water and my chin tremble. I hated it. Feeling so exposed and pathetic, even in front of him.

Not when I knew I was supposed to be stronger. I'd failed him yet again. I'd let them get to me. I couldn't hold it in.

But, at least this time I hadn't almost killed anyone. Running was better than murder, right? Didn't that count as progress?

Er, well, in my case, anyway.

"Why didn't you tell me you couldn't write?" he asked, and I could tell by his tone alone he was treading lightly.

Not wanting to push me close to that edge.

"You didn't ask," I mumbled. "Nobody sits around giving lessons to urchins."

"Fair enough. But you've got to tell me these things. Otherwise, I can't prepare you for what's coming," he said.

I pursed my lips sourly. He was right, but he was wrong, too. He should have known no one was ever going to go out of their way to teach a Viperi orphan something like that.

"Well, I can't read, either." I crossed my arms and looked away.

"We can fix that."

I snorted. "Who can? And what's the point? It's over, isn't it? I'm done. I can't be a member of the Zenith's Call."

"That's not true," Roxus countered, his tone deepening with disapproval.

"But Domitri said—"

"*Domitri* doesn't make the decisions in our order," Roxus interrupted, biting every word sharply.

I blinked up at him, watching the clouds of wrath slowly dissolve away from his squared, rugged features. He combed his fingers through his hair and rubbed at his stubbly chin like he was trying to rein in his temper before he spoke again.

"I met with him and Mistress Orvana. Things are going to change. He's been relieved of any teaching involved with prospects for the foreseeable future. Someone else will be instructing you all in divine lore."

I couldn't hide my total shock. "What? Really? Because of me?"

"Because of many things. He's been on edge lately due to the tensions with the Tibran Empire spreading closer to the Southern Kingdoms. That doesn't excuse his behavior, but hopefully some downtime will clear his head," Roxus replied. "Perhaps he can return his focus to more present matters— like teaching his own prospect."

My mouth scrunched in disgust.

Domitri had a prospect? Gods, who was that unlucky?

"On that same note, however, I think I have a solution when it comes to your reading and writing. Incidentally, it might also help you with your apparent complete lack of social skills. You need to be as keen with your words and smiles as you are with a blade."

I frowned. What was he talking about? I had plenty of social skills.

Fine. So maybe not the *friendly* kind.

Ugh.

Roxus shook his head, muttering under his breath. He made a big grunting, heaving show of standing up and stretching his back before he shuffled to the door. Pausing there, he waved a hand to call me along with him.

I trudged after him, hissing a few Viperi curses under my breath as I walked ahead of him out into the hall.

I only made it a few steps before I stopped, my thoughts once again twisting and writhing in my head like a knot of thorns. Everything felt so heavy. So out of control. But knowing he was standing there, right behind me, was strangely … comforting.

Like he was protecting me, even now.

And it was immediately terrifying.

"Why do you keep doing this?" My voice came out so small and broken.

It made me sick to my stomach.

"Doing what?" he asked as he stood close behind me.

"Forcing them to give me more chances? Can't you tell I'm not cut out for this? I can't be something I'm not. I can't be anything good," I murmured. "Domitri is right. I'll never be accepted by anyone there. You're wasting your time."

"Is that really what you think?"

I bobbed my head once.

Heavy, tense silence settled between us for what felt like an eternity. Maybe it was only a minute, but in that time, I could feel every one of my heartbeats like a hammer to my throat.

At last, I heard the rustling of fabric behind me, as though he were fishing through his coat pockets. Then another golden brown pastry, topped with a crust of sugar crystals, appeared right in front of my face.

"You're downright pitiful when you're hungry, you know that?" he chuckled.

I scowled at the pastry, my senses now focused on every delightful nuance of butter, cinnamon, nutmeg, and a hint of cream.

Really? Had he even heard anything I said? Was he just brushing me off?

I reached out for the pastry, cursing fiercely under my breath. Before I could even touch it, Roxus jerked it back.

"I'm not wasting my time," he said, his tone suddenly serious. "I told you from the beginning this wouldn't be easy. I told you they'd come for you. And this is only the beginning, Violet. It's going to get worse before it gets better."

A tingle of fear churned in my stomach. My hands curled into sweaty, trembling fists at my sides.

He was right. I knew that. Mistress Orvana would only

tolerate me for as long as I managed to keep my instincts under control. But how long would that be?

"I don't think I can do this," the words slipped past my lips so quickly I couldn't stop them.

"I *know* you can," he countered.

A sharp pain in my chest made me wince and my shoulders draw up closer to my ears. "You're wrong."

I could hear that devilish smirk in his voice. "Rarely. Domitri is right, though. You'll never be accepted by anyone else—not unless you start working on accepting yourself first. You can't change what you are or where you came from. But you can change what you do now. You can become something better or worse. Your choice."

My pulse boomed in my ears. I wanted to look back, to meet his gaze, but I didn't dare move an inch. Not when heat crept over my face like the glare of a sunrise and my chin kept trembling like crazy.

"Yes, I've forced them to give you more grace than the other prospects. Call me sentimental, but I think we can afford some wiggle room for a starving girl I scraped out of the bottom of a dog kennel in the city prison," he said. "But I'm not a miracle worker. I'm just the guy holding the carrots—er, pastries. You still hold all the power over your destiny. So I suggest you go ahead and make up your mind about what you want out of life."

Every word from his lips squeezed around my heart, tight and warm, like a hug I'd never felt before. It made my shoulders drop and my breathing slow. My mind, so tangled up with worry and fear, seemed to settle. All those thoughts went quiet.

It was ... peace.

A peace I'd never felt before.

A peace I knew I'd never deserve.

"I'll keep trying," I promised, my voice catching.

"Good." He lowered the pastry.

I grabbed it before he could pull it away again and crammed it into my mouth. The explosion of rich flavors, warm and delicious, made my eyes roll closed.

Roxus was grinning wolfishly as he strode past me and continued down the hall. "Come on, then. Time to learn a new trick."

I trotted after him. Something about that proud spring in his step made my stomach swim with uneasiness. He was up to no good.

Great. What now?

When we reached the first floor and stepped into the front sitting room ... I finally saw it.

Or *her*, rather.

I lurched to a halt, staring straight into the pale, moon-shaped face of the coppery-haired girl. The same one who also happened to be a prospect, like me.

Her wide doe eyes studied me, shining in a dark green color like ivy leaves. She never looked away, even as Roxus strolled over to stand beside her and cross his arms.

He arched a brow at me disapprovingly and tipped his chin in a gesture for me to come closer.

I had to swallow the urge to growl and bare my teeth at her as I advanced a few more steps and stopped again, still well out of her reach if she decided to lunge at me.

What, by all the gods, was this?

"Violet, I believe you already know Chrysa," Roxus said, motioning to her. "Or you've seen her, at least."

I scowled and didn't reply.

Neither did she.

"Turns out, you both need some improvement. You need someone to teach you how to read and write. She needs someone to tutor her in combat. A trade of skills seemed like the logical way to resolve this, and Mistress Orvana agreed."

What?! He wanted me to teach her swordplay? Sparring? Hand-to-hand combat?

I balked and choked out loud. "B-but that's—!"

"Your best option for improving your situation at Arx Eburna. You're not the only one receiving their fair share of suspicion and rejection by the other prospects," Roxus corrected firmly, his glare forbidding as he motioned to Chrysa again. "She is a former Tibran slave."

My mouth clamped shut.

Locking gazes with her again, I searched every one of her features for some clue. How had I missed that?

As though she could read my thoughts, Chrysa pulled aside her thick, waist-length red braid to reveal the gnarled, pale branded mark on the side of her neck. The symbol of the Tibran Empire. Sweet gods.

She really had been a Tibran captive.

And judging by how much the scar had faded, she had either been with them for a long time ... or on the run.

I wondered which was the case for her. According to Roxus, Tibrans didn't let their captives go easily. Deserters were hunted down and brutally executed.

Chrysa finally lowered her gaze to the floor as she arranged her braid back over her shoulder, hiding the mark from plain sight. Her brow scrunched, drawing up in a look of earnest tension. Maybe she didn't like being exposed like that.

At least she could hide it, though.

I couldn't hide what I was so easily.

"You are welcome to do some of your lessons here, rather than at Arx Eburna. But I'd encourage you both to consider taking advantage of all the resources there. You'll have access to parts of the library to study divine lore and history before your final trial on those subjects," Roxus continued. "And the sparring room has more to offer than my home for training."

"You mean *miracle-working?*" I countered, using his own

words from before. It was a tall order to expect I could teach
her all the intricacies of combat and swordplay in only a few
months.

"To get you reading and writing in two languages may
require a little divine intervention." Roxus narrowed his eyes
slightly, giving me that unspoken look of warning.

"Two languages?!" I balked.

"If you want to be considered for the Zenith's Call, you at
least need to know Sokraal and Rienkan," he said, referring to
the human and elven languages. "It'd be better if you knew
Avoran, too, but that might be a miracle too far with so little
time."

All the wind rushed out of me at once.

Suddenly, teaching combat seemed like the easy part.

I eyed Chrysa more carefully, wondering if she was even
going to be able to teach me one language, let alone two.

The scrunched, uncertain expression on her freckled face
didn't give me much confidence.

But neither of us had a choice.

"Fine," I agreed.

Chrysa looked at Roxus and nodded without saying a
word.

Hmm. Come to think of it, I'd never heard her say
anything at the assessments, either. Not even to the other
prospects. I wasn't sure who her patron was, but I had never
seen her talking to anyone else.

How was she going to teach me anything if she didn't
speak?

Taking a cautious step forward, she extended a hand out
to me.

I stared at it, noting every old scar flecked across her wrists
and fingers. Marks from shackles?

I frowned harder, steeling every strained nerve and forcing
myself to take her hand and shake it.

"Good. Get to work, then. You've got plenty to do." Roxus wore that stupid, smug grin as he stepped away from us, ruffling my hair on his way back upstairs.

Right.

I drew my hand back from her and sized her up again. She was a lot taller than me, like everyone else at Arx Eburna, but that didn't matter. If she made a false move, I'd see it coming a mile away.

Former Tibran slave or not, it didn't matter. This girl couldn't be trusted. No one could. Chrysa was no different from all the other prospects who still whispered at my back like I didn't have ears.

Better ears than all of them, in fact.

And I'd damned to the deepest pit of the abyss before I let her even dream that we were allies, let alone friends.

Viperi did not have *friends*. And that was all I'd ever truly be in their eyes.

Now, I'd just have to hope I could prove that to Roxus without getting my throat slashed as soon as my back was turned.

Thirteen

"Again—and get your weight off your heels! Do you want to die or something?"

My voice echoed through Roxus's sparse training room. It wasn't much, just some training dummies and a rack of practice weapons, but it would do for now.

I stood, arms crossed and brow aching from hours of disappointed scowling, as I watched Chrysa flounder through another sequence of forward strikes. We'd been at this for nearly three hours, and I now had a full appreciation for how much work this was going to be.

Chrysa handled a blade like she'd never touched one in her life. Her movements were too slow. Too chaotic. She hesitated on every strike—probably second-guessing herself each time.

It was a hot, stinking mess.

Now I had to figure out how to clean it up. Easier said than done. I'd never taught anyone combat before. I barely remembered learning it myself. Viperi were trained from the moment we could walk, and we didn't have that kind of time at our disposal.

We'd have to settle for passable rather than perfection.

I sighed as she blundered to a halt in the final pose, holding her practice scimitar up in a high parry.

Her green eyes flickered to me, waiting for my critique, as she sucked in ragged breaths. Her face was so flushed I could barely see any of her freckles, and her hair stuck to the sweat drizzling down her forehead and neck.

Too bad I wasn't exactly brimming with compliments for that performance.

"Sloppy," I snapped. "Do it again. Control your breathing. Quit locking your elbows. Feel the stability in your core. Focus. You need to be thinking one move ahead, at least."

Chrysa dropped her arms, still panting as she wiped her face on the sleeve of her tunic. She made almost no expression, keeping a veneer of slightly sweaty indifference no matter how hard I pushed her.

Interesting.

"These are not the same drills my patron has shown me," she said, her voice soft and surprisingly small.

I had to concentrate to keep my mouth from falling open.

That was the first time she'd said a word to me.

It took a few seconds for me to recover my composure. I managed a convincing dismissive snort as I wafted a hand.

"Because your patron probably has no idea what he's doing. Or she, I guess," I quipped. "Who is your patron, anyway?"

"Domitri," she said and angled her face away, like she knew how I was going to respond to that.

Rage poured through my body like I'd swallowed a bucketful of cinders. It made all my nerves twitch at once, and my muscles draw tense. I ground my jaw, stifling a growl.

Seriously? Roxus had brought *Domitri's* prospect here to train with me?!

Of all the rotten, sneaky, back-handed—

"For the record, he protested this. He didn't want me to be anywhere near you or Roxus. But Mistress Orvana insisted, and I did not object," she added quickly.

All the fury in my blood went cold in an instant.

She ... hadn't objected? Why not? Anyone else would have, right?

None of the other prospects wanted anything to do with me.

"He is not a kind man." Her voice quietened, becoming hardly more than a whisper.

Something about her tone, and the dejected, faraway look on her face made my insides quake. What did that mean? Did he despise her, too? Was he cruel to her?

"Why stay with him, then?" I questioned.

"I have no other choice. No one else would take me in. Not all of us are found by people who leave pastries out for us after we train."

Heat crept over my cheeks. Roxus was kind to me. He was gentle, but always kept a certain distance. Whether out of respect, fear, or simply a desire for his own privacy—I didn't know. I hadn't thought about it all that much.

Now I had to wonder ... who was he *really?* Why was he so different from Domitri and all the other patrons who openly despised me?

Another question stung at the back of my mind. Something Chrysa might actually know the answer to.

The day of my combat assessment, Domitri had nearly killed me. I'd seen his body glowing with a soft halo of blue light, and then again when we were in the auditorium. What did that mean? Could she see it, too? Could anyone else?

Or was there something wrong with me? Something worse than just being a Viperi?

The thought made that pit in my stomach go sour. My

toes curled inside my boots and my mouth pinched sourly. I'd seen lots of things glow blue since I'd come here. First the symbol on the door, and then some of the torches.

None of it made any sense.

And I had no idea how to begin asking Chrysa about any of it, or even if I should. Asking the wrong questions could be dangerous. I didn't need any extra problems.

"I'm not suggesting we become friends," Chrysa murmured suddenly as she fiddled with her practice scimitar, still avoiding eye contact.

"Then what are you suggesting?"

Her lips pursed thoughtfully. At last, she glanced at me and gave a shrug of her wide, willowy shoulders. "Tolerance? At least for the sake of training. We need to demonstrate to the others that we can work peacefully with others, even if they can't with us. We need to make it obvious to the Mistress that *we* are not the problem—*they* are."

Oh.

I worked my jaw from one side to the other, studying her round, freckle-dusted face for any signs of deception. She seemed to search mine with the same intense curiosity. I wondered how strange I looked to her.

Had she ever seen a Viperi before?

"Fine," I agreed. "I suppose that makes sense."

The corners of her mouth twitched, hinting at a cautious smile. "Good. Then can I ask you something?"

"I guess." I turned away, giving her my shoulder as I strolled to the rack of practice weapons and chose the other scimitar.

Might as well show her how to do these sequences properly again.

"Why did you leave the rest of the Viperi? I thought they all lived in big cavern-cities far underground all the way in Nar'Haleen," she said.

I froze, my fingers brushing the worn leather of the hilt. The truth rose from deep in my chest like an inky, putrid tide.

I knew full-well what the other prospects and agents thought. They assumed I was a spy. That I'd come here by choice.

Not even Roxus knew the truth, though.

I hadn't come here because I wanted to.

My mother and I never had a choice.

"I didn't leave," I growled softly, keeping my back to her. "I was exiled."

"Exiled? Why?"

Seizing the weapon tightly in my grasp, I faced her with a stony scowl. My fingers squeezed at the scimitar's hilt until my whole arm shook, knuckles blanching and palms sweating.

Trust for trust.

"Because the only thing Viperi hate more than the gods and peoples of the surface, is imperfection in their own ranks. I was found to be imperfect, and the brood father gave the order to have me exterminated," I hissed bitterly. "My mother defied his ruling and we were both exiled, which among our people is a fate worse than death. It is to die in shame, separated from the clan, unwitnessed and without honor."

I left out a lot of details. I didn't tell her how the rest of our clan chased us out, shooting arrows tipped in poisoned, barbed points so that we would be weak and injured by the time we reached the surface.

I didn't tell her how my mother perished under the glare of the unforgiving desert sun, leaving me alone in the golden dunes.

I didn't expect her to understand—not the significance of any of that, or how much each word of it burned in my throat. I'd never said any of this out loud before, mostly because I knew no one else would really care what the truth was. They'd cling to their own theories. They'd prefer rumors to the much-less-scandalous reality.

I glared at Chrysa through the glittering bits of dust that drifted through shafts of late evening sunlight ebbing through the narrow windows on the far end of the room. And for a long time, neither of us spoke. The smell of sweat and old wood hung thick in the warm air. The faint echo of the wind howled over the roof.

Then I saw her hand reach up to the gnarled scar on the side of her neck, hidden by her thick hair. Her gaze panned away, thin gingery brows drawing up in a look of anguish I didn't understand.

But I felt it, too.

The pain of the past like a rotting wound deep inside. Festering. Aching.

Echoing forever.

"The Tibrans invaded my home when I was little. They murdered my family. They took me far away," she whispered. "And I know I should hate them. I should want to murder them all for what they did. I shouldn't feel guilty about running away."

Her evergreen eyes shut tightly for a moment, as though she were trying to bear down and brace against that inky black tide that smothered from within.

"But I do. Because for all their cruelty, after everything they've done and are still doing, they are all just like me," she said. "We were all strangers strung together, stolen from our homelands and forced to fight or grease the wheels of Lord Argonox's war machines. We only had each other."

Her eyes opened and she stared back at me again. My heartbeat skipped, not sure what to make of the strange softness in her expression as she added, "Until now."

Trust for trust.

We were both monsters, after all.

Suddenly, I realized why Roxus had brought her here. I knew why, in spite of Domitri being a pig-faced moron, he had allowed us to train together. This wasn't just about swapping skills.

However devious and manipulative he might be, Roxus knew the truth.

He knew we needed each other if we were ever going to stand a chance of starting a new life. We might never be friends. But everyone needed allies, and we were both in dire need of someone to be on our side.

It made my heart feel strangely tight, as though it were being squeezed in a giant fist and twisted deep inside my chest. I struggled to breathe and looked down at my boots. I didn't want her to see my eyes tear up. I didn't want her to see that I felt anything at all.

For Viperi, feeling was a weakness.

Gods, I was becoming the softest one of all.

"I'm going to show you the maneuvers again," I managed stiffly, clearing my throat to keep my voice from catching.

Chrysa nodded. "I'll try harder."

"No, try *better*. Doing the wrong thing harder isn't going to make any difference," I grumbled. "Light feet. Firm grip. This is a dance, not a charge. Keep your joints loose and your movements fluid. The blade should become an extension of yourself."

Chrysa still didn't get it. Hours later, she hadn't improved much at all. I didn't know if I'd be able to get her ready for the trials. Four months wasn't much time.

But I would try.

And when the time came for us both to stand before the Mistress of the Call, maybe it would be enough. That was the only hope I had to cling to now, even if it went against everything I'd ever been raised to believe.

Viperi didn't tolerate "good enough."

There was only perfection or punishment.

But I wasn't with them anymore. I had to adapt. I had to become something new if I wanted to survive. Not a feral street urchin. Not a brutally efficient assassin.

I had to learn to become a Zenith's Call ... no matter what the cost.

FOURTEEN

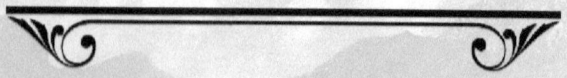

I was doomed.

I knew it even before I spotted her that Chrysa was already waiting in the Krin'Moir by the time I arrived at Arx Eburna at dawn.

Unlike me, she had to stay in the temporary dormitories here since her patron, Domitri, also lived here within the temple grounds.

Apparently, lots of the agents opted to do that, keeping close to their studies and chasing down missions—whatever that meant. Roxus was still being vague, dancing around the truth of what the Zenith's Call really did.

Annoying beyond belief.

But after more than a month, and watching several other prospects be dismissed for lack of ability, it felt like that answer was closer than ever.

They had tested all the prospects on stealth, putting us through obstacle courses in darkened rooms where we had to cross floors littered with glass bottles or hanging glass balls that would clink and clatter if you made a wrong step. Easy—if you happened to be able to see in the dark.

Which I could.

I'd also breezed through their assessments of sleight of hand. Pick-pocketing is all that had kept me fed for the last several years, after all. I could slip coins from pockets or purses, weapons from belts, and get away before anyone was the wiser.

To test us, they'd lined up a group of Vindexori and elder agents, challenging us to determine which one had a large red glass gem in their pocket and swipe it.

I'd passed with flying colors.

To my surprise, so had Chrysa. She had more skill in the subtle arts than I'd ever suspected, but maybe that was something I could use to keep improving her combat ability.

Now, unfortunately, came the thing I hated most. The thing I'd been struggling with for the last three weeks. My certain doom.

Reading and writing.

Ugggh.

Today was our first day back in the auditorium for instruction in divine lore and history, and I couldn't hold back a long, groaning sigh of defeat as soon as I spotted Chrysa already standing there with that same look of faraway indifference she always wore. Only when I got closer did she offer a painfully forced, stiff smile.

I took in a deep breath of the thick, mineral-tinged air and sighed loudly.

Gods just end me now. Couldn't we just drop the fake pleasantries? This was going to be misery and we both knew it. As bad as she had been at combat, I was ten times worse when it came to learning how to write. My penmanship was horrible, and I got lost trying to spell anything more than one syllable.

Ironically, reading came fairly easy. I was improving every day and had a good handle on Sokraal.

Rienkan was much harder, though. All of the elven languages sounded faster, more complex, and almost musical. The sounds were completely different from the common tongue and even Viperi.

Chrysa didn't speak it, either, though. That made teaching me impossible, so Roxus had employed Leruna to come and tutor us both a few times a week. How on earth Roxus got Domitri to agree to that, I still had no idea. Maybe he was glad for any upper hand he could get for his prospect.

Honestly, it was just nice to not be taking those lessons alone. And as it turned out, Leruna was full of wisdom when it came to some of the languages. She was a Rienkan elf, so she could teach us all the proper pronunciations and spellings. More than that, though, she spent time explaining how all the elven languages were connected because they all stemmed from the Avoran tongue. Once she revealed that, and pointed out how we could logically break down some of the words to determine their meaning between all the elven languages, everything snapped into focus in my mind.

I learned faster. It all just ... made sense, suddenly. Like a veil had been lifted from my eyes and I could see how all these elven languages had evolved over the eons.

And I realized, the human tongues shared that connection —although far more loosely. The Tibran language was the mother tongue to all the common human languages, except for Vordegan, which was its own basket of harsh, sharp, guttural sounds that were frankly alien-sounding compared to any other language I'd heard.

Fortunately, I wasn't expected to learn that one. Thank the gods for that.

Chrysa and I poured all our attention into memorizing the words, sounds, and syntax rules. She caught on quickly, too. But not as fast as I did. Apparently, I had a special talent for languages.

But now we'd be assessed on our improvements. I had to sit in that room again, surrounded by all the other prospects, and try to write out the names of all sixteen gods, their histories, symbols, and notable myths or histories about them.

Ironically, we'd learned a lot of that information from Leruna, as well. Since she served the temple of the sea goddess, Undae, she was full of stories of ancient divine history.

But, gods, I hoped they wouldn't be grading my work on spelling. Chrysa said mine was still atrocious.

I trudged over to fall in step beside her with a nod of greeting. "You're early."

"You're late." She nodded back, standing straighter with her deep green eyes focused ahead as we made our way to the Eternal Hall.

I scowled. "Roxus held me up. He was going on about not panicking if things go wrong this time."

"He's not here today?" she sounded concerned. Maybe she thought I was going to freak out again, too.

Fabulous.

"Not until later," I said.

"Running more of those mysterious errands?" Chrysa gave a bemused snort.

I sighed and rolled my eyes. "Always. The man comes and goes like the wind."

"You think it's on Zenith's Call business?"

"I don't know," I admitted with a shrug. "Probably. But he doesn't talk about anything personal with me."

She threw me a sideways look with her thin brows slightly raised. "Never?"

"Nope."

"So you really don't know anything about him?" she pressed. "I mean, haven't you ever been tempted to snoop around and find out?"

I couldn't resist a coy smirk. "Yeah. I did. And he totally caught me."

She snickered and covered her mouth. "What did he say?"

"Nothing revealing about himself if that's what you're hoping." I laughed, too. "It really doesn't bother me. He doesn't know much about my personal life, either. I've never even told him about being exiled. He hasn't asked, either. I don't know, maybe he's waiting for me to volunteer it."

Her mouth twisted thoughtfully to one side and she stopped right outside the doorway of the auditorium. "I bet that is what he's waiting for."

I arched an eyebrow. "You think?"

"Yeah, definitely. It's a sign of trust. Maybe if you open up some, he will, too."

I had to think about that. She could be on to something.

Still, the idea of just waltzing into his office one evening to dump my entire life's story on him felt … weird. Weird and insanely uncomfortable.

Was that really what he was waiting for?

Hmm.

I jerked some as Chrysa nudged me with her elbow. She nodded into the auditorium. "Look."

I did, half-expecting to find that Domitri was lurking in there, waiting to shock us all with his return to the classroom. But, no. There was a new woman standing behind the lectern —one I had never seen before.

A Lunostri elf.

My heart gave a frantic flutter at the sight of her, and dread settled in the pit of my stomach like a stone to the bottom of a frozen lake.

I'd never seen a Lunostri elf outside of Nar'Haleen. They didn't travel much outside their nomadic villages, scattered across the Valley of the Gods and moving with the sun. Some kept to the ancient temples, or in hidden cliff-bound cities.

But I couldn't recall ever seeing one this far to the west.

Her dark ebony skin was painted with beautiful silver runemarks, and her slender pointed ears were studded with glittering crystal earrings. She looked a lot younger than any of the other patrons I had seen and wore the sweeping silken robes of a scholar. Curators, Roxus called them.

Masters of the ancient texts and keepers of arcane lore.

Bizarre. And slightly unnerving, considering how Lunostri felt about Viperi. We came from the same region, and our ancestors had warred many times in the past.

In fact, of all the surface races living throughout the Southern Kingdoms, the Lunostri were perhaps the only ones that might give the Viperi pause.

Gods help me.

She wasn't what Chrysa was pointing at, though.

There were more prospects missing.

Had they all been dismissed? Why? Had something happened?

"Only thirteen left," Chrysa whispered.

My mouth twisted into a tight, sideways frown. I had known from the start not everyone would make it to the end to be accepted into the Zenith's Call. I just hadn't expected it would be so few. Fates, we had a little less than three months left.

Would anyone actually make it to the end?

Would I?

"Everyone, find a seat and we'll get started." The Lunostri woman behind the lectern was looking right at me, her yellow-green eyes shining in the ambient light of the sconces all around the chamber.

Great.

This would go exactly how I envisioned, then—with the same embarrassing passive-aggressive misery I'd come to expect whenever I had to deal with any of the other patrons.

And this time, Roxus was nowhere in sight if anything went wrong.

Lovely.

The Lunostri woman smiled, nodding to me slightly.

I sucked in a sharp breath. What did that mean? Was she greeting me?

No. Surely not.

Was there someone else behind me she was looking at instead?

I glanced over my shoulder, but found no one.

Definitely me, then.

Sweat prickled on the back of my neck as I lowered my head and followed Chrysa down a few steps and into the first available seats. The cold of the wood against my back sent a shiver down my spine.

Or maybe that was just the panic.

Once everyone had settled in, a tense silence filled the room. It made every tiny hair on my body stand on end.

"Varri'dasha, everyone. I am Curator Faera," the Lunostri agent said, giving the common Sokraal greeting to us. *May the gods watch over you.*

I sat stiffly in my chair, braced for any sudden movements. Just in case. Hopefully, the gods weren't watching me too carefully.

"I will be instructing you all in divine lore and history from now on," she went on in a smooth, airy voice. "But more importantly, I will be advising you on your true purpose here. The true purpose of the Zenith's Call."

Another bitter chill raced up my spine.

We were finally going to learn the truth? The reason we were all here? The reason Roxus had pulled me out of that miserable prison?

My pulse quickened and I bounced one of my legs, fidgeting with the quill on my desk as Faera spoke.

"You may have noticed that there are fewer and fewer of you every day, as some of your peers have already been found wanting and dismissed, or chosen to leave of their own accord. Those of you who remain are our best prospects for future agents of the cause. But after what I'm about to tell you, some of you may decide this is not the life you want."

I stole a sideways glance at Chrysa.

She was nibbling fiercely on the inside of her cheek, brows knitted and hands in her lap.

Well, I wasn't the only one on edge.

"If that's the case, you're welcome to leave. No one will fault you for it," Faera said. "Because the path that lies before you, the one that will bring you into the order of the Zenith's Call, is one of dangerous secrets and grave consequences. It is one of pain. Of solitude. Of sacrifice."

Heavy silence filled the room with a tension I could almost taste. Like a mouthful of bitter sea spray, it made my lips press together and my eyes narrow.

They really weren't assassins. Gods, by the sound of it, they weren't even mercenaries.

So what were they, then? And why did Roxus believe I could be one of them?

"Before there were the Southern Kingdoms, before any of the god stones were forged, there was the Zenith's Call. There were those who sought the gods, not as priests and priestesses, or humble temple keepers, but as an extension of their will. They were the keepers of the holiest secrets. The protectors of sacred relics. The guardians of divine gates."

Faera strolled away from her lectern, pacing at the front of the auditorium as her sharp, yellow-and-green eyes flickered over each of us again. Appraising. Looking for the smallest reactions.

"And after the War of the Stones, when all of Reatia had seen the might and fury of the divine realm that had cracked this mortal world in two and left it eternally scarred, we endured," she said, her voice softening with grim reverence.

I sucked in a breath, feeling the weight of each word like a stone stacked on my chest.

"Ages have passed, have changed the face of the mortal world. But we must remain unchanged in our purpose. We must become whatever the situation requires," Faera said. "Sometimes we are teachers. Sometimes liars. Sometimes mercenaries."

Every eye in the room followed her as she made her way back to her lectern at the front of the room and faced us all with an expression of calm resolve. "We are thieves. Vagabonds. Spies. Scholars. Acolytes. Secret keepers. Even assassins, when we must be."

I stiffened in my seat as her frosty-hued gaze fixed squarely on me again.

"But first, and always, we are guardians. We protect the deepest secrets of our world's history that can never be lost or allowed to fall into the wrong hands. Such things could mean the end of the world as we know it," she declared. "We defend that ... even if it costs us our very last breath."

I tried not to be too obvious as I swallowed against the knot forming in the back of my throat. Somehow, it felt like she was asking me if I was ready for that sort of commitment or not.

And I ... didn't know.

The commitment didn't scare me. But trusting the commitment of everyone sitting around me—believing they would have my back all in the name of some shared cause.

I didn't know if I was willing to risk that.

I was still just a Viperi to them. A monster in their midst they were forced to tolerate. Why would they ever want to trust me?

I had no idea.

And I didn't have much time left to figure it all out.

"That is why we train you to fight—because what you learn now may be cause enough for some to try to kill you. They may try to torture you for what you know, and we must be certain that you are ready to kill or be killed rather than surrender these secrets," she explained, her brow drawing tense and earnest.

I sank a little lower in my seat. So that was it. That was why they'd tested us on combat straight away.

The weak and hesitant need not apply.

"That is why we will educate you in all areas of divine lore and history, because the survival of the entire world may depend on your ability to recall these facts," she continued. "That is why you must speak languages from all corners of this world, so that you may pass through these lands when necessary."

Oh boy. That did not bode well for me, then. How much longer I have to get a handle on those subjects? I was learning, yes, but it was slow.

Gods, no wonder Roxus thought I needed extra help.

"We will require you to lie and deceive, to pass through the fabric of every community as smoothly and silently as a ripple upon a pond. We expect a level of stealth unmatched by any other organization this world has ever seen, because we walk where no one else can." Faera put her hands on her lectern, staring down at it for a moment as though gathering her thoughts.

Then she gazed out at all of us again, her gentle smile never quite reaching the deep, haunted depths of her eyes.

Chills swept over me, making my skin prickle and my heartbeat clash like thunder in my chest. That was a look I knew all too well.

It was the expression of someone who had seen, and

survived, horrors untold. Things that probably would have sent most of us screaming from the room.

And she was just a *scholar* here.

"To remain and be further trained, you will leave the rest of your life behind and never return to it. Your family. Your friends. Anything you were or had before will be surrendered for this cause. You will become Zenith's Call and nothing else, until you draw your final breath," she said, her eyes still searching every face sitting around the room.

But no one moved. No one made a sound.

In that silence, I was sure Chrysa could probably hear my heart pounding.

I didn't have any of the things she was talking about. No home. No family. No belongings. I was raw clay, so long as I could keep my instincts at bay.

Is that why Roxus had chosen me?

I didn't know.

"Before we continue our lesson, I would ask that if there is anyone in this room who is not prepared to die to save a world that may never know you existed ... you must do us all the grace of leaving. No one will fault you. There is a reason so few of us exist." Faera stood straighter, her lips pressing into a thin, straight line.

And we waited.

A minute passed. Then another. My mind raced like a gushing stream, smashing into ever-frenzied thoughts as I tried to make sense of why Roxus had brought me here in the first place.

Yes, I could fight. I had nowhere else to go—nothing better to do with my life. No purpose. No place. These people could give me both.

But was I ready to become some sort of divine guardian?

What did that even mean?

Would they ever accept me, or would I always be kept at arm's length?

A chair scraped over the stone floor on the far left.

I flinched, sucking in a sharp breath.

Everyone stared as an elven boy stood, his expression skewed with teary-eyed frustration, and walked silently out of the room.

Then there were twelve.

Another prospect was eliminated, this time of his own choosing.

And I had no idea if I would be next.

FIFTEEN

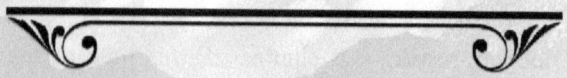

Two more prospects were gone.

The moment Chrysa and I stepped through the entryway into the library, we swapped a quick, sideways glance.

Hmmm. This couldn't be a good sign.

It hadn't been that long since our first lecture with Curator Faera, and now only ten of us remained. Gods, we still had roughly two months left to go before we had our final trials.

Sinking into the empty seat next to Chrysa, I stared down the long table that stretched almost half the length of the library's main chamber.

A few other prospects sat around, immersed in their studies and thumbing through ancient volumes of divine history. They didn't even stop to glare at me anymore.

Did that mean they were finally getting used to me? Or were they just too worried about their own survival in this elimination process to care what anyone else was doing?

Eh. Probably the latter.

The days had all begun to run together, and sometimes it

seemed like every second of my life was now already planned for me. Smothering and frustrating, at times. But I couldn't deny it also came with a sense of strange calm.

I'd never had a purpose before. Not in a long time, anyway.

Chrysa and I spent our mornings in the sparring room, and I taught her everything I could about combat until one of the elder agents called us to whatever lessons they'd prepared for the day. Sometimes they had more assessments, probably to gauge our progress. But the final trials were still roughly eight weeks away.

Hopefully enough time for both of us to improve more.

The afternoons were open for our discretion. Or, at least, they would have been—but Roxus had set us up on a rigorous schedule for swapping our lessons with more training, reading, writing, and tutoring with Leruna until late at night.

After that, Chrysa returned here, to Arx Eburna, and I surrendered to a bath with Delthene scrubbing her oils and potions into my skin and hair. She'd force me to eat another meal, usually a bowl of hearty stew or porridge, before I finally collapsed into bed. Body exhausted and stomach full, it was impossible to fight the pull of sleep.

But the next day, I'd do it all again. And again. And again.

Chrysa dumped an armful of huge, leather-bound books in front of me like an avalanche and groaned.

"Today, we start on the Foregods. I'm betting Faera will quiz us on everything before the War of the Stones this week," she murmured. "She seems far more focused on the divine lore than the languages. I wonder if that's because the expectations for learning the languages aren't as strict as knowing the lore?"

I sighed so hard it made my lips flap. She might have been bright-eyed and eager when it came to all this studying, but my brain already hurt.

"The good news is, very little is written about the Foregods. So you won't have to read much." Chrysa plopped down into the seat across from me and slid one of the thick, dusty tomes my way.

She swiped another for herself—one about ancient Avoran enchantments. The sorts that apparently could be found in all the ruins and temples throughout the Southern Kingdoms.

"And the bad news?" I could tell by that subtle smirk on her lips that she was holding back something crucial.

"It's all written in Avoran."

Ugggh.

I lay my head face down on the book and groaned louder. I took a deep breath, inhaling the musty aroma of the yellowed parchment and aging leather.

Gods strike me down right now, right here, in this hell pit of learning.

This would take an eternity.

With all the extra help studying and practicing from Chrysa and Leruna, I now had a good handle on both Sokraal and Rienkan. I could hold conversations, write letters without misspelling everything, and Leruna said my accent was decent enough.

But Avoran was an unholy nightmare of a language, and I understood completely why it had died out as soon as those fancy flying elves had all gone north—replaced by the other, simpler elven tongues who altered and abbreviated a lot of the words to make them much easier to say.

Curse them and their unnecessarily complex alphabet straight to the abyss.

Leruna explained that the Avoran language was the closest to that of the gods, the first words ever spoken upon the surface of the world. She promised that, at some point, I might feel a connection to it because at our very core, we were all descended from one of the five peoples—the five mortal races first created to walk the surface of this world.

Obviously, the Avoran elves were one of those races. All the other races of elves had come from them, even if they all looked very different now. Some of them had even warred against one another in eons past.

The mysterious rajinna, who could do all manner of incredible and powerful magic, were another of the five peoples. I'd never actually seen one, but I'd heard they looked strange. Some said they even had tails like a lion and horns on their heads.

Bizarre. But mostly myth, at this point. Supposedly, they were all but extinct after ages of being hunted and enslaved for their magic.

Then there were dwarves, most beloved of Giaus. They lived far to the west, deep in their mountain halls cut from the heart of the earth. They didn't care much to explore or expand beyond their homeland, so seeing them this far east was rare. I'd only glimpsed a few in my lifetime, coming and going with the merchants at the harbor.

Humans were the most common, of course, and had mixed with just about every other race to form some sort of new one. According to what I'd read, they had originally come from the east, in the area of Tibrus. But it hadn't taken them long to expand all across Reatia.

Now, you couldn't swing a cat without hitting one.

And ... then there were the Viperi.

My kin.

We were often mistaken as nothing more than a human sub-race. I guess in some ways, we were. Especially if any of the old stories about our nasty origins were actually true.

I crossed my arms over the book and let my chin rest in the crook of my elbow. My thoughts circled back to that book I'd found in Roxus's office—the one with Viperi symbols inside. He'd said there was very little written about them.

No one wanted to study us and I couldn't blame them. We had been created to be an evil god's perfect army. A combination of the foulness of Vescor's malice and humans who had willingly volunteered to be warped in his name in exchange for power.

And we hadn't changed much since then, even after two thousand years.

The Viperi still hungered for blood, relished in treachery even against our own, and despised all those who walked the surface world. We were murderers and liars. We relished power and dominance in every aspect.

That very thing—that relentless need for dominance—was what had driven me and my mother from our clan. It had killed her and condemned me to this life as a savage outsider.

Even if I'd wanted to go back and rejoin my foul kin, which I didn't, they would have butchered me on sight. Viperi were forbidden from speaking about our people, society, traditions, and life within the clans to anyone from the surface. I'd already revealed more than enough about myself to earn a traitor's death several times over.

Not that it mattered, really.

As far as my old clan, or my father knew, I was long dead. Nothing but sun-bleached bones in some desert canyon. Not a threat to any of them anymore.

"What's wrong?" Chrysa asked without even looking up from the book she was reading. Indifferent as ever.

Another deep sigh made the papers in front of my nose rustle. "I was just thinking ... Roxus had a book in his office with things written in it about the Viperi."

Her keen emerald eyes darted up, as sharp and direct as arrow points. "You think he was researching you?"

I shrugged. "Probably. And why not? He probably wanted

to know if his new Viperi pet preferred only the fresh blood of my enemies for my food, or if some from the local butcher would do."

One corner of her mouth curled up into a wry little grin. "You're awful."

"Apparently."

"Seriously, though. What was the book about? What did it say?" she pressed.

"I don't know. I couldn't read it then," I reminded her. "I just recognized some of the symbols on the pages."

"Symbols of what?" She sounded genuinely curious now. Her chair creaked as she sat forward some.

Something about it made an embarrassed heat prickle on the back of my neck. I scratched at it as I sat up a little straighter in my seat. No one had ever asked about the Viperi before. At least, not unless they were preparing to accuse me of something awful.

But Chrysa wasn't like that.

"The Eye of the Foul Father," I mumbled with the frayed corner of one of the book covers.

"And what is that?" She frowned, tilting her head to one side slightly with her eyes narrowed.

As though she had read the answer in my expression before I said it out loud.

"It's a sacred symbol to the Viperi, going back to the Dire King Zarexius." I kept my voice down so that it was hardly more than a whisper. Gods, I did *not* want any of the other prospects to overhear me talking about this stuff.

The last thing I needed was them accusing me of trying to recruit someone to my evil cause.

"Who is that?" Chrysa whispered back as she leaned in closer.

BAM!

Out of nowhere, a hand slammed down between us.

I couldn't hold back a scream as I floundered back.

Chrysa jerked away, too. She opened her mouth, like she was about to start yelling. Then her eyes went wide, and she seemed to shrink as her shoulders trembled. Her face went from flushed, scarlet fury to ghostly pale in an instant.

It was the most expression I'd ever seen on her face.

Utter terror.

"Why don't you answer, pitathi? Go on. Tell us who the Dire King Zarexius was." Domitri sneered down at us, his hand still planted on the table between us like a forbidding wall.

All eyes in the library were suddenly on me. The other prospects. The scholars standing around, observing and helping. The Vindexori guarding the doorway.

But all I could see was his tall, impending form looming over us, wreathed in that eerie bluish glow that hung around him like an aura.

What was it? What did it mean? Why did it make all the breath seem to freeze in my lungs?

"Well?" He snickered. "Don't hold us in suspense. Answer now, or consider yourself dismissed."

My mouth opened, but nothing would come out.

Could he really do that? Dismiss me from being a prospect without Mistress Orvana's approval?

I stole a glance at Chrysa. She hadn't even blinked, and still trembled like she was ready to bolt at any moment.

My chest shuddered with a frantic breath.

Run.

"*Do not* look at her," Domitri snarled louder, leaning down to get right in my face. "You think she can help you? You think anyone in this place would actually want to save you?"

All I could do was keep gaping at him like a beached fish.

BAM!

He slammed his hand down on the table harder, making books jostle and papers fly.

"Answer me, pitathi!" Malice churned like inky dark water in the depths of his eyes. His sharp features drew into a half-snarling grin, one eyebrow arching up expectantly.

Control. I had to stay in control. No running. No fighting.

I had to stay calm. This was a test I couldn't afford to fail again.

"They say he was the father of the Viperi," I managed hoarsely.

Domitri's eyes narrowed into vicious slits, his long nose wrinkling in a grimacing scowl. "And? Don't stop there. Tell us exactly what he did."

Run, Visha.

Roxus. Gods, where was Roxus?

"H-he ... he made a deal with Vescor, Foregod of the Void. He traded his soul for an army of perfect soldiers." My voice shook and halted, the words tangling in my throat.

"Perfect *monsters*," he corrected, hissing every word through his teeth. "The most efficient, brutal, and evil creatures to ever slither across this world. The Viperi. Isn't that right?"

All I could do was swallow hard, feeling my throat jump as my heart hammered harder and faster in my chest.

"You lot were bred in the void, children of hunger and greed, soulless and empty just like the dark god who seeded you," he seethed. "And when your king was felled in the War of the Stones, you were cursed eternally to the depths of the earth by Paligno."

Domitri pushed away from the table, his sweeping robes swishing as he strolled a few feet away before turning on a heel to face the long table. His face seemed to twist strangely, that bluish glow becoming brighter for an instant. It made the tips of his fingers alight, and I couldn't look away.

I couldn't move.

Everything below my neck seemed to go steadily numb.

"You were banished to the dark, never to see the light again. And yet, here you sit ... defiling this holy ground with every breath you take." He spread his arms wide, gesturing to the dimly lit library. "Someone, please, tell me why we allow this?"

No one said a word.

But it didn't matter.

I could feel their disgust like a silent fog creeping in around my ankles. Every second, it grew stronger, thicker, and deadlier.

They knew the truth. No more whispered rumors. Just plain historical fact.

I knew what came next. They would all turn on me. They'd hunt me down. They'd want to destroy me. That's what Domitri wanted.

If he couldn't drive me out, then he'd convince the rest of the prospects to do it for him.

I couldn't give them that chance. Out—I had to get out. Somewhere else.

Somewhere safe.

You must run, Visha. Faster than you ever have. They will not spare any mercy on you, my beautiful, wicked daughter.

But I couldn't. Domitri stood between me and the only way out of the library.

Nowhere to run. Nowhere to hide.

That only left one option.

"You should not be here," Domitri hissed bitterly, leaning down so close I could feel his breath on my face and see all the angry pink veins on the whites of his eyes. "Slither back to whatever putrid cave you crawled out of, girl. You will *never* be Zenith's Call."

My lip twitched. A growl kindled in my throat. My tongue traced my pointed incisors.

I snarled at him.

My senses came alive, honing in on everything around me. The soft hiss and crackle of the oil lamps and torches. The muted gasps and whispers of the other prospects watching.

That wavering glow around Domitri seemed to grow brighter—clearer, even. I could smell the tinge of nervous sweat in the air as he withdrew slightly, the tiniest step, as though he could sense the shift in my mind.

From prey ... to predator.

Just like he wanted.

My heartbeat slowed, and my gaze flashed to the quill resting in an ink bottle before me. Not a weapon. Close enough for me, though.

And lethal when rammed through someone's eye into their brain.

Perfect.

I started to move, to reach for it.

Two seconds. I could end him, and never have to see that awful sneer curl over his lips again.

A hand grasped my wrist an instant before I could touch the quill.

I bared my teeth, snarling into Chrysa's face as she stared back at me, face pale and eyes wide and desperate.

"No," she whispered, squeezing my wrist harder. "You *cannot*."

I froze.

Holding her gaze, my face twitched. The growl in my throat fizzled. I sucked in a sharp breath.

Oh, gods. She was right.

What was I doing?!

I snatched back, glancing between them as all the wind seemed to rip the breath from my lungs at once. I-I couldn't lose control. I couldn't let him bait me.

I had to go.

Run, Visha!

My mother's voice roared like a stormy wind in my brain. It tore at the thin, frayed threads of sanity barely tethered to the cracking foundations of my soul.

"Even more useless than a pitathi runt believing she can join our holy order," Domitri chuckled darkly, "is one who does not even have the guts to kill. No wonder your kin cast you out."

I tore away from my chair and fled, taking the central aisle in seconds and bursting out of the library and into the Eternal Hall.

As I sprinted for the grand vestibule, I could still hear Domitri laughing with wild delight.

Like he loved seeing my terror.

Like he couldn't wait to see what he could do to me next.

Sixteen

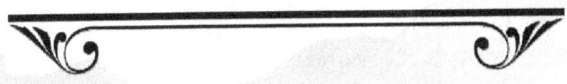

I couldn't do this anymore.

Sitting under the shade of a huge palmetto in the Nai'Pol's largest rooftop garden, I kept my arms wrapped around my knees. The words replayed over and over, mingling with that delightfully wicked grin on Domitri's face.

As though he could sense every speck of my agony and gobbled it up like sugary wine.

I hated him.

To my very core—to the deepest, most wicked parts of my soul—I *despised* that man.

And there was absolutely nothing I could do to stop him.

"You know you can't hide up here forever."

I looked up, my whole body jerking with a surge of panic as Chrysa approached. She carried all our books and scrolls, as well as her own, and dropped them onto the ground between us. She settled into the soft, cool grass with her legs crossed.

My mouth fell open, words tangling in my throat so all I could do was make shocked choking sounds.

How had she known where I was? Why had she followed

me here? What, by all the gods, did she want from me? To humiliate me even more?

"I am *not* hiding," I snarled, showing her my pointed canine teeth as she dared to sit down across from me.

"Fine." She shrugged. "Sulking, then."

I growled low.

"I'm not scared of you, you know," she added, casually picking at her nails and refusing to meet my gaze.

"You should be," I warned.

She finally glanced up, those deadpan green eyes seeming entirely unimpressed. "Why? Because you'll hurt me? Kill me?"

I narrowed my eyes.

She snorted and looked back down at her nails. "I've heard all that before from people a *lot* scarier than you."

Ugh. Right.

Tibrans.

"How did you even find me?" I grumbled, leaning forward to rest my elbows on my knees.

"Wasn't hard," she replied as she sat down next to me. "You tend to stick out in a crowd."

"There's no crowds here."

She gave one of those slight, far-too-subtle smirks. "Exactly. Makes it even easier."

For a long time, we just sat in silence, staring over the beautiful terraced gardens that filled the space between the airy temples with lush green plant life and trickling water rushing through canals to fill reflecting pools. My eyes drifted over the white marble statues of the gods, studying each one.

Undae, Goddess of the Sea.

Paligno, God of Living Things.

Proleus, God of War.

Adiana, Goddess of the Moon.

There were others, of course. Several more. But I couldn't

see them from where we sat, watching the sun begin to sink beyond the glittering sea. It smeared the horizon with shades of soft lavender, pink, and deep red.

"I don't understand," I murmured quietly.

"Don't understand what?" Chrysa didn't look away from the red, rippling orb of the sun that glowed brighter as it slowly sank.

"Why Domitri agreed to have us train together if he despises me so much," I said. "It doesn't make any sense. Even if Roxus did some fancy talking to convince Mistress Orvana it was a good idea, why did he agree?"

"You're assuming they gave him a choice," she pointed out.

"Is that what happened? They didn't give him a choice?"

Her brow creased some, furrowing ever so slightly. I couldn't tell if it was in thought ... or dismay.

"I don't know. He doesn't tell me things. He's not like Roxus," she answered at last.

I snorted and looked away. "Roxus isn't exactly a fountain of truths."

"Maybe not, but he's made it very clear that he supports you. He would tell you if there were something dangerous heading your way," she clarified. "He cares about what happens to you."

"And Domitri doesn't? About you, I mean."

Her shoulders drew up slightly and her lips pressed together, betraying her unease. Or maybe that was dread?

It was hard to tell with her. All of her expressions, and most of the time her words, were so muted and difficult to read. Guarded.

Like she'd spent a lifetime stuffing down everything she thought and felt so deeply no one would be able to discern it.

"He's unhappy with me. Especially now," she murmured.

"Because you stopped me from losing it and murdering him in the library?" I asked, trying to make light of it.

But she didn't laugh or smile.

She nodded once.

I frowned. "He *wanted* me to attack him?"

"If you attack one of the patrons or even a Vindexori outside of combat training, they would have no choice but to dismiss you," Chrysa explained. "Or worse."

Hmm. Fair point.

But still ... he was willing to take the risk that I might kill him? Or was he that confident he could beat me in a fair fight? He had gotten the upper hand with me before, yes. But I'd also been injured already by then.

On level ground, I had no doubts I could spill his innards all over the library floor. That conniving little weasel.

"Will he punish you?" I dared to ask.

Chrysa didn't say it—not out loud. The answer was clear enough on her face, though. For once, that veneer of composed indifference cracked and I saw the truth spill through.

Her jawline tensed. Her face paled some, and she swallowed hard.

He would punish her severely.

"Will he beat you?" I pressed, feeling the coals of my rage starting to glow deep in my chest.

"Stop it," she warned, her tone suddenly sharp.

What?

She fixed me with a steely look of warning that made me recoil some.

"Do not ask those questions, Violet."

I glared back at her. "Have you told Mistress Orvana? I don't think he's allowed to—"

"It doesn't matter," she cut me off quickly. "You should

know that better than anyone. What happens to people like us does not matter."

I winced, feeling every word like a steel-pointed blade in my heart.

Gods, she was right. I was so stupid. I should have known better. I was Viperi. She was a former Tibran. Neither of us had any recourse except whatever grace our patrons were willing to fight for.

I was lucky. Roxus would fight for me.

But Chrysa apparently didn't have that same assurance from her patron. There was no one coming to save her. No one built her up when this training tore her down.

Chrysa was far more alone than I'd allowed myself to see.

The memory of those other Tibran refugees I'd seen at the harbor echoed through my mind. The elder man falling to his knees to weep on the docks. I could still hear his cries mingling with the shrieks of the gulls—still see the tears leaking down the aged, wrinkled sides of his face.

Cries of grief, of relief, of terror.

And freedom.

"How did you manage to escape the Tibrans?" I asked, fully expecting her to refuse to answer.

She didn't owe me any explanations, even if I'd told her a little about my past and how I'd wound up separated from the rest of my kin. I didn't exactly have a face most people trusted right away ... or at all.

Chrysa's mouth pinched shut, twisting to one side and then the other. She picked at the corner of the cover of one of the books piled on the ground between us.

"I just got lucky," she said so quietly I hardly heard her.

I didn't dare to move, to make a sound. I didn't want to do anything to disturb her as she stared down into her lap, expression twitching and changing so fast I couldn't tell what she might be thinking.

Or remembering.

"The Tibrans don't spare time on training the people they take from the lands they conquer. They call it conscripting. Those of us who weren't fit for combat were given other jobs within the ranks. As you've seen, I'm lousy with a blade, so they taught me to fletch arrows and assist blacksmiths with patching armor and shields for reuse." Chrysa kept her tone hushed and quick, her eyes darting back and forth as though seeing those memories flash by.

I frowned, realizing now that was probably why she'd handled a bow decently before.

She'd spent some time around them.

"Our legion was anchored off the coast of Elondia, preparing for the initial assault. It was the dead of night. The night was so quiet. Then the Elondian navy attacked out of nowhere," she said. "Everything was chaos. They hit our ship with cannon fire, and we started to sink. Everyone was running. Screaming. Dying … "

She started fidgeting with the end of her long, light-red braid. The ends of it spiraled, making little ringlet curls. I wondered if all of it was that curly, but I'd never seen her wear it in anything but a tight braid over one shoulder to hide her brand.

"I was flung from the deck when one of the cannonballs hit. I'm not a very good swimmer, but I managed to make it to a piece of floating wreckage. I clung to it for two days, drifting in the open sea. Hoping I would die. Then a fishing boat from Nar'Haleen found me."

"A fishing boat? That's quite a stroke of luck." I just had to be sure I'd heard that right.

Undae must have really been watching over her to be discovered in so many miles of empty ocean before she died of dehydration and exposure.

Chrysa dipped her chin lower, brow set in a look of focus.

As though it took everything she had to keep her emotions, her true feelings, from reaching the surface.

"Eventually, I wound up in Rienka. Domitri found me there, sorting fish in the harbor," she murmured, her voice tight around each word as though they stung her. "He saw my brand and brought me here."

I chewed on the inside of my cheek, mulling that over. Something didn't quite feel right. She was leaving out details —that much I could tell—but why would Domitri decide just having a Tibran brand made her the right fit for the Zenith's Call?

"What were you before the Tibrans took you?" I asked, trying to keep my tone as indifferent as possible.

No need to arouse her suspicions, too.

Chrysa gave a small shrug. "I don't remember much of anything from my life before. I was four or five when I was taken. Some of the others said I came from Noltham. They teased me about what a privileged life I had enjoyed before, about being the daughter of some noble. But I don't remember any of that."

"Was Chrysa your real name?" I probed a little further. "Or one the Tibrans gave you?"

"It's my real one." Her gaze flicked up to me, then, eyes as keen as an eagle's. "What about you? Violet doesn't sound like a Viperi name."

My heart gave a frantic twist deep in my chest, feeling suddenly so heavy I could barely draw a breath.

Trust for trust.

Truth for truth.

I had to try.

Turning my body away and giving her my shoulder, I rubbed at the back of my neck. Anything to keep from meeting her gaze when I answered, "It isn't."

"Does Roxus know?"

I shook my head.

"You don't have to tell me," she added quickly. "I get it. We train together. That doesn't make us friends."

My mouth twisted to the side like I'd bitten into something sour. Crap. She had entrusted me with some pretty vivid details of her life, more than I'd offered about mine. And I couldn't bring myself to even tell her my real name?

The name I'd sworn to leave behind.

Didn't she deserve that much? After everything Chrysa had been through—

"I don't need sympathy," she grumbled, scowling at me like she was reading my mind again. "Or vengeance. I just have to get through this. And I will. I have before."

I looked down. "I know."

"If you really want to help me, then let's just keep doing what we've been doing." She stared off across the gardens again, her chest heaving in slow, steadying breaths. "Focus on what's ahead. This is far from over, for either of us."

Right. We were only halfway through the training period, and after that, the challenge of the final trials loomed like a forbidding wall. We had no guarantee of even making it to that point.

All we had was whatever mad courage we could muster to make it through the next day.

"I'm not asking you to be friends," Chrysa clarified, fixing me with one of those apathetic stares that probably scared the ever-loving crap out of the other prospects. "I'm not even asking you to trust me. Not fully. But if we can become allies against them—the patrons and the other prospects—then we can survive this."

"You want to be *my* ally?" I nearly choked in surprise.

She nodded.

Good gods above, what was happening?

I had to admit, the fact that she had already stuck her neck out in my defense was alarming and confusing. I'd never expected anyone to do something like that for my sake, let alone Chrysa.

But she'd stopped me from making a huge mistake. From taking Domitri's bait. And she'd likely have to pay the price for that now.

It gave me the smallest kernel of hope.

"Sooo ... I'll watch your back, if you watch mine?" I just had to be sure.

Chrysa nodded again.

I hesitated, trying to envision what that would even look like. The two unwanteds rallying together in the name of dodging a gruesome death in the streets of Rienka or the pit of some prison? Hmm.

It wouldn't win us any affection with the rest of the prospects. But it might win some respect.

And that I could live with.

"Fine," I agreed.

Chrysa held out a hand for me to shake. "I cannot stop Domitri from targeting you."

"I'd prefer if you gave me some insight on how to deal with him myself." I shook her hand once, sealing our pact, and quickly looked away. "Or a good slap if I start to lose it again."

She chuckled quietly and pulled her hand away.

Only I wasn't kidding.

"When he does that, tries to provoke me to fight, it's like every reason to go through with it is whispering in my head at once. Sometimes I can't hear anything else," I admitted.

"He is an elder agent. You must submit, no matter how awful it is or what he says to you. He enjoys defiance because then he is justified in exacting whatever punishment he chooses and no one will protest—least of all for your sake. You can't give him that. You have to stay in control."

She might as well have slapped me in the face.

Gods, that ... was that what she had to do every day?

Eying Chrysa carefully, I wondered over the scars that flecked her jaw and collarbone. She had one at her hairline, too, that was more gnarled but mostly hidden by her bangs. I wondered how many had come from the Tibrans.

And how many Domitri had given her.

She was stronger than she looked. She might be useful, after all—especially as an ally.

Or maybe I was just being a fool again.

Time would tell, and ours, I knew, was growing short.

Our race for survival, to secure a place within the Zenith's Call, had only just begun.

SEVENTEEN

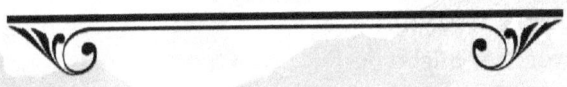

I could *read*.

Not just simple sentences or the watered-down notes that Chrysa provided me to help me catch up with all the lessons and studies we did on divine history and lore.

I could read the actual books—*by myself*.

Sokraal, Rienkan, and Avoran—it didn't matter. I could read them all now, and write almost as fluently.

It was like the floodgates of my mind had been flung open wide.

I devoured the texts on the pantheon. I pored over all the histories of the Foregods, and the War of the Stones that had bound the deities' power beyond a boundary called the Sivanth. I read ballads of battle, of the great hero Jaevid Broadfeather, a famous dragonrider who had finally ended the Law of the Stones and released the gods' power back upon the earth.

There was so much to discover, and each page felt like a new journey.

And thankfully, it filled the time when Chrysa was gone.

After my almost-outburst in the library, when she had spoken out and interrupted Domitri's taunting, Chrysa had hinted that she might have consequences to face. She'd suggested that defying him had cost her in the past, but had warned me not to push the issue any further.

That's why I hadn't gone looking for her or asked any questions when she disappeared for almost a week.

I had a feeling that the more I asked and looked for her, the worse it might be for her. Others would notice my concern. They'd probably tell Domitri, and he might punish her more severely.

After five days, though, I began to worry. To wonder if she was gone.

Had she been dismissed for defying her patron? Or something far worse?

I didn't know. And I couldn't even ask anyone about it.

The other prospects still hated and avoided me like a disease. The other patrons mostly did the same, with a few exceptions like Curator Faera. Ironically, she was the nicest to me out of all the patrons overseeing our trials and training.

But I didn't dare point any fingers or ask any questions. I couldn't afford to put any wrinkles in the silky smooth surface of my life right now.

Telling Roxus that I'd nearly gone on a murder spree in the library seemed like a bad idea, too. For all he knew, I was improving beautifully. Handling myself and my studies like a respectable member of society.

I didn't want to disappoint him anymore.

Sitting in the Eternal Hall with a giant tome about the origins of the Foregods balanced on my thighs, I took my time perusing every page. I'd just gotten to a rather interesting chapter about the so-called Vault of Whispers—an impenetrable chamber supposedly hidden somewhere in these very ruins. The book described that it had once held artifacts of incredible divine power and unspeakable danger. Wonders that could wreak havoc upon the mortal world if they fell into the wrong hands.

Nonsense, of course. But interesting.

The cool stone of the large statue of a winged Avoran warrior felt strangely soothing to my back as I leaned against it. Too bad the noise of the other prospects playing at combat training like a bunch of kittens squabbling for the same ball of string was so loud in the next room.

Not much had changed on that front.

Typical.

If those were the fighters the gods were relying on to protect their most precious secrets and artifacts, then Fates help us all.

"Don't you look busy," a familiar voice mused.

I glanced up to find Roxus striding toward me, his hands deep in the pockets of his long coat and that wistful, knowing grin crinkling the corners of his eyes.

Weird. He didn't usually show up to walk me home until well into the afternoon.

Hmmm.

"Not really." I sighed and closed the huge book. "Curator Faera has already gone over most of this in her lectures."

"She's nothing if not thorough," he chuckled in agreement.

"Which is why her giving our final trials in divine lore and history is utterly terrifying." I groaned and ran a hand through my hair. It had grown out so that it brushed my shoulders, finally. Too bad it still wasn't quite long enough to be tied back in a ponytail.

At least, not one that didn't slip out whenever we practiced combat.

"Where's Chrysa?" he asked, glancing around as though

he suspected she might be hiding out behind another nearby statue.

"Still gone," I murmured.

His smile faded, that veneer of casual calm melting at the corners of his features. His jaw worked to one side, eyes shimmering with that look of devious thought as he stared off across the Eternal Hall.

Like he was already plotting something.

Oh boy.

"Well, I've got a new lesson for you to learn today. Come on." Roxus snapped his fingers and motioned for me to follow.

I bounced to my feet and quickly gathered my belongings, cramming all my books and rolls of parchment into a leather haversack Delthene had given me.

I jogged until I could fall in step beside him, and we walked side-by-side toward the great vestibule with the huge fountain of the Fates in the center—Krin'Moir, as they called it.

I'd gotten used to this place, with all its mysterious oddities. The blue flames of the torches and lamps, the shadowed crouching statues that flanked nearly every room, and the constant heaviness of moist, cavernous air in my lungs. Sometime during the last two months, it had begun to feel comfortable.

Almost like coming home.

Almost.

"Where are we going?" I asked as I followed Roxus up the grand staircase that led to the hidden door—one of only a few ways out of the complex.

And the only one I was permitted to use as a prospect.

"Hard to explain, easier to just show you." He gave me another one of his typical, cryptic responses.

Ugh.

I scowled. "You could at least try?"

"Probably."

"Why do you do this? Do you just enjoy watching me squirm?"

One corner of his mouth quirked up.

I took that as a "yes."

I crossed my arms, muttering Viperi curses under my breath and stomping into each footstep angrily as we made our way down from the high, terraced temple grounds and into the streets of Sol'Karr. That jerk. Didn't he have anything better to do than play mind games with me?

Apparently not.

With the wind tousling his shaggy brown hair, Roxus kept his hands buried deep in his coat pockets as he swaggered along the sidewalk. He led the way down the steep avenues to his house and paused just outside the door.

He nodded for me to go in ahead of him. "Drop the bag and get changed."

I arched an eyebrow. "Into what?"

"You'll see."

More mind games. Fantastic.

I shot him a perfectly venomous glare on my way in, muttering more curses as I topped the stairs. Flinging the door to my bedroom open, I stopped mid-step as soon as I spotted it … spread out on the bed and sparkling beautifully in the late evening light.

My new leather armor ensemble—the one he had ordered from the tailor. I'd totally forgotten about it.

But there it was, in all its black, deep purple, and silver-threaded glory.

I was practically salivating as I dropped my bag and rushed to the side of the bed, stroking the intricate embroidered filigree up the bodice from the hips to the bust. It had matching designs on the sleeves and the thighs of the leather leggings.

There was a similarly embroidered black silken hood attached to the back of the tunic I wore under the bodice, and it hid my face under a veil of shadow when I pulled it down low.

The tall, heeled black boots came just above my knee and fit so snugly they practically felt like a part of my body. Everything fit flush and perfectly, soft and flexible, with reinforced plating hidden in the forearms to deflect blade strikes in a pinch. Flawless. Beautiful.

Absolutely lethal.

I did a little spin in front of my dressing mirror, then dropped into a low crouch to test the give of the material. Perfect. Gods, the new leather had been oiled so well it didn't even squeak when I moved.

"Goodness, girl. You look like a murder waiting to happen," Delthene sighed sadly from the doorway.

I couldn't hide the smile that spread so wide on my face that it made my cheeks ache when I turned to face her.

"Just be careful tonight, dear." She shook her head slowly.

"I will," I promised, knowing full well that was probably a lie. Especially when I still had no idea what Roxus had in store for us tonight. But if this was the desired attire, then I was all in.

Bring it on.

I skipped past Delthene back down the stairs to where Roxus was still waiting by the door. He grinned around the long wooden pipe he held in his teeth as soon as he saw me.

"Oh? Where'd that sour little frown go, eh?" he teased.

I elbowed him in the ribs as I sauntered past. "I must have left it in my other clothes."

His grin widened, and he blew a perfect smoke ring into the air. "Good. Let's go, then. We'll miss the main event."

Main event? Were we really on the hunt for someone? Doing mercenary work?

Or was this something else entirely?

My heart pounded frantically and my stomach fluttered at the thought, but I knew better than to ask. He was all secrets and surprises this evening. I doubted anyone could pry the truth out of him a second before he wanted to give it.

Pulling my new hood down low to hide my smirk, I walked alongside him farther into the city proper. We passed the merchants closing up their shops for the night in the market district as the sun sank beyond the far horizon. Lights glowed from the windows in the upper levels of the narrow, smashed-together buildings that crowded every street and square.

Hardly a soul walked the cobblestone sidewalks that fed through the residential and market districts down into the harbor proper. Thick evening fog rolled in from the bay, filling the alleyways and harbor-side streets like silvery smoke. It snaked around my legs and curled in the wake of my breath as we hit the main, twisting road that ran along the perimeter of the bay.

With the docks and ships on one side of the street, and the other side packed with more closely stacked buildings and shops, we shuffled along quickly and made our way toward the southern end of the docks. There, the buildings that faced the towering, ghostly black silhouettes of the massive ships seemed less refined.

The paint was peeling off their old, cracked plaster walls and the glass of their windows was wavy with age and spotted with sea spray. The farther we went, the more lights glowed in the first and second-level windows of each narrow building. Even from outside, I could hear it—the music, shouting, screeching laughter, and clattering of dishes.

Taverns, dive bars, and inns with sprawling dining rooms. Dozens of them lined the dockside road, booming with activity as all the sailors, dockhands, pirates, and fishermen moved indoors to drink away the day's worries.

The sorts of places a girl could get in a lot of trouble.

I smirked up at Roxus and squinted one eye, silently asking him what the heck we were doing here.

He just shrugged and clapped a hand onto my back, steering me toward one building with a wooden placard hanging over the door depicting a crow with a mug grasped in its talons. The Rook's Roost—a place I'd seen before as an urchin surviving on these very streets. But not one I'd ever dared to enter, mostly because it was a well-known pirate and mercenary hangout.

These sorts of folks didn't tolerate starving children picking their pockets. Especially not ones with red eyes and teeth like fangs. A rich merchant would scream and make a loud fuss about being robbed, but a pirate? Well, he might just put a knife in your back for it.

I gulped the knot of nerves that hung in the back of my throat as Roxus all but shoved me through the front door.

Gods help me. This wouldn't end well. What was he thinking?

Hood or not, and all my shiny new clothes aside, it was still *very* obvious that I didn't belong here. Surely he realized that … right?

The rusty hinges on the warped, old wooden door screeched as we entered, announcing our arrival to a room packed from wall-to-wall with sailors, barmaids, minstrels, and scoundrels. It was the sort of place you tasted as soon as you walked in. The sour brine of sweat, pipe smoke, and stale ale stung my eyes and made my nose run.

From the sunbaked fishermen with fish guts crusted on their hands, to the Rienkan pirates with colorful beads and charms braided into their long black hair and pierced through their pointed ears, no one even looked up as we muscled our way down the crowded bar. Roxus got a few shouts of greeting as we made our way to a doorway at the very back.

He just nodded back, lifting one hand in greeting but keeping the other firmly planted right at the base of my neck. Almost like he was worried I'd make a run for it.

A legitimate concern, really.

We pushed through the doorway from the main tavern area into a dimly lit staircase that plunged down into the gloom. Something heavy thudded against the floorboards, coming from down below where that staircase ended. Not a beat, like a drum. No, it was too irregular.

What, then?

"Eyes open," Roxus said as he nudged me down the stairs. "And try to relax."

Relax? *Relax?* Was he kidding?

At the base of the steep, spiraling staircase, two towering men in patched-together armor thrust out their arms, blocking our path through another doorway obscured by heavy tapestry that hung across it like a curtain. Light ebbed from underneath. The sounds of impact and crowing, booming shouts from a crowd thudded like a pulse under my feet.

Roxus didn't waste a second.

He pulled two golden coins from his pocket and another large, circular medallion with the Zenith's Call symbol engraved into it. The door guards greedily snatched up the coins, but left the medallion, and stepped aside to let us in.

Brushing back the tapestry, Roxus motioned for me to go in ahead of him. My knees froze up immediately. I glanced between him and the two big bouncers that had begun eyeing me up and down like they were trying to figure out who, or what, I was.

I didn't give them time to work it out.

Lowering my head, I hurried through the curtain into a

room roughly double the size of the one upstairs. Then I stopped again, my legs locking up solid and my breath catching in my chest.

Gods have mercy.

It must have been a cellar once because there were still massive ale casks and wine barrels lining all the walls. But every inch of the place had been modified into something like a small amphitheater with seating levels crowded with tables and chairs all around a central, deep pit in the middle of the room.

A fighting pit.

Big iron torches affixed to the walls filled the place with wavering golden light, illuminating crowds grouped around the tables to watch the fights down below. Buxom barmaids carried trays of food and drink to each level, chatting up patrons with dazzling smiles and flirty winks. They wore their blouses low and their skirts hiked short in the front, catering to a crowd of thugs and vagrants that had apparently come here for a variety of entertainment.

Some of the figures seated around the tables looked like well-to-do merchants in fine doublets with noble ladies on each arm. Others were clearly pirates, cutthroats, mercenaries, or slave lords. All sipped from wine goblets or gulped from frothy ale tankards. They tossed coins down on their tables to place bets on a fight raging in the pit down below.

A portly human man with a large mustache stood on a platform just behind the makeshift arena, calling for final bets. He shouted about the fight in a booming voice, commenting and urging the crowd to put their money in before the final call.

None of that was what made my feet stick fast to the floor, though.

It was *him*—the young man squaring off with a muscle-bound brute down in that small arena.

The one who looked straight at me, locking gazes as soon

as I stepped into the room, and smirked from one pointed ear to the other.

My heartbeat skipped.

I'd never seen him before in my life. And yet, for that fleeting instant, it felt like I did. Like we had met somewhere or in some lifetime before.

And I was already in way over my head.

EIGHTEEN

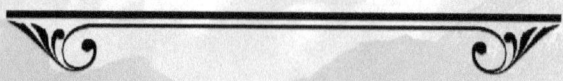

I had never seen anyone like him.

But just the sight of the young elven man, wearing nothing but a pair of light linen pants, made my insides feel squishy and strange.

He closed in on his opponent with his wide shoulders hunched and fists raised, head tipping from one side to the other to stretch his neck. That look on his hard, sharply angled features—a ruthless, killing cold in his eyes— made my skin prickle with a strange heat.

Sweet Fates.

Who was this guy? And *what* was he? Not a Rienkan elf, not with that dark, chestnut-golden hair. Not Lunostri, either, with that lightly tanned skin.

"He's the current arena champion. His name is Declan," Roxus called down into my ear over the noise. Probably reading the strange mixture of shock and embarrassed terror on my face as I stared at the man.

Not like I could do much to hide it since now my cheeks were burning like someone had lit my hair on fire.

"Come on. This'll be a good fight," Roxus coaxed as he hauled me along to an open table near the door.

I staggered along, unable to pry my eyes off the elven man as his focus flickered back to his opponent. I almost tripped trying to sit down, caught in awe as he moved with all the grace and power of a stalking lion.

Declan must have been well over six feet tall, and every inch of his body was corded with lean, hard muscle that rippled with every lightning-fast punch. His broad chest shone with sweat in the torchlight, adorned with swirling black and gray tattoos of dragons that went from his wrists to his pectorals and up his throat to just under his chin.

Most of his sweaty, brownish-gold hair was shaved down short on the sides, with a length portion on top pulled back into a messy little bun on the back of his head. Not a style I'd seen anywhere in Sol'Karr before.

So where had this towering elven brawler come from?

A whoop went up from the crowd as Declan pounded his fists together, snarling at his opponent—who wasn't altogether small, either. The other fighter didn't have the height, but he more than made up for it in sheer bulk. His neck was as thick around as his whole head, and he barreled toward Declan like a charging bull.

Coins hit the tables before the first punch landed. The shorter, stockier man struck fast, but Declan had more reach and was lighter on his feet. He dodged and ducked, moving on the balls of his feet so that every one of the man's hits missed.

They moved in a blur, kicking up the sand on the arena floor as they brawled. Declan scored two jabs on the man's face, but the proximity cost him. He took one solid hit to the gut and an uppercut across the jaw that sent his head snapping back. His expression glazed over for a second, as though the punch had dazed him.

The stocky man hit him again. And again. It sent Declan

rocking back on his heels. He staggered, managing to catch himself against the side of the arena.

The bulkier man gave a triumphant bellow, pumping his fists into the air and stoking the crowd into a frenzy as he prowled toward where Declan still seemed to be gathering his wits.

Gods, was this the end? He was supposed to be the champion of this arena, right? What would happen if he lost?

I leaned forward in my seat, trying to get a peek at his face.

Then Declan slowly lifted his head ... and he grinned like a madman, blood oozing from his nose down over his lips, and dove back in.

My pulse skipped and stalled, kicking frantically in my chest.

He whirled around and rushed his opponent head-on.

In seconds, they were on the arena floor, wrestling and growling like two rabid wolves. More coins hit the tabletops. People around the arena shouted. The mustached man calling the fight yelled for final bets.

And I heard it—the sound that had resonated like thunder under my feet.

As Declan pinned the stouter man, he pounded his fists into his trapped victim's face over and over. Each time, the spectators around the arena stamped their feet. My body jolted, cringing in response.

Blood sprayed the sand. Declan shouted, snarling out a feral string of curses as his handsome face twisted in a look of pure rage.

But the man pinned beneath him was trapped, taking blow after blow. The caller counted down.

"ONE!" The crowd screamed along with the caller.

Declan drew back, cocking a fist. He drove it down, aiming for the man's face again. Out of nowhere, the stocky man pinned beneath him threw up an arm and deflected the blow.

"TWO!"

The brawnier man tried to deflect, but Declan's punches hit like a blacksmith's hammer pounding an anvil. Relentless. Powerful.

Each impact made my toes curl inside my new boots.

"THREE!"

The room erupted. Coins flew. Patrons shouted, toasted, or screamed in dismay.

Across the table, Roxus chuckled and took a long drag from his pipe. He puffed a few satisfied smoke rings into the air before waving down a barmaid and ordering two tankards of ale and a pot of spiced tea.

She winked and gave him a flirty pat on the arm as she pocketed his coins and hurried off. She returned minutes later with our drinks, a battered iron teapot with a porcelain warmer heated by a small stubby candle underneath, and a wooden cutting board with a loaf of fresh, sliced sweet oatbread and cheese on it.

The tea, I assumed, was for me, so I went for that first. I'd never cared much for ale, anyway.

Pouring a cup from the small teapot, I took a cautious sip and savored the rich flavors of the citrus, clove, and cinnamon that warmed the back of my throat down to my stomach. Delicious and savory, just the way I liked.

Roxus took one of the pints and began to drink, watching the crowds move around us as the sandy arena was cleared and raked smooth for the next fight. He sank deeper into his seat, draping one of his arms along the back of it with a lazy, sly grin.

I eyed the second, untouched pint of ale.

Hmm.

He was a scoundrel, yes, but I didn't think he was the sort to buy drinks for someone my age.

So who was that for?

Before I could even open my mouth to ask, the open chair next to mine slid back and Declan poured his lithe, tall frame into it with a hoarse little chuckle. His leg bumped mine as he sprawled in the seat, still breathing hard and slick with sweat from his fight.

Good gods. He hadn't even bothered to put on a shirt. And his nose was still oozing blood!

I gaped, choking on my breath, as his presence—the smell of his earthy musk, the size of his long-limbed frame, and strong body heat—overpowered all my senses at once. He didn't say a word as he swiped the other tankard off the table and immediately chugged half of it in one long gulp.

I flinched when he smacked it back on the table and sighed deeply, combing his lengthy hair away from his face.

"A decent performance," Roxus mused, still puffing away on his pipe.

"*Decent* would've spared me that crack to the nose. To what do I owe the pleasure?" Declan took a few deep breaths, as though trying to come down off the adrenaline rush, before his vivid green eyes panned to me.

He probably thought I didn't notice the way they darted over me quickly, sizing me up from head to toe. Hah.

I narrowed my eyes back at him slightly, just so he'd know I noticed.

It made a wide, roguish smile bloom across his handsome, albeit bruised and sweaty face. My heart nearly stopped altogether.

"Been a while since I saw you fight. Figured I'd come see if you're still getting your face kicked in properly or if they've finally stuffed you back in the kitchen with the rest of the losers," Roxus jabbed.

Declan probed gingerly at his nose, which was turning a frightening shade of purple on one side and underneath his eye. Gods, was it broken? Did he need a healer?

I didn't dare ask.

"They like a good show, and I'm more than used to getting my butt whipped so long as it pays," Declan said.

"There's the hot-headed mercenary brat I know," Roxus laughed, his gaze flicking to me as he waggled his eyebrows.

Oooh. So this guy was a mercenary?

Somehow that didn't shock me, given what I'd just seen.

Still, he seemed awfully young to be retired from that line of work. He was obviously older than me, sure, but he couldn't have been more than twenty.

"I didn't realize you had any children, Rox," he said, those keen eyes slipping me another distinct sideways glance.

"I don't," Roxus replied with a smirk. "At least, not any I'm aware of."

"Then who's this you've brought along?" Declan wiped his chin on his tattooed forearm, managing to smear blood across his chiseled cheek in the process.

Roxus arched a brow expectantly in my direction, tipping his chin up in an encouraging gesture.

O-oh. Right. Okay.

"M-my, um, my name is Violet," I stammered, my voice cracking.

Uggh. Gods strike me down right now.

Why couldn't I stop staring at him?!

Focus. Get it together.

His piercing gaze panned over me again, sharp brow furrowing as his eyes lingered on mine for an extra second. Probably noticing their color now. A curious little frown put a crinkle right at the top of the bridge of his nose.

"Don't tell me this is the girl we discussed—the one you want me to train with?" He looked back to Roxus.

"Seems like you could use an opponent worth your time," Roxus said as he swirled his tankard and took another sip. "Or at the very least, one that will last more than two minutes."

Declan's thin lips curved into another devilish smirk. There was something knowing sparkling in the depths of those razor-sharp green eyes. Almost like he could see right through me.

Like he knew what I was capable of.

"And you think she can hold up against me that long?" he baited.

Roxus didn't even look up from his pint. "I'd bet good coin on it."

Declan downed the rest of his tankard and dropped it on the tabletop before he stood and gave another half-hearted wipe at his nose. It didn't help this time, either. Now he had blood smeared on his chin, arm, and cheek.

"Then I hope you brought enough gold, old man, because I'm going to want two more of those," he warned, tapping his fingers on the rim of the empty mug before he faced me. "Next round, girlie. No backing out."

I still hadn't managed to close my mouth before he turned on a heel and swaggered away, weaving his way through the crowd like a tower of perfectly efficient muscle.

Wow.

"Just in case you're wondering, he's half Holvradix elf," Roxus murmured, seeming to enjoy every second of my awkward, gawking silence.

My head whipped back to glare at him. "I wasn't."

"Suuure," he cackled. "You think I didn't notice you staring at him like a slab of raw meat? I guess I shouldn't be surprised. He's only a little older than you, I think. Might be seventeen now."

"*Seventeen?*" I wheezed. "No—no, no, no. That is a whole, *grown* man. Don't play games with me."

Roxus just laughed. "Holvradix elves grow big, and he's actually small for his age since he's only half their blood."

"And what's the other half?"

He shook his head slightly, maintaining that smug, wolfish grin. "Not my story to tell. You'd best do something about learning to breathe when he's around, though. Might make things awkward if he goes in for a grapple-hold."

I whipped around in my seat to face him. "Wait—you're not serious about me fighting him, are you?"

"You've regained a lot of your strength over the last few months. You've put on healthy weight and muscle. It's time for you to get a proper workout, not just playing around with basics with Chrysa. We both know that's not a challenge for someone of your skill."

The smugness glinting in his beady brown eyes made me want to lunge the rest of the way across the table and throttle him.

"I'm not fighting in a brawler's pit in the cellar of a pirate tavern!" I fumed.

"No, you're *auditioning as a training partner* in a brawler's pit in the cellar of a pirate tavern," he corrected. "Big difference."

I licked my teeth behind my lips. Gods help me, I'd kill this man.

"He's more than twice my size," I snapped.

"Which would probably matter if you weren't Viperi," he countered.

"He's way stronger than me."

"And you're way faster than he is."

"I hate you," I growled.

He grinned. "No, you don't."

"Shut up."

I slumped back in my chair, staring down at the two new figures who were now swapping blows down in the pit. I couldn't see where Declan had gone. Probably off somewhere downing more free drinks before we fought.

Ugggh. Fates. This was ridiculous.

The sound of coins clattering onto the table drew my glare back to where Roxus sat, still holding that pipe between his teeth.

I scowled. "Are you seriously betting on my fight?"

"Might as well make a little money while we're here," he said.

"You don't get paid for being a secret guardian of the gods?" I huffed, crossing my arms and glaring back toward the arena.

"No. The temple funds our missions, helps with our gear and outfitting when they can, and provides us with some basic necessities like food if we choose to live within the order," he mumbled around his pipe. "But we all have to keep up appearances to the rest of the world and do what we can for work between missions."

"Like betting on pit fights?" I snorted.

"Not usually. I prefer mercenary work when I can get it. Keeps the larder full and the wine cellar stocked. But I haven't been able to do much of that lately. Had my hands full with a certain little red-eyed troublemaker."

He flicked a meaningful glance up at me.

I stuck my tongue out at him.

"Just do what you do best, and keep those instincts under control. This is a fight for dominance, not a duel to the death," he warned.

An uneasy feeling squirmed in my stomach like I'd swallowed a live eel. Roxus really wasn't kidding. He was going to make me fight this guy—knowing full well it would push my self-control to the very brink.

Too late, I realized ... that was probably the whole point. He was right about my training with Chrysa. It wasn't a challenge. I wasn't going to improve by only sparring and practicing with someone far below my skill level.

But Declan?

He clearly had skill. Someone had taken great care in teaching him combat, I just wasn't sure who. His style was so brutish and abrupt. Explosive, even.

Fates, I didn't know how this would go. It had all the right ingredients for disaster. He was a fireball on a collision course, and I was a powder keg ready to blow. It felt like Roxus was cramming us both in a bottle and shaking it just to see what happened.

And now, I had absolutely no way out of it.

NINETEEN

This would be ugly.

But ugly is exactly what the crowd huddled around their tables, watching each fight and stacking little towers of coins onto their tables, wanted.

Violence.

Blood.

A battered, bruised victor.

My heartbeat thrashed wildly in my chest as I approached the arena, feeling the grit of the sand between my bare toes. Heeled boots wouldn't serve me in a fight like this. But the rest of my ensemble? Well, might as well break it in properly.

They had already combed the blood-spattered sand smooth, erasing all evidence of the previous fight by the time I reached the edge of the pit and jumped down into it.

Landing in a crouch, I tested the depth of the sand with my fingers. I needed to know how much it might slow my steps since speed was one of my only advantages in this fight.

I hardly noticed when the whole room went silent.

Across the arena, Declan stood with his arms crossed and

his head tipped to one side, grinning at me like he was cherishing my innocence about what was about to happen.

I frowned, feeling those instincts already straining at the tethers of my sanity.

Stupid. This was stupid.

I would lose unless I let those urges take over. How else was I supposed to keep the upper hand against someone so much bigger and stronger?

My gaze flickered up to where Roxus still sat at our table, legs crossed and lips pinched tight around his pipe's mouthpiece. That deep crease in his brow put a knot in my chest. Panic.

He was concerned, too.

Or, at least, that's how it looked from where I was standing.

Should I stop? Call this off?

"Esteemed lords, ladies, and guests—tonight, we have an exquisite treat for you!" The caller's voice rang out through the silence.

Oh gods. Too late.

"Your beloved champion, Declan the Destroyer, will face an opponent so cunning, so voraciously evil, her kind is rarely beheld by our mere mortal eyes walking these blessed streets!"

My shoulders dropped. Seriously?

I shot Roxus a furious glare.

His head tilted back slightly, eyes squinting at the corners like he was suppressing a smile.

That jerk.

I'd show them evil.

"The Pitathi Murderess!" the fight-caller boomed, motioning to me.

I stood, ignoring the rancorous booing and screeches of dismay from the crowd as I fixed my stare upon Declan again.

Flexing my arms and legs and testing the give of my new leather armor, I rolled both of my shoulders out and gave my neck a good stretch.

"To the count of three! Face off, and both of you mind the rules. No killing. No weapons. No magic." The caller motioned for us both to come to the center of the arena.

Standing before Declan, I got a fresh appreciation for just how big he was. Not bulky or brawny—no, his frame was far more lean and efficient in build. No less intimidating, though, since I was literally more than a foot shorter and easily over a hundred pounds lighter. Probably more.

He stretched out a fist, offering to bump mine as a gesture of goodwill.

I arched an eyebrow, doing my level best to look wholly unimpressed before I lightly tapped his fist with my own. "Declan *the Destroyer?*"

He rolled his eyes. "Yes, it's stupid. I didn't pick it."

I couldn't hold back a smirk. "Didn't try to change it either, though."

"At least mine rhymes, Murderess," he taunted as he shifted his weight from one foot to the other.

Riiight. How many times had he been hit in the head, exactly? Too many, apparently, because that did not rhyme at all.

But I hadn't come down here to give him a grammar lesson.

"Consider me green with envy," I quipped instead.

I took a calculated step back, easing my weight onto the balls of my feet as I critiqued his every move. Looking for weakness. Hoping for some dumb luck.

I probably should have been praying, too, but in my personal experience, the gods didn't pay any attention to the prayers of Viperi.

"I don't normally hit little girls." Declan gave a playful

wink as he flexed his own powerfully sculpted shoulders and brought his fists up.

"Me neither, so this ought to be interesting." I took another step back and sank into a crouch, never breaking eye contact as I took a measure of his every breath.

His grin widened.

My heart gave another ridiculous little flutter. Ugh. Annoying.

Focus—I had to keep it together. He was about to try to punch my face black and blue, after all.

But, hey, what else was new?

"FIGHT!" the mustached caller yelled, spreading his arms wide over us.

My mind instantly snapped to silence, hearing nothing of the roaring crowd. Feeling nothing but the vibrations under my bare feet, rattling the tiny grains of sand, and the ebb and flow of my breathing.

Smelling the metallic tinge of bloody mist still hanging in the air from the previous fight.

I could use those instincts. Only a little.

Just enough to give me the edge I needed to put this brute of a man down on his rear.

Declan surged in, much faster than I'd anticipated. So he did have a bit of speed, after all.

He must have been holding that back in the previous fight.

In less than a second, he was in my space. His first swing was cautious, though. Testing.

I ducked to the side and kicked into a roll, coming up beside him in a blur and landing a jab on the side of his ribs before I dipped back out of reach.

He grunted at the impact, but didn't falter, and immediately whirled on me. He spun in for a leg sweep that missed by less than an inch.

Curse it—he really was faster than I thought.

If he pinned me, it was all over.

I had to stay light on my feet and well out of his reach.

The crowd hollered as Declan pursued, making more tactical strikes with his fists and forcing me into a retreat. I bit down hard, pulse throbbing in my neck as I darted in suddenly, hitting the sand on my knees and sliding through the gap between his legs and coming up behind him.

A swift kick to the back of his knees made him stumble, and I lunged for the back of his head, landing two solid punches before I sprang back.

BAM!

Something caught me across the cheek as I stood. Too late, I saw Declan's face mere inches from mine. The wind left my lungs in a burst as he slammed into me and flung me down onto the arena floor.

"You're slippery, I'll give you that," he snarled as he drew back a fist aimed right for my face.

I bared my teeth and snarled, planting both my knees in his chest and twisting so his blow glanced wide, hitting the arena floor instead of my head. The impact rattled my brain like pebbles in a jar, and I blinked hard.

Close—that was too close.

I had to get away.

"You must be merciless, Visha."

My mother's voice sizzled through my brain like lightning on the ocean. Every muscle in my body locked up. The instincts roared, seeping into my veins—fuel to a fire I could scarcely control.

"You are Viperi. You will kill or be killed."

Something snapped in my brain. A tether pulled too taught for too long.

And I fell into the inferno, seeing nothing but red flame.

Declan reared his fist back for another blow, and I flung an arm out, catching him around the neck and bashing my skull into his so hard my vision swam.

He faltered, gasping. His eyes went wide in a daze.

It was the only chance I needed.

I wriggled free of his grasp and kicked up into a low crouch. I bared my teeth and let that molten fury wash over me, watching him stagger to his feet.

There! An opening.

I surged in, wrapping a leg around his and driving an elbow into his gut. He growled a curse, stumbling some but managing to keep his footing. I felt his abdomen tense, his breath catching, as he prepared for another strike.

I threw myself into a full backbend, his punch sailing over my head so close I felt the breeze, and drove another kick up into his jaw.

Declan's head snapped back and he let out a string of curses in Sokraal.

Blood spattered the arena floor.

The crowd roared.

Coins clattered, hitting the tables by the fistful and spilling onto the floor.

I flipped backward, executing a flawlessly tight landing in a crouch, and immediately kicked off—rushing him head-on.

I went for his legs again. I had to get him onto the floor somehow, where his size wouldn't help him and he'd lose some of that punching power along with the leverage. Taking out a knee would be the easiest method.

BAM!

He caught my cheek with a solid jab as I struck. Everything went white. My ears rang.

I staggered, struggling to recover and blink away the stars that winked in my vision.

All the wind rushed out of me as one of his powerful arms

took me by the waist and slammed me down onto the arena floor flat on my back again.

Curse it!

He locked his legs around me, pinning me in place and drawing back another powerful fist aimed at my head. His green eyes were wide, blood oozing from a fresh cut on his swollen chin.

"Tap out!" he commanded, hesitating to make that final blow.

I growled back, hissing with my pointed teeth still bared.

Viperi did *not* surrender.

"Do it!" he roared. Something twitched in his expression, making his features skew with a frantic desperation I didn't understand.

I wouldn't.

He would have to hit me. To kill me.

Before I killed him first.

Declan hesitated, fist cocked and chest heaving for manic breaths.

I slipped one of my shoulders out of socket—a Viperi skill I hadn't used in ages. Immediately, his hold on me was loose, giving me an inch or two of room.

And that was all I needed.

I spun in his grasp, twisting my body around, catching his upper abdomen with a solid elbow straight to the liver.

I heard him suck in another wheezing breath. His grip slackened just enough I could coil my legs beneath me and push up with all my strength. I hauled his much larger body off me and slammed him down onto the arena floor.

This was it. My chance to snuff him out.

I locked my thighs around his neck, hooked my ankles together, and squeezed his windpipe like my life depended on it.

Because it did.

He would die—not me.

He pitched wildly, face turning blue ... then purple. He gasped and grabbed at my legs, rolling us both across the sand —doing everything he could to fling me off.

But I didn't let up. I didn't let go, even when he managed to catch my ribs with a frantic punch.

Pain exploded in my side. I screamed. But I didn't let go.

"ONE!" the caller shouted.

Declan floundered for another second, then I felt his whole body tense.

Oh no.

"TWO!"

The crowd whooped as he stood up suddenly, wearing me like a shawl still wrapped around his neck, and barreled straight for the pit's wall like a charging bull.

Oh gods—was he insane?! He would knock us both unconscious!

I clung to his head like a terrified squirrel, unable to hold back a scream of protest as he slammed us both into the wall at full speed.

I hit first, my head cracking off the wall and all the breath was crushed from my lungs by the force of the hit.

Instantly, the world went sideways.

My body went slack and everything seemed to spin in a whirling vortex of blurred chaos. The screaming of the crowd grew louder.

Up! Gods, I had to get up!

Where was Declan? Was he about to pin me again?

Smears of color seemed to blur around me as I blinked, suddenly aware that I was lying on my side in the sand.

A dark shadow fell over me. I squinted up, my teeth clenched as the sickly sweet flavor of blood oozed through my mouth. Had I bitten my tongue?

"N-not ... bad, kid," a familiar male voice panted hoarsely over me.

Declan.

Somewhere nearby, the caller shouted again. "THREE!"

I caught a clear glimpse of his bruised, bleeding knuckles an instant before they sailed straight for my face.

Then everything went completely dark.

TWENTY

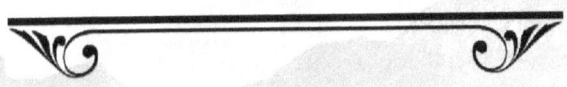

"Come on. That's it, girl. Wake up."

My eyes flew open as someone patted my cheek, coaxing me out of the dark and back into the glare of the torchlight.

I lay sprawled on the arena floor like a starfish, warm blood running from my nose and lips all down the sides of my face. I coughed and sputtered, choking in a frantic breath as the hazy collection of faces leaning over me finally came into view.

Roxus and Declan stared down at me with mixed expressions of concern.

"She's back." Declan sighed, his hard features going slack in relief. "Fates, girl, you gotta learn when to tap out."

I managed a groggy, blood-smeared grin.

Not dead. Not yet, anyway.

Roxus rolled his eyes, lifting a hand like he was gesturing to the mustached fight-caller to let him know I was, in fact, not dead.

I groaned through my teeth as Declan scooped his arms under my back and knees, lifting me out of the sand and holding me against his strong chest.

If it didn't feel like my head might explode with intense, pounding pain, I might have blushed.

Ugh. Embarrassing.

"Gotta hand it to you, girlie, you got more fight in you than I thought," he muttered as he carried me to the edge of the pit. "I see why he picked you. Good thing I passed on the invitation—you're much better suited for the Call."

I managed to lift my head and shakily stare up at him. What was he talking about? Roxus had asked him about becoming his apprentice before me?

So I was his second choice? And why had Declan refused?

Did he know something I didn't about becoming a member of the Zenith's Call? Was there something else Roxus hadn't told me?

For whatever reason, that thought put a sharp sting of fresh pain through my chest.

I squirmed, trying to sit up on my own, but Declan's hold on me tightened.

"Take it easy. You were out cold for a few minutes," he growled, so low I could feel the vibrations in his chest against my ear.

It made my whole face burn.

"Hand her up," Roxus called from somewhere nearby. "Can she walk?"

"Y-yes," I hissed through my teeth.

"Stubborn brat," Declan fumed under his breath as he passed me up to Roxus like a ragdoll.

He had no idea.

My legs wobbled as Roxus eased me onto my feet. Leaning against him, I took deep breaths and tried to focus past the ringing in my ears and the pounding of my pulse that made my eardrums ache like they might burst.

Probably another concussion.

Fantastic.

I tried not to listen to the taunts of the crowd as Roxus helped me hobble back to our table. They spat all manner of names and slurs, promising next time I'd be lucky if Declan let me leave that pit alive. Somehow, I doubted that.

Oddly enough, he didn't seem to want me dead. He'd had more than enough opportunity to see to that, and no one except Roxus would have taken issue with it.

My mouth twisted to one side, catching a glimpse of his long, lean form striding across the arena to exit on the other side. He didn't even acknowledge the roaring cheers or chants from his captive audience. His mouth stayed set in a firm, bitter frown.

Almost like he was sulking.

He'd won, though, hadn't he? What was there to sulk about?

"How's your head?" Roxus asked as he helped me ease down into my seat.

"Hurts," I grumbled.

"I don't doubt it. Here." He slid a small goblet in front of me filled with what looked suspiciously like wine.

I flicked him a dubious glare that made my head throb with sharp pain again.

He scowled back and nudged the cup closer to me. "It's got a healing remedy in it. Trust me, you want it in wine. The taste on its own will make you throw up."

Ugggh. Fine.

I muttered a few choice Viperi curses as I cradled the cup in both hands and took a tentative sip. My mouth scrunched and I nearly gagged as the powerfully bitter flavor, like pure swamp sludge, burned my tongue and throat.

Gods, what was in this? It didn't taste anything like the remedies Leruna provided.

"It's Lunthardan," he explained as he eased down into his

seat across from me. "They keep it in reserve here in case someone goes a little too far. Works fast."

I glowered into the cup, hating that I already felt a little better even after one sip. Curse it. Why did he have to be right about everything?

"Declan agreed to train with you," Roxus announced. "Twice a week, until you can handle more."

I stared at him over the rim of the cup. "What about Chrysa?"

"You've nearly done all you can for her," he said. "She's solid in her basics now. You can still spar and train with her at Arx Eburna, if you want. Mistress Orvana shouldn't have any issue with that, since you've gotten along well so far. But we're going to have to shift our focus to your improvement, not just hers."

"Is this because Domitri is punishing her for getting too friendly with me?" I dared to ask as I choked down another sip of the wine-and-healing-sewage concoction.

Roxus didn't answer, keeping his focus on his long smoking pipe as he stuffed it full of fresh dried herbs and lit it.

I took that as a "yes," though.

"Is she even still a prospect?" I probed, wondering if he had seen her or Domitri since the incident in the library.

"Yes. She ought to return tomorrow, and you two can get back to work," he said.

For whatever reason, hearing that made my throbbing muscles relax some. I sank deeper into my seat and took another awful sip from the goblet.

"They're going to be giving the other prospects final trials in combat soon, so you need to take each training session with Declan seriously. He knows his stuff, and he can help you in the areas where you have some weaknesses," Roxus warned.

"I thought I didn't have to take that trial after what happened before?"

"You don't, but I wouldn't put it past them to make you an opponent, just for spite." He nodded to my cup. "You need to finish that."

"Worried you'll be seen carrying your bruised and bleeding second choice prospect out of a pirate bar?" I baited, letting my tone carry an edge.

His eyebrows rose. "Second choice?"

"Declan told me you asked him about being your apprentice first."

"I did," he confirmed. "Years ago, right after he first made his appearance on the mercenary scene."

Oh.

Well, Declan hadn't mentioned *that* part.

"Why did he refuse?" I rubbed at the back of my very sore neck.

"You'd have to ask him that."

Hmmm. Maybe I would.

"You lost control again, didn't you?" Roxus asked suddenly.

I froze mid-sip. My gaze flashed up and fixed on his as I sat, paralyzed. Everything below my neck seemed to go totally numb. I couldn't even feel myself breathing.

Oh no.

How did he know that?

"Don't give me that look," he murmured as he blew a smoke ring into the air between us. "You tried to kill him. I've watched you fight enough now to recognize the difference."

I sank even lower in my seat, wishing I could melt into the floor.

"I'm so—" I started to whisper, but he cut me off right away.

"I don't want apologies. I want you to do better. That's why you're going to start training with him. If you can't handle being pushed to the limit without losing your head, you can't be Zenith's Call. It's that simple," he said. "Declan is the only one I know of who can bring you to that point and still come out on top. As far as I'm concerned, *he* is your final trial."

Oh ... so that's why he wanted us to train together.

My stomach clenched and bound up into a tangle of aching knots.

I stared back down into my goblet, finding my reflection on the rippling surface of the dark red wine. My face was bruised again, and there was dried blood around my nose and mouth. I looked horrific.

Like the filthy monster I was.

I flinched and almost fell out of my chair as a hand grasped my shoulder and shook it roughly. I whipped around to find a heavyset man dressed in fine silken robes and a silver-scaled belt leering down at me. The frilled lace of his collar almost hid the folds of his neck that spilled down onto his chest, not disguised at all behind his sparse, graying beard.

My heart stopped cold.

I was instantly lost in the depths of his ruthless dark eyes. Like windows into the deepest pits of the abyss.

A hell I knew all too well.

"Well, well. That was quite a fight." The heavyset man grinned darkly. "Quite a whelp you've found, Roxus."

"Varri'dasha, Sulam," Roxus replied dryly, his expression becoming as cool and distant as the surface of the moon. "Don't tell me you lost coin on it, as well."

Sulam gave a throaty, hacking laugh and squeezed my shoulder so hard his knuckles blanched between the many glittering stone rings he wore.

But I didn't dare make a sound.

Under the table, my knees shook. I could feel that cold tide of pure, primal panic rising within me.

"In my own arena? Of course not. I know a good fighter

when I see one. Just as I know a pathetic weakling, too," Sulam replied in his throaty, rasping tone. "Tell me, does this Pitathi whelp belong to you?"

Roxus's eyes pinched tighter at the corners. His jawline went solid, as though he were biting down on that pipe to keep from snarling. "I don't deal in slaves. You know that's not a habit we have in common."

The sneer that deepened the wrinkles around Sulam's mouth sent a shock up my spine like I'd been struck by lightning.

"You deal in more than you realize, I think." He snickered and gave my shoulder one more vice-grip squeeze. "Take care. I'm sure we'll be seeing each other again soon."

Roxus only answered with a small nod, his gaze smoldering with thought as he watched Sulam lumber off into the crowd.

Only when he disappeared did I feel the tingle of fresh terror return to my legs. Spots danced in my vision and I stuffed my hands under the table so Roxus wouldn't see them shaking.

Out of all the slimy criminal lords slithering through these streets ... why did it have to be him? Why did it have to be his tavern? Shouldn't he be out somewhere in the gods-forsaken desert, scraping more desperate souls out of the sand so they were forced to be his thieving slaves?

"Violet?"

I flinched when Roxus said my name. A cold sweat ran down my neck as I sat, quivering and wringing my hands under the table.

His eyes darkened. "How do you know Sulam?"

It wasn't a question.

It was a demand.

But I couldn't get any sound to come out as I stared

blankly back at him, my mouth opening and closing as I choked on every sound I tried to make.

"Violet," he said my name again, more softly this time.

Under the table, I felt his rough, strong hand gently clasp mine.

"You're all right," he said.

I wasn't.

Not with Sulam still somewhere in this place, probably watching me right now. Enjoying my terror. Relishing my panic.

I guess Roxus could tell.

"Let's go home," he said and immediately stood. He kept a protective hand on my back as he walked right behind me through the crowd.

I tried to focus on taking each step, staying steady, and not looking around to see if Sulam was nearby. It was better not to know. Otherwise, I might break into a mad sprint.

We'd almost made it to the tapestry-covered doorway when another voice called out to us. We both turned to see Declan striding over, his swollen, battered face nearly unrecognizable now. Had he been fighting in the pit again? Gods, I hadn't even been paying attention.

"Leaving already?" He glanced between us, those light green eyes like the sun through spring leaves in the torchlight.

"She's still in training, so we have an early start tomorrow," Roxus said, waving him off. "I'll send word about setting up a training routine for you two."

Declan seemed to deflate some, his broad shoulders dropping as he kept a worried frown fixed on me. "Right. See you later, then."

He stretched out a hand toward me, offering to bump my fist against his. A gesture of truce, I knew.

But I couldn't do it.

I cringed back slightly, unable to stop tears from welling in my eyes as I met his gaze. I just wanted to leave. To be anywhere but here.

To be somewhere safe.

When I didn't move or say anything, Roxus gave me another gentle nudge toward the door. "We'll be in touch," he promised.

"Okay." Declan withdrew his hand and nodded in agreement.

There was no mistaking the concerned frown as he glanced all around, as though he could sense something in this room had set me off.

But Sulam was nowhere in sight.

And I was desperate to get out before he returned.

Lowering my head, I sped toward the doorway and ducked through without ever looking back. Roxus followed, right on my heels as I made my way up the stairs, through the tavern's dining area, and back outside.

Only there, with the strong ocean breeze filling my lungs and teasing through my hair, did the tension in my chest begin to ease.

I would not go back there.

Not ever.

Roxus didn't say a word as we walked home, shadowing my steps like a towering specter. I could almost feel the heat of his stare on my back, like he was frantically trying to read every single move I made.

I was too tired to bother hiding anything, though.

By the time we reached his home, I carried my boots upstairs to my room and shut the door without saying good-night. He didn't follow.

Apparently, neither of us felt like talking anymore.

The house was already dim and quiet as I shambled across the room. I didn't see Gibb anywhere. Delthene was probably asleep, then. He liked spending his nights in there with her.

Stupid cat.

Just this once, I wished he would come curl up with me.

I peeled off my new armor, leaving it all in a heap on the floor, and washed the blood off my face in the basin by my dressing table. Then I crawled into the soft reprieve of my bed. The silken blankets closed around me like a cool, caressing sea. My head hit the pillow, and I couldn't keep my eyes open.

My thoughts circled and spiraled, twisting around everything I'd learned. Declan. Chrysa.

Sulam.

It all mixed together like paint until it was nothing but a muddied mess. And I was left drifting, wondering, waiting. Hoping it could all be fixed somehow.

Could *I* even be fixed?

I didn't know.

Some things, when broken, stayed that way. Usually beautiful things.

But I had never been beautiful. Viperi couldn't be beautiful, could they?

Lying on my back, I surrendered to the pull of that swirling void deep in my chest. The one that dragged me down into darkness again.

I couldn't keep letting these phantoms rule me. I had to get control. Roxus was right—I hadn't gotten any better at it.

And gods knew I was almost out of time.

* * *

It was another dream. A nightmare. I knew that.

And yet my heart ached, feeling it like the pierce of an arrow's point being twisted in my chest.

It was just a dream—but the memory was all too real.

I couldn't run any farther.

Every step made my legs howl in agony. My feet were cut

and battered, burned on the hot sand and jagged stone, so that every step left a footprint of blood behind.

My mother sagged at my side, the arid wind snatching in her long white hair as her ruby-red eyes stared wildly around us. Her lips were swollen and split, turning a strangely dusky shade of purple. Her face had gone ashen days ago.

I didn't understand why.

How long had it been? Where were we? Where could we go?

I didn't know, and part of me knew she didn't, either.

We ran for the setting sun, huddling in shady crevices in the rugged desert canyons whenever we could. But those places were growing harder to find. There were no more cacti or prickly bushes. No signs of life anywhere.

No hope for miles in any direction.

My mother staggered. She let out a garbled, hoarse cry as she fell into me. On her hands and knees, her whole body shuddered strangely. Convulsing.

I crouched down beside her, trying to get her back to her feet.

She weakly shoved my hands away, her face spasming and twitching as she stared back at me. Her brow drew up, her sun-reddened face looking more like raw meat now than the porcelain perfection it had been before.

She cupped one of my cheeks in her hand. *"G-Go, Visha."*

I shook my head, seizing her arm and trying to drag her up again. "Not without you."

The harder I pulled, the more she seemed to go slack until she lay on her back, sprawling on the sun-scorched stone.

Her body twitched and trembled, eyes searching wildly as though she couldn't see me.

"Mother?" I cried, sinking to my knees beside her and trying to use my body to shield her—to give her some small fragment of shade from the sun's oppressive glare.

Her scarlet eyes blinked hard, focusing on my face for a fleeting second. Her expression skewed like she wanted to sob. But neither of us had tears left now.

She grasped my hand, lacing her fingers through mine.

"*Run*," she gasped brokenly. "*You must run. Never stop running.*"

"No, Mother," I begged. "Please, you have to get up. We have to keep going."

Her pupils went wide, gaze fixing on my face but seeming so far away.

"*You ... must ... l-live, Visha.*" My mother's cracked, bleeding lips barely moved, her breaths rattling as her grip on my hand went slack.

Her expression emptied, as though she were looking at something far away.

No.

NO!

I clung to her, my hair snatching around my head in the howling winds. The hot sand filled my nose, my eyes, and my throat as I screamed for her. Over and over, until my throat was raw.

But her eyes stayed wide and fixed. Her body was limp. Her breath was gone.

My mother was gone.

As though the scorching desert storm had already carried her spirit far away.

And I was left behind, seeing nothing before me but an endless, brutal world that I couldn't survive in.

No matter how fast or far I ran.

Something on the far horizon caught my eye. A glint like metal catching in the sunlight.

I staggered forward, letting out another desperate cry as the line of merchant wagons seemed to materialize out of the rippling heat like a mirage. My only hope.

The only path forward.

Surely it was better than death?

I ran, leaving my mother's motionless body behind. My lungs throbbed like they were being torn apart. My body burned. My feet throbbed.

But I ran with every shred of strength I had left.

Straight into the squeezing, brutal grasp of slavers ... and the man who ruled over them like a chortling, fallen god.

The man who called himself Sulam.

The man who would haunt my nightmares until the day I could finally carve the final breath straight out of his wicked chest.

TWENTY-ONE

I t was getting worse.

Every night, the dreams came. They dug deeper and deeper into my mind like a worm into an apple, eating away at me a little bit at a time. I could hardly keep my eyes open if I sat still for too long. Gods, it was a battle just to make it through a meal without winding up with my head in my plate.

Studying was impossible. I sat up by lamplight, fighting to read the same paragraph, only to startle awake when the book smacked me in the face.

How was I supposed to fight like this?

I didn't know, and I was out of time to figure that out. Declan was coming. And today, I didn't know if I could survive another match with him—even a practice one.

My body still ached in places from the last time I'd faced him in that fighting pit. My arms and legs felt too heavy. My head throbbed. But if I didn't show up, if I didn't give it everything I had, I didn't want to think about the consequences.

Sitting at the table across from Roxus and Delthene, I stirred at the bowl of spiced fish stew with my stomach clenching and squirming. My mind replayed flashes of my foul dreams. Sulam's toothy smile. Domitri's snickering laughter. My mother's whispering voice.

I couldn't keep doing this. Something inside me would break. And what then?

Was I going to snap? Or collapse?

I didn't know.

"Should I have something prepared for after they've finished?" Delthene chatted idly, but I could feel her worried gaze on me like the glare of the noonday sun.

"You know he'd happily eat us out of house and home," Roxus muttered. "Especially after this one's given him a proper challenge."

I glanced up, meeting Roxus's cautious smirk. Like he could tell I was an inch from fracture.

I glanced between them, trying to figure out who or what they were talking about.

Oh. Right.

This was about Declan coming over for our first official combat lesson.

I sank lower in my chair and went back to stirring at my bowl of stew, hoping it would at least look like I was eating so Delthene didn't fuss at me.

"You ready?" Roxus asked suddenly.

I cringed and forced myself to take a bite. At least then I could get away with a small nod since my mouth was full. The warmth of the rich spices mingled with the bright flavors of citrus lemongrass, and I pinched off a piece of the lightly crisped flatbread and popped it in my mouth, too.

Roxus's smile faded at the corners, mouth pressing into a tight, dissatisfied line. His gaze held mine for one long, heavy second before he turned his attention back to his bowl without another word.

Like he wasn't buying an inch of my response.

Curse it. I couldn't hide anything from him, could I?

I finished picking at my dinner and trudged upstairs, refusing to even glance at my reflection in my dressing mirror as I pulled on a white linen shirt and leggings—suitable attire for sparring.

Down on the first floor, the front door opened. Voices and footsteps echoed up the stairwell. My heart hit the back of my throat like I was trying to swallow a lemon whole.

He was here.

Cold sweat prickled on my skin. My heart pounded, kicking like an angry mule in my chest. Gods, I'd barely walked away from my last little match with Declan.

How the heck was I supposed to fight him at all when I felt like an empty husk?

Someone rapped their knuckles on my bedroom door and I bit back a curse, whirling around just in time to see Roxus stick his head inside.

"He's here," he muttered. "You all right?"

I nodded again, grinding my teeth as a swell of heat tingled up my spine and out through all my fingers.

Strange. It almost felt like ... anger.

Was it? Or were my nerves running wild?

I wasn't sure until the instant I stepped into the doorway of the sparring room alone and saw him there.

With his back turned, Declan stretched his long, powerfully corded arms over his head and flexed his shoulders like he hadn't heard me enter the room. He'd opted for a similar ensemble of loose linen clothes, a tunic and breeches, and no shoes. But the dusky bruise along his neck and cheek looked new.

Another souvenir from a fight in that pit?

I didn't ask.

I couldn't even make a sound thanks to that knot of white-hot emotion still lodged in the back of my throat. I tried to breathe. To swallow it down. But it burned like hellfire, singing a path down to my heart.

Rage—it was rage.

He worked for Sulam, fighting in the pit every night. He filled that putrid man's pockets with coin won off the blood of every opponent he crushed. Coin Sulam probably used to buy more slaves.

I took a step closer, my fists clenched into shaking fists at my sides.

Declan's towering form froze. He held eerily still. Then his head slowly turned to flick me a glance back over one of his powerful shoulders.

"Well, well. Quiet as a cat, aren't you?" A crooked grin split his mouth.

He had no idea.

I narrowed my eyes, stalking around him with every muscle tense and every one of my senses ablaze with primal focus.

"Not even a hello?" He clicked his tongue disapprovingly. "Roxus warned me you were out of sorts. Don't tell me you're still angry I won our last match."

I made a straight line for the rack of practice weapons and hesitated, my fingers brushing the hilt of a short, curved scimitar. Hmm. That was new.

Had Roxus put this here for me?

I narrowed my eyes and picked the dulled weapon up, giving it a spin over my hand before I let the supple leather of the hilt settle in my palm.

Balanced. Light. Versatile.

Perfect.

"Seems like you have an acceptable handle on armed combat," Declan observed as he swaggered over with his arms crossed over his broad chest.

I snorted. "Acceptable?"

His wolfish grin widened. "Compared to the rookie half-wits you've been training with—yeah, sure. *Acceptable.*"

I faced him, arms crossed to mimic that cocky pose, and acutely aware that I was scarcely half his height. Gods. How was he only seventeen—three years older than me?

Impossible. Either his age was wrong ... or mine.

Maybe both, since my being fourteen was essentially just an educated guess.

"You won't need that today. We're starting with hand-to-hand. Your stamina needs work," Declan announced as he sauntered off to one of the sparring circles marked in the center of the room.

My lip twitched. I squeezed the hilt of the practice scimitar tighter. *Pfft. Acceptable.*

I'd show him acceptable.

Placing the scimitar back on the weapon rack, I rolled my shoulders and stretched my neck out as I prowled closer, never breaking that steady eye contact. Poised for any sudden movements.

"I'll admit, your style's not anything I've seen in the pit before. Definitely not something the Zenith's Call uses, either. The Viperi teach you all that?" he asked.

My heart gave a strange, twisting lurch, and it took everything I had not to let it show.

He had said Viperi.

Not Pitathi.

Had Roxus warned him about that?

"Yes, mostly," I said. "The rest I learned trying to survive beatings by other bullies like you."

He chuckled darkly. "There are no other bullies like me, girl."

"Apparently. Is that why you left your people? Did they run you out?" I sank into a defensive stance across the sparring circle, waiting for him to make the first move.

His eyes darkened for an instant, something like the smallest ember of wrath sparking in the hard lines of his rugged features.

"No," he muttered.

Hmmm.

I'd read a little about Holvradix elven tribes in books on divine lore, but it seemed to be a hodgepodge of guesses and rumors mostly. Apart from their long-standing hatred for their neighbors, the Avoran elves, the Holvradix people kept to themselves in the wild frozen mountains far to the north. They didn't trade. They didn't tolerate outsiders.

They didn't leave their homeland.

So what was he doing here, working for the absolute scum of the earth?

I needed to know.

Roxus had mentioned he was only half Holvradix. What was the other half? And how had he wound up so far south— kingdoms and oceans away from the mountain halls of his kin?

"Light hits. No wrestling maneuvers. This is a warm-up, so keep on your toes and don't stop moving," he warned as he advanced, his fists already up.

I set my jaw, heart still pounding in my throat. I waited for him to step within a five-foot distance before I lunged. Head-to-head, fist-to-fist, I stood no chance whatsoever. He had me on reach. He had me on raw power.

But I did have speed on him.

Diving into the fight, I swung one lightning-fast jab after another, growling each time he easily deflected my hits.

"Slow down," he snarled. "You're gonna burn out early doing that. Think."

I spat a Viperi curse, cutting him a defiant glare, and went *faster*. More hits, sharp and swift, aimed at his head.

BAM!

All the wind rushed out of me and I staggered as he popped a sudden, stern punch straight to the pit of my stomach. I bent over, wheezing and cursing furiously as he stood over me.

"This only works if you listen to me. Otherwise, we're both wasting our time here," he fumed. "You seem a little extra spicy today. Still sour about losing our last match?"

I glared up at him, still trying to catch my breath. Gods, he wasn't even sweating. Had he just been toying with me in our fight before?

Or had all those restless, sleepless nights finally caught up with me?

Regardless, that molten knot of emotion seemed to singe through all my sanity as I forced myself to stand upright and raised my fists.

Declan's sharp green eyes darkened, as though he could somehow sense the exhausted desperation humming through my veins.

"You gonna do what I say this time?" he demanded.

"Just shut up and fight!" I snapped.

His expression cooled instantly, chin tilting up as he took a step backward and crossed his arms again. Digging his heels in.

"Not until you tell me what's going on here," he said. "You coming at me like a rabid weasel every round isn't going to make you a better fighter."

I dove at him, swinging wildly as the wildfire in my blood caught.

He caught my fist in mid-air and twisted me around, spinning me like a dance partner faster than I could blink and pinning me into a headlock right against his chest.

"Gods, girl, what's wrong with you?!" he shouted. "Calm down!"

I wrenched myself free of his grip and darted out of reach.

My chest heaved in furious, ragged breaths. My head swam with rage and exhaustion.

I couldn't hold it in anymore. The words broke past my lips like a spray of burning venom. "How can you work for Sulam? Do you have any idea what he does to people?!"

Declan didn't move. He stood strangely still, staring at me with his eyes wide and expression slack.

Seconds passed, and all I could hear was the hissing of my manic breaths and the rush of my blood boiling.

Then his head bowed slightly, eyes boring into mine with a quiet fury that sent a pang of real fear racing up my spine.

"I'm flattered you think I do it by choice," he growled low.

I hesitated. "Don't you? How much does Sulam pay you? And how many opponents die at your hands?"

His lip curled as he looked away, brow locked in a deep, disgusted scowl. "Just square up and do what I say. Roxus has already paid me for this session, and we don't have all night."

I straightened, squaring my shoulders and refusing to look away. "We do if it means I'm deciding whether or not I can trust one of Sulam's sleazy henchmen. I'd rather take my chances on my own than take advice from a thug who probably spends his nights bathing in coin still wet with the blood of slaves and captives."

He was on me faster than I could blink.

Snatching me by the front of my tunic, he practically dragged me up onto my toes so he could yell right into my face. "HEY! You don't know anything about me—so how about you watch your mouth!"

My heart pounded like mad, skipping and stalling as I stared straight into his flushed face. I should have been scared. Terrified.

But I couldn't shake that infernal rage.

Seizing his arms, I dug my nails into his skin and hissed back, "How can you fight for him? How can you do his bidding like some collared attack dog? Do you have any idea who he—"

"I DON'T HAVE A CHOICE!"

All the wind rushed out of me at once. It snuffed out the flames of my anger and sucked the breath from my lungs.

I hung completely still in his grasp, caught in his frenzied glare while his hand gripping my tunic shook. It was a look I knew from the inside out.

It was terror and frustration. It was confusion and pain.

But, gods, it didn't make any sense.

"So... what are you saying? That you're a slave? I don't see any chains," I managed to sputter.

He dropped me like a rotten tomato.

I landed in a heap at his feet, watching him turn away and storm to the other side of the sparring circle. Like he had to get away—to put some distance between us—before he snapped.

"Not all chains are so easy to see," he murmured, his tone a soft rumble like distant thunder. "Make no mistake—my collar is tight and the leash is short."

I sat, still panting as I tried to get my shaking legs to cooperate long enough for me to stand up again. "W-what do you mean?"

Declan turned his back, as though he didn't want me to see the look on his face. It didn't matter, though. I could hear the utter brokenness in his voice. I could feel the aura of pain and shame wafting off him like heat from molten metal.

"Sulam has my little sister. She's a slave in his house. As long as I keep my head down, as long as I keep winning him coin in pit fights, he won't touch her."

I held perfectly still, feeling the impact of each word like a blade stabbed straight into my chest. That was why he fought so hard. That was why he spent every night wrist-deep in blood with his face bashed black and blue.

He didn't have a choice.

"That's why you turned down Roxus's offer to join the Zenith's Call," I realized aloud.

His head turned slightly back toward me, but he didn't meet my gaze. All the furious tension in his densely muscled body had gone slack. His arms hung limp at his sides. His brow smoothed as his expression dissolved to something distant and empty.

"I know one day I'll lose my edge. Some new pup will come along, fresh and fit for the fight, and that'll be it. Sulam will send me to the Caldera, and gods only know what will happen to Nora," he said quietly.

I frowned. "What's the Caldera?"

A faint, ironic smile tugged at his lips and he finally glanced my way. "The end ... for fighters anyway. It's an arena on Kosaar. But the fights aren't like the pit. It's to the death."

A memory prickled at the back of my mind. Something I'd tried to forget.

I had only spent a short time under Sulam's thumb, but his henchmen liked to brag. They'd mentioned something about an arena where blood sport won more coin than any vagrant or sell-sword could imagine.

That must have been the Caldera.

More than a minute passed as we stood in silence, staring at one another from across the sparring circle. My mind raced, sorting through everything he had said. It all made sense now.

Except for one thing.

"Why doesn't the Zenith's Call help you?"

Declan let out a heavy breath. He strode toward me, his features still creased with uncertainty as he offered a hand to help haul me back to my feet. "They're not like that. They don't monitor all the crime and wrongdoing in the world. Haven't you learned that yet?"

I had, of course. I'd learned a little about what the Zenith's

Call did—what they considered to be their true calling. It just... felt wrong.

"But they could help. They should," I grumbled.

Declan chuckled and gave me a rough pat on the back that nearly made me trip and fall again. "You're gonna make a lousy agent."

"What?"

He shrugged and stepped back into a fighting stance. "That sense of justice—it's adorably unbecoming for a guardian of divine secrets. For a Viperi, too."

I pursed my lips sourly. "Thanks."

"Seriously, though, you need to cool off the pace today. We're gonna work endurance and technique, and it's gonna take some time," he said. "Now, can we get to work, please?"

I looked down at my own hands, watching my fingers shake from the aftermath of all that adrenaline. My head still felt sluggish. Maybe taking it easy was a good idea.

"Fine," I agreed. "But I still think you're a thug."

Declan's gaze flickered with sadistic glee as he waved me in, taunting me to come closer and fight some more.

"You can think whatever you want about me, half-pint. Just do what I say and keep moving." He snickered. "With a little luck, maybe we'll make a *real* fighter out of you, after all."

Somehow, I didn't think he would give me a choice. I'd either learn ...

Or he'd beat me to a pulp with that same stupid grin on his face the whole time.

Gods help me.

I sank deeper into my stance, forcing my focus inward to the burning fatigue in all my muscles and the throbbing of my pulse in my fingers and toes. I had to put everything I had into this.

"He has my little sister."

The words echoed in my head as my eyes locked with his, louder than the rush of my blood, louder than the panic that tightened in my chest.

I'd assumed so much about him.

And I'd been so wrong.

Now, everything had shifted. Declan wasn't my enemy. He was a prisoner. And that terrified me more than anything, because he was undoubtedly the strongest person I'd ever met. If someone like him was trapped, chained to the heel of a monster like Sulam, then what hope was there for anyone else?

What hope could there possibly be for a Viperi urchin?

TWENTY-TWO

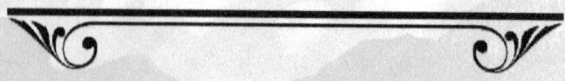

Die—I was going to die.

Every muscle screamed. Every breath felt like fire in my lungs. But I couldn't stop.

Declan wouldn't let me stop.

"Arms up! Keep your feet moving!" Declan snarled over me. He paced back and forth, shouting at my back as I slammed my swollen, throbbing fists into the straw practice dummy over and over.

Right jab. Uppercut. Back leg strong and left hook. Left Jab. Another right. Leg sweep.

My heart pounded against my ribs, my vision blurred, and my head thrummed with splitting pain. Sweat poured down my back and soaked my hair. My lungs ached. My whole body burned, every muscle drawn tight.

But I couldn't stop. Not with Declan looming over me, watching. Judging. Waiting for any sign of weakness.

Each strike was like a bellows' breath to the flames of my soul, and I'd never burned so bright.

Where was this strength coming from?

Was it me, or was it just primal fear of what would happen if I failed? Could it just be pure spite?

I didn't know.

After only four training sessions with Declan, I couldn't deny the difference. Everything was changing so fast.

We'd fallen into a steady routine, and I had to admit, I probably looked like an eager puppy waiting for him to hit the door in the afternoons we'd set aside for these lessons. It made the long days, skulking in the back of every room at Arx Eburna while the other prospects and patrons leered at me, a little more bearable.

So, yes, I was eager to get back when I knew I had a combat lesson with Declan in the afternoon. A little too eager, maybe.

I couldn't help it, though. Not when the changes were so obvious. My endurance had more than doubled. I could spar with Declan for nearly an hour before the fatigue, and one of his classic gut punches, sent me face-first to the ground.

My appetite had kicked into overdrive, and Delthene had tripled portions just to keep me from raiding the larder in the middle of the night. Because of that, I put on more pounds of muscle. My clothes got tighter as my frame filled out, blooming to a new life I'd never seen before.

I looked less like a half-starved child and more like a powerful young woman.

Or so Delthene claimed.

I decided just to take her word for it. Er, well, until I realized my leggings were too snug in the thighs and hips. Oops.

Another pleasant side-effect of being completely exhausted: I slept.

I collapsed into bed every night after my bath and didn't even dream. I guess there was only so far the nightmares could chase me before my weary mind finally gave up torturing me every night.

And I was more than glad for that sweet surrender.

A scream of furious energy tore through my teeth as I surged in for the final three strikes. Two jabs to the face and a right hook sent the practice dummy flying back against the wall with a crack.

I dropped back into a crouch, arms still up, and sucking in growling breaths.

Someone clapped.

I looked, expecting to find Declan giving me one of those patronizing smirks that made me want to hit him as hard as I had that straw dummy.

Roxus stood in the doorway, slowly clapping. A knowing smile, like the flash of a spark off flint stone, glinted in his eyes as he glanced between us.

"Impressive," he purred smugly. Like this was all going according to plan.

"She's full of nothing but fire, spite, and vinegar," Declan agreed. "The Zenith's Call would have to be stock-full of fools not to take her. I've never seen anyone with that kind of speed."

I shot him a sideways glare as I still fought to catch my breath. "You've not met many Viperi, then."

Declan shrugged. "Fair enough."

"Regardless, I appreciate the effort, Declan," Roxus said. "I hope you'll be willing to keep this up even after the trials are finished. I need her to keep that edge ... and the control."

"Of course. She's the first sparring partner I've had in a while that actually gives me a challenge." Declan swaggered over to drop one of his big, rough hands onto the top of my head. He drew it back quickly, making a face when he realized how sweaty and gross my hair was.

Served him right.

"Go ahead and wrap it up for the day. I've got something

to discuss with you, and she's got company," Roxus announced as he stroked at his stubbled chin.

I frowned, glancing my patron up and down. Company? What was he talking about?

Unless ...

My heart gave a frantic flutter. Hope squeezed at my chest, crushing the breath from my lungs for a moment.

Roxus held my gaze, watching me and apparently reading every nuance of my expression with that same, wistful smirk on his face. He nodded slightly, as though he knew exactly what I was thinking.

Oh, gods.

Chrysa was back!

"Meet me in my office." Roxus waved a hand at Declan and walked off, disappearing back into the hallway with his hand back in the pockets of his long coat.

The wind rushed out of me, like I'd been holding my breath ever since that day in the library when Domitri had last singled me out. The day Chrysa had spoken up in my defense. The last day I had seen her.

Was she all right? What had happened? Was she coming back to Arx Eburna to train again? Where had she been all this time?

Questions swirled in my brain, leaving me standing frozen in numb silence.

Until Declan thumped my ear.

"Hey, let's cool down. Stretch out. You know the rules— no skipping steps," he scolded.

I winced and shot him a glare. "Fine."

Sitting across from him in the sparring circle on the worn wooden floor, I hurried through all the stretches he had shown me to loosen up my arms, legs, core, and back. I tried not to watch as he did the same, although much slower.

I ... did not succeed.

It was hard not to be impressed at the range of flexibility he had for ... well, for as big as he was. Usually, muscle-bound men like him struggled to even touch their toes. Or, that's what I had seen in the past from the burly city guards, anyway.

Declan was unique. Like me.

Or, at least, that's sort of how it felt now—like we were on opposite ends of the same bizarre spectrum. The spectrum of social oddities in the Southern Kingdoms. What would our ancestors have thought of us training and sparring together?

It made me smile a little.

"I can honestly say your smile is almost as frightening as your snarl. I'm guessing you've got a friend waiting for you downstairs?" Declan asked with an eyebrow arched.

I wrinkled my nose at him. I knew him well enough now to recognize that the relentless teasing was his strange, annoying way of showing affection. People he didn't like, he ignored outright.

"Friend is a strong word," I murmured sheepishly.

He laughed. "It's a weird one coming from you."

"Aren't we friends?" I dared to ask.

I only half meant it. I knew things were incredibly transactional between us. Roxus paid him for these training sessions. He might not come here or have anything to do with me otherwise.

But knowing what I did about him now—about his little sister and his entanglement with Sulam—I couldn't help but feel a certain kinship to him.

A certain *sameness* that I didn't quite understand.

Declan hesitated. The taunting grin on his lips faded some, and he used stretching out his legs as an excuse to look away. "You seem to know Sulam well enough to understand that's a dangerous word for someone in my position."

I did. But I still wanted to know.

Because it would change things for me, too.

"You don't need to worry about him using me as leverage against you," I reminded him. "I can handle myself."

"That's not what I'm worried about."

Oh.

Wait—was he worried that Sulam would try to use *him* as leverage against *me?*

Hmmm. I hadn't considered that. But he was right, it did pose a problem.

One I'd never had before.

Too late, I realized it didn't matter. If that was the kind of extortion Sulam chose to use against me, it would absolutely work.

I would not be able to stand by and watch him do something awful to Declan.

That realization sent a shockwave through my brain and rattled the foundations of my soul. I hadn't known Declan very long. Not even as long as Chrysa.

But I cared what happened to him.

I cared a *lot.*

Gods ... I really was going soft.

"Hey, look, it's fine." Declan kept his voice low and hushed as he stood. His chest swelled as he took in a deep, steadying breath, and then offered a hand to pull me up, too.

It wasn't fine. Not even close.

"I can fend for myself, too," he said. "So keep those sad, teary-eyed looks to yourself, yeah? I don't accept invitations to pity parties."

I couldn't hold in a snort. That jerk. I shook my head and gave him a half-strength punch in the arm. It didn't even jostle him.

"You arrogant sow's end," I muttered. "Roxus should have warned me what he was really getting me into, setting me up to fight you in that stupid pit."

Declan just grinned and gave me a taunting pop on the

back of the head before he swaggered away to gather his cloak and boots. "That's the thing about fighting, kid. You're not always gonna know who's really on the other end of your blade. Taking a life isn't a small thing. Neither is sparing one. Never make that choice on a whim."

I followed behind him at a distance, standing by and picking at my nails while he laced up his boots. "Where did you learn to fight, anyway?"

"In the pit mostly. But my father was a member of the Darksteel Guard out of Tibrus. My mother was a Holvradix elf. They both taught me a thing or two before they realized I was a hotheaded brat who liked blood on his knuckles."

I blinked, unable to mask my surprise. His *mother* was the Holvradix elf? And his father had been a Tibran? Interesting ...

"How did you wind up here?" I asked. "I ... I guess I've never actually met someone from Tibrus before."

His smile had gone cold with focus as he kept his voice low. "And you won't. None who will claim it anyway. Not with Argonox acting like a bloodthirsty lunatic."

Fair enough.

"My father was sent on a conquest. Since he was a member of the guard, he couldn't refuse. But maybe he saw what was coming because he paid off some of his superiors to get my mother, sister, and me out of the kingdom," he explained. "We made it all the way here. Thought we would be safe."

I didn't have to ask how that had gone. He wouldn't have been fighting for his and his sister's lives in Sulam's pit if things had gone well, after all.

"Where's your mother?"

"Dead. Plague took her on the ship."

My heartbeat skipped. "I'm ... sorry."

He didn't look my way as he finished lacing his boots and stood. "Why? It wasn't your doing."

My mouth scrunched, trying to decide how to respond. The right thing to say.

It didn't come naturally to me like it seemed to for other people.

"I know what it feels like. Losing someone that way, I mean," I whispered at last.

Declan's deep, evergreen eyes finally locked back onto mine. The edge to his grim expression cut like steel straight to my core. "Seems like you know what it's like to be under Sulam's greasy thumb, too. How long did he have you?"

I had to think about that for a second. "A year. Maybe less. I'm honestly not sure."

He nodded slightly. "And you just ... escaped?"

I shifted my weight, fidgeting with the rough, peeling calluses on my knuckles. "Funny thing about having no one to care about is you don't have any leverage for someone like Sulam to use against you. And being Viperi means death threats don't really carry much weight. There are things worse than death. Honestly, I don't think he knew what to do with me at the time."

He did a terrible job controlling that worried little furrow that made his brows crinkle together. "So, you what, just walked away?"

I shrugged. "More like ran, hid, and never looked back. I thought I'd never see him again. I hoped I wouldn't."

"Sorry for the reunion."

I traced the points of my incisors with my tongue behind my lips. "It's not your fault. According to Roxus, I'm 'not good at talking to people.' So not even he knew about it before we went to the pit."

Declan didn't reply, but I could feel his gaze on me as I turned and made my way across the sparring room to the door.

He stayed silent, trudging along like a giant golem until we reached the hall. Then he stopped and turned to face me. Something quietly fierce dimmed his roguish features, making his jaw and shoulders tense.

"That *friend* downstairs—do they know all this about you?" he asked quietly.

"No. They know some, but like I said, I'm not good at talking to people," I admitted. "She only knows a little about why I had to leave the Viperi."

Declan gave a slow, affirming nod, but that intense focus never eased as he glanced past me toward Roxus's office. I could feel my heartbeat throbbing in my fingertips as his throat jumped with a stiff swallow.

"Be careful," he warned in a low whisper. "About what you say, who you say it to, and who else might be listening. The Zenith's Call are oath-sworn to the gods. But this kingdom's crawling with people ready to ram a blade into anyone they can if it suits their agenda ... or whatever god they claim to serve. Don't give them anything to misconstrue."

My toes tingled, squirming against the worn wooden floor as I stared up at him.

He was right, of course. I was Viperi—the gods' favorite enemy. A spawn of darkness and deceit. I couldn't afford to misplace my faith in someone, not with my life on the line. One wrong word could make me a martyr for a cause I wanted nothing to do with.

"I'll be careful," I promised.

His mouth scrunched to one side like he didn't quite believe me.

Or maybe he knew, somehow, it might already be too late.

TWENTY-THREE

Chrysa wasn't herself.

Not like before.

The instant I stepped into the sitting room and spotted her, sitting at the low table with a cup of steaming herbal tea in her hands, all the hairs on the back of my neck prickled. A chill ran up my spine. She looked up at me, her eyes utterly empty and her expression eerily blank.

Almost like she didn't recognize me at first.

Her cheeks were hollow, and a faint dusky bruise around her neck looked strangely like fingermarks.

Like someone had tried throttling the life out of her.

I didn't know what to say.

My hands clenched as I stepped closer, every instinct screaming in my head that something was wrong. But all I could whisper was, "Chrysa?"

"I'm okay," Chrysa said at last, murmuring the words over the rim of her teacup.

I stiffened. Sinking slowly down onto the smooth velvet cushion across the table from her, I waited while she gingerly sipped from the small porcelain cup she cradled. Delthene's special ginseng and honey tea, by the smell of it.

"You don't look it," I dared to challenge.

"I am," she said, firmer this time. "I knew what might happen. I was willing to take those consequences. And I'm fine, Violet. So you can quit looking at me like that."

"Like what?"

"Like you pity me. Like you're ready to storm out of here and go on the warpath. I don't need pity. I don't need to be avenged, either."

Confused, angry emotion bristled in my chest like a knot of white-hot thorns. I was ready to track down Domitri and twist his head off like a tomato from a vine—Chrsya wasn't wrong about that. But something in her tone kept me rooted in place. Stuck. Bewildered.

"If you'd just tell Roxus what's going on, maybe he could —" I started to protest, but she cut me off.

"No. I have to endure this—I *will* endure it. We're almost to the end of our trials."

"It's not right."

"Life rarely is," she muttered bitterly. Her mouth wobbled some. "Not for people like us."

I couldn't argue that.

But she wasn't like me. She wasn't Viperi. She deserved better.

Seconds of tense, uncomfortable silence passed before she finally put the teacup on the table and forced a thin smile. "Looks like you've got a new training partner."

I sank lower in my chair. Somehow, her knowing that felt like I had betrayed her somehow, even if it wasn't the same at all.

"Roxus set it up. He said it was because he wanted me to keep improving in combat, but I'm not stupid. I think he just wanted me to get used to being pushed to my limit so I don't break and lose control of my instincts so easily." I sighed, sinking back in my seat.

"Well, whatever the reason, you look ... a lot better. Healthier," she said.

I bobbed my head. "I feel more solid. More grounded."

"Good."

"I've been reading more, too," I added.

Her smile was real for an instant. It made her whole face seem to glow. "Even in Avoran?"

I couldn't hold back a little impish smirk. "When I don't have any other choice."

"I'm glad." She leaned across the table, fixing me with an intensely earnest stare. "I'm glad you're finding yourself."

Somehow, it felt like there was more she wanted to say—something she was holding back with all her strength. Whatever it was, she kept it back. Pushed it down behind that veneer of dejected cool, indifferent calm.

A mask the Tibrans had probably forged in her many years ago. The thing that had kept her safe so far.

I understood that.

"I came by because I wanted to let you know I'll be back at training tomorrow. Hopefully, you'll still want to practice together," Chrysa said, her gaze drifting around the dimly lit room as though she were taking it all in.

"Of course," I agreed. "Is that ... going to be okay for you?"

I wasn't sure what new rules Domitri might have given her for being around me. Given what had happened, he likely wouldn't want her exposed to me anymore. Not when I'd proven to be such a *bad influence* already.

"It'll be fine," she assured.

Hah. I doubted that. Arguing it with her was probably pointless, though.

"I guess we'll just pick up where we left off, then. Tomorrow? Usual place?" I suggested.

She bobbed her head.

Curse it all. I hated this. I hated sitting in the lukewarm atmosphere between us, wading through stiff conversation, all while avoiding the obvious. She wasn't okay. She wasn't safe. Nothing about her situation was usual.

And, gods, there was nothing I could do about it.

Not without putting her at even more risk, anyway.

We sat and shared tea for a few hours, pausing only when Declan and Roxus shuffled by on their way out the front door into the night. Declan's expression stayed steely as he cast Chrysa a long, appraising stare on his way past. I couldn't tell what he was thinking any more than I could tell what the space between stars might hold.

As soon as the door closed behind them, Chrsya cleared her throat and began to stand. "I guess I should get going, too. It's late. We've got to start early tomorrow."

I frowned down at my half-empty teacup. Somehow, Delthene's soothing mixture of fragrant teas hadn't quite put my nerves at ease this time. There probably wasn't enough tea in all the Southern Kingdoms for that now.

All my thoughts stayed tangled up in my head, knotted and messy, as I stood and saw her out. Standing in the doorway, I watched her silhouette stride off into the foggy latenight streets with my arms crossed.

I didn't move or look away as Delthene's footsteps approached, their familiar cadence giving her away long before I heard her sigh deeply right behind me.

"Poor child," she murmured quietly. "It's a shame. Truly a shame."

She must've noticed the bruises on Chrysa's neck, too.

"Why doesn't anyone help her? Couldn't Roxus do something?" I asked, more to myself than to her. I didn't expect her to know about the intricacies of the social politics at work in the Zenith's call.

"It's not for me to say," Delthene answered quietly. "But if I had to guess, I suspect that Roxus has dedicated himself to seeing you through this difficult time, first and foremost. He's not the sort to divide that kind of attention or go back on his word once he's set his mind to it. Perhaps, once you're on your feet and don't need his help, he might be able to do something for her."

My frown deepened. I chewed on the inside of my cheek as I watched the curling fog swallow all traces of Chrysa's form. I decided Delthene must have been hinting at my extremely tentative acceptance within the Zenith's Call. Maybe Roxus was concerned that pushing any other issue with Mistress Orvana might be a step too far. It might put my security in the order in danger.

But that was only a guess.

"In the meantime, don't feel badly because you were chosen to be saved, child," she whispered. "That you were spared a bitter fate is not a weight you ought to carry. It was not your choice that put that girl where she is, and it's not your responsibility to save her. Not when you're still learning to survive yourself."

I glanced back, studying the grim resignation that creased Delthene's aging features. Somehow, in that moment, she seemed ancient. Eternal.

Like she was gazing back at a shadow of her former self, dissolving away into the night.

"She must follow her own path," Delthene said. "And we must accept that in her journey, we might not be the heroes meant to save her, merely the guides meant to walk alongside her. To love her through it. That is the true price of friendship, my dear."

"It feels wrong," I admitted.

She put a hand on my shoulder. "The right thing doesn't always feel good."

"It should."

Delthene laughed softly. "Yes, I agree. What a wretched world the gods have wrought for us. Or perhaps we're the ones who make it wretched."

"Now you sound like Leruna," I muttered.

"Hah! You may be right. In any case, it's long past time for you to get to the bath. I could smell the sweat all the way from the cellar," she scolded.

Delthene fussed at me up the stairs to the washroom, going on about how I ought to show my hair a little more attention now that it was getting longer. She warned that soon she'd have to show me how to put kohl around my eyes and color on my lips, and that Roxus ought to allow me more time for things like that instead of insisting I spend every spare minute fighting.

According to her, just because he'd resigned himself to looking like a weather-beaten old shoe didn't mean he should expect me to.

I tended to agree, but there wasn't a lot of extra time in my days for personal grooming. Not right now, anyway.

I soaked in the tub a little longer than usual, rinsing my hair in the jasmine oils Delthene provided. The steaming, fragrant water soothed every sore muscle. Too bad it didn't do much to put my mind at ease.

I replayed every word Chrysa had said over and over in my mind, picking through her cryptic excuses or veiled hints about what she'd been doing all this time. It was too easy to get carried away envisioning the worst.

And Delthene was right. I couldn't help her. Not yet. Not when I was in a precarious position, too.

I couldn't save her unless I saved myself first.

I just had to keep my eyes on the end goal. I had to keep

forging onward. I had to become Zenith's Call, and then I could do something about Domitri. I could become a horrifying menace in his life the same way he was in hers. I could be the iron grip around his throat.

Only, I'd leave more than a few bruises behind.

I bared my teeth, unable to stop a low growl from rumbling in my chest at the thought.

I didn't know how or when I'd stumbled across this twisted sense of justice. It certainly hadn't come from the Zenith's Call—or the Viperi, for that matter. And it was extremely inconvenient since it lit the fires of my internal rage so quickly.

But I had to get it under control. I just had to bide my time. Wait.

And pray nothing happened to Declan, Chrysa, or anyone else I cared about that might push me over the edge once and for all.

Delthene was right. Survival had to come first. But every step I took away from Chrysa felt like a betrayal. A failure. A nail in my own coffin.

One day, if I didn't do something, I might lose her for good. Declan, too.

That thought burrowed deep into my heart like a splinter that would fester and ache. How many people could I lose before the walls I'd patched together in my soul finally broke?

And when all that scorching rage poured out of me ... what would be left? Anything?

Or would I be broken beyond repair?

TWENTY-FOUR

Her form was utterly ruthless.

Fast. Smooth. Nearly perfect.

Nearly.

It would be enough to satisfy the elder Zenith's Call agents, though, and that was all that mattered. Chrysa was a blur of speed and power. Watching her now, I almost didn't recognize the girl who'd struggled through her first combat assessment on our first day.

She'd improved on nearly every front and had gone from floundering through strikes and parries to moving with lethal efficiency. She held herself with a confidence that set her far above the other prospects.

With enough time and practice, she might even be up to Viperi standards.

But as I watched her fight, a knot of prickling, bitter heat smoldered in my chest. I should have been proud. But part of me wondered—worried—that I might have gone too far.

I couldn't forget that emptiness I'd seen in her eyes when she came back. Like the Chrysa I knew was gone, and the person staring back at me was an empty shell.

She had seemed normal in all the days since, though. We carried on with our usual routines like nothing had ever happened. She smiled and scolded me about my fumbling attempts at speaking Rienkan.

Maybe I was being too paranoid. Or was I just projecting my insecurities and guilt about her situation?

Gods only knew, and I was too focused on my own survival to sort it out now.

I couldn't afford to lose my focus—my grip on the here and now. One slip might send me plummeting, and I'd wind up back in that prison cell with nothing but an executioner's sword to look forward to for all my work.

I smirked, watching Chrysa duel with the third elder. She dodged his strikes easily, weaving around him like a ginger blur. After this, we would both be marked as approved in our combat capability trials.

Then all that remained was proving our knowledge of divine lore and ancient geography.

Neither were subjects I was necessarily smitten with, but I'd gained enough understanding through my hours of studying to feel pretty confident about being able to pass whatever trial Curator Faera put in front of me.

Turns out, you couldn't swing a stick in this part of the world without smacking into some ancient ruin from the long-diminished empire of the Avoran elves. Practically everything in the Southern Kingdoms was built upon the ruins of their ancient cities, temples, and palaces. Some, like Arx Eburna and the temple above it, were more obvious than others. And like Arx Eburna, there were many more hidden below the surface of the golden dunes or flourishing jungles holding secrets that had been kept hushed for thousands of years.

Secrets every member of the Zenith's Call was sworn to keep.

I'd known about some of the subterranean ruins before-hand. The Viperi had been, er, *repurposing* some of them for a long time. My clan had lived in a place like that. Granted, I'd never paid much attention to any of the details of it at the time. I couldn't recall if they'd been former palaces, temples, or something else.

Now, it didn't matter.

Chrysa toppled her final opponent with a swift leg sweep and pinned him, taking the match in less than a minute. A smattering of reluctant applause went up from the other prospects and patrons standing around watching. Many of them cast me sideways glares like this was all my fault.

It definitely was.

Our weeks of practice had finally paid off. I'd built her up from practically nothing, and now no one could refute that my combat prowess was just a fluke of being Viperi. Like I'd been born with every skill I'd ever need and hadn't spent years of my own life getting beaten to a pulp by clan elders.

Ridiculous.

I squared my shoulders and stood straighter, unable to withhold a proud smirk as Chrysa made her way to Mistress Orvana. The Mistress of the Call put a hand on her shoulder, regarding her much more softly and kindly than she ever had me, and gave Chrysa her approval.

I wasn't good at reading lips in the common tongue, so I couldn't tell exactly what Mistress Orvana said. Whatever it was, it made Chrysa's cheeks flush a little and she nodded in return. Compliments, maybe?

For whatever reason, that made me proud, too.

Chrysa had passed the combat trial and could move on. Now, I had to do the same with the divine lore and whatnot.

I kept my expression controlled and indifferent as Chrysa approached her patron, Domitri. He didn't even look at her as he spoke, keeping his eerie gaze locked onto me, instead. Like he knew his presence, wreathed faintly in that glowing blue aura, put all my nerves on a razor's edge.

I still hadn't asked her anything more about him. Not even if she could also see that odd blue light that seemed to follow him like a wavering halo. Sometimes, it almost seemed like nothing but a trick of the light.

Other times, I wondered if I should finally bring it up to someone. Roxus, at least. Could everyone see it? Did it have something to do with an artifact he carried? Zenith's Call sometimes used ancient artifacts on their missions. Maybe that was it.

Domitri's scorching glare bored into mine from across the room, and I didn't dare blink or look away. He wouldn't rattle me again. Not so easily.

At last, Chrysa gave him a small bow and turned away. Domitri's lip curled, twitching like a dog about to snarl. Then he turned away, too, and started for the door that led back out into the Eternal Hall.

I guess he was only sticking around for what he was absolutely obligated to—his own prospect's trial—and nothing more.

Ugh. Good riddance.

"Well done," I murmured as Chrysa jogged over to stand next to me. "Still a little slow on the right parry."

"I know, I know. Gods, I'm *so* glad that's over," she panted, her face still flushed and damp with sweat.

We stood together, watching a few other prospects battle through their trials. Two did decently, although their form was still sloppy. A third stumbled on the archery challenge, falling from the latticework and landing wrong. The crack of his ankle on impact was telling enough, even before he began wailing in pain.

He wouldn't be returning for a third try.

We filed out of the sparring room along with the rest of

the remaining prospects after the last match, making our way out to the temple grounds for what had become our daily tradition of having lunch in the shade while we aired out our sweaty fighting leathers.

I'd noticed a while ago that Domitri apparently didn't provide much for Chrysa to eat. She had to rely on the dining hall for all of her meals, and lunch wasn't always a guarantee for her. I'd also made the mistake of mentioning that where Delthene could overhear, so now she always packed plenty of extra in my bag.

We split grapes, cheese, and little balls of seasoned rice formed around centers of pickled vegetables and curried meat. Chrysa always apologized for eating some of my food, and I always rolled my eyes and insisted she take whatever she wanted.

I looked forward to it. To how normal it all felt. Simple, honest, and completely mundane—all things I'd never had before.

We swapped stories about our lives, intentionally avoiding the horrible bits that no one wants to say out loud. I told her about my mother, who was equal parts conniving, vicious, and protective when it came to me. That, I had learned, wasn't the same as loving. My mother's intensity about my success within our clan—about proving to my father that I was the best of his offspring—had a direct impact on her standing among our people.

It hadn't been the same for Chrysa, apparently. Life with the Tibrans was brutal. But the captive soldiers and slaves formed their own sort of family. Trauma bonding—that's what Chrysa called it.

"Sort of like us now?" I asked around a cheekful of food.

She made a thoughtful face. "Yeah, now that I think about it. I guess it's sort of the same."

"Well, for what it's worth, I do like you, and not just

because of our trauma," I added without really thinking about it. "I never really had a friend before I met you."

Chrysa went still. Her eyes widened some as she stared at me for a few uncomfortable seconds. "Never? Not even another Viperi?"

I shrugged. "Viperi don't have friends."

"Not even among family members?"

I snorted and cast her a sideways smirk. "*Especially* not among family members."

"I see," Chrysa looked down at the little bunch of grapes in her hand. "I did have some friends before, but no one like you. No one who really knew me."

I understood that. "You should meet Declan. Then you'd have two friends. He's an idiot sometimes, but he's ... good."

Her mouth pinched up right before she popped a few grapes into it.

"He seems exhausting," she mumbled.

"He is," I agreed. "And loud. And he sweats a lot, which he blames on being half Holvradix elf. Apparently, they're made for cold climates? Whatever. It's gross."

She giggled and nearly choked on her mouthful of grapes.

Chrysa seemed a little quieter, like she had slipped off into deep thought, as we finished our lunch and went shuffling back down into Arx Eburna. I didn't push her, though. Not when my mind was already spinning.

I was practically sweating by the time we made our way into the auditorium for what would be one of Curator Faera's last lectures before her final trial. Time was running out. The pressure among the nine of us still under consideration was so thick it was nearly smothering—like being wrapped too tight in a thick wool blanket.

As we made our way to our desks, I caught the mutter of that word as someone whispered close behind us.

"*Pitathi.*"

It wasn't a taunt this time, though. Someone was talking about me, not to me.

Someone who didn't want me to overhear.

I glanced back, trying to be casual, and searched the faces moving along behind me.

His gaze caught mine for one second too long—the same older boy who'd shouted in my face on my very first day here. Something dark and ominous twinkled in his eyes, although he did a good job of keeping his expression neutral as he turned down another row of desks and sat down.

Hmmm.

It could be nothing. They probably talked about me all the time. Especially now that I was one of the few remaining who stood a chance at becoming Zenith's Call.

But I couldn't shake the cold spike of dread that twisted in my gut as Curator Faera approached the lectern and began to speak. Were they all plotting against me now? Coming up with a way to drive me out of the Zenith's Call before my final trial?

I'd have to be more careful. I'd have to keep my head down and—

"Magical talents passed down through ancient bloodlines have become far more rare since the War of the Stones," Curator Faera said, her airy voice carrying through the auditorium.

I stiffened.

Great. Was she going to talk about the special gifts Viperi were born with, too?

Granted, none of them were especially magical. Being able to see body heat was something even some common animals could do. Not that special. The hyperflexibility was a little more bizarre, I guess, but certainly not magical.

I wasn't stupid enough to think either of those would be a welcomed discovery by the rest of my peers, though.

Just a few more reasons for them to think I was a monster in their midst.

"Of course, the people with these gifts are usually quite secretive about them. But the nature of our cause means we like to keep a close watch on them, particularly so they are not abused or forced to do ill with such abilities," she went on. "Rajinna are perhaps the most notable, and their inborn magical talents are profound, diverse, and overshadow most all other races across Reatia."

I sank a little lower in my seat as Faera panned her gaze around the room, hoping she might briefly forget I even existed.

She stared right at me.

Crap.

"But there are others who also possess some enduring magical heritage. Other gifts, unfortunately, have seemingly disappeared over the centuries," she said.

"What about Pitathi? They must be able to do all sorts of foul magic," someone spoke up from behind me.

It made a hissing chorus of snickers go up around the room.

I had to suck my teeth to keep from snarling. I didn't even have to look to know who it was—that same stupid boy who had taunted me on my first day.

Faera blinked, seeming surprised. Then her features crinkled with a disapproving frown. "*Viperi* are a bit of a mystery, even to us. They've always been very insular and forbid mingling with outsiders. Much of what we know about them is hardly more than myth ... or ill-founded rumor."

Her eyes went steely as they focused on the boy, as though silently daring him to produce some proof of anything he thought about me.

It made my whole head flush with heat and I sank even lower in my chair. My heart pounded hard and heavy in my chest, each beat sending a rush of cold sweat prickling over my skin.

But it wasn't my mother's voice that filled my head this time.

"Choose," my father's tone bit like the crack of a whip through my brain.

I cringed and shut my eyes tightly.

No—no, no, no. I had to stop this. Focus. Breathe.

He wasn't here. Not really.

I opened my eyes, looking frantically over at Chrysa in the seat beside mine.

She slowly shook her head, like she could sense my panic. Like she could see me being shoved closer and closer to the brink.

"Do not look at her! Do as I command! CHOOSE!"

I cringed again.

Run. I had to run. I had to—

"Get it under control, girlie," a new, gruff voice huffed through my thoughts. *"Angry doesn't make you stronger, and scared won't make you faster. Think."*

Declan.

My shoulders instantly relaxed. A slow, shaking breath left my lips as the fires in my chest smoldered down. It left my ears ringing and my hands shaking.

But I was calm. In control.

"Violet?"

I glanced up, jolting in my seat when I noticed Curator Faera was standing right next to my desk with her brow drawn up in concern.

One peek around the room and I realized ... I was the only one in it. Well, apart from Curator Faera. Had the lecture already ended? Oh. Gods. How long had I been out of it?

What else had I missed?

Where was Chrysa?

"Is everything all right?" she asked.

I scrambled up and gathered my things. "F-fine! I was just thinking—remembering something. I should go."

"Right, well, there's something I need to give you first," she said with a thin, unconvinced smile.

"Oh."

I hesitated, unable to keep my gaze from flicking between her and the door as she motioned for me to follow her down to the lectern.

Hmmm. She'd always been fairly nice to me. Maybe this wouldn't be so bad.

I made my way down the steps to join her, watching her rummage through her stack of belongings: papers, a few books, a corked bottle of ink, and a collection of quills.

"It's nothing bad, I assure you," she laughed as she searched. "It's not really a gift. More of a request, I suppose. But I thought you might find it interesting and I didn't want any of your peers getting their hands on it."

I couldn't suppress a suspicious frown as she finally produced a thin, black leather-bound tome. The front cover was blank, but the spine had a very familiar symbol leafed on it in silver.

The Eye of the Foul Father, the symbol of the Viperi.

I stared at the book in her outstretched hand, wondering if this was some sort of test. If I took it, was I proving that I was a conniving little villain in their midst?

"It's a history," she explained, her expression quirking with awkward apprehension. "All that we know about the Viperi, actually."

Well, that explained why there couldn't have been more than a hundred pages in the whole thing.

"I already know their history," I replied quietly.

"I'm sure," she said. "Just as I'm sure it's rife with those ill-meaning rumors, unfounded myths, and untruths. I was hoping you might take it and make corrections."

I arched an eyebrow. "You mean you want me to correct the mistakes?"

Faera nodded eagerly. "The Zenith's Call are meant to be truth-keepers. It's long overdue that we keep the proper truth about your people, too. You are the first chance we've ever been given to actually get an accurate accounting. If you're willing to, of course."

My hand still shook some as I took the book from her, feeling its weight as a lot more than just a flimsy little book.

The weight of my people's reputation and the understanding of the rest of the world.

"I'll try," I whispered. "But I haven't been with them since I was little, and I don't have good memories of my time there."

Her smile widened, making her odd lime-yellow eyes shine. "I understand. I'm not asking you to write words of praise or condemnation. Just the truth."

Right. That might have made me feel better ... except that the exploits of kin didn't need much embellishment in order to be perfectly horrific.

The truth was more than enough.

Frowning down at the book, I mulled it over for a few seconds more before finally asking, "Why?"

"Why what?" Curator Faera had gone back to fumbling around, looking for something in her leather bag of belongings and the scattered pile on the lectern.

"Why do you care to know the truth about the Viperi? Rumors and myths seem more than enough for most other folk, Zenith's Call or not."

She stopped and blinked at me, seeming thrown by the question. Or maybe it was just because I'd never said much of anything to her before now. Her ebony skin seemed to flush deep rose around her cheeks for a moment.

She looked away, tucking one of her locks of braided hair behind a pointed ear as she murmured, "It's not for me, to be honest. That's all I can say for now. Soon, though, I'll be able to tell you more. Once you've been sworn in properly."

I narrowed my eyes. Was she saying she thought I would become Zenith's Call? That I could really pull this off?

Like an idiot, I dared to hope.

"Ah! Here it is!" Faera gave an impish giggle as she produced a long, elegant feather quill. The long peacock feather shimmered beautifully, and it was tipped with an ornate nib. That wasn't what made me stare, though. Not even when I noticed the tiny lines of writing etched into the nib.

The quill glowed faint blue as she held it out to me proudly.

"It's enchanted," she announced. "It never runs out of ink. It's Avoran—something I found on an expedition years ago. Use it, if you like, and consider it a gift of good faith."

I stared at it, watching the way that eerie aura of blue light ebbed from it even as she waved it around right under my nose. Weird. It sort of reminded me of the glow that came off Domitri, albeit a lot fainter.

"Is that why it glows?" I asked without thinking.

"What?" She paused, tilting her head to one side curiously.

"The quill." I nodded to it. "Does it glow because it's enchanted? Or because it's Avoran?"

Curator Faera's lips parted, eyes slightly wider now. Her gaze flicked quickly between me and the quill. She made a few sounds, but stopped before she got any words out, like she couldn't decide what to say.

"I don't see any glow, Violet," she whispered at last. "What do you mean? Do you see it glowing?"

My heartbeat gave a frantic skip, seeming to jump from

my chest to my throat in an instant. All I could do was nod slightly.

She couldn't see it? Could anyone else?

"What else do you see?" She stepped in closer, keeping her voice hushed. "What else glows? Anything in this room?"

I shied back, putting some distance between us. I didn't like it. Not the way she kept moving closer, or that intensely curious expression like a cat that just cornered a canary. Nope. Not one single bit.

"N-Nothing," I lied.

"It's okay," she urged. "You can tell me."

I shook my head slowly. "Nothing," I repeated.

She knew I was lying. I could see it written all over her disappointed frown. Like all the light in those vibrant Lunostri eyes had gone dim.

"Violet, I—" she began to plead.

BANG!

We both jumped when the door to the auditorium suddenly whipped open.

A dozen Vindexori poured in, rushing down the stairs with their crossbows aimed right at me. Behind them, Mistress Orvana stepped into the room with her face flushed and eyes wide in fury.

"There she is! Take her immediately! Use whatever force you must!" she screeched.

I staggered back, my pulse already kicking like mad in my chest and sending currents of adrenaline like molten metal through my veins. Oh, gods. What was happening?

Run—I had to run!

Curator Faera used stepping in front of me as a distraction to swipe the book and quill from my hands, almost like she didn't want anyone else to catch me with them. I didn't have time to question it, though.

"What is the meaning of this?" Faera argued as the Vindexori encircled us.

They shoved her out of the way as they closed in like a noose of black leather armor and cold steel.

I sank low, baring my pointed teeth. One of them I recognized, even with that silken shawl covering half his face. I'd dueled him before. Beaten him before. I could take him down a second time. Then I might be able to make it to the door before—

"Stay out of this, Faera. It doesn't concern you," Mistress Orvana warned as she strode down the steps with her head held high.

Faera shouted back, but I couldn't understand a word of it.

Not when the Vindexori descended on me like a pack of ravenous wolves.

They surged in, and I dipped and fought, landing a few successful strikes that sent my attackers reeling and wheezing. It wasn't enough, though.

Not with so many on me at once.

A crossbow string snapped and pain exploded in one of my thighs. I screamed as my knee gave out, everything immediately going red as those primal instincts threatened to tear through all my common sense.

I had to get away.

They would kill me otherwise.

And I might kill a few of them, too.

I tried putting weight back on my leg only to find it crumpled again. I stumbled, catching myself against the back wall.

Nowhere to go.

Trapped.

"You're making a mistake!" Curator Faera cried over the chaos. "She's just a child!"

I snarled, struggling to balance on one leg as the Vindexori tackled me, wrenching me around and seizing fistfuls of my hair to pin me against the wall.

I screamed, probably sounding more like a feral animal than a person, as two of them—much bigger men—seized my arms and slapped iron shackles tightly around my wrists. Another forced a rag into my mouth to muffle my cries.

"Silence, Pitathi scum," Mistress Orvana hissed, her lip curled in disgust. "The only mistake made here was allowing her to defile this place with her presence—a mistake I will now see corrected. Get her out of my sight!"

My heart pounded as I forced myself to hold her gaze. I couldn't hide it—my terror. My anger. My confusion.

I didn't know what was happening. But whatever game Mistress Orvana was playing, I was already caught in it.

TWENTY-FIVE

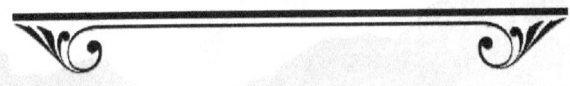

W hy?!

Why was this happening?

I twisted and kicked, feeling both my shoulders slide easily out of socket as I tried to slip from their grasp.

It didn't work.

The pain in my thigh blurred my vision. Terror squeezed at my chest, wringing every last bit of air from my lungs. The two big Vindexori dragged me down dark and twisting hallways, the rest of their band following close behind with crossbows still aimed right at me. No escape.

Not this time.

My mind whipped in a frantic spiral, trying to make sense of it. Why were they doing this? Where were they taking me? Where was Roxus?

Did he even know about this?

Blood ran in warm streams down my leg from the crossbow bolt that still stuck out of my thigh. Every step sent a pang of fresh, hot agony up my spine.

A whimper of pain leaked through my clenched teeth as they gripped me harder and shoved me through a narrow doorway into a dimly lit room.

No. Not just a room.

A cell.

The stone floor was cracked and crumbling, and only a single blue-flamed torch flickered in a rusted iron sconce against the far wall. No windows. No other doors. Nothing apart from a heavy wooden chair set right in the middle of the room and the thick odor of minerals in the cold air.

One of the Vindexori grabbed me by the hair while they forced me down into that chair and clamped heavy metal shackles on my wrists and ankles.

The chair's arms were stained with something dark and old. Blood.

Immediately, everything spun. My vision blurred, and I could barely force in a breath.

Oh, gods, was this a *torture* chamber?

My heart beat wildly. I wrenched against the shackles, growling as the rough metal bit into the skin of my wrists and ankles. Curse it!

Six of the Vindexori stayed in the room, stepping back to stand in formation along the walls surrounding my chair from all sides. They kept those crossbows aimed at me, their eyes winking like cold stars in the near dark.

Then *she* entered.

Mistress Orvana slid silently into the room, her expression empty of everything but cold wrath. Her glare fixed on me as she paced a slow circle around my chair, lip curling when she finally stopped to stand right in front of me.

"How did you do it?" Her voice snapped over me like the crack of a lightning bolt.

I barked a hoarse, shaking laugh. Was she kidding? I didn't even know why I was here!

BAM!

My head snapped to the side as she slapped me across the face so hard it felt like my eyes might pop right out of their sockets.

"Do not mock me, you vile creature. Tell me how you did it!" she hissed.

"I have no idea what you're talking about!" I yelled back.

She straightened, expression blanking in surprise for a second. Then her deep, burnished golden eyes narrowed. She seized my chin, forcing me to look directly back at her.

"What manner of fool do you take me for? I see through your lies, Pitathi. Not in a thousand years has anyone managed to open that door. Yet you arrive and suddenly someone has nearly breached it? Did you think I would write it off as mere coincidence?" she seethed.

I glared back at her, my cheek still throbbing with warm, stinging pain. What, by all the gods, was she talking about? A door? There must have been a few thousand doors in Arx Eburna—and I knew about precisely ten of them. The ten I was actually allowed to use.

Mistress Orvana must have been able to sense my confusion because her hold on my chin tightened. Something like desperate determination twisted her fair features and made one of her eyes twitch.

"Tell me the truth now, and perhaps I'll spare your life. Did they send you here for something in that vault?" she demanded.

"I don't know what you're talking about!" I snapped. "I don't know about any vault!"

BAM!

My other cheek flared with hot, stinging pain as she hit me again.

"You vile, lying little beast," she muttered as she stepped back, appraising me with her arms crossed. "No one else walking these halls has any reason to tamper with the Vault of Whispers. No one apart from the Surotrix possesses the knowledge of how to open its door. No one else can even see it. Did you really think you could just tamper with it with such crude magic and succeed?"

Mistress Orvana spat on the ground in front of me, her chest now heaving with deep, furious breaths.

My mind whirled with that information, frantically trying to piece it all together. To make some sense of why I was being blamed for what sounded like a failed theft attempt.

The theft of an ancient magical vault, apparently.

"To break into the Vault of Whispers would be a feat for the ages," she murmured, almost like she was talking to herself rather than me. "It would require a depth of skill unlike any this order has seen since before the War of the Stones. One befitting of a trained Pitathi assassin."

Oh ... oh no.

A cold shiver spread from my head down to my toes.

I wasn't an assassin. I knew that. But based on what she and the rest of the order had seen from me, I could understand now why they'd jumped to that conclusion. I was a far better fighter than the rest of my peers. Better even than most of their agents.

To them, I definitely looked like assassin material. I'd even aspired to become just that when I'd first arrived here.

But there was no way I'd ever be able to convince her that I wasn't one.

Or that I hadn't tried to break into that vault.

I sank into the wooden chair, my arms and legs going slack against the shackles as that truth settled over me like a cold frost.

My life was as good as forfeit, wasn't it?

Not even Roxus could help me now.

Would anyone tell him what happened to me? What about Chrysa and Declan?

"There is no other explanation. Only this," Mistress Orvana said, as though she were trying to convince herself.

I kept my gaze down, determined not to let her see my eyes well up as she prowled closer.

"Only you."

"Keep telling yourself that." It took every last shred of my nerve to lift my head and glare back at her, hissing every bitter word through my teeth.

She glared back at me, her whole face twitching with an erratic mixture of rage and uncertainty. One of her hands drifted down to the long, silver dagger belted to her hip. Like she intended to end this matter right here, right now.

CRACK!

The door flew open, banging off the wall and sending the nearest two agents floundering for their weapons. Mistress Orvana whirled around, that dagger in her hand.

My heart dropped to the soles of my boots, and all the wind rushed out of me at once.

Roxus filled the doorway with his tall, lanky figure and billowing brown coat. His eyes were icy steel as he glared at Orvana, lip curling back into a half-snarl.

He stood motionless for a second, like a tower of wrath, glaring between us. Then his voice filled the chamber like a clap of thunder.

"You dare break the ancient laws and interrogate a prospect without their mentor present?" He growled low, shoulders hunching in aggression.

Like he might lunge at any moment.

A pang of dread shot straight to the pit of my stomach. Panic made my fingers go numb and my blood run cold.

Bad—this was bad.

Something about him was off. Dangerous, even.

But he was here. Gods, he'd actually come for me.

Now, I just prayed he would believe me even when no one else did.

* * *

Any moment now, the room would explode.

Into what, I wasn't sure. Shouting. Violence.

Both seemed perfectly plausible.

That look on Roxus's face, like every ounce of warmth and joy had been drained from his features so that nothing but a void of fury remained, put every single one of my nerves on edge. I'd never seen him look like that.

And it terrified me.

Orvana straightened, her neck arching and shoulders drawing back in defiance. "I am the Mistress of the Call, I reserve the right to—"

Roxus cut her off immediately. "To what? Cast aside six thousand years of tradition and sacred law? You don't have a single shred of evidence that she had anything to do with this."

Her mouth snapped shut.

No one made a sound.

My pulse raced in a wild blur, so fast and frantic it made my vision spot.

"You've greatly overstepped the rules of your station," he rumbled ominously. "And you've tested my patience to its limit. Perhaps you'd like to settle this in the old ways?"

He nodded to the blade in her hand.

Mistress Orvana's grip on the weapon tightened. I could have sworn, for the briefest instant, fear flickered in the depths of her golden eyes.

"You'd really risk everything for this creature?" Her tone was haughty. Confident.

But I could see her hand shaking as she sheathed her dagger again.

Roxus's lip twitched. A low, beastly sound came from his chest like the rumble of a war drum's beat.

Or the warning growl of a beast.

Mistress Orvana's stance went stiff, freezing as some of the color drained from her face. Her lips pressed into a thin, tight line and her throat bobbed as she swallowed.

"Do you even know what she did?" Mistress Orvana snapped.

"Do you?" he countered. "Because it's my understanding that there's been nothing credible found at the scene. No trace of the culprit. You're operating on nothing but suspicion and bias."

"I'm operating on two thousand years of ample evidence her kin has provided!" Mistress Orvana thrust an accusing finger at me. "I don't care how you dress her, or whether or not you've managed to housebreak her. She is no different. We can only expect malice and treachery from anyone of that blood!"

"Then I suppose I suffer from the delusion that the Zenith's Call still upheld their oath to welcome anyone willing to oath themselves to our sacred cause," Roxus snarled, taking an aggressive step closer. "Or was that a ruse you toted simply to secure my allegiance?"

Mistress Orvana jerked back like she'd been smacked. She blinked, mouth opening a few times, but not managing to get any sound out.

"If that's the case, then I should withdraw my oath now," he threatened. "We both know you need my help a lot more than I need yours."

Orvana's mouth pinched up bitterly, cheeks puffing and turning red. She stared back at him in silence for what felt like a horrible eternity before she whirled around to cast me one more scathing glare of warning.

"Take her, then," she snapped. "But rest assured, I will be conducting a *thorough* investigation. I want to know her whereabouts every second she has been in Arx Eburna."

"At my side or attending her training sessions," he answered quickly.

I stared past Mistress Orvana, unable to stop my chin from trembling as I finally met his darkened stare. With his rugged features still drawn into a look of withheld rage, I hardly recognized him.

But I knew he was lying.

He hadn't spent every second at my side, and we both knew it. I'd been left to my own devices here in Arx Eburna plenty of times. So why was he telling her that?

I didn't dare ask or even make a sound as he muscled his way past her, leaning down to open the shackles on my wrists and ankles.

His gaze halted on the crossbow bolt still sticking out of my thigh. His jaw clenched and brow knitted in quiet fury, but he didn't say anything as he slid his arms under my back and knees, carrying me like a child against his broad chest.

My heart gave a frantic, sharp twist as the musky smell of his coat filled my nose. Was this the man I trusted to protect me? Or had I just been pulled from one prison to be tossed into another?

I didn't know. All I could do was pray he might believe me.

"How long do you dream this can go on, Roxus?" Mistress Orvana seethed as she watched him carry me toward the door. "You know I will get to the bottom of this—one way or another. I cannot risk the security of our entire organization on your desperate efforts to protect a Pitathi."

I felt his body tense. His jaw worked from one side to the

other, as though he were fighting to keep his temper from breaching the surface of that smoldering scowl.

"Come to your senses," she reasoned, her tone a bit softer and more pleading, "before you doom us all."

Roxus didn't look back and kept his glare trained straight ahead as he carried me out of the chamber. It was only once we had stepped through the doorway, I heard him mutter quietly, "With you leading us, we are already doomed."

TWENTY-SIX

I didn't understand him.

Not even a little.

Why, by all the gods, did Roxus believe I was innocent when absolutely no one else did?

Why did he even care?

Well, fine, so maybe Chrysa would believe me, too. But none of the other prospects or elders did—especially not now that Mistress Orvana had me hauled off in shackles.

Just the thought turned my stomach to sour mush.

Apparently, all the other prospects and many of the patrons had witnessed the whole thing. Gods. As if it wasn't awkward enough already whenever I walked into a room.

How could I ever face any of them again?

I stayed quiet as Roxus carried me through the dim, winding halls of Arx Eburna, only bothering to keep track of where we were once we crossed through the Eternal Hall. I caught a glimpse of Chrysa's pasty, horrified face as we made our way out.

I'd have a lot of explaining to do later.

Roxus all but kicked in the door that led down another

narrow passage to a flight of stairs and into a chamber I'd never seen before. This one, besides being off to itself and eerily quiet, had only a few small rooms closed off by hanging tapestries that covered each doorway. The heavy spice of incense hung thick in the air, mingling with the rich aromas of other herbs—things I didn't recognize but made my eyes water.

Ducking past one of the hanging tapestries, Roxus carried me into a small room with a single, low bed against the far wall. The table beside it was arranged with a pitcher, two copper cups, a stack of clean towels, and a lamp made of panels of colored glass.

"Stay here," Roxus warned as he set me down on the bed.

"What is this place?" I managed through chattering teeth. I couldn't stop shivering. Gods, what was wrong with me?

"The infirmary," he replied, his tone low and sharp. Annoyed.

At me?

I couldn't tell.

Roxus didn't say anything else as he strode out of the room, leaving me to sit alone on the edge of the narrow bed.

My mind raced. My body shivered. I clenched fistfuls of the stiff, white sheets and stared at the wooden crossbow bolt sticking out of my leg. Until then, I hadn't realized just how deep it was. Crap.

Pulling it out would hurt.

Was I in shock? Is that why it didn't hurt more right now? I mean, yes, it was painful. But I could bear it.

For now, anyway.

"Just do what you can. I'll have a healer look after it once I get her home," Roxus's voice carried down the hall.

"You're not coming in?" an unfamiliar male voice asked.

"I'll be back for her in an hour," Roxus muttered, almost like he didn't want me to overhear. "Business to settle, first."

Uh oh.

I tensed, still gripping the edge of the bed like my life depended on it as another tall, leanly-built man brushed back the tapestry and stepped into the room with a basket of supplies in his arms.

He wasn't as tall as Roxus but had a similar build beneath his long, silver and green robes. He didn't look a day over twenty, with wide shoulders, squared human features, and light blond hair cut off at his shoulders. Part of it was pulled back into a little half-ponytail to keep his shaggy bangs away from his dark blue eyes.

Something about his broad, easy smile was strangely disarming—like he was someone I'd known for years.

"Now then, you must be Violet," he said as he approached and set the basket down on the table next to the bed.

He knew my name? How? Had Roxus told him?

"Have we met?" I dared to ask.

He shook his head as he began pulling items out of the basket and setting them out in an obsessively careful line— small knives, needles, thread, bandaging, and bottles of strange swirling liquids.

Medical supplies.

"Not at all," he chuckled. "But I've spent a lot of time patching up your handiwork. You've sent several Vindexori my way with all manner of bruising, sprains, and a few broken ribs.

Oh.

Oops.

I hung my head lower, looking away as he moved closer and stared at the arrow bolt sticking out of my leg like a fork from a side of ham.

"Looks like one of them got the better of you this time," he said, something gently teasing in his tone.

My mouth mashed sourly, but I didn't answer.

"I'm Kaedan, by the way. I've got a feeling we may be seeing a lot of each other from now on," he added as he returned to his wares, pouring out the contents of a large decanter into a small bowl. It looked like water, clear and liquid, but the acrid smell instantly made my eyes water.

"I didn't realize the Zenith's Call kept healers," I murmured.

His smile widened, crinkling the corners of his dark, cobalt eyes. "They keep all manner of people at their disposal. We've even got a fellow herding chickens out back."

"Maybe I ought to try for that job, instead," I grumbled.

He laughed again, shaking his head some as he wrung out a clean white cloth in the bowl.

"I have a feeling you're a tad overqualified for that," he said.

I wasn't so sure anymore.

"All right, Miss Violet, you'll want to prepare yourself. I've got to widen the wound to cut that bolt out so it doesn't take a hunk of your leg along with it. It's not going to feel great, even with a potion to numb the area," he warned and held up another small vial of something that swirled in hues of blackish purple.

I frowned. "What's that?"

"A mercy," he replied. "Drink it all in one go and lie back. It'll knock you for a loop."

I took it in a shaking hand, tugging the cork off the top and daring to sniff it.

My nose wrinkled and my throat went dry. Putrid and sickly sweet, the liquid burned all the way down as I threw my head back and downed the whole vial in one swig.

Ugh. Vile.

I scarcely had time to flop back onto the bed before the whole room began spinning and weaving. Darkness gathered in the corners of my vision and my ears rang. A strange, tingling warmth spread through my chest and down to my toes.

Everything seemed to slip away, farther and farther, until there was nothing but that spinning, tickling heat and the steady pounding of my heart ...

And the echoes of memories I'd fought to bury years ago.

* * *

"You must do this, Visha," my mother's trembling voice whispered at my side. *"Whatever he says, you must not question."*

She gripped my shoulder like she was afraid I might suddenly disappear.

Or turn and bolt.

I had never met my father before. Brood Fathers seldom had anything to do with their offspring, except to cull the weak and defective. But that usually took place right after birth.

I was now in my ninth year. Too old to be culled.

Right?

"Why do none of the others have to?" I questioned.

"Because the Brood Father commands it," she answered quickly, gaze darting ahead to the two massive chamber doors looming before us. The gates to his private chambers.

A place I had always been forbidden to enter.

Until now.

I caught a glimpse of our reflections wavering in the polished black stone walls. Even the doors shone like flawless obsidian, their surfaces etched with depictions of twisting serpents entwined around thorny branches.

"You must not speak to him. Do not look in his eye," she warned, drawing me closer to her as we passed into the chamber beyond, slipping through the doors like silent wisps

of shadow. *"Submit immediately and do not move unless he commands it."*

My stomach gave a frantic twist. What was happening? Why had she brought me here?

Had I done something wrong?

I didn't know.

My mother fell silent as we sped down the grand corridor, passing massive columns of onyx and alabaster that loomed as big as nightmares in the near dark. Only the faintest light from two golden braziers standing at the far end of the room gave off an ethereal glow. It made the deep shadows dance. Sculptures of winged beings cut from pure black glass lurked just beyond the light, as though desperately trying to twist themselves free of the darkness.

Our darkness.

At the far end of the chamber, on a raised dais, I saw him. He stood behind a long stone table, seated in a chair of polished bronze and fine black velvet. My sire. The leader of our clan.

The Brood Father.

I swallowed hard.

With his hands resting on the curled arms of the chair, his eyes glowed in the weak light of the braziers as red as fresh blood. His long, sharp features didn't so much as twitch as we approached. No expression. No movement.

My heartbeat quickened. A cold sweat prickled on the back of my neck.

His eyes narrowed ever so slightly—as though he could hear my blood rushing faster the closer we got to the dais. He raised a hand, and immediately my mother stopped, jerking me to a halt right next to her.

We both fell to our knees in full submission, ankles crossed and foreheads pressed to the cold stone.

"Rise," he commanded, his tone deep and smooth like the slice of a scimitar in the crisp air.

We stood but kept our heads bowed low.

"You—approach me."

I dared to steal a glance upward, my heartbeat skipping when I found him pointing directly at me. Oh, gods.

My knees shook as I cast one last pleading look at my mother and stepped away, staggering toward him with all the grace of a newborn fawn. My heart beat so fast it felt like it might punch straight out of my chest and land on the table as I wobbled to a halt before it.

My father's stare hit me like a chokehold, strangling all the air from my lungs. He was ruthlessly handsome, albeit a little older than I'd expected. His pointed jaw was clean-shaven and his long, shock-white hair hung in smooth locks down to the center of his chest like bolts of white silk.

The golden rings on his fingers glittered as he gestured to the table between us, where three palm-sized coins lay on a piece of black velvet. Each one of them seemed old and battered—probably ancient—and had the same engraving on the front depicting the Eye of the Foul Father.

But only one of them caught my eye.

My gaze lingered on it, and I bit back the urge to reach out and touch it just to be sure it wasn't an illusion or a trick of the light.

"Choose," the Brood Father commanded.

I dared to flick another quick glance up at him. Was this some sort of gift? A blessing? Or a rite of passage my mother had not told me about?

"She has shown no sign or symptom, my lord," my mother blurted, her tone frantic. *"I have kept close watch in case she showed any indication of—"*

"Silence," the Brood Father boomed, his voice filling the chamber like the biting snap of a whip.

My fingers curled into shaking, sweaty fists as he leaned forward, jaw tight and gaze smoldering with sudden intensity, all focused directly on me.

"Choose," he repeated.

I looked down at the coins again, all three set in a straight line. They were identical in size and shape. The engravings were the same. Only the one on the far right was different—so subtly, I didn't know if anyone else could even tell.

Maybe they couldn't. Maybe that was the whole point.

Was I meant to pick that one? Was this a test? Would doing it prove my worthiness?

My mind raced and my pulse pounded harder and harder against my ribs. What should I do? What was the correct answer? I-I didn't know! I—

I looked back at my mother, hoping she would give me some clues.

Instantly, there was a big, powerful hand crushing around my neck. My father moved as fast as a striking serpent, leaning across the table and gripping my neck so hard I couldn't make a sound.

"Do not look at her! Do as I command! CHOOSE!" he yelled into my face, baring his pointed canine teeth.

I stumbled as he let me go with a shove, and motioned to the coins again, his expression skewed with primal rage.

I wouldn't get another chance. I knew that.

So I held my breath, steeling every frayed nerve, and pointed a trembling finger to the coin on the right.

The one that glowed faintly with a pale blue light.

* * *

Pain stole the breath from my lungs as soon as I opened my eyes.

But, gods, I'd never been so glad to wake up with two legs.

Lying on my back on my bed, I set my teeth against the pain that throbbed from my thigh—the place where I'd been shot by the crossbow. Thankfully, the arrow was gone. But it must have been a deeper wound than I thought because the pain thrummed so deep it felt like it hummed straight down to my bone.

A whimper leaked past my lips as I gripped fistfuls of my blankets. Tears welled in my eyes.

Fates, I couldn't take this. Not without—

"Here, you need to drink this," Roxus's voice murmured close by.

I blinked groggily, barely able to make out the shape of him sitting at my bedside. He moved in closer and cradled the back of my head, helping me sit up and holding a small cup to my lips.

I cringed as the bitter tonic burned down the back of my throat. A flavor I knew all too well now.

I guess Leruna had come by and left more of her healing remedies. Ugh. Disgusting.

"W-why does it h-hurt so much?" I managed to rasp.

"Apparently, Viperi bones are more dense than we realized. The arrow tip shattered when it hit your femur. Took Kaedan a few hours to dig out all the shards," Roxus explained. "One narrowly missed your artery. Kaedan said you were very lucky."

I did not feel lucky *at all*.

"Leruna has already come to look after your recovery. She left some healing tonics that should speed things along. But as long as you're taking them, you're not to leave this bed. Not without help."

No argument there.

Lying flat on my back, surrounded by soft downy pillows and the cool caress of satin sheets, I let my eyes roll closed.

Everything seemed to spin slowly, and the throbbing agony in my leg gradually went numb.

So did everything else.

My thoughts were a hazy blur. I couldn't even remember how I'd gotten here. It didn't matter, though. I was safe here.

For now.

Silence settled through the room. I breathed in the soft, faint brine of the sea floating in from my bedroom balcony.

I wasn't even sure if Roxus was still in the room until I heard him ask, "Did you do it?"

I opened my eyes. My jaw clenched and I forced my head to turn enough to look him straight in the eye.

He stared right back, his expression stony and empty of all emotion.

"Did you try to break into the Vault of Whispers?" he asked again.

"No," I answered.

He leaned forward some, resting his weight on his elbows as he sighed deeply. "All right."

"You believe me?"

"You haven't given me any reason not to," he said.

My mouth scrunched. True, I had never just outright lied to him before. But there were times when I hadn't told him the whole truth, either.

Lying by omission, I guess.

"It's over, isn't it?" I murmured. "My training and being considered as a member of the Zenith's Call—it's all over, right?"

I wasn't stupid. Mistress Orvana wouldn't want to allow me to go back after this—even if I had nothing to do with whatever had happened to the so-called vault. It didn't matter. She had already decided I was guilty, even before they ever put me in that chair.

"Do you want it to be over?" Roxus asked suddenly, his tone much softer and more cautious than I expected.

I hesitated, fixing him with a wide-eyed stare he would probably assume was fear or panic.

Honestly, it was a little of both.

"I-I ... I didn't think I'd get to go back," I stammered. "You mean Mistress Orvana would really let me?"

"It's not up to her. Not solely," he replied. "She's busy conducting her investigation, but I doubt she will find anything of merit to implicate anyone, let alone you. No one just wakes up and decides to crack an ancient, magically sealed vault. Whoever is to blame has spent a long time planning this. I doubt they'll be sloppy enough to leave behind evidence, especially after their first attempt failed."

I frowned, watching that keen, sharp light flicker in his brown eyes. Like he was putting all the pieces together at lightning speed. Seeing things no one else could.

He was a lot smarter than he let on.

"You think they'll try it again?" I guessed.

"Why wouldn't they? Especially with all eyes now on you as the most likely culprit." He made a scoffing sound in his throat.

I looked back up at the ceiling above my bed, feeling the heavy thudding of my pulse like stones stacking on my chest. Every beat made it harder to breathe.

Roxus was right.

Guilty or not, all eyes were on me. And whoever wanted in that vault had the perfect scapegoat. The perfect distraction to try again. They'd probably wait until I went back to training, just so I looked even more guilty—heck, that's what I would have done.

Fates. I couldn't go back, could I? Not until the real culprit had been caught. But what if they never were? Or what if they just kept waiting?

A warm, rough-palmed hand grasped my arm gently.

"Hey, let's not worry about it now. Rest. Delthene is on orders not to let you leave this room alone and to see that you take the tonics every four hours." A faint, halfhearted smile tugged at Roxus's mouth.

I couldn't do anything but stare back, my thoughts still a vortex of worry.

His expression hardened some, brows knitting together in a contemplative frown as his eyes searched mine. Almost like he was trying to see through me, down to the whirling storm that consumed my mind as fierce and furious as a hurricane.

He squeezed my arm a little. "Violet, I know what it means to have no one in your corner. To be forced to put your faith in people you hardly know and have that faith betrayed. But I want you to know this as absolute truth—until you give me a reason not to, I will always have your back. I'll believe you even if no one else does. That's what family does for one another. Understand?"

Tears welled in my eyes. I couldn't stop my chin from trembling or that weight from growing heavier and heavier on my chest. But I couldn't look away.

Not when that gaze felt like the only lifeline I had left in the whole mad, terrible, wretched world.

"Trust for trust," I managed hoarsely.

His smile was real then. "That's right. Trust for trust."

I nodded, fighting back sniffles.

"Get some rest," he urged, giving my arm one last reassuring pat before he stood and started for the door.

I gulped against the hard knot in my throat. "Roxus?"

He paused at the doorway and glanced back. "Yes?"

"My name ... it's Visha," I whispered shakily, my eyes squeezing shut as tears left warm trails down the sides of my face. "But please don't call me that. I like Violet. Like the flower."

"Violet," he agreed. "Like the flower."

I could hear the smile in his voice.

His footsteps retreated. The door clicked shut. And I was alone in the silence, feeling nothing but those cooling wet trails on my cheeks and the dull ache and throb of pain in my leg.

But the weight on my chest was gone. My pulse slowed. My body relaxed into the silky embrace of the sheets and pillows.

I trusted Roxus—maybe more than I should. Okay, so, definitely more than I should, considering I still knew next to nothing about him. It could all go bad. One wrong word, one false move, and it could all fall apart.

And what then?

Mistress Orvana, the other prospects, Domitri, and some of the other patrons—they wanted me to be a monster so badly. And, gods, I was getting *so* tired of running.

Maybe it was time to prove them right.

To fight back.

I let out a long, slow breath, feeling the faint throbbing in my leg like a reminder.

Ugh. No. I couldn't. I knew better.

Every step I took through Arx Eburna was practically a walk on a hair-thin wire. I had fought tooth and nail, let Declan beat me senseless over and over, for some sense of control over those urges. I couldn't throw it all away.

No matter what they did or said, I had to keep that control. I had to stay focused.

Or I might lose a lot more than just my chance at becoming Zenith's Call.

I lay there, the pain in my leg muted but still present. But it wasn't the physical wound that scared me the most—it was the look on Roxus's face before he left. There was something

there, something hidden beneath the anger and determination.

A darkness I couldn't quite name.

What did he know that I didn't?

Twenty-Seven

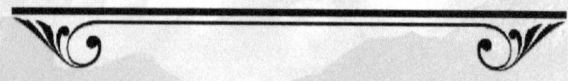

"Hey, you gonna pass out or throw up?"

I looked up, sweat rolling off the end of my nose and dripping from my chin, and glared at Declan with every ounce of energy I had left.

Which sadly ... wasn't much.

Five days after my arrest in front of all the gods and prospects at Arx Eburna, Leruna had finally given a *very* reluctant blessing for me to return to training.

Or, a lighter version of it, anyway.

I was supposed to take it easy for the next week to give my leg time to fully heal. But I guess Declan hadn't gotten that news. That, or he knew better than to go easy on me. Wounded or not, I'd push myself to the brink before I rolled over and let him win a match.

Today, however, he hadn't come by looking for our usual fight.

He'd all but dragged me out of the house and insisted we go on a "run" together—which I truly had not realized was something anyone would do just for the sake of exercise.

But here I was.

After two grueling hours of chasing him down alley-ways and along the narrow, twisting streets, we came to a lonely stretch of beach tucked away in a cove on the far side of the island. Here, the shallow waters lapped peacefully at a broad sandbar of pristine white sand that must have kept the ships from bothering to moor. A few elven fishermen stood way off from shore, their pants rolled up and their arms full of fishing nets they tossed out into the shimmering water.

Against the failing light of day, Declan finally stopped and stood at the edge of the water. His tunic and hair were soaked through with sweat, but he didn't even look winded as he watched me tromp angrily through the sand after him.

My calves howled. My thigh throbbed with fresh agony where my injury was now hardly more than a fading pink scar. My lungs ached with every wheezing breath.

Maybe I would throw up, after all.

"Need a breather?" he chuckled as he strolled over to watch me still struggling to breathe.

I raised a shaking hand and gave him a rude gesture.

"What did you expect? I'm half your size! I take three steps to your one!" I fumed.

He just laughed louder. Standing with his hands on his hips and the sea wind teasing through his dark golden hair, Declan watched me struggle the last few yards over the sand, grinning wolfishly the whole time.

Big jerk.

Hobbling over the sun-warmed sand to stand next to him, I stood straight and tried to focus on keeping my lungs open and each breath controlled. In and out. No fainting. No puking.

After a few minutes, I quit seeing stars. My leg still throbbed, but it was bearable now. More of a dull ache than a sharp pain. I'd had worse.

"Roxus said you'd be returning to your training at Arx Eburna tomorrow," Declan said. "Ready for that?"

"Sure," I lied and rolled my eyes.

It was a stupid question, though. Going back there would be like walking straight into the deepest pits of the abyss. Everyone except Chrysa and maybe Curator Faera hated me there. I doubted my very public detainment and interrogation would do much to improve my reputation.

"Worried about it?" he asked.

I shrugged and stared out across the rippling horizon, watching the sunlight dance over the waves.

"Well, what's the worst that could happen?"

"They take me back down to that interrogation cell, torture, and kill me before Roxus hears about it," I answered sharply, flicking him an irritated sideways glare.

His eyebrows quirked upward. "That's ... really specific."

"And extremely likely," I muttered.

"Is it, though?" He stepped closer.

I pursed my lips, trying to decide if he was teasing or not. Sometimes Declan was hard to read—probably because he hid behind those sheepish grins and brash smiles like someone wearing a porcelain mask.

But that ruse didn't work on me now that I knew what he was hiding.

Reaching into his pocket, Declan took out a small metallic sphere and offered it. It wasn't any larger than a chicken's egg, and the seam around the middle suggested maybe it would split open if I twisted it.

"Take it," he urged. "But don't open it. Not unless you need it."

I frowned and carefully plucked the sphere from his hand. "What is it?"

"An advantage," he replied. "In case you need it. Throw it on the ground. It'll open and you'll get a few seconds of a black smoke cloud. It'll blind everyone around you—but I'll warrant it won't have that same effect on someone with body heat-vision."

A crooked, conniving grin twisted up my lips as I studied the little sphere, turning it over to admire the way the sunlight glittered off its smooth silver surface.

"Where did you get this?" I looked up at him again.

His features twitched, tugging into a tense, uncomfortable grimace for a brief second. "Sometimes it's good to have friends in low places, right?"

"That's the only kind I've got." I pocketed the tiny smoke bomb.

"Gotta start somewhere, right?"

Hmm. He was right, I guess. Until now, I hadn't had any friends anywhere.

"Thanks," I said quietly.

"Don't mention it—seriously, don't. Roxus might come after me if he knew I was slipping you things like that. It certainly won't do you any favors if they catch you with it ahead of time." He rubbed the back of his neck and shifted his weight uncomfortably.

"Hey, listen, I don't need *your* help looking guilty to the Zenith's Call. I'm doing just fine at that all on my own." I smirked.

He shook his head, doing an awful job of holding back another grin. "Right. Well, in case you do find yourself in another tight spot, maybe it'll help."

Gods, he had no idea. Really, he didn't. I didn't know how much Roxus had told him about my situation with the Zenith's Call, but I was willing to bet good coin it wasn't everything. I couldn't be caught in Arx Eburna with something like this in my pocket. As far as almost everyone there was concerned, I was the one going after the vault. I was guilty —no matter what Roxus said.

Sure, my time suffering these trials was almost up. They'd have to make a final decision about me soon. But I wasn't stupid enough to dream that things would suddenly be better and they'd all just let their grudges go and accept that I had earned a place among them.

Things would get worse before they got better.

If I even survived at all.

I'd have to tuck this away in my room where Delthene and Roxus might not find it. I couldn't be caught with it.

Declan stayed quieter than usual as we made our way back to Roxus's house, walking along the shore with the warm, turquoise waters lapping at our ankles. The wind snagged in my hair, blowing it around my face as I watched the elven fishermen flinging their nets out and reeling in slender silver-scaled fish each time.

They didn't give us a second glance as we passed by and started up the beach and back into the steep, craggy path leading into the city.

At the crux of the first switchback in the narrow trail, I looked back just in time to see the shapes of three large creatures bounding through the bigger waves beyond the cove. Their brilliantly colored scales gleamed as bright as gemstones in the light of the setting sun, powerful necks arched, and strong tails lashing with impressive speed.

Hippocampi—a beautiful, wild, and ethereal mixture of land and sea. They sort of resembled horses, only with fishlike tails and finned necks and forelegs.

The Rienkan elves had mastered taming them long ago. I'd only ever seen them from afar like this, though. It was hard to imagine riding one over the waves, leaping and diving with effortless grace.

Maybe someday.

As the sun sank beyond the sea and the moon rose higher, Declan led the way back into the harbor and off through the markets. He kept off the main streets since neither of us looked altogether commonplace and acceptable strolling around together. A known pit-fighter working for a crime boss and a Viperi urchin? Hah! We certainly made quite a pair.

My mind wandered as I stayed close behind him, keeping my head down in case anyone noticed my eyes or teeth. The hair wasn't as much of a problem, really. But red eyes and pointed canine teeth gave me away pretty quickly.

Better to play it safe.

A block from the house, Declan stopped so suddenly I crashed right into his back.

What the—?

I leaned sideways to peer up at his face, but he kept a cold, focused scowl trained straight ahead. I followed his line of sight all the way to Roxus's front door ... where a slender woman in a long, dark cloak was rushing outside.

I froze. From that distance, even with my ability to see heat-light in the dark, I couldn't pick out her features. Not when she had the hood of her cloak pulled down so low. Her movements weren't familiar as she stepped quickly from the front door with an armload of books, looking up and down the street before hurrying off into the night.

Thankfully, she didn't seem to notice Declan and me lurking in the shadows nearby. He'd picked the perfect spot to stop before we were exposed by the ambient moonlight.

I was still trying to decide if it was safe to take a breath when Roxus stepped in the doorway. He lingered there with his arms crossed, watching the woman go with his grim expression cast in stark relief by the lamp hanging overhead.

Strange.

Was it Leruna? Surely not. I would have recognized her gait, and she had no reason to be skulking around like that. Not when she'd come over so many times already.

The woman was too tall to be Chrysa.

So who else could it be?

"Friend of yours?" Declan's voice was so low and faint I barely heard him.

Almost a growl.

"I only have three, and you're one of them, so no." I bumped his arm with mine, hoping to nudge him onward.

He made a sound that could have been a cough or a snort. I couldn't tell which.

"I'm flattered. Wanna make another lap around the block? Follow and see who it is?"

I gnawed at the inside of my cheek. Part of me *did* want to do that.

But another part knew that Roxus wouldn't like it. I couldn't exactly afford to lose one of my three friends. Especially not the one giving me a roof over my head.

Better to keep quiet and observe. Maybe I'd find a clue inside.

"No. Let's just go," I answered at last. "Looks like he's waiting on us, anyway."

"That's unusually cautious of you." He slid me a skeptical sideways look.

I sighed deeply, already feeling that jittery tingling in my extremities as the nerves took hold. "After what happened last time, I can't afford *not* to be cautious from now on."

Declan nodded, his features hardening into a thoughtful frown. He led the way up to the front of the house, waving a greeting to Roxus as we neared the door.

"Well, she survived," Declan joked, giving my shoulder a playful shove that nearly sent me flying sideways.

Big, dumb, overly strong idiot.

Glancing between us, Roxus's expression remained ominously indifferent. No telling annoyed eye-twitches or disarming smiles. He might as well have been one of those statues in the temple at Arx Eburna.

Crap.

"Delthene's got some leftovers set aside for you in the dining room," Roxus said and stepped back into the house.

My stomach clenched, gurgling anxiously at the prospect of having to sit there and try to eat while they made awkward small talk. Like even a few bites might make me sick.

Ugh. No thanks.

"Actually, I think I'm just going to go to bed," I muttered as I shuffled past, darting around both of them in the front foyer and heading straight up the stairs.

I didn't give them the chance to protest, but I could feel Roxus's suspicious glare on my back nonetheless.

Fine. So he wasn't wrong. I had other priorities at the moment, though.

Halting at the top of the stairs, I waited until I heard their conversation and heavy footfalls drift off into the dining room before I dared to stick my head back into the drafty stairwell. All clear. Good.

Time to investigate.

I took off my boots and crept on silent bare feet down to Roxus's office, avoiding every spot where I knew the worn, wooden floorboards would creak. The door was cracked open a little, so I pushed it a few inches more—just far enough to slip through.

Inside, everything was in its usual state of chaotic disarray. Books and scrolls piled on every flat surface, and embers smoldered low in the hearth. Strange artifacts crowding shelves, hidden amongst cobwebs and layers of dust. Things that hadn't meant much to me previously.

Now, after months of careful study in history and divine lore, I could recognize ancient bronze statuettes of Avoran design, intricate Nar'Haleenan mechanisms meant to chart the planets and stars, and complex bits of Tibran weaponry.

Marvels he'd probably collected during his work on missions for the Zenith's Call.

Only one thing looked out of place.

Right in the middle of his desk, a small bronze box, roughly four inches in diameter, sat on a piece of fine white linen. It was hardly bigger than a jewelry box, but it didn't seem to have a lid or latch anywhere.

And it glowed.

The small cube glowed with such a bright blue aura it made every hair on the back of my neck stand on end.

I'd never seen anything shine that intensely before.

What the heck was it? And why did Roxus have it here? I'd never noticed it before. Had that woman with the books brought it?

I paused before the cube, leaning around to admire how every side of it was covered in geometric runic designs. Not Avoran. Not from Nar'Haleen, either.

It had to be Tibran. Everything about their design work was hard, sharp, and angular. It had a forceful abruptness to it you couldn't mistake.

Strange.

What was he doing with a Tibran artifact?

Nibbling at my bottom lip, I reached out to lightly graze a fingertip over its tarnished, golden surface. The old metal was smooth and oddly warm.

"It's just a replica," a deep voice spoke right behind me.

I leapt back from the desk, my heart in my throat.

Roxus leaned in the doorway, the lines and creases in his features seeming deeper and heavier than usual. Tired, even.

Gods, how did he do that? How did he move around without making a single sound?

"O-of what?" I managed to wheeze.

His mouth mashed up into an indifferent frown as he shrugged. "We aren't sure yet."

"We being ... the Zenith's Call?" I guessed.

He just shrugged again.

Glancing back down at the cube, I watched that constant glow ebb from all those runic marks that covered every side of it, and couldn't hold back a frown.

"And you're sure it's just a replica?" I dared to ask.

Roxus's eyes narrowed slightly. "Reasonably. Why?"

My mouth quirked from one side to the other. I knew I should tell him. But then again, how could I even be sure he didn't see it glowing, too? Curator Faera hadn't known about her quill, sure. But that didn't mean no one else did, right?

"What is it, Violet?" Roxus pressed, taking a step into the room.

My heartbeat skipped. I shook my head and backed away farther. No, no, I couldn't risk it. One wrong word, one false step, and I could lose everything.

"Nothing. It just looks very fancy for a replica," I fibbed instead. "But I guess the Zenith's Call wouldn't just let you take a real, magical ancient artifact home."

My laugh was thin, broken, and painfully forced. Like the panicked shriek of rusty wagon wheels.

Roxus didn't laugh or smile back.

"True," he muttered, his tone sharp and slightly bitter.

Oh. Oh no. Had I made him angry? Did he know I was lying?

Trust for trust.

I shut my eyes tightly for a second. Calm—I just had to stay calm. Roxus had no reason to suspect I saw anything different than he did.

"I-I should go get a bath before bed," I rambled nervously, scuttling by him back toward the hall. "I get to go back tomorrow, right?"

"Right."

I had one foot in the hall when he suddenly called out again.

"I can't go with you to Arx Eburna in the morning. But I'll be there as soon as I can. Apparently, Mistress Orvana has some new policies she wants to put in place in the name of ... everyone's *security*."

I hesitated, staring back at him over my shoulder.

He didn't look back at me, though, and stood still in front of his desk, gazing down at the cube. There was something oddly defeated in the way his broad shoulders drooped and his head bowed slightly. Like he was deep in thought, trying to solve a problem that had no solution.

A pinch of unease in the center of my chest made my heartbeat skip.

"I'll be fine. On my best behavior," I promised.

Once again, Roxus didn't answer. Maybe he hadn't even heard me.

He stood eerily still, all focus trained upon the small cube sitting on his desk.

I held my breath until I got to the washroom and shut the door. With my back pressed against it, I sank slowly to the floor and sat with my knees close to my chest. Everything seemed hazy. Faraway.

Distant compared to the problem that loomed like a moon right in front of my face.

I couldn't keep lying. Especially not to Roxus. Too much was at stake now. Time was almost up, and I was so close to the finish line.

One little lie could keep me from crossing it.

I shut my eyes and leaned my head back against the door. Tomorrow.

I'd tell him the truth about what I saw tomorrow.

About the quill that Curator Faera had given me. About the cube. About Domitri.

And then I'd face the consequences.

They might lock me up again. Or take me back to the prison where Roxus had found me. It might be the end of everything.

They might even kill me.

But I had no choice now.

Tomorrow would change everything. I couldn't keep running from myself—from my destiny. I could keep hiding it, either.

Tomorrow, I would finally come clean about everything.

And maybe, *hopefully*, I wouldn't lose everything because of it.

Twenty-Eight

here was a special seat in the abyss especially reserved for Mistress Orvana.

Or, at least, there should have been.

The thought of her being lashed to a chair in the middle of a crackling pyre was all that kept me sane as I strode back into Arx Eburna, feeling the weight of every stare crushing down on me. They weren't just watching me—they were waiting for me to make a wrong move. To lash out. To be the monster they'd all heard about.

And if I wasn't careful, I knew I might prove them right.

Every muscle in my body clenched hard when I saw them. My stomach dropped. My steps slowed until I finally stood, staring down a group of patrons and Vindexori blocking the doorway leading onward into the Eternal Hall.

Fantastic. This day was already off to a great start.

"Mistress Orvana has decreed there will be no entry without a chaperone, and no traversing the grounds unless you are in a group of three with other prospects or a patron," one of the Vindexori snarled.

Ugh. Of course she had.

I crossed my arms. "Well, who is going to be paired with me?"

Their expressions stayed steely, bitter, and forbidding. Seconds passed, and none of them volunteered.

Ah. Okay. So *that's* how this was going to go.

Mistress Orvana knew I only had one friend among the other prospects—not enough to meet her criteria. And other than Roxus, no other patrons would ever volunteer to babysit me. As usual, he was off running his mysterious errands, and I had no idea if I'd even see him before I got back home tonight. I'd already made myself infamous among the Vindexori, too.

"Then what am I supposed to do?" I argued, my heart already pounding with frustrated force against my ribs.

"That's your problem," one of the patrons scoffed and pointed back the way I'd come. "Off with you!"

My lip twitched, and I bit down to suppress a growl. Bunch of idiots. Did they really think this would keep me out? As soon as Roxus got wind of what they were doing, he would—

"What seems to be the problem here?" a familiar voice, smooth and oily, spoke over my shoulder.

Dread like a blast of arctic cold made my body freeze. I sucked in a sharp breath, not daring to look past my shoulder as I felt his presence looming right behind me. Watching me with all the practiced, calculating vicious hunger of a viper circling a caught mouse.

Domitri leaned down, his breath stirring my hair as he whispered, "Having trouble, are we, pitathi?"

My heartbeat skipped.

"No," I managed stiffly.

Leave. I had to leave before—

His hand snapped out and grabbed my arm, squeezing so hard it felt like he might snap it. Gods, how? He wasn't especially big or strong-looking.

So why did it feel like someone was squeezing my arm in a vice?

"What, did you think we would just welcome you back with open arms? Did you dream that we'd keep tolerating your presence no matter what you did?" he hissed quietly. "We might not have the evidence to prove you're the one tampering with the vault, but rest assured, you will make a mistake. And when you do, no one will be rushing to your rescue."

My whole body burned. Every primal instinct fused into my brain railed and roared at the seams of my control. I twisted and jerked in his iron-strong grasp.

But there was no escape.

I forced myself to look—to meet his wretched, gleeful sneer.

Fear hit me like a punch to the throat and I couldn't breathe or make a sound.

Domitri's eerie, glowing face stared straight back at me, inches from mine. His features rippled like a reflection on a pond, and his smirk suddenly darkened to a void of pure wrath, as though the veil over his true intentions had suddenly been dropped and I got a glimpse of every terrible thing he wanted to do to me.

The faint blue light that wreathed his features seemed to intensify like the glare of the sun. His smile was too wide, almost as though it had been stretched. His eyes were sunken. His cheekbones were too sharp.

He almost didn't look human at all.

"Who do you think will mourn you?" he snapped, his voice so quiet, I doubted anyone else standing around could even hear. "Who would mourn a monster? Perhaps we should find out."

My ears rang. My whole body seemed to go numb. Staring up at Domitri, it was as though the rest of the world had faded to a faraway blur. I was captive. Trapped with this monster.

Gods, couldn't anyone else see it? The way his features melted and warped like soft clay?

"W-what ... are you?" I whimpered, my voice shaking.

Domitri's eyes narrowed suddenly. Suspiciously.

Then they went wide—too wide.

His face paled. His mouth opened.

But Domitri didn't get a word out.

"What, by all the gods, is going on?" Curator Faera demanded as she pushed her way to the front of the group of other patrons and Vindexori.

Her gaze flashed between Domitri and me, spotting where he still had that iron grip on my arm, squeezing me so hard his knuckles were white.

Fury took her delicate features like an all-consuming fire. She muscled her way past the last patron, seized Domitri by the shoulder, and shoved him away from me.

I ducked away as soon as his grip on my arm went slack, rushing to the side of the doorway.

"How *dare* you put hands on a prospect in such a manner," Curator Faera shouted loudly enough that everyone else standing in the Eternal Hall, prospects and even a few more Vindexori that had been passing on patrol, stopped to stare.

Oh, gods. This wouldn't be good.

I pressed myself against the wall, praying silently that I'd just disappear. Or turn invisible. Or melt into the floor. I'd take whatever means of escape I could get.

That was when I spotted Chrysa through the crowd, almost like she had been trying to get to me, as well, but the other patrons had blocked her path. She stared at me with a pasty, haunted expression, her mouth hanging open and a book gripped tightly to her chest.

"I'll have you know that the pitathi girl was about to violate the mistress's direct orders and enter the Eternal Hall without a chaperone!" Domitri yelled back, straightening quickly.

He stood nose-to-nose with Faera, glaring back at her with his body tense and fists clenched.

She didn't blink, though. Her expression cooled to a frosty, meaningful stare that made my skin prickle with unease. "Was she? Or did you and the rest of these idiots really believe you could entrap her with rules she hasn't even been informed of yet? Tell me, was this your idea? Or Mistress Orvana's? Perhaps we should go ask her now, hm?"

Domitri's eyes were round and crazed as he made choking, balking noises. "H-how dare you fling such accusations at me!"

A rush of whispers and murmurs went through the crowd.

Curator Faera waved her hand in his face dismissively. "Spare me your petty theatrics, Domitri. I'm in no mood for them. You've not been in your right mind for months now."

He jerked back, blinking and balking like she'd just slapped him.

Faera didn't spare him a second glance, though.

"I have volunteered to be her chaperone until other arrangements are made. So stand aside and save your sputtering." She turned on a heel, leaving him in awkward silence, and motioned for me to follow.

The crowd parted for us, but I could feel the heat of every seething glare burning at my back like a branding iron. It all but left a scorched taste in my mouth as I made my way into the Eternal Hall behind her.

"Oh, thank gods. I was afraid we'd be too late," Chrysa gasped as she ran over to walk beside me.

Wait—had she been the one to bring Curator Faera over?

Wow. I really owed her one this time.

Glancing over my shoulder, I caught a glimpse of Domitri's blue glow through the dispersing group of patrons and Vindexori, his heated scowl still focused squarely on me.

That is, until he noticed Chrysa at my side.

Rage twisted his features, warping them and making that blue aura around him flicker like heat waves off sun-roasted cobblestones. It put a knot in the pit of my stomach so tight my breath caught.

He must have guessed that Chrysa, his own prospect, was the one who'd helped me.

Again.

My mouth mashed and screwed up. I fought to keep my voice from shaking as I leaned over to whisper to her. "He saw you."

Chrysa's expression had gone foggy, as though all the energy and life had been drained out of her. She stared blankly ahead as she whispered back, "I know. It's okay."

It wasn't. We both knew that.

But what could I do?

What could anyone do?

Staring up at Curator Faera as she strode proudly ahead of us, shoulders back and head held high, a frantic hope lit in my mind like a lone candle in a stormy night. Maybe she would listen to us. Maybe she could help.

I dared to hope.

I had no idea if Faera was someone I could trust. Odds were, she had some sort of motive. A plot I'd never see coming.

But I was running out of options.

Options ... and time.

I waited until we were well out of earshot before I dared to say anything to her. Once we passed through the Eternal Hall, heading for the doorway to the auditorium where she was giving her daily lecture, I reached out to lightly tug on Curator Faera's sleeve.

"I-I, um, I appreciate you ... helping me back there," I stammered like a complete idiot.

She stopped abruptly, her yellow-green eyes as keen as an owl's as she glanced between Chrysa and me. Her mouth set in a tight, uncertain line as she let out a deep sigh. "Don't thank me just yet. I can't save you from every hostile word here, but I can assure you are following all the ridiculous rules they contrive for you."

I sagged some, weight sinking into my heels. I didn't have the guts to tell her that was a lot more than any other patron was willing to give me here. Well, other than Roxus, of course.

"I'll chaperone you today, as I promised Roxus I would. But I will also search for a third prospect to accompany you and Chrysa on your remaining lessons, as I've my own work to look after," she added quickly.

Chrysa and I swapped a dubious sideways look.

She really thought she could find *another* prospect willing to associate with *us*?

Well ... Fates help her.

Cause gods knew no one else would.

* * *

Gods, Fates, and all things holy.

Anyone but *him*.

As the few remaining prospects wandered out of the auditorium, Chrysa and I stopped side-by-side and stared at where Curator Faera was talking to an older boy.

The same one that had given me problems on my very first day here. The one who'd called me out during the combat assessment. The one who constantly whispered foul names at my back when he thought I couldn't see his stupid face snickering and grinning gleefully.

Only, he wasn't grinning or snickering now.

Standing at Curator Faera's lectern, I glared at him and wished, with all my heart, I had the ability to light him ablaze with just my eyeballs.

He glared right back, his arms folded over his chest, and his chin tilted upward with proud disgust.

I hated him. I hated his stupid dark hair cut short over his round human ears. I hated his beady little dark eyes that were a little too close together, and that pompous Damarian accent whenever he spoke.

Something about him reminded me of a vicious hamster. Stupid. Conniving. Just intelligent enough to be truly annoying, but it would still be socially frowned upon to murder him in cold blood.

My lip curled and it took everything I had not to storm from the room, new rules be cursed.

"Chrysa, Violet, I believe you know Varren. He's agreed to be the third member of your little group to ensure you stay out of trouble," Curator Faera announced. "I realize this is not an ideal situation for any of you, but let's try to make the most of it and endure. Soon, this will all be behind us and we can go our separate ways."

Her stiff, uncomfortable smile wasn't fooling me. She didn't seem to like this arrangement any more than we did.

But why, by all the gods, had she picked Varren?

And why had he agreed?

A bemused snort from Chrysa made the rest of us glance her way. She stood with her hips cocked and head tilted, staring him down with a smug half-grin. "This was the only way you could pass divine lore, wasn't it?"

You could have heard an evil hamster sneeze.

Varren puffed up, shoulders hunching and face flushing beet red.

Curator Faera raised a hand swiftly, hushing us before the fight even got started. "Now, now—yes, there are terms to his agreement to help. He will be given passing marks on the divine lore assessment. But this is a fair exchange, I believe, all things considered."

"And if he suddenly decides not to be helpful?" I asked.

"Then the offer is rescinded and he will take the final trial test along with the rest of you," she clarified.

I snorted and shook my head.

"He won't back out on us," Chrysa said, still sporting that wry grin.

I arched an eyebrow at her, wondering where she was getting all this confidence.

"He'd never pass the Avoran translations otherwise," she explained. "I've heard him *attempting* to practice in the library. He's terrible at it. This is his only shot at getting around the trial."

Varren's face had gone from red to a lovely eggplant purple. He worked his jaw from one side to the other, every angry word he wanted to yell practically sizzling in the air around him like a furious little thunderstorm.

To his credit, though, he managed to keep his stupid mouth shut.

"I'd advise all of you to keep the terms of this arrangement secret," Curator Faera warned, her tone weary with defeat. "Should news of it get back to Mistress Orvana, you'll likely all be expelled without question. Understood?"

Chrysa and I nodded.

Varren, after taking a few breaths through his wide nostrils like a raging bull, nodded, too.

And just like that, my fate was secured. Tethered to hope by a thin, frayed thread ... otherwise known as Varren.

But it was the only hope I had at the moment. It was the only thing keeping me from Domitri's vicious machinations.

For now, anyway.

And only as long as Varren managed to keep his big mouth shut.

TWENTY-NINE

Having Varren following Chrysa and me around was about as much fun as dragging a dead cow around behind us.

He refused to talk, offering only eye rolls and snorts to anything we said. I gave up coaxing him into conversation a lot faster than Chrysa did, though. I guess she was holding out hope he'd come around eventually—especially when she offered to tutor him in Avoran.

He didn't take the bait, though. Stubborn idiot.

Unfortunately, I needed him—needed his continued cooperation. For him to keep his word. But Varren wasn't an ally. He was a liability.

That thought alone made my blood run cold.

After three days, his resolve hadn't faltered, but he did seem less ... enthusiastically angry about the situation. The other prospects avoided him now, too. Whispers followed us down every corridor. The patrons and Vindexori stared at the three of us like they were watching a trio of dark spirits drift through the halls.

A typical day for us, really.

It seemed to rattle Varren, though, even if he didn't want to show it. He trudged along after us, lagging behind a few paces with his head down like he hoped no one would recognize him.

I felt a minuscule, *teeny* fragment of sympathy when he tried to sit next to some of the other prospects during Curator Faera's last official lecture, only to have them all quickly gather their things and move several seats away.

Ouch.

Varren sat alone, head down, and arms draped limply in his lap for the entire lesson. He didn't even bother taking notes this time. Since Curator Faera had agreed to pass him for his help in co-chaperoning me, he didn't really need to.

The class dragged on, and I found myself spending more time watching his private parade of misery than actually listening to anything Faera said. A mistake, probably. But at this point, a few extra hours of lecture probably wouldn't decide my fate when it came to her final trial exam. Either I knew the information at this point, or I didn't.

And I was reasonably sure I did.

"We will be having the final trial examination in five days," Curator Faera concluded. "If you should need any additional help, you may stop by my office in the morning hours. Best of luck to you all."

She motioned for everyone to go, her gaze panning the auditorium as everyone stood, murmuring and gathering their things. Then she stared straight at me and waved, gesturing for me to approach her lectern.

I swallowed.

Oh great. Had she noticed I wasn't paying attention? Or was this about something else? Something worse?

Dread stirred in my stomach, souring it like wine that had been left out in the heat far too long, and I slowly shoved all my things into my leather bag, before trudging down the steps toward her. Chrysa followed almost immediately, and Varren lagged around at the door, waiting and still within earshot.

"You two may wait outside," Faera insisted, looking at my companions as though silently daring them to push the issue. "Violet and I need to have a discussion."

"Is she in some kind of trouble?" Chrysa demanded, her tone already defensive.

Curator Faera's smile was not reassuring at all. Something about it seemed cold, distant, and almost worried. "Not at all. It's just that I don't like to discuss critiques of assignments publicly. Please, you can stand outside the door and wait. She'll be with you in a moment."

Gods—would I?

Based on that look, I couldn't tell.

But Curator Faera had always been reasonably kind to me. She'd come to my defense against Domitri, and she'd arranged this whole bargain with Varren. Surely she wouldn't try anything bad, right?

My heartbeat fluttered as I watched Chrysa and Varren leave, feeling the closing thud of the auditorium door behind them like a judge's gavel on my chest.

Only then did I dare to steal a glance up at Faera's face again.

Her expression was an utterly unreadable blank slate, like maybe she was lost deep in thought.

For a few painfully awkward seconds, we just stood in silence, both staring at the door on the far side of the empty sloping rows of desks. I could feel my pulse throbbing in my fingertips. My throat had gone dry and stiff.

But I didn't dare to move or make a sound. Not until she did.

At last, Curator Faera cleared her throat and straightened, turning slowly to face me. Her expression stayed tense, brow crinkled with strained uncertainty I still didn't understand.

Then she reached into the pocket of her robe and produced a pair of silver coins.

My stomach plummeted to the soles of my boots. All the blood seemed to drain away from my extremities, leaving me numb and cold as I stared at the two identical coins resting in her palm. The same size. The same sort of scuffed tarnish on the engraved details of a beautiful woman's profile.

Only one of them glowed faint blue.

"These are called stemma. They were a form of currency long ago, but more than that, they were signets of the wealth and power of specific households in the ancient world," she whispered, her gaze fixed unblinkingly on me.

I bit down hard, fighting to keep all the panic down. Don't think. Don't remember.

Don't hear his voice again.

"It's said that some of the stemma coins were forged by the first houses of the Avoran elves themselves, made from blessed metals, and infused with divine magic." Faera moved closer, still watching my every move—my smallest reaction.

"It's been theorized that these coins would still emanate magic, even thousands of years later."

I took a step back. My heart pounded so hard it made my head feel like it might burst or I'd start bleeding from the ears. But I couldn't look away.

My eyes stayed fixed on that coin—the one that glowed faintly.

"You can see it, can't you?" she pressed, her voice quivering with urgency. "You can see which one is real? And which is a forgery?"

Tears welled in my eyes. I took another step back, slowly shaking my head.

Her expression fell, despair and desperation skewing her fair features as she begged, "It's all right, Violet. Just tell me, please. Tell me what you see."

I didn't want to. I didn't know her. Not well enough to divulge something like this. What if it got me punished again? Or kicked out altogether?

I'd come so far. I couldn't throw it all away over a stupid glowing coin.

I couldn't be exiled again.

"I-I don't see anything," I muttered and turned my face away.

"I know that's not true," she countered. "You saw it before when I gave you my quill. I suspect you've seen it many times throughout your life. Maybe you thought it was nothing. Or perhaps you didn't realize that you were the only one who could see it. Gods, I bet there are hundreds of things in this place that still emanate ancient magic."

My mind spun, whirling frantically as I tried to think. To remember all the things I'd seen glow with that strange blue light since I'd been here.

The torches around Arx Eburna.

The mark on the secret door when Roxus had brought me here.

Domitri.

The quill.

The weird cube on Roxus's desk.

And now this.

I flinched as she took another step closer, putting the coins right in front of me. "I can't help you if you aren't honest with me."

"Why does it matter?" I snapped suddenly, fixing her with a glare of warning. "So what if I can see it? It ... it doesn't mean anything!"

"It means everything, Violet," she insisted. "You now know the history of your kin. How you were made as an army by the dark god Vescor, gifted to Zarexius, the Dire King, to carry out his campaign against the rest of the gods. The one your people call the Foul Father. But what you might not realize is that Zarexius himself was a mighty sorcerer, and Vescor granted him many boons of power."

"Y-you're saying this is something I got from him? That I'm related to the Foul Father?" My voice broke, faltering under the weight of that accusation.

"Perhaps," she said quietly. "You might be a very distant ancestor and could have inherited a lingering kernel of his power. It's certainly something we could look into. We could discover the truth together."

It couldn't be. There were so many clans of Viperi living all over the Southern Kingdoms, deep underground in the long-forgotten halls of ancient cities. I couldn't possibly be someone like that.

Unless ...

Unless I was.

And that was why the Brood Father had tested me. Why he had needed to know. Because such a thing—such a mighty gift—would overshadow his authority. I would be a closer kin to the Foul Father.

A more suitable ruler, worthy of ascending to his throne.

A rival he could not tolerate.

My gaze fell on that glowing coin, staring at the beautiful engraving of the elven woman's face, wreathed in lilies, and wearing a crown tipped with stars. A fragment of a lost empire.

Just like me.

My hand shook as I pointed to it, mouth mashing flat as I tried to keep my chin from trembling. "That one," I answered. "It glows blue."

Curator Faera gasped faintly. Her hands seemed to be trembling some, too, as she turned both coins over, revealing that the glowing one had the same face on the opposite side ... but the other had the symbol of the Zenith's Call.

A forgery.

"Gods and Fates," she breathed in awe. "Violet, I ... I believe you have the gift of runesight."

A swell of bitter cold chills took my body like the rushing pull of an ocean tide, dragging me under and tossing me recklessly. Runesight? What did that mean? Was it good? Bad?

Would it get me in trouble?

I guess Curator Faera could sense my confusion because she swiftly pocketed the coins and put her hands on my shoulders. She bent down, drawing me in close enough that she could look at me eye-to-eye. "It means you can see magical auras. This is a marvelous discovery. Make no mistake about that."

It did not feel very marvelous. Dangerous, more like it.

"It is certainly a trait that would be highly valued by the Zenith's Call. Gods, it might even seal your entry to the order regardless of how you perform on any other trials. But you must not tell anyone about this, Violet. Not yet. I've got a lot more research to do, and I want to be absolutely certain I've got my facts straight."

"Not even Roxus?" My stomach gave a fluttering flip.

She frowned slightly. "He doesn't know that you've seen things glowing?"

I hung my head a little. "I never told him. Or anyone. Not until now."

"Then, yes, you should tell him. But *only* him. Understand?" she said, giving my shoulders a gentle, reassuring shake. "I understand now why he chose you as a prospect. You're a very special girl. You're going to do great things in the Zenith's Call, Violet."

I wanted to believe that. More than anything, I wanted to know that I belonged here. That I had a place. A purpose.

A home.

I could see how this so-called ability could be a great boon for the Zenith's Call. And yet, I could also see the risks. It wasn't just a splendid divine gift. It was a tether to the most hated figures in history.

Evidence that I'd sprouted from the very root of all evil.

I had a hard time believing Mistress Orvana would be as thrilled and amazed when she found out. I had to step carefully—more so than ever before.

One wrong word and this could all end terribly.

But something else in the back of my mind still stung with worry, digging in like a thorn I couldn't pull out. A question I had to ask before I lost my nerve.

"What about Domitri?"

Faera blinked, brow knitting with confusion. "What about him?"

I rubbed at the back of my neck, not sure how to phrase this, or even if I should.

Too late now, though.

"What about him?" she repeated, that confusion quickly hardening to concern.

"He glows, too," I confessed.

Her eyes widened slightly. "What do you mean?"

"His whole body, but especially his face," I said.

Curator Faera opened her mouth, but a frantic scream ripped through the room so loudly it made us both jump.

A scream from beyond the door.

Chrysa's terrified, desperate scream.

THIRTY

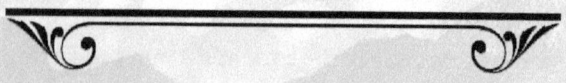

I'd never heard Chrysa scream like that.

For a split second, everything froze—my heart, my breath, my thoughts. Then, panic exploded in my chest, and I ran.

I didn't—couldn't—think. All I knew was she was in danger, and I couldn't lose her, too.

I bolted up the sloping stairs to the back of the auditorium and flung the door open wide.

On the other side, Varren all but fell against me. I guess he'd been standing there with his back pressed to the door. He cursed and spat as he floundered, his face plastered with a look of pasty horror.

But Chrysa was nowhere in sight.

I whirled on Varren immediately, letting him see every bit of fury crackling in my red eyes.

"Where is she?!" I snarled.

He put his hands up and stumbled back another step, bumping against Curator Faera as she joined us just outside the door.

"WHERE?" I yelled louder.

"I-I—" he stammered stupidly, glancing back and forth between us and the exit passage that led out of the Eternal Hall. "Her patron—he came for her. Yelled at her in some other language and smacked her a few times. Then he dragged her off that way."

Rage lit like a furnace in my chest. My breathing deepened and my hands curled into fists.

I'd kill him.

Patron or not, he wouldn't get away with it. Not again.

Not while I was around.

"He struck her?" Curator Faera gasped in horror.

Varren nodded frantically, almost like he was worried we wouldn't believe him. "Yeah, he ... he got her by the neck and pinned her to the wall. He was yelling at her, but I couldn't understand any of it."

"That insufferable beast," Faera hissed, flashing me a no-nonsense glare of warning.

Like she knew I was dancing right on the edge of losing all my sanity.

"You will both go to Krin'Moir and sit by the fountain and wait for me to return, do I make myself clear?" she commanded.

I couldn't hold back a scowl of defiance, tracing the points of my incisors with my tongue behind my lips. Stupid. This was stupid. I should be going with her. Chrysa was *my* friend!

"I mean it, Violet," she warned, her tone sharp as she thrust a finger toward the exit. "Trust me and do as I say. You know as well as I do that Mistress Orvana will grant you no mercy if you try to take this matter into your own hands. This is something for the elders to sort out, and believe me, we will. We will find Domitri and Chrysa and see this rectified."

She meant it.

I could hear it in her voice and see the steely determination written all over her face. Her ebony cheeks were flushed deeply, and her mouth was pinched into a tight, furious frown.

And she was right—I had no choice but to sit on my hands and let her sort this out. If I got involved, it would only make things worse. I always seemed to make things worse.

But, gods, I *hated* it.

I despised feeling useless, like my hands were tied and I was being forced to watch this disgusting charade from the sidelines.

It didn't help that, even if Faera meant well, I doubted any of the other patrons would care what happened to Chrysa. They hadn't before. So, why would that change now?

Wrath like a summer storm sizzled and boomed in my head as I followed Varren into Krin'Moir. I kept my head down, using my shoulder-length hair as a sort of curtain to hide my face as we passed into the cavernous chamber. The Vindexori glared at us, bristling at my presence, but saying nothing as we approached the gleaming stone fountain of the two dragons in the center of the room.

Plopping down on the ground at the base of it, I picked at the lacing on my boots and let my imagination run wild. It wasn't hard to picture every violent, agonizing thing I wanted to do to Domitri. It was a lot harder to think about what he might be doing to Chrysa, though.

I just prayed Curator Faera found them soon.

"I, uh, I'm sure they'll find her. And she'll be fine."

I looked up slowly and found Varren sitting a few feet away, his legs criss-crossed, and his head bowed low, too.

I narrowed my eyes. Seriously? He was talking to me now? He'd been dragging behind Chrysa and me for days without saying a single thing to either of us.

"Like they've helped her before? Don't be stupid. They won't do a thing to stop him. They never have. The mistress doesn't care what anyone does to us," I muttered bitterly. "And what do *you* care what happens to her, anyway?"

His head turned slightly, just enough I caught a glimpse of one dark eye glancing my way. "Well, I mean, she's not ... like you."

I snorted and rolled my eyes. What a waste of breath.

"Although ... I admit, neither of you are what I was expecting," he mumbled so low I could barely hear him.

"What? Not stirring cauldrons filled with our enemies' entrails?" I scoffed. "Or making sacrifices to the dark god and pledging our allegiance to the forces of evil?"

His brow rumpled with a flustered frown. "I never said you stirred cauldrons."

"Well, there's some fresh material for you to work with, then. You're welcome." I leaned forward to rest my elbows on my knees.

Minutes passed, and neither of us spoke. I lost myself in the constant rush of the cool waters sliding over the sculpted dragons. Each second seemed to douse the fire in my soul, leaving me chilled, damp, and small.

"Why do you want to be Zenith's Call, anyway?" Varren asked suddenly, his voice thick with frustration again. Like he'd been sitting over there stewing over that one question all this time.

"Why do you?" I deflected.

It wasn't like I owed him any answers.

"I saw Nar'Haleenan soldiers sack a temple to Eno in Mathros. They were drunk out of their minds. They dragged all the priestesses out, stripped them naked, beat them, and cut their hair. They burned their songbooks. It was disgusting." His frown deepened, putting a darkness in his eyes like the deep shadow of poisonous memory. "Then four men in black armor showed up out of nowhere. No one knew who they were—but the soldiers were terrified of them. They fled imme-diately and never came back."

I couldn't hold back a bemused smirk. "Vindexori."

He nodded slightly.

"Nice to hear of them doing something useful for once." I went back to fiddling with my bootlaces.

"Well?" Varren was staring at me now, those beady eyes prying into me like he was trying to read my mind. "What about you?"

"Nothing as dramatic as that," I deflected again.

"I would think it would have to be something pretty substantial."

Ugh. He wasn't going to let this go, was he?

Fine.

"Because I don't have anything else," I fumed, meeting his stare with a tiny fraction of the fire and cinder I'd been holding back all this time. "I don't have the luxury of choosing from a variety of noble professions. I can't be a baker. Or a seamstress. Or a fishmonger's wife. No one wants a Viperi serving them ale, washing their bed linens, or pruning their garden. According to everyone else, I'm only fit for two things in this world—slitting throats and breaking bones."

He drew back some, almost like he thought I might hit him.

Part of me wanted to, even if I knew it wouldn't do any good. The patrons had been trying to smack some sense into him for weeks without much progress.

"Unfortunately, I was born with an inconvenient dislike for injustice, which— as you can imagine—does not make me very popular with my own kin or anyone else in the criminal world. But that's not enough to make me tolerable to the rest of you folk, either," I went on, letting all the angry words spill out of me like rotten eggs from a basket.

Splat.

"So, here I am, trying to survive torment from idiots like you every day, all while hoping there's some light at the end of the putrid tunnel of my life." I sat, fully bristled, my chest heaving in quick, furious breaths.

Varren didn't move. With his eyes wide and mouth open, he just stared at me with all the intelligence of a pigeon looking at a bread crust.

"I'm not evil enough for my own kind. And I'm not good enough for yours," I finished, lowering my voice and looking away again. "But I'm willing to bet the Zenith's Call needs people in their ranks who aren't afraid to do the dirty work ... because those drunken soldiers don't always just turn tail and flee, do they? That means they need someone good at slitting throats, breaking bones, and not feeling bad about it later."

"You'd really do that?" he asked. "You'd kill Nar'Haleenan soldiers for attacking a temple?"

One corner of my mouth twisted upward into a menacing smirk. "If Roxus tells me to? Absolutely. With pleasure."

Varren made a sound, something like a sputtering suppressed chuckle. Weird. "*Pfft*. You're insane, you know that?"

"Don't be jealous because your left parry still sucks." I leaned back against the side of the fountain and stared up at the ceiling.

A few seconds later, he finally spoke up again. "Just my left parry? Or ... is there other stuff?"

"*So* much other stuff."

"Like what?"

"For starters, your footwork is incredibly sloppy. That's why you trip all over yourself."

"I have big feet," he protested, grumbling under his breath.

"Not big enough to make that excuse legitimate."

He crossed his arms and leaned back, too. "Fine. What else?"

"You take your eyes off your opponent to watch your own hands. Your weapon should be an extension of yourself. You don't need to stare at it."

"Well, what about—"

Varren didn't get a chance to finish that thought.

From across the chamber, Roxus's voice carried like a tolling bell, shouting my name.

I snapped to my feet immediately. My heartbeat pounded with wild hope as I ran to him.

Thank the gods—he was here. He could fix all this. He could find Chrysa.

He had to.

Roxus caught me as I rushed him, grasping my shoulders and holding me out at arm's length. He looked me over and spun me around, assessing for any signs of damage like someone inspecting a spring lamb.

"Are you all right?" he demanded, cutting a suspicious glare to Varren.

Varren, on the other hand, was doing his very best potato impression, staring at us with those wide, empty eyes like he wasn't sure why anyone would ever want to touch me on purpose.

Roxus's whole demeanor seemed to droop a little with what must have been relief when he saw I wasn't bruised or bleeding this time.

My whole head burned with embarrassment. I wriggled, trying to slip away with a little bit of my dignity intact. Gods, didn't he see everyone watching?

"I'm fine! But Chrysa is—"

"Faera told me what happened," he interrupted. "We're going home, right now. You don't need to be anywhere near this until we have a resolution."

I drew back and scowled. What? Seriously? But she was my friend! I had to be here when they found her!

"Don't give me that look," he scolded, keeping a hand on my shoulder and steering me toward the grand staircase. "Whatever madness has taken Domitri, I can't have you anywhere near it. Mistress Orvana will sort this out."

Oh. I seriously doubted that.

"And if she doesn't? If she turns another blind eye? You saw the state he left Chrysa in last time, and no one did a thing about it!" I seethed. "He'll do it again! You know he will!"

Roxus's jawline hardened, expression dimming fiercely as he urged me toward the exit. "I can't do anything to protect her—just you. *You* are my only concern."

"NO!" I screamed.

Well, it was more of a snarling screech of frustration. But it made the Vindexori guarding the doorways tense. Roxus's expression cooled, his grasp on my shoulder tightening and his brow locking into a deep, forbidding scowl.

"Do you take me for a fool? The eyes of the order are on you as we speak, so consider your next words carefully," he warned in a low, eerily calm voice. "Do you really think barging into Mistress Orvana's office and slinging accusations without any evidence is going to get you far?"

"Varren saw it happen," I fired back, pointing at where he still sat at the base of the fountain. "Is that not evidence?"

"Perhaps. And, believe me, I'll deal with him right after I'm sure you're safe," Roxus said. "But not a second before. So turn around and march, girl. The sooner I get you home, the sooner I can start sorting this mess out."

My mouth screwed up. My eyes stung. All I could do was glare back at my patron with my teeth clenched.

Gods, I hated it. That Chrysa was in trouble. That I hadn't been there to help her. That I had to hide away in my room and wait like a coward.

But most of all, I hated that Roxus was right.

I stole a glance over my shoulder, meeting Varren's confused frown where he still sat by the fountain.

It wasn't right. Curse it—it wasn't fair!

Curse him, he'd better help Roxus. He'd better tell the truth about what he saw. He'd better be the most helpful he'd ever been in his entire life.

Or I'd make sure he paid for it in *full*. Slowly. Painfully.

Viperi-style.

Even if it might cost me absolutely everything.

Roxus's hold on my shoulder tensed, as though he could sense my temper stoking hotter and hotter. My eyes welled as we neared the exit, and all I could think about was how I was failing her—Chrysa—again. Leaving her behind. Abandoning her.

My pulse boomed in my ears, drowning out everything else as we reached the door.

If I couldn't protect her, my best friend, then what good was I?

THIRTY-ONE

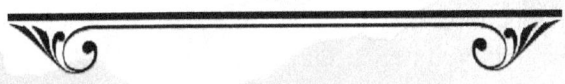

Gods, I hated secrets.

And now Roxus was sitting on them like a proud mother hen.

I hated waiting. I hated feeling useless. I hated not knowing what was happening or whether or not Chrysa was okay. She had no one else to help her. I was the only one who really understood what she had been through.

But what could I do?

The frustration boiled through my brain, sending wave after wave of sizzling energy through my body. My chest was sore from my pulse pounding so hard for so long. My feet were numb and my jaw ached from clenching my teeth against frustrated screams.

I didn't know how much more of this I could take.

Roxus was right—the more involved I got, the worse it would be for Chrysa. I was the reason Domitri had come after her in the first place. He had seen her in the crowd and probably quickly figured out she was behind Curator Faera's prompt interference on my behalf.

Once again, Chrysa had come to my defense to shield me from her own patron's wrath.

And once again, she would pay for it in blood and bruises. Maybe worse.

And what was I doing about it?

Nothing.

Sitting on my bed with my legs crossed and a heavy, leather-bound tome on ancient Nar'Haleenan temple structures spread out in my lap, I glared at the lines of tiny, faded ink. Gibb lay asleep, curled up like a big orange pastry roll on the pillow beside me. Close by—but just out of reach.

Stupid cat.

Even with him purring deeply near my head, I couldn't relax. I couldn't even think straight. My heart pounded in my ears, refusing to calm down, no matter how many chapters I read. My blood ran as hot as molten metal.

This couldn't go on forever.

It had been hours now. The sun was already setting, drawing long shadows across my bedroom floor. The evening breeze stirred in the drapes hanging over the balcony doorway, carrying in the faraway calls of seagulls and the soft scent of the sea.

The sudden sound of the front door opening and closing downstairs nearly made me fall off the bed. Flinging the old book aside, I bolted for the hallway and darted down the stairs. I was breathless and tripping over my own feet when I hit the bottom landing and found Roxus hanging up his old coat.

"Well?" I demanded, my heart beating out of my chest.

He didn't turn around. His head bowed some and his wide shoulders rose and fell, like he was taking in a deep breath to prepare himself.

Meanwhile, I couldn't breathe at all.

Talk, curse it! Say something!

"It seems Domitri and Chrysa are not in Arx Eburna," he replied at last, his tone soft and cautious. "He must have taken her somewhere in the city, but no one knows where else he might have established a private residence. We were all under the impression he lived solely on the temple grounds."

I took a few staggering steps closer, my legs wobbling as everything below my knees seemed to go numb. "What? You're sure? Did you search his chambers?"

Roxus finally turned to face me, his expression slack with exhaustion that deepened the creases in the corners of his eyes. He rubbed at his thickly stubbled chin as he lurched past me toward the sitting room, avoiding eye contact the whole way.

"Yes, Violet. We did a quick walkthrough of his apartment, just for safety measures," he said softly—carefully. Minding every word. "But we didn't toss the place looking for evidence. We've no right to invade his privacy like that, especially when nothing else in the place looked off."

I narrowed my eyes, critiquing every subtle change in his body language and expression as he settled into a cushion next to the fire pit and began stoking the coals with a long iron poker. I had to figure out if he was lying or dancing around the truth.

Gods, he was a hard man to read, even when he wasn't trying to be vague. His expression remained distant, the light in his gaze dim and overshadowed with deep thought.

"What about Chrysa's room? Did you look there?" I pressed.

He sighed and nodded.

I slowly sank down to sit on the cushion across the fire pit from him, my hands gripping my knees so tight my knuckles ached. "And? What *did* you find?"

"Well, we didn't find blood spatter on the walls, if that's what you're worried about," he dodged, still avoiding eye contact as he tossed a few more pieces of wood onto the fire. It sent a shower of little sparks up into the air between us.

I pursed my lips bitterly. Of course, they wouldn't find anything like that. Domitri was a vicious, conniving monster —but he obviously wasn't a stupid one.

Not the sort to leave obvious evidence lying around in the open.

Roxus made a noisy, grumbling sound and tilted his head back to look up at the ceiling as though praying for patience from some divine being. Then he *finally* looked me in the eye.

"A bed made with clean blankets. A trunk of folded clothes. Practice weapons on a rack by the door," he recalled. "She had a brush on the dressing table and a stack of books from the library. But that was it, Violet. Nothing about any of the things we found seemed off. If anything, it was far cleaner than I expected, given the state of your room."

He was one to talk. I'd seen what a wreck his office constantly was.

He was telling the truth, though.

I could see it written all over the hard-carved edges of his face.

But something about it—about the way his sharp brown eyes fixed so earnestly on mine—made my heartbeat skip and my hands go clammy. It felt off. Wrong.

Like trying to put a shoe on the wrong foot.

"Domitri's chambers were no different," he muttered and turned his focus back to the fire. "He lives in one of the patron houses in the temple grounds. It's a small apartment, so it's not like there was much there to look through in the first place. No wine cellars to stash bodies in. No staircases hidden behind bookshelves."

I chewed at the inside of my cheek, watching him more closely than ever. His jaw had gone tense, making a vein stand out in the side of his neck and a muscle feather in his cheek. I'd only ever seen him do that when he was supremely irritated.

Or when he was biting back words.

He was holding something in.

"What aren't you telling me?" I demanded before I could even think about it.

His expression emptied, going cold as he fixed me with another heavy stare that made a bolt of panic race up my spine.

"What aren't *you*?" he countered, his tone sharp and accusing.

I stiffened like he'd smacked me across the face. He might as well have. He had never used a tone like that with me before. Admonishing.

Accusing.

I was about to protest. To argue. Then it hit me—the obvious reason.

He'd been looking for Chrysa and Domitri, so that meant he'd probably run into Curator Faera. She might have let it slip or hinted that there was something I needed to tell him. Something I'd been hiding for a while now.

But ... how? How was I supposed to confess something this big?

My heart twisted in my chest like someone had seized it and was trying to rip it from me like prying a stubborn apple off a branch.

I sank lower in my seat, my spine seeming to turn to gooey mush under the weight of his gaze. Only the crackle and pop of the flames in the fire pit filled the tense silence as the warm light of the dancing flames flickered in his dark eyes.

"Roxus, I-I ... " my voice hung in my throat, caught in a thick tangle of emotion that made my vision blur and my chest feel tight.

I had to tell him. I knew that. But would it even matter now? Would he ever trust me again?

Or had I already ruined everything?

"Violet, I know that there are things in your past you haven't told me," he said suddenly, his tone soft and low. Comforting.

The Roxus I knew—the one who had found me in that putrid dog cage in the prison.

The one I trusted.

"I don't expect you to come out and tell me everything that's ever happened to you right away. Some of it you may never tell me, and that's fine. But when it comes to your safety or your place in the Zenith's Call, there are some things you *have* to tell me," he said firmly. "I can't advocate for you otherwise. Understand?"

I nodded slowly.

"So?" He arched an eyebrow expectantly.

"How much did she tell you?" I hedged. Better to test the waters first to see how deep I was in.

Now both eyebrows were up. "Who?"

Uh oh.

I sank down even lower, wishing I could just melt into the floor altogether. "You talked to Curator Faera, right?"

"No."

Crap.

I bowed my head and picked at my floor cushion's silky tasseled fringe. "I ... I didn't know until today. What it was, I mean. She said it's called runesight."

One of Roxus's eyes squinted ever so slightly. His jaw worked from one side to the other. But I couldn't tell what that skewed, almost twitchy look on his face meant. Was he angry? Frustrated? Confused?

"She said it means I can see magical auras. I-I wasn't quite sure what she meant, but ... but I was going to tell you! I swear! I just didn't know how." My mouth screwed up. I clenched my teeth so my stupid chin wouldn't tremble.

I wouldn't cry about this. No matter what. I'd done this to myself. Now, I'd take the consequences.

"And this is something you've been able to do the whole time?" he asked quietly.

I nodded again. "It only happened one other time before I came here. But everything here is so weird and different that I thought it was normal. I thought everyone could see it."

Roxus leaned forward some, his voice deepening gravely as he asked, "Who else knows about this?"

My mind raced, frantically trying to remember who else might have noticed. Had I ever mentioned it to Chrysa?

"I-I, um, I think only Curator Faera. She was the one who told me what it was. She wanted me to tell you as soon as possible."

His shoulders relaxed slightly, but the deep crinkle of concern between his eyes didn't smooth. Not a good sign.

"Chrysa?"

I shook my head—even if I wasn't completely sure.

"That Varren boy?"

I shook my head.

No. Definitely not. I hadn't even really spoken to him until today. We hadn't exactly swapped intimate secrets.

"Good. Tell no one else," he warned. "I mean, *no one*. None of the other patrons. None of the other prospects. Not the healer. Not even Delthene."

I stiffened, a cold chill climbing every inch of my spine. It stole the breath from my lungs and made my throat feel stiff and numb.

"Is it ... bad?" I rasped shakily.

Roxus studied me, his expression finally softening some. "Not yet. But we need to be careful."

"I'm sorry I didn't tell you sooner," I murmured, looking back down at the fringe of my cushion. I twisted the little silky tassels through my sweaty fingers again and again.

It didn't make me feel any better, though.

"It's okay," he said.

But it wasn't.

I could tell just by the way he poked fiercely at the fire, arranging the coals and sending little bursts of sparks into the air between us. That grim, discontented frown on his thin lips, and the way he kept rubbing at his neck, jaw, and chin, put all my nerves on edge. He was usually so hard to read.

And yet this had him *very* obviously worried.

"I smelled blood in Domitri's apartment," he growled suddenly. Bitterly. Like the words had slipped past all his better judgement.

Every little hair on my body stood on end. My pulse skipped sloppily, as though stumbling over his words in a mad, desperate sprint.

"W-what?" I stammered hoarsely.

"I couldn't find the source. I paced every room twice. No sign of it. Not a speck of dust out of place. But the smell was strong. Old. Like it had been there a while."

He bit each word angrily and glared into the crackling flames. Something about the way the glow rippled across his rugged features and his shaggy brown hair fell around his shoulders made him seem ancient.

It almost distracted me from the obvious.

"Wait—you can *smell* blood?" I blurted.

He wrinkled his nose a little and flashed me a small, secretive grin. "You're not the only one with a few tricks up your sleeve."

I stared at him, waiting for an explanation.

Normal humans didn't have that good of a sense of smell, did they? And he certainly didn't look like an elf. Or a dwarf. Rajinna had horns and tails, so that couldn't be it. Viperi always had red eyes—*always*—so there was no way he shared my own kin's blood.

So *what* was he?

"Don't strain yourself," he muttered. "It's not that important."

I crossed my arms. Maybe it wasn't to him—but it mattered to me. He knew almost everything about me now. And I still knew next to nothing about him.

So much for trust.

"My nose isn't what it used to be, but I can pick up on blood easily. I couldn't toss the place searching for it, though. Not with the Vindexori breathing down my neck," he continued. "Mistress Orvana will require more proof of foul play before she allows anyone to do that. But Domitri has not been himself for a good long while, and I'm not the only one who's noticed."

"Curator Faera said something like that, too," I recalled. "But what do you mean? He wasn't always this violent, or ... ?"

Roxus rubbed at the back of his neck, seeming to mull it over before he answered. "Before he turned up with Chrysa, Domitri was a private fellow. Dedicated to his work. He could be ornery, but he kept to himself and didn't cause a ruckus. I certainly never saw him raise a hand against anyone in the order, let alone a prospect. He wasn't that sort and preferred books to blades ... and people, for that matter. We were shocked he had even taken a prospect on in the first place."

"So what changed?" I asked, hanging on his every word with my heart pounding like mad. This was more than anyone had ever told me about Domitri. Maybe I could figure out why he hated me so much.

Er, well, apart from the obvious issue of me being Viperi.

Roxus's mouth quirked to one side thoughtfully. "He went on a mission into some uncharted temple grounds to the west months ago, and when he returned ... "

"What?" I urged. Gods and Fates, it was irritating when he just trialed off like that. I needed answers!

Roxus scratched at the top of his head, tousling up his thick, wavy hair as he sighed deeply. "It's not for you to worry about. I've already told you too much," he said at last. "Go on and see if Delthene needs help with dinner."

I scowled, clicking my teeth a few times as I tasted every angry word I wanted to scream, burning like cinders in my throat.

He was shutting me out? Now?! This was *everything* I needed to worry about!

AUGH!

I snapped upright, pounding my feet into the worn, creaking floorboards as I stormed out of the room and back upstairs.

Stupid—it was stupid! I had every right to know.

And gods only knew what Domitri was doing to Chrysa right this second.

But, no, Roxus wanted me to stand around cooking? Trusting that it would all just work out?

I slammed the door to my room so hard that Gibb jumped up, his back arched and tail puffed. He hissed as I marched past him, whipping the doors to my armoire open wide. My chest heaved in hard, fast breaths that made my vision spot. I could still see it hanging there, though.

The beautiful black leather ensemble that had been crafted especially for me.

I had no choice.

I had to do this.

I ran my fingers over the beautifully embroidered sleeve, tongue tracing the point of my incisors at the same time.

It was reckless and foolish—but I had no other choice. Chrysa had put herself at risk twice on my account. If I didn't return the favor, then what good was I?

No better than scum like Sulam and Domitri.

And I would *not* be like them.

Maybe I was nothing more than a filthy Viperi, with the blood of a thousand murderers running through my wicked veins. But I would give everything I had to help her get free of Domitri once and for all.

THIRTY-TWO

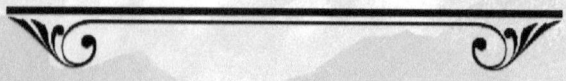

Wicked, secret, dangerous things always required the cover of darkness.

That was why I had to wait until late in the night, when the house fell quiet and I knew Roxus was gone and Delthene was sound asleep, before I dared to slip out of bed.

My bare feet hit the worn wooden floor without a sound, and I picked my way carefully across the room. Already dressed for the occasion, I had been extra careful to hide my beautiful, oil-black leathers under the thick, downy blankets when Delthene came in to wish me goodnight. All I needed were my boots and weapons.

Er, and no small amount of luck.

I pulled my boots on and laced them quickly, then picked up a small dagger from where I'd hidden it under the edge of my mattress. I didn't have any substantial weapons, but I had managed to get my hands on a small silver dagger—something I'd found in the pocket of Roxus's old coat after dinner.

It was hardly bigger than a letter opener, honestly. I'd just have to make do.

Hopefully, I wouldn't even need it.

After all, my primary goal was to free Chrysa. Fighting was secondary, and if I was careful, I could avoid it altogether.

I'd start with searching Domitri's quarters myself for evidence. Maybe Roxus wasn't willing to risk anyone's anger by "tossing the place," but I was. That might be the only way to find any real clues about where he might have taken her.

Pulling my long black cloak off the back of the chair beside my bed, I fastened it around my shoulders and pulled the hood down low.

Time to go.

I ducked through the balcony doors and closed them gently behind me, taking a few slow, steadying breaths before leaning over the edge of the railing. Three floors up. Roughly forty feet high. Enough to make my knees a little weak. My stomach swirled and fluttered, and my heart quaked deep in my chest.

No time to get nervous, though.

Chrysa was counting on me.

My balcony hung from the far side of the house, almost out of sight from the main road. Going down here would be a safe bet for climbing down, but I couldn't afford to get caught right outside the front door.

I set my jaw and turned around, looking up toward the roof. A lot of the houses and buildings in Rienka had rooftop gardens, and Roxus's was no exception.

I'd start there.

With an angled leap off the railing, I caught the eaves of the roof and easily hoisted myself up. I crawled carefully over the roof's stone railing, ducking into the cover of the potted palms, ferns, and little fruit trees Delthene loved to prune. She loved having tea here in the afternoons, and I'd spent enough time with her to know that our roof was only six or seven feet from the neighbor's terrace.

Close enough that she sometimes chatted with their housekeeper while she sipped at her favorite sweet jasmine tea.

Only ... the neighbor's house was a level shorter.

An easy jump, even for me.

I didn't even need a running start and sprang from the railing to the neighbor's garden like a flying squirrel. I landed and kicked into a roll, absorbing the impact and keeping low in case anyone heard the impact of my landing. Then I froze—waiting. Heart pounding. Cold prickling shivers running from my feet up my legs from the impact.

Seconds passed. Then a minute.

No noise. No rush of footsteps or voices coming to investigate.

Perfect.

I stood and went straight to the edge of the garden, making another tactical jump to a lower balcony on the far side of their house. From there, it was an easy descent to the street, and I landed in a low crouch behind a line of ornamental shrubs. Not even the snap of a twig.

I took the backroads and darkened side streets all the way to the temple grounds, moving like a wisp of shadow through the night. I knew every stretch of path to the entrance to the lavish, terraced gardens of Arx Eburna. Getting to it wouldn't be hard. I'd walked it with Roxus more times than I could count now.

But once I got inside?

Yeah. That would be the challenge.

Roxus had mentioned that Domitri lived in one of the patron apartments within the temple grounds. I'd seen them in passing, of course, and while getting inside them wouldn't be difficult ... getting inside them unseen and finding Domitri's specific door might be.

Then there was another problem—a more recent one.

Ever since the last attempt on the vault, Mistress Orvana

had tightened security considerably. Vindexori prowled the temple inside and out at all hours of the day and night. They were well-trained and organized. Also decent in a fight, as long as their opponents weren't Viperi.

Fortunately, they were also predictable, and I'd been watching them do patrols since I'd first arrived here. Chrysa had always enjoyed it when we took our lunch breaks outside in the gardens. She liked the trees and warm island sunlight. It was a lot different from her homeland, apparently.

And even more different than the inside of a Tibran ship.

I stalked through the night, keeping low and fast, blending into the shadows whenever the heavy thud of footfalls or clunking of armor grew too close. The streets were all but empty, with only a few figures lumbering down the sidewalks at this hour. Probably drunken dock workers staggering their way home.

Nothing noteworthy.

But the closer I got to the temple, the more my pace slowed. The more I marked the faces I spotted meandering the streets, just in case I saw someone I recognized from Arx Eburna. I couldn't afford to get sloppy now.

The streets gave way to the pristine manicured gardens of the temple grounds at the very crest of the hill. Here, the wind was stronger, blowing in from all sides of the island. It carried the muted fragrance of the flowers growing throughout the temple grounds and the faint flavor of sea spray.

I hesitated at the threshold, bathed in the sterling wash of a moon that stared down over me like a lidless silver eye. Somehow, it felt like the stare of that gleaming white-silver orb penetrated every part of me. Like it saw through my flesh down deep to my shriveled, black, blood-thirsty heart.

I licked my teeth again, testing the points of my sharp incisors with the tip of my tongue. Viperi teeth. Fangs leftover from our days as demons, some said.

Right now, I sort of wished that were true. If I'd been half-demon, I might have had some more useful tricks up my sleeve —something better than a tiny little dagger and a fool's hope.

My heart pounded slow and fierce, making my fingertips throb as I prowled down a line of hedges on the border of the temple's first terrace. Surveying the sprawling gardens, bathed in a mixture of warm golden torchlight and the streaming silver from the moon, I picked out a path forward and searched for my final goal.

My eyes narrowed. There it was.

Two terraces up, standing right amidst the towering pillars and marble sculptures of the gods, the patron apartment buildings were far more understated than the rest of the temple grounds. They might as well have been dormitories, as far as I'd heard, with each of the three-level buildings boasting about ten separate dwellings each. Plenty of room for any Zenith's Call who preferred to live close by.

Well, except for the Vindexori. They were required to live in barracks in the cavernous depths of Arx Eburna itself.

Thank the gods I wasn't trying to break in down there. It would've been nearly impossible.

Shifting my weight to balance on the toes of my boots, I watched a pair of Vindexori guards stroll by, armed to the teeth with crossbows and short swords. They passed my little hiding spot amidst the bushes, and I held my breath until they'd strolled several yards away.

Whew.

Fixing my gaze on the apartment buildings, I finalized my plan. Square and unassuming, the sides of each building were lined with windows and small, modest balconies that looked out across the temple grounds. Nothing grand, but climbable in a pinch.

I'd have to try it.

There were only two main entrances leading in and out of

each building, and both would likely be guarded. Maybe even locked. I would be hard-pressed to take out any of the guards without the others being alerted to the disturbance of an attack or my attempt at lockpicking. Not with so many of them on the grounds.

That just left one option.

The rooftop gardens again.

I narrowed my eyes on the nearest of the buildings. Two terraces meant I'd be ducking at least five, maybe six, patrols of Vindexori.

Curse it.

But I had no choice. Better make it fast.

I coiled my legs, flexing my fingers, and switching over to my heat-vision with a hard blink. I could do this. Fast and clean. Make as straight a path to the nearest apartment building as possible, get to the roof, and start searching for Domitri's place befo—

A powerful hand slammed onto the back of my neck, scuffing me like a puppy, as a second clamped down over my mouth.

"Do. Not. Scream," a low, growling voice murmured right against my ear.

My body went completely stiff in terror, my heart seeming to freeze mid-thump. Adrenaline poured into my veins, stilling all my senses and making my blood rush. I bit down hard on the hand over my mouth, digging my fangs into thick, callused fingers.

The figure grappling me growled low, a humming, rumbling sound against my ear like a roll of thunder.

But he didn't let go.

Gods and Fates ... it wasn't possible! Had the Vindexori found me already? Or was it Roxus? And how?!

Tears of reckless fury blurred my vision. My throat burned

like I'd swallowed sour wine, and I couldn't stop my shoulders from shaking as I bit down harder.

"Stop that," the man's voice warned. "Fates, you're such a menace."

Wait—I knew that voice, didn't I?

"I'm not gonna ask what you're doing out here, and don't you dare tell me. Plausible deniability. But you should know, if I spotted you this easily, you're not doing a great job of being sneaky, girl."

I released the hand from my bite and whipped my head around, scowling into the darkness behind me.

Declan frowned back, his big form curled close enough to me that I caught the scent of his sweat.

Sweat ... and blood. And not from where I'd just bitten him like a feral cat.

I didn't need my heat-vision to make out the deep bruising on his strong jaw or the fresh split in his impressively swollen bottom lip. No wonder I hadn't recognized his voice at first. He looked like he'd taken several hard hits to the face and neck that must have made his speech rougher than usual.

He looked down at the two fresh, bleeding holes in his pointer finger in dismay, then cast me an accusing scowl. "You *bit* me," he fumed quietly, like he couldn't believe it.

"You snuck up on me," I hissed back.

"That doesn't mean you get to bite me like a rabid raccoon."

"What are you even doing here?" I demanded in a whisper.

His frown deepened, putting an angry little crease right between his eyebrows. "You're asking *me* that? Seriously?"

I narrowed my eyes, holding his unrelenting glare. Unlike Roxus, Declan's expressions had gotten infinitely easier to read. And that little furrow in his brow wasn't suspicion. Or even accusation.

It was ... exasperation.

And pure, unfiltered stubbornness that could rival the gods.

Ugh. Fine.

"It's a long story," I seethed quietly, turning my gaze back out across the temple grounds. "I can't tell you more than that. Not right now. Just trust me—I have to do this."

He didn't let it go. Not that easily.

"Have to do what?"

I bit down hard, steeling myself for that rush of anxiety that prickled all through my chest. Uncertainty. Dread.

Gods, what was I even doing here? If I got caught, they'd kill me. Butcher me like an animal right on the temple steps.

"I need to get into one of those buildings over there," I whispered, motioning to the patron apartments in the distance.

Declan peered over my head, his bruised, bleeding mouth quirking to one side in a thoughtful gesture that must have hurt. Whoever he had faced in the pit tonight had really done a number on him.

"Which one?" he asked.

My shoulders drew up slightly. "I'm not sure. I thought I'd start with the closest one. I ... I have to find Domitri's apartment."

He rolled his eyes as he sank back down into our now shared hiding spot. "See, this is why Zenith's Call doesn't do this kind of stuff alone. You'll spend all night going from door to door, you dolt."

I wrinkled my nose and showed him a particular finger of my own.

He didn't retort, though. Not about my gesture, anyway.

"I knew when I spotted you slinking down the street you were up to no good. Fates, I had no idea you were out to ruin your whole life tonight," he murmured, wringing his hand through his shaggy hair. His knuckles were swollen, split, and bleeding, too.

"Only if I get caught," I countered sharply.

He made a sound somewhere between a snort and a chuckle.

With a weighty sigh, he stood and brushed off the seat of his pants. "Follow me in, but keep hidden. I'll figure it out."

My pulse skipped, and I couldn't stop my eyes from widening.

"You're ... helping me?" I squeaked.

"Oh, make no mistake, girlie. This is not charity. You owe me *big time*." His tone was ominous.

"What are you going to do?" Part of me knew I shouldn't ask.

Like he said—plausible deniability.

"Oh, you know, something stupid, as usual," he grumbled as he stomped out of the shrubbery and into the winding path that led up to the first terrace. "After this, I'll have to lie low for a little while, so don't come looking for me. I don't want this traced back—the last thing I need is Sulam questioning my loyalties."

I nodded slowly, wondering just how closely Sulam did watch him. Did he track all his movements? Spy on his relationships? Did he know that Declan came to train with me? Or had Declan come up with some lie to cover for it?

Now wasn't the time to dive into that, though. One crisis at a time.

I sucked in a deep, shaky breath. Gods help us.

Declan's sweat-drenched tunic clung to his skin, betraying the way every thick muscle in his back and shoulders rippled as he rolled his head from one side to the other, stretching his neck. Impressive. I couldn't help but admire him some, rising in the moonlight to tower over me like a column of battle-hardened muscle.

Then he flicked me one last, meaningful glare over his shoulder and forged forward.

Straight into the temple grounds ...

Yelling and waving his arms like an absolute maniac.

My jaw dropped. My pulse took off frantically as heat flushed through my cheeks, and I sank lower into the bushes. Sweet holy gods above. Had he lost his mind? What in all the abyss was he doing?!

It didn't take ten seconds for the Vindexori to descend upon him like a pack of wolves, encircling him with their hands on their weapons at the front of the second terrace. Declan shouted at them, still waving his arms and making a scene. His size and battered, bloody state must have been enough to give them pause, however, because they didn't shoot him on sight.

A minor miracle I'd have to remember to thank the gods for later. I honestly hadn't planned on murdering any Vindexori tonight, but a startling jolt of fury sizzled in my chest when I realized ... if I had to, for his sake, I'd burn this whole place to the ground and kill every Vindexori in it.

Oh no.

Gods. First Chrysa. Now him.

I really was going soft.

A few temple priests hurried over next, confused and flustered when they saw Declan raving and covered in fresh wounds like a madman.

"That worm-eaten scoundrel had me *ROBBED*!" Declan's voice boomed suddenly. "You go and ask him. Better yet, bring the sorry sack out here to face me like a man!"

"Who?" One of the priests glanced around, utterly bewildered. "Fates preserve us, what are you on about? This is a holy place! And it's the middle of the night!"

"Weren't any of you listening?!" Declan shouted, his arms still waving like stockings blowing on a clothesline. "It was

Domitri! He actually thought I wouldn't know he was the one who sent those thugs! HAH! Now drag him out here—and tell him to bring all my coin with him!"

I dropped my head down, putting my face in my hands.

Gods above—*this* was his plan?

I was totally doomed.

"Now then, everyone, just calm down! We'll sort this out," an elder priest huffed. "Domitri isn't here. We've been searching for him, but—"

"I thought he just returned?" another, much younger priest spoke up. "I saw him leaving Mistress Orvana's office not ten minutes ago. They must have found him, although I'm not sure where or how. He looked rather angry, so I did not stop to ask."

My stomach dropped.

What? They ... They had found him? Here in Arx Eburna?

But that—how? When?!

How could he just come and go like a wisp of smoke without anyone noticing? And what about Chrysa? Was she still missing?

It didn't make any sense. My hands clenched hard, nails digging into my palms as I listened.

The elder priest blinked in shock, glancing between Declan and his holy cohorts. "He's been found? What of the girl? Wasn't his young prospect missing, as well? Curator Faera was quite earnest about finding her."

The young priest shrugged. "I did not see her. Perhaps that is what Mistress Orvana intended to speak to him about?"

Heat tingled over my skin.

Missing—Chrysa was still missing.

The elder priest puffed an annoyed sigh that made his lips flap, as though this entire debacle was beneath him. "Go and fetch him, then. Check his quarters first, and do it quickly.

We've sacred rites to conduct at dawn, and I've no interest in spending the night out here arguing with drunken vagrants," he said, shaking his head and waving a hand to a Vindexori standing nearby.

Two of the black-clad guards stalked off, making their way toward the middle of the patron apartment buildings.

My eyes nearly rolled right out of my head. My heartbeat skipped, and I clenched my fists so hard my nails dug into my palms.

It was ... actually working.

I had to follow—now.

Stalking through the night, I made sure to keep hidden by the tall bushes or in the deep shadows of the statues and buildings as I tailed the two Vindexori all the way to the door. Cold sweat drizzled down my neck as I stood, waiting for them to open the door and step inside. Out of sight.

My only chance.

As the door began swinging shut behind them, I stole one last glance at Declan before I dared to dart forward, sprinting for the closing gap.

He was still raving and waving his arms, standing in the middle of the guards and priests like a big, angry, blood-spattered giant.

All the distraction a girl could ever hope for.

Fates, I really did owe him.

I swept through the doorway without so much as a rustle of fabric and immediately dropped low into a crouch in the heavy shadows within the apartment building's narrow foyer.

The door clicked shut.

The two Vindexori guards prowled onward, never looking back.

Perfect.

All the wind seemed to rush out of me at once, making my vision flicker with winking bright spots for a moment.

Breathe—I just had to breathe. Think. Focus.

But I couldn't. My thoughts churned as my pulse clashed like cymbals in my ears. The drain of adrenaline left me feeling cold and queasy, and I leaned back heavily against the wall to steady myself.

Shutting my eyes tightly, I pulled at all the stray threads of my thoughts. My self-control. My sanity. I had to weave them all back into place, one thread—one second—at a time.

When I opened my eyes, I could hear myself think. More than that, I could hear the movements of the Vindexori. I bit down hard, focusing forward as their footsteps retreated up the staircase at the far end of the foyer.

Now, I just had to follow them to Domitri's front door ... and pray no one noticed me. Gods only knew what would happen if the Vindexori realized I was following them.

Something far worse than dismissal from the trials.

A fate not even Roxus would be able to save me from.

I shut my eyes tightly, forcing all the Viperi curses that screamed inside my head like a flock of angry crows to finally go quiet.

Focus. Breathe.

Chrysa was counting on me. I was in far too deep to second-guess myself now. Forward was the only way out. Evidence against Domitri was the only thing that might save me if I was discovered.

So I sprang from the shadows and ran for the stairs.

THIRTY-THREE

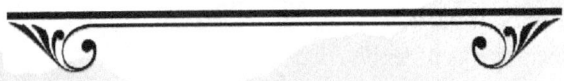

I couldn't breathe.

Not when the Vindexori might hear.

Following scarcely ten paces behind the two fully armored guards, I moved like a shadow stretched far behind them, silently following their every step.

I couldn't risk making any noise. No wrong steps. No rustles of fabric or even the smallest gasp. Nothing but absolute perfection.

I had become the dark, letting it permeate through me straight down to my soul. My senses were awake, drawn as taut as spider's silk so that I felt every slight sound, every flinch of the floorboards beneath my feet or murmured word, like a vibration on my skin.

The Vindexori murmured to one another, stomping their way up two flights of stairs and down a long, dimly lit hall on the right. I kept going up, though. Darting across the landing, I stopped at the second step going up with my back pressed to the wall. My muscles burned, flexing and releasing with swells of adrenaline as I slowly slid down the wall, sinking low into a crouch.

My tongue writhed in my mouth, feeling dry as I traced my pointed teeth and leaned slowly to the side—just far enough to peer around into the gloom with one eye. A glimpse was all I needed.

They stopped at the fourth door on the left and knocked. The rap of armored knuckles off wood cracked through me, making my pulse swell.

The floor shuddered faintly under my toes as the door whipped open suddenly.

I froze.

A harsh voice hissed in the dark—one I recognized immediately. It made every hair on my body prickle at once.

Domitri. Fates, it really was him.

He was here.

"What is the meaning of this? Do you have any idea what time it is?" he seethed furiously.

The Vindexori guards stammered through an explanation, urging him to come down into the temple gardens to address a "large, angry man covered in blood."

I smirked in spite of myself.

Domitri spat a string of curses.

Fabric rustled. A door shut and the telltale metallic clatter of keys clinked. Then the footsteps approached. Three heavy figures striding closer and closer.

I whipped back into my hiding spot, slipping silently a few more steps up toward the next floor and holding perfectly still. I watched as Domitri and the two Vindexori passed just a few yards away, hurrying back downstairs.

They didn't even glance my way.

As soon as I heard the main door open and shut, I moved like a wisp of pure night, prowling to the door and dropping into another low crouch. I slipped the dagger from my belt and worked at the lock. The Fates must have smiled on me, or merely enjoyed watching me flail, because the lock gave easily. I hesitated.

Too easily?

My pulse thundered in my ears. Surely he wouldn't trap his own door, would he?

I didn't know.

And it was far too late to stop now. Not when I was this close. Chrysa, gods curse it, she might be right on the other side of this door. Even if nothing had happened, even if she was perfectly fine, I still needed to see her with my own eyes. I needed to be sure she was okay.

I studied the ghostly orange glow of Domitri's handprint still glowing on the metal knob. The imprint of his body heat still lingered there.

Whatever happened down below in the gardens, it likely wouldn't last long. I had to do this fast.

Sliding the blade back into my belt, I slowly twisted the knob and pressed the door open. It swung in without so much as a creak or groan. Good.

I only opened it as far as I needed to slip inside, then shut and locked the door behind me with a simple twist of the bolt. No need to give myself away immediately if Domitri came back sooner than expected.

I turned, my night vision sweeping the small sitting room. No lamps burned, although the coals in the fire pit off to the right glowed with radiant heat-light. It bloomed bright before my eyes, revealing the shapes of furniture and two doorways leading off on opposite ends of the room.

Fast—I had to be fast.

My senses stretched out to the corners of the space as my breathing slowed. My lungs opened to the close, stagnant air, as though no one had opened a window in quite some time.

Hmmm.

Where was the smell Roxus had mentioned? The reek of blood? I couldn't detect it at all.

Gods, was his nose *that* much better than mine?

I frowned to myself.

He really wasn't human, was he?

I went for the doorway on the left first, finding a modest kitchen area and a window that let in streams of moonlight from outside. Not a plate out of place, though. No dishes in the small porcelain sink. But also no traces of food anywhere. Odd.

He had to eat, didn't he? So where did he keep his food?

I almost missed it.

One casual glance to that closed window, and the moonlight sparkled off something lining the sill.

Nails.

Many of them.

He had nailed his windows shut?

My jaw tightened. My stomach fluttered. I couldn't think of a single good reason to do something like that unless you were trying to keep someone from escaping.

I looked around a little more, but other than a small washroom that looked similarly untouched, there wasn't much on that end of the apartment. No evidence of washing blood away. No evidence of blood at all.

Until I stepped into the narrow hallway on the opposite end of the apartment.

It hit me so suddenly, my eyes watered—the stench of old, rotting blood. Of rot.

Of carrion.

There wasn't an urchin crawling the gutters of this city that wouldn't know that smell.

But where, by all the gods, was it coming from?

Unlike Roxus, I didn't have a pair of Vindexori breathing

down my neck, watching my every move. I had to be fast, but I could be thorough.

I checked the first door I came to and found it unlocked. Inside, the simple room seemed to be laid out just as Roxus had described earlier. Definitely suited for Chrysa.

The trunk at the foot of the bed had changes of her clothes folded neatly inside, and their musty smell suggested no one had worn them in a long time. There were brushes and combs on the dressing table, and a few books on her night-stand about the Foregods and Avoran enchanting, but nothing personal.

And no blood.

I looked under the bed and found a spare pair of boots. There was also a small box with three simple glass vials with cork stoppers inside. A quick whiff of the sickly sweet contents made my lip curl—healing tonics. Not unlike the ones Leruna had given me.

And these were very condensed. More potent.

One of the bottles was nearly empty, with only a swallow's worth left inside.

Hmm.

I quickly put them back, my mind churning as I gave the room one last, long look. Something felt off about the entire space. Roxus was right. There were no personal touches. Nothing that made it specifically Chrysa's.

I couldn't recall Chrysa wearing any of the clothes in that trunk. But, then again, I'd never paid all that much attention to what anyone else wore. Even the books were fairly generic— material we all had to study as prospects. Studies on Avoran magic, history, and divine lore.

It could have been anyone's room.

Was it ... staged? Simply made to look like this was where she lived?

I couldn't shake that nagging suspicion as I dashed into the next room.

Instantly, every muscle in my body locked up solid as the smell hit me like a punch to the jaw.

Blood.

The stench hung like a fog of rot in the air, so strong my eyes welled, and I bit back the urge to gag.

This—*this* was where it was coming from, somewhere in this room.

Domitri's room.

It was bigger than Chrysa's. Much bigger. A four-post bed stood against one wall, with bedsheets rumpled and still faintly glowing with warmth. He'd been lying there when the Vindexori knocked.

Gods, how could anyone bear to sleep in here with it reeking so badly?

I moved deeper into the room, studying every detail. The windows were nailed shut here, as well. An especially large nail had been hammered into the lock on the only door leading out onto the small balcony, jamming it. Over the top, I noted that a long curtain rod held only the torn remnants of a curtain, as though someone had snatched it down in a hurry and left only a few torn bits behind on the wooden rings.

But there was no sign of the curtain anywhere.

The armoire had normal clothes inside, but smelled incredibly stale. Untouched for a long time. Just like the clothes in Chrysa's room.

A fine layer of dust had settled over every flat surface, from the dressing table to the bookshelf packed tight with more historic, leather-bound volumes. A small writing desk was piled with scrolls and stacks of parchment, most blank, and all covered in that same thick layer of dust. The ink pot had been left open so long it had dried out with the quill still perched in it.

If I hadn't known better, I would have said this place had been abandoned for a long time. Sealed off and left to decay.

But Domitri had been in here mere minutes ago.

And that stench of blood ...

I paced toward the bed, surveying it with my lip curled. I could faintly see the outline of where he'd been lying still glowing dull orange. He was staying here, clearly. But not eating in the kitchen. Not using the washroom, not opening windows, touching any of his books, or writing anything at his desk.

And where was Chrysa?

None of it made sense. I was missing something.

Something big.

I could feel it like a hard knot of cold iron lodged in the pit of my stomach.

I stood in the middle of his bedroom, slowly scanning every corner as I turned in a circle. What was it? What was out of place? What didn't belong?

And where was that gods-awful smell coming from?

The doorknob rattled in the sitting room.

Every muscle in my body went as solid as stone. My heartbeat thrashed to a frantic halt.

Oh gods.

Domitri was back—he was unlocking the door!

Hide. I had to hide.

Right now.

Without thinking, I dove under the bed. It wasn't as tall as mine, but still high enough off the ground that I could wriggle beneath it without making much noise. I had scarcely managed to drag myself into the heavy dark beneath it when I heard the front door open.

Footsteps moved in the next room, crossing the space.

Coming straight for me.

A voice muttered bitterly, hissing furious words through clenched teeth in a language I didn't recognize.

Not Rienkan. Not Avoran.

But definitely Domitri's voice.

I held perfectly still, holding my breath as I lay on my stomach, feeling every flinch in the floorboards under my body as he paced the room and muttered to himself in that strange language. My heart pounded, slow and hard against my ribs.

The smell—holy gods, it was so much worse now. Stinging my eyes and forcing bile up in the back of my throat. I moved to clap a hand over my nose and mouth.

And then I felt it.

Something cold, wet, and sticky slowly seeping through my leathers.

A puddle beneath me.

It was on my hands and now smeared on my face.

I shakily drew back my hand, trying to wipe it off. But it just smeared more. Gods, what was it?

Light bloomed through the room as though he were lighting lamps.

I could see his boots move to the bedside and pause. I prayed to whatever god might actually hear a Viperi and have pity on me that Domitri would leave again.

He didn't.

He hissed and spat furiously. Then the bed above me flinched, and I saw the backs of his legs. He was sitting on the edge of the bed directly in front of me.

My breath snagged in my throat.

Every muscle in my body clenched at once.

And then I saw it.

The weak light of the lamps fell over my hand, revealing the smeared goo of old, congealed blood. Thick like jelly and putrid, caked all between my fingers. On my face. In my hair. Coating my clothes.

I was lying in a huge puddle of it.

Panic screeched wildly through my brain. The urge to pitch wildly, to writhe free of my hiding place and try to get it off.

But I couldn't. I couldn't move. I couldn't scream.

My eyes welled as I bit down hard against the urge to vomit.

Still—I had to stay still. Control that blinding hurricane of terror. Breathe slowly, carefully. Think. I was down here, and there was blood everywhere.

Why?

Rolling my head to the side, I peered around under the bed and found the source of it. By the weak light ebbing in from the lamps, I could see the shape of something large and dark lying in the largest part of the dark, gooey puddle.

A big, rolled-up pile of dark fabric.

The curtain?

It had to be.

My stomach bound up in sharp, twisting knots as I spotted a pale hand clenched in a fist peeking out from one corner of the fabric. The hair on the knuckles and wide fingers made it seem masculine, and I didn't need to see the rest of the body to know that whoever had been wrapped up in that curtain had been dead for a good long time.

The hand was already decomposing.

But why was it clenched like that?

I tried to breathe quietly through my mouth, battling against that urge to throw up as I reached to shakily and carefully pry the cold, stiff fingers open.

My pulse dropped to a slow, pounding ache low in my chest as I saw a lock of torn hair tangled in the hand's frigid grasp. Long, black hair.

And something else.

The light caught over something small and golden,

clenched so tight in the dead man's fist. Like holding onto it had taken his last bit of strength before he was swept beyond the Vale.

A ring.

No—not just a ring.

A *signet* ring bearing the emblem of a serpent twisted around a letter T.

Everything stopped. My ears began to ring.

I couldn't look away.

I knew that symbol. I'd seen it before many times in our divine lore studies—seen it burned into the flesh on the side of Chrysa's neck.

The emblem of the Tibran Empire.

THIRTY-FOUR

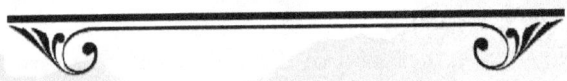

I t wasn't Chrysa.

Wasn't her hair clenched in the dead man's fist. Wasn't her body wrapped in the torn curtain and thrown haphazardly under the bed and left to rot.

She wasn't here.

So where was she?

Who was the dead man lying mere inches away from me, his blood soaking through all my clothes?

And how, by all the gods, was I going to get out of here?

All the windows were nailed shut. The balcony door, too. That meant I'd either have to break glass and make an extremely unstealthy dive out into the temple grounds, or I'd have to find a way to get to the front door.

That meant getting past Domitri, who was still sitting on the edge of the bed.

While my mind whirled through all my options, scrounging desperately for some sort of plan, I carefully pried the ring from the dead man's hand and slipped it into my pocket. I'd take it to Roxus and tell him everything I had found.

It was my only piece of real proof, and hopefully it would be enough to keep him from going into a full rage when he realized what I'd been up to.

But there was one more thing I couldn't leave this apartment without.

The corpse beside me wasn't Chrysa. But I *had* to know who it was. Domitri might decide to dispose of the body, and what then? It would be my word against his.

No—I needed that final damning piece of information when I revealed everything to Roxus. Even if it wasn't someone I recognized, I needed a description.

My throat burned, my stomach rolling ominously, as I reached out to tug carefully at the rolled-up curtain. Just a little. I only needed to see the face, or rather, what little of it was left. Enough to get a description.

My nerves quivered as the fabric rustled. The body shifted. I froze.

The bed above me didn't move. Neither did Domitri's legs.

My whole body trembled as adrenaline rushed through my body, passing through every part of me like an invisible current.

Seconds passed.

I swallowed a scream as Domitri stood suddenly.

Oh no.

He'd heard me. That had to be it. He'd heard—

Domitri began walking away from the bed. He left the room without another hissing, furious word.

Reeking air rushed into my lungs.

This was it. My only chance.

I pulled the curtain harder, yanking it down swiftly and revealing a decomposing face frozen in an expression of horror.

Everything went numb.

My heart stopped.

The flesh was graying and decayed. The eyes were sunken. The features were warped with rot.

But I still knew him right away.

No doubt. No question whatsoever.

The dead man wrapped up in the curtain and stuffed unceremoniously under the bed was someone I knew. Someone I'd come to hate with every fiber of my being.

The same long dark hair, smooth and pulled back. The same jawline. The same thin, scowling brow.

Domitri.

Confusion hit me like a lightning strike.

How? How could it be him? Here, dead, right in front of me?

No—no, this wasn't ... it couldn't ... It didn't make any sense.

My chest heaved in ragged, frantic breaths. My mind spun. My pulse kicked recklessly at my ribs.

My ears rang so loudly I didn't hear him come back into the room. I didn't notice his footsteps stopping beside the bed. I couldn't hear anything—see anything—except for that face.

His face.

Dead. Right in front of me.

It stared back at me with milky eyes and a slack jaw. A withering nose. Skin rotting away like wet paper, dotted with black spots of old blood.

If this was Domitri, then ... then who ... ?

A hand surged under the bed, moving as fast as a viper's strike, and seized my braided hair with startling strength.

I screamed, pitching wildly as he dragged me out across the bedroom floor.

"What have we here? A filthy little rat has found its way into my home!" The still-living Domitri sneered as he flung me down, his whole body emanating that eerie flickering blue light—an aura of pure magic.

"You," I growled through my teeth as I scrambled to get up. "Where is Chrysa?"

Domitri threw his head back in a laugh, immediately kicking down against my ribs with his heel before I could stand.

The impact knocked the wind out of me. Stars danced before my eyes.

Up. I had to get up. I had to fight.

Had to escape, whatever it took.

"Is that why you came?" he snickered. "Looking for your friend locked away in here like a maiden in a tower? And what would that make you? A noble hero to save her?"

His laugh was ice through my heart. Stabbing agony.

It stoked a fire deep within me.

One I'd barely managed to hold in.

Domitri reared a foot back, ready to kick me again, but I was ready for him this time.

I bared my teeth, whipping into a wrestling maneuver Declan had shown me many times. I grappled his other leg—the one now bearing all his weight—and brought him to the floor with a *thud* before he could land that kick.

He let out a bellowing cry as he hit the ground on the flat of his back, and I lunged with a scream of fury.

My blood roared in my ears, blotting out all common sense. All thoughts of escape. Of delivering my evidence to Roxus.

All I wanted was blood—*his* blood.

For every bruise he'd put on Chrysa's skin. For every venomous word he'd spat at me. I didn't know who or what he was, but I was willing to bet he'd bleed just like anyone else.

I swung at him, fist aimed at his neck.

"You disgusting little beast!" Domitri roared suddenly, his voice a cacophony of pitches and tones that all seemed to mash together into a horrible disharmony. He thrust a hand out toward me, and the air between us exploded.

The burst of vicious cold from his outstretched hand hit me square in the face and sent me rolling head over rear. Brilliant light flashed in the air.

I smacked off the armoire and crumpled to the floor, my vision swimming. The coppery warmth of blood filled my mouth. It oozed from my nose as I tried to get to my feet, wobbling and weaving as the room spun slowly.

Wh-what was that? More magic?

How?

By the abyss, what was he?

My head lolled as I tried to look up at him, catching a glimpse of his sneer wavering within that rippling blue light before he slammed his fist into my cheek.

Pain exploded in my jaw. My eye felt like it might burst free of its socket as I slumped sideways.

No! Up, curse it—I had to get up!

I staggered, my weight against the armoire as I hauled myself up, still tasting blood. I bit down hard, willing my vision to clear. A feral growl leaked past my lips as I surged for him again.

VOOOM!

Another low, concussive explosion of magical energy, like a shockwave, threw me to the floor. Harder this time. My lungs seemed to crush in on themselves. I couldn't breathe. My head throbbed, and my vision swerved in and out of focus.

"You thought you could come slithering in here and best me?" His voice thrummed in the air, sending splinters of pain rippling through my skull as I fought to keep conscious.

My vision snapped into clarity as he seized a fistful of my

hair and dragged me to my knees, leering into my face. His features warped, and his smile stretched too wide. His teeth became long and pointed. His eyes burned deep, molten yellow.

"I-I ... see ... you," I rasped bitterly.

His expression hitched, his smile cracking slightly.

"Y-You ... are *not* Domitri," I spat.

A strange, insane rage twisted his features. He rushed me, seizing my throat in his hand and lifting me easily off my feet as though I were nothing. My back creaked with fresh agony as he slammed me against the wall, pinning me by the neck.

His lip twitched and his eyes widened, pupils dilated and hungry.

"You will not spoil my work," he muttered as he squeezed harder.

I couldn't breathe. I couldn't feel the ground even with my toes. But by all the fates, I wouldn't let him kill me so easily.

Magic be damned.

I pulled the dagger from my belt and stabbed him in the forearm. The blade crunched through flesh and tendon, and Domitri let me go with a savage howl of pain.

I hit the floor with a desperate gasp, drinking in the putrid air as he staggered back, clutching his arm. Through my swimming, weaving vision, I saw his form ripple like a blue mirage. Domitri's features melted away, and his stature swelled in height and muscle. Something strange protruded from his head.

Horns? I-I couldn't be sure.

And there wasn't time.

This was it—my only chance.

"Where is she?" I demanded as I shambled toward him, still gripping my blade as the world seemed to tilt sideways. "Where is Chrysa?!"

His laugh was a rippling, foul melody that made my brain throb again. He stretched a hand toward me, each finger tipped in a curled, pointed nail. Claws?

Domitri snapped his fingers with a deafening *crack*.

The flash of blue light blotted out everything for a second.

My legs buckled instantly.

The dagger slipped from my hand and clattered to the floor.

I could barely feel the wooden floor under my cheek as I lay sprawled on my side. Whatever he'd done—whatever magic he was using—I couldn't resist it. It burrowed into my mind like a worm into an apple. It writhed in my skull, sending waves of agony through me.

I let out a ragged, broken scream.

"Oh, little viper. You do have some bite in you, I'll grant you that." His voice was everywhere. In my head. Slithering through every inch of my body, scraping its talons over my brain and up my spine.

I wailed again.

No! Oh, gods, no!

I-I couldn't ... I couldn't fight it. I couldn't get him out of my head!

His boots stepped right before me, making the old floorboards creak under his weight. He squatted down and grasped my chin, forcing me to meet his gaze.

And I saw him—really *saw* him.

Not Domitri. No blue aura wreathing his form. Not even human.

Something else.

A being with long black horns peeking through wavy black hair, and long pointed ears as sharp as a knife's edge. With dusky blue skin and fanged teeth. His yellow eyes seemed to simmer with crazed malice as he considered me, a cruel smile splitting his bowed lips.

Rajinna. He was ... a rajinna.

A shapeshifter. A wielder of magic older than the bones of the ancient Avoran halls beneath our feet.

And no one knew. No one else could see past his magical disguises.

No one except me.

Furious tears welled in my eyes. A hate I couldn't fathom boiled in my veins.

His smile widened.

"You see, little beastie, I cannot let you interfere any further. We've come too far. Risked too much. You've meddled enough, and I am bored of this game," he purred low.

It took everything I had, every shred of my will, to spit at him.

He chuckled and shook his head. "And to think, she asked me to spare you. Sympathy. Such a futile human emotion," he scoffed.

My failing vision found his other hand as he put it right in front of my face. My pulse boomed as I felt the gathering of magic like a chill in the air and saw the smallest kernel of white-blue light forming right before his open palm.

Die. I was going to die.

Right here in this room.

And Roxus would never know the truth of what happened. No one would. He might just roll up my body with Domitri's and stuff me under the bed.

My chin trembled. Fear seeped into the foundations of my soul.

Help—I needed help.

"Do not let them see any weakness in you, Visha. Weakness will be crushed. Destroyed. It will suffer a long and painful death."

It was too late. This man, whoever or whatever he was, had seen me, had seen my weakness. My terror.

I couldn't run. I couldn't hide.

Doom had finally found me.

So I shut my eyes tightly, seething one last curse as I waited for the killing blow.

BAM!

The heavy bang of the door cracking off the wall in the next room made both of us flinch.

"Master Domitri?" someone shouted. "What's going on? We heard screaming and—"

The rajinna man's expression tightened. He spat a curse in a language I didn't understand and dropped me onto the floor. All I could do was lie there, my head still reeling, as he scrambled away from me and clutched at the place on his arm where I'd stabbed him.

"In here!" he wailed frantically, doing an excellent job of sounding pathetically terrified and not like he was about to blast my head off my shoulders with his magic.

My jaw tightened, every fiber of my being screaming in outrage that never made it past my lips as I watched his form shimmer. A glow of blue magical light rippled over him, and he took on Domitri's face again. His horns, teeth, and long lion-like tail vanished behind the face of the dead man stuffed under the bed.

The man he'd been impersonating all this time.

I let out a strangled, furious cry.

Footsteps approached hurriedly. Armor and weapons clattered.

Vindexori?

Curse it all.

They stormed into the room, filling it with black leather armor and smoldering glares. I couldn't even count how many because of how my head still spun, but I did catch the glint of crossbows being aimed at me.

"She ... she was hiding in my room! She attacked me as soon as I came in! She tried to *kill* me! I-I barely managed to throw her off!" the fake Domitri whimpered as they helped him stand up.

That disgusting liar. It made me absolutely sick.

But there was nothing I could do except groan and struggle weakly as the Vindexori descended on me, pinning me down and immediately shackling my hands behind my back.

"Stop ... he's ... he's lying," I protested hoarsely as they dragged me to my feet. "He's not even Domitri!"

No one listened. Why would they? I was a filthy Viperi. I'd been nothing but trouble since I had first darkened their door.

They whipped me around and patted my armor, looking for hidden weapons. They turned out my pockets.

My stomach dropped to the soles of my boots as I saw one of them pull the Tibran signet ring out and hold it up to the lamplight.

Oh gods. No.

"A spy!" The fake Domitri gave an exaggerated gasp of horror. "She's a Tibran spy!"

I felt the room shift, as though a freezing wind had swept through the small space. They all fell silent, looking at the ring. Looking at me. Horror and hate was as thick in the air as the stench coming from that rotting corpse.

"I am not," I insisted, voice trembling.

I knew it wouldn't matter. They'd never believe me. But, gods, I had to try.

"Look under the bed! Just look under there and you'll see none of this is true," I pleaded.

None of them listened.

The Vindexori crammed a rag into my mouth, muting my

cries, and then two of them seized me by the arms. They began dragging me from the room.

I wrenched against their hold, twisting around just enough to catch one last glimpse of the imposter Domitri's face—of a cold, calculating, and triumphant smile curling over his lips.

Like he relished every second of my misery and knew that I would be put to the sword as a traitor for a crime he would get away with.

And it all clicked into place in my mind.

The vault.

He was the one who had tried breaking into the Vault of Whispers.

He'd almost succeeded once. Now, he'd get to try again while all the eyes of the Zenith's Call were fixed squarely on me.

A primal noise left my throat, muffled by the rag that had been stuffed roughly into my mouth.

This rajinna man, with all his magical prowess, would get away with everything—with murdering the real Domitri, deceiving the Zenith's Call, torturing Chrysa, and breaking into their most sacred vault to steal only gods knew what.

Something the Tibran Empire wanted.

But what?

I didn't know. And at this rate, I'd never find out.

As the Vindexori dragged me from Domitri's apartment and hauled me out into the night, I was met with more of them gathered outside. They glared at me over their black shawls, muttering to one another with their hands resting on their weapons. Waiting for me to make a wrong move.

Probably hoping I would.

The crowd of a dozen or so Vindexori parted, stepping aside as a long figure made her way to the front. Dressed in a cloak haphazardly thrown over her floor-length nightgown like she'd rushed straight from her bed.

Mistress Orvana stood before me, her expression already pinched tight with seething anger as she eyed me up and down. Then the Vindexori presented her with the signet ring they'd found in my pocket.

Her face went pale. Her eyes widened and her lips parted in silent horror.

And I knew, at that moment, not even Roxus could save me now.

THIRTY-FIVE

Part of me had always known I'd wind up in a prison cell again.

I just hadn't expected it to be for a crime I hadn't actually committed.

My life was full of terrible little surprises lately.

Last time, Mistress Orvana had dragged me down into the depths of Arx Eburna to see me chained up and interrogated because *someone* had tried breaking into the Vault of Whispers.

This time, however, she made certain I was delivered straight into the hands of Sol'Karr's city guard, locked in the deepest pit of their dungeon. A place worse even than the dog cage I'd been locked in previously.

Probably so Roxus wouldn't know where I was.

Little did Mistress Orvana know, he wasn't even aware I was outside the walls of his home. As far as Roxus knew, I was still in my room, lying in my bed and glowering sulkily at the ceiling. He might not even realize I was missing until morning.

And by then ...

I stared straight ahead, my body aching from the beating

I'd already taken at the rajinna man's hands and the Vindexori after. They'd taken my fine leathers, leaving only my thin linen undershirt and leggings, so I could see the extent of the damage.

The magic was one thing, and it left dark bruises with strange, spidery edges. But the Vindexori had taken great pleasure in softening me up for the interrogation to come.

My lip was split and swollen. Blood oozed from my nose. That first kick when the imposter Domitri attacked must have cracked a rib because every breath sent a sharp pang of agony through my side.

Gods only knew where he was right now. And Chrysa ...

I bowed my head. My hands writhed in the shackles that held them to the floor. They'd kept my chains short this time. No cell with iron bars, either.

No, they'd learned their lesson about how to hold me.

The tiny room had no windows and only one heavy iron door that didn't even have a handle on this side. No way to pick the lock, even if I had been able to try. They'd shackled my wrists and ankles, affixing them to metal hooks hammered straight into the cold stone floor. The chains were so short I couldn't even stand.

I had to sit, crouched like an animal amidst the rotting bits of hay and filth.

How long had I been down here?

It must have been hours. Maybe the sun had already risen.

Maybe Roxus had noticed I was gone.

Would Mistress Orvana even tell him what had happened? Or, at least, what she believed had happened?

The lies that imposter was spouting like a spider spinning silk.

Lies that I'd gotten tangled up in like a blasted housefly.

The door lurched with a heavy clunk, and the rusted hinges creaked and moaned as it swung inward. I squinted as light from the hallway spilled in, revealing four hooded figures in long black cloaks. Their faces were hidden deep in shadow, but my heat- vision could still pick out noses, mouths, and chins.

I recognized Mistress Orvana right away.

Three swept wordlessly into the room, her included, but the fourth remained at the door, pulling it closed with a low boom that echoed off the stone walls and ceiling.

I steeled my nerves, fixing my face in a hard scowl at the floor in front of me.

I wouldn't break. No matter what they did to me, I would not break.

Not at *her* hand.

One of the figures—probably a Vindexori—lit a torch and held it aloft. The wavering light filled the tiny room and made my eyes sting, but I could have sworn something about his face seemed familiar.

Too bad the low hood of his cloak still hid most of his features. Maybe he was one of the agents I'd sparred with. Or one I'd seen stalking the halls, watching me with disapproving glares.

I didn't know. And it didn't matter.

"Seal the door and see that no one enters. No one can interfere once we begin the rite," Mistress Orvana commanded. "Itanus demands sanctified ground."

I couldn't hold back a snort.

Sanctified ground? *Here?* In this cesspit of a prison cell?

Was she stupid or just that desperate?

I didn't know what she meant by any of it—the rite or the mention of the ancient foregod, Itanus. But I could guess it wasn't good when she produced a thick silver collar and held it out at arm's length. The surface of it shone in the torchlight, adorned in interwoven rings of runic etchings that spanned from a large jewel so black and flawless it looked like a shard of pure night. If it was an artifact of Itanus ... it very well could be.

I swallowed against a rising tightness in my throat.

Mistress Orvana began murmuring prayers, her voice like the rustling of leaves in the wind, as the third cloaked figure paced a circle around us and sprinkled what looked distinctly like salt on the ground behind them. If what I remembered about these rituals was true, it was pure salt taken from the Deadlands to the west. Remnants of an ancient sea lost to the War of the Stones.

Salt that supposedly also held remnants of the blood of the gods—a powerful component for concentrating divine power.

Only when the circle was closed did she brush back the cowl of her cloak and stare at me, her expression rigid and deeply creased with determination. As though she, too, had come this far and wouldn't stop now.

My heart sank.

So, it was desperation, then.

Not good.

Her hands were trembling faintly as she stepped closer to me, clasping that thick silver collar around my neck like another shackle. It closed with a soft click, but that tiny sound shattered over me like a clap of thunder. The weight of it made me off balance. I wobbled to stay upright.

"Now we will get to the bottom of this," she muttered quietly, like she was talking to herself. Working herself up for what was to come. "With or without your cooperation, we will have the truth. No one can deceive the God of All-Past. Not even a Pitathi."

"I am *not* a spy," I snapped angrily as she stepped outside the salt circle. "And that man is *not* Domitri. You're all being tricked. He's a rajinna, and he's working for the Tibran

Empire! He wants something in that vault! He failed to get it once, but he will try again!"

Mistress Orvana turned her back, taking something from the hands of the other cloaked figure. A large, silver-plated book.

She never even glanced back as she replied coolly, "Funny. He said the exact same thing ... about *you*."

My breath caught.

Of course he had. They'd never trust my word over his.

I worked my jaw from one side to the other, studying every tiny feature of her face. Searching for a kernel of doubt. A fragment of hesitance.

All I found was cold resolve as she opened the tome and began to recite the ancient prayers. Pleas to Itanus to grant his blessing over the ground before her.

The circle of salt began to glow faintly, an arc of ominous blue light as the magic took hold. A glow only I could see, probably.

Chills swept over me. A feeling like I was about to plummet from a high place swirled in the pit of my stomach. Flipping and flipping, it left me queasy as I set my jaw and kept my gaze locked onto her.

If she was going to do this, then I'd make sure she never forgot my face.

Heat from the collar bound around my neck wafted up the arch of my throat. Hotter and hotter. My body trembled out of my control, and black smoke began to curl from that single dark jewel. It boiled and curled, twisting through the air like a living thing.

It snaked around me, slithering around my head and surging for my nose. A smell like camphor invaded my senses. It overwhelmed me and made everything slide into a numb calm. I couldn't feel my body. The room seemed to glaze over as though I were staring through a frosty window pane.

Mistress Orvana bristled, her body rigid and her expression drawn in controlled terror. Maybe she hadn't expected this to work. Or, more likely, she'd never done it before and wasn't sure what the effects would actually look like.

I could only guess by the way my mouth gaped, shoulders dropping and head lolling slowly back beyond my control, that it must have been bad. A horror.

"N-now then. You will answer my questions." Her voice hitched slightly and she cleared her throat as she closed the tome and handed it off to one of the Vindexori.

The world seemed to slip farther away. Darkness crept into the corners of my vision. I fought, trying to stay within myself. But that power, as ancient as the foundations of the earth, took me inch by brutal inch.

Mistress Orvana stepped closer, right to the edge of the salt circle, and narrowed her eyes upon me. "Whom do you serve?"

Everything slid into bottomless black. Caught in that vortex, the dark seemed to bite and pull at me, tossing me end over end like a whirlpool. I couldn't hear or see anything. Even my pulse had gone quiet to the rushing roar of it.

An eternal abyss.

Fear gripped me like fangs at my throat, squeezing tighter and tighter. Crushing the life from me. Smothering the soul in my chest.

Air—gods, I needed air!

Lost. I was lost, wholly and completely. Within the awful, churning darkness. Within this brutal, terrible world.

Within myself.

Anguish seemed to stomp out the last few embers of my heart, crushing them to nothing.

I was going to die. I would be in this horrible in-between forever, forgotten and unwanted. No one came looking for a Pitathi urchin. No one wanted—

"Hello there." A deep, warm voice thrummed through me like a ray of pure sunlight.

His voice.

Roxus.

"What if I could offer you something else? A different path."

Breath rushed in, filling my lungs as I gasped wildly. My eyes flew open, filling with the yawning dark and feeling it pass through my body like nails into my skull.

Then, far away, I saw it. The faintest light winking in the abyss like a single star through roiling storm clouds.

A flickering blue glow to guide me home.

My only way out.

"Trust for trust," he warned gently.

I bit down hard, focusing all my thoughts—all my will on that tiny speck of light.

"Trust for trust," I repeated.

And I meant it. To the very core of my entire being, I trusted him. He had found me in that dark once before. He had seen me as something worthy. Something with potential and purpose.

And I would not let him down ... even if it meant crawling back to him on my knees and begging forgiveness. I would become that person he thought I could be.

Even if it cost me everything.

THIRTY-SIX

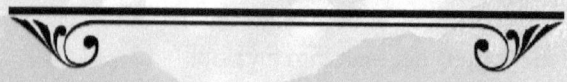

A wild gasp left my lips as everything suddenly snapped into focus.

The cold stone against my cheek. The chains still shackled to my wrists and ankles clattering as my body trembled out of control. The crushing silence in the cell.

Here—gods help me, I was still here.

But alive.

I scrambled to sit up and immediately vomited.

It wasn't food that came up, though. Black, sticky tar-like ooze splattered the ground in front of me. It reeked like camphor, too.

"Easy," a deep voice murmured over me as a warm hand pressed to my shoulder, steadying me. "Get it up. Come on. Breathe deep."

I looked up shakily, hardly able to focus on the hooded figure of a Vindexori stooping over me. The same one that had seemed so familiar before crouched down right at my side, his mouth set in a grim, hard line. I recognized that sour expression even as I turned to throw up again.

Varren.

Why was he here? Why was he dressed like a Vindexori? Wasn't he still a prospect like me?

Or, like I had been, I guess.

I doubted I'd ever be one again after this.

"Look, we're all doing things we're not necessarily proud of these days, okay?" he muttered as though he'd read the skeptical confusion in my expression.

I made a scoffing sound as I spat more of the black ooze onto the stones. "H-helping traitors and s-spies?"

His scowl deepened, making a muscle twitch in his jaw as he offered the end of his cloak to wipe at my face and chin. "You look gross," he growled.

"So do you." I managed a bleary glance at his attire. "Why are you … ?"

"Don't ask questions you don't want to know the answers to," he scolded quietly, his eyes darting toward the door. "Look, we don't have a lot of time. Mistress Orvana is going back to Arx Eburna. She's furious. Apparently, you didn't give her the answers she wanted, even with the help of that artifact."

A groggy smirk slid over my lips. "You mean, I didn't confess to being a Tibran spy on a mission to rob her precious vault?" I drawled. "Shocking."

"No," he confirmed. "But now she believes that Roxus is the real culprit. That he's been using you as a distraction. She left to gather a company of all her highest-ranking Vindexori. They'll go straight for his estate."

I rolled my eyes.

"Is he … ?" Varren let his voice trail off suggestively, but his tone was surprisingly sharp and convicting.

I leveled a heavy look at him, holding his stare and letting him see the truth in my eyes. "No. Domitri is to blame for this. Or rather, the person wearing Domitri's face."

"That's what you told Mistress Orvana, too. A rajinna sorcerer, right?"

I nodded once.

He muttered a curse. "She didn't believe it, although, I can't understand why. The artifact she used to interrogate you only allows for the recollection of facts. No lies, just the truth of the past."

Somehow, that wasn't surprising.

"And what about the other girl? Chrysa? Did you find her?" he pressed.

My stomach rolled, threatening to have me puking again just at the thought of what might have happened to her. He'd killed the real Domitri. He'd beaten her before.

Gods only knew if she was still alive.

All I could do was shake my head slowly.

Varren spat another curse and began fumbling through the many pockets of his black leathers. He pulled out a single sliver of twisted black metal, holding my gaze in an unblinking stare as he placed it on the ground right next to my hand.

"You wait until I'm long gone, understand?" he warned. "They can't know it was me."

My chest heaved as a weight, like stones being stacked on my chest, seemed to make every breath a fight. He was ... giving me a way out?

I narrowed my eyes slightly.

"We're even now," he said solemnly.

I glanced at the metal shard. A crude thief's tool.

And I understood.

Sliding my hand to the side, I covered it with my palm and nodded slowly.

Varren stood and pulled down the cowl of his cloak again. He didn't say another word as he hurried for the open door and pulled it closed behind him.

Well, *almost* closed.

I didn't miss how he left less than half an inch of gap there. Just enough for me to wedge the door open. Getting through the rest of the prison would be a challenge, yes. But not one I'd never taken on before.

I closed my fist around the black twisted metal pin as my heartbeat turned to thunder in my chest.

Mistress Orvana hadn't gotten what she wanted from me, so now she was on the warpath. Searching for her next alternative culprit. Going after Roxus with a host of Vindexori.

Leaving the Vault of Whispers practically unguarded.

I knew what I had to do, and the clock was already ticking.

If I were a conniving, vicious Tibran spy looking to steal sacred artifacts from an ancient vault guarded by divinely-charged guardians, this is exactly when I'd make my strike.

I gnashed my teeth against the rise of fury like ash in my throat.

He'd gotten the best of me in that apartment. I hadn't known about his magic or what to expect to find there. But I couldn't afford to be so clumsy this time.

I waited until I heard Varren's steps retreat. Silence crept in, and the darkness of the prison's dungeon rolled over me like an all-consuming tide.

With one hard blink, I switched to my heat-vision and drank in the details of the room. The place where he'd knelt still glowed faintly. The now-broken circle of salt, too.

It was more than enough to see what I was doing, and I picked the cuffs on my wrists in seconds. Freeing my ankles went even faster, but I staggered as I stood. My legs wobbled dangerously with every step, knees threatening to buckle as the world tilted and spun for a few seconds.

I braced myself against the wall, waiting for it to pass.

Think—I had to think. Getting out of here was the first problem. Then ... Then I had to go home.

Home.

The word hit me like a dagger to the heart.

I'd never truly had one of those until now. A place that wanted me, welcomed me.

Roxus had given me so much. But that alone was worth far more than any training from the Zenith's Call.

He'd picked me to bring into his home so I could share it with him. So I could join his family and be a part of the world without shame.

Tears stung at my eyes.

Roxus was my chosen family, and I'd fight to my very last breath to get back home. If Varren was right, Mistress Orvana was on her way there right now.

I had to get there first. I had to warn Roxus. I had to tell him the truth about everything before it was too late.

I just prayed that, after all that had happened ... he would still believe me.

Thirty-Seven

My legs burned and sweat already slicked my skin and drizzled down the sides of my face as I ran.

I had to be fast—fast and utterly ruthless.

That was the only way I would make it out of this place alive.

I repeated that over and over in my head as I sprinted up the winding stairwell, ascending from that putrid hell to the prison cell blocks above.

I knew how to dodge city guards. I'd been doing just that for years because my life depended on it.

Now, that same harrowing reason drove me forward and called forth every primal instinct from the deepest corners of my mind. I was death and shadow haunting those halls, moving silently down each corridor.

I halted in a sharp corner, using the shadows at my back to wait and listen. My senses stilled, reaching out like invisible fingertips to trace along the halls ahead of me for any sound or movement. Voices carried from the prison barracks. Three, all male, and slightly slurred.

Probably city guards on their down shift, drinking off the night's patrol before they tumbled into their cots for the night.

Slipping from my hiding spot, I crept along the wall and made for the opposite end of the hall. Not a single one of them even looked up as I stepped quietly past the open doorway to the barracks.

So far, so good.

But the real challenge lay around the next corner, where Captain Evrol's office undoubtedly held something I could not leave this place without.

My leathers.

It was stupid, probably, to risk retrieving them from the evidence lockup in the big cabinet behind his desk. But, curse it, those were *mine*. I would have them back.

My bare feet didn't so much as whisper over the cold stones as I stalked toward the door, pausing when I heard the faint scuffle of movement from the other side. He was inside, jabbering away with someone. I'd have known his voice even in the depths of the abyss.

"It's customary to wait until dawn," a rough, unfamiliar voice grumbled in a tone like rubble rattling in a bucket. "Displeases Clysiros."

"You think I give a rat's tail what some mythical monster prefers?" Captain Evrol scoffed. "Keep your childish fantasies to yourself, and do your job. Besides, it's just a Pitathi. Not a person."

My stomach turned, twisting and shuddering like I'd been run through with a shard of ice. My lips twitched, instinctively drawing back to bare my teeth.

"On your orders, then." The other man gave a resigned sigh.

The executioner, then?

I wasn't sure until the door burst open. Flat against the wall with the opening door swinging my direction to hide my position, I peered through the crack between the hinges to see the two men blunder out.

A big, stocky man draped in dark robes emerged first. He kept his head down, but I still caught the glimmer of the torchlight off a mask of solid silver cut in the shapes of two bird wings that covered most of his features. His long, black leather apron reeked of old blood.

Definitely the executioner.

Not even a step behind him, Guard Captain Evrol moved with all the grace of a drunken ape. He had a stiff leg, I knew, that made him shuffle strangely if he'd been on his feet for too long—something I had noticed from my previous stay here. Likely a bad knee. Probably an old war injury.

It would make him slow if this went poorly.

I waited, holding my breath, as they moved down the hall and turned the corner I'd just come from. Heading for my cell?

Curse it all—I only had seconds before they realized I was not in there anymore.

I bit back a curse and whipped around the door, darting into his office. I vaulted easily over his desk, sending papers scattering as I dropped into a crouch before the big, solid oak cabinet that spanned from floor to ceiling. All eight of its doors were locked, but thanks to Varren, I had brought my own special key.

It took ten seconds, maybe a little more, to pick the lock on the first one. I flung the door open and scoured inside, raking through the contents. Purses. Small messer swords. Daggers. Clothing.

But none of it was mine.

I snapped my teeth angrily and moved to the second door. Gods, this would take too long. Time—I needed more time.

The second lock gave in quicker, and I furiously pulled the items out in fistfuls. More small blades, some crudely hewn from old rusted cutlery or pitchfork prongs. Jewelry. Shoes. A haversack that clinked strangely. Leather armor.

But still nothing that belonged to me.

Shouts echoed far down the hall outside.

Adrenaline immediately poured through my body, setting every nerve afire.

I sprang over the desk again, whipping the door shut with a bang I didn't even care if Captain Evrol or the other prison guards heard. He'd find me soon enough, regardless. I threw the lock and rammed one of those crude shivs into it to jam it hard. Then I seized the heavy mahogany chair from behind his desk and wedged it under the handle.

It wouldn't hold for long, but it might buy me a minute or two.

I dashed back to the cabinet and unlocked as many of the doors as I dared, flinging them open and scouring the contents in a frantic blur.

Then the familiar glimmer of fine silver thread caught my eye.

A gasp of relief seeped through my lips like a kettle hissing steam as I yanked them free. My boots were behind them, and I stuffed everything into the haversack I'd found. Flinging it over my shoulders, I ran for the only window, seizing a large brass paperweight on my way.

"Get it open!" Captain Evrol thundered from the hall outside.

"It's jammed! It won't budge!"

"WHAT?!"

Shouts and bangs vibrated against the office door as I hurled it into the windowpane that overlooked the courtyard —the same one that held the executioner's block. The window where Captain Evrol watched every execution from behind the safety of that polished pane.

Glass shattered.

BANG—BANG—BANG!

They were smashing through the door, and I caught the motion of the large, curved edge of an axe as it slammed through the wood and sent splinters flying.

"Again! Hit it again, you fools!" Captain Evrol bellowed.

CRACK!

I dared one last glance back over my shoulder as I scurried through the window, just in time to see the captain sticking his big head through a fresh hole in the middle of his office door. He gaped down at the jammed lock, the chair wedged under the handle, and then straight at me.

His face went purple, eyes bulging in rage.

I smirked and made a vulgar gesture.

Then I leapt through the broken window. The crisp night wind snagged in my hair as I ran along the eaves of the prison's roof and disappeared into the night.

There might be hell to pay for that later—especially if Roxus didn't believe anything I said about Domitri and what I'd found at his apartment.

I couldn't worry about that right now, though.

I had to get home. I had to tell Roxus about everything that had happened. I had to convince him to help me. I had to do everything I possibly could to stop Domitri and find Chrysa ... even if I had to do it all on my own.

Thirty-Eight

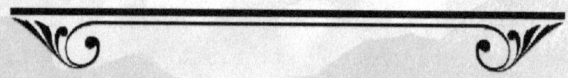

My knees nearly buckled when I reached the front steps of Roxus's home.

My home.

There wasn't time to be sneaky about it. As far as I could tell, I'd made it here before Mistress Orvana and all her Vindexori. But that didn't mean they weren't mere minutes away.

No time to waste.

I burst through the front door, expecting to find Roxus sitting in the living room or Delthene bustling about.

But there was no one there.

No one waiting in the front sitting room. No one in the kitchen or dining room. Not even a single lamp was lit on the main floor.

Terror pierced my chest like a spearpoint, snatching the air from my lungs as I stood at the base of the stairs. My heart pounded madly, making my vision swim.

Oh, gods, no. Had I been too late? Had Mistress Orvana already come and hauled them all off?

Something rustled upstairs, and I whirled around to find

Gibb sitting on the landing, his feline eyes aglow in the weak light. He stared back at me, unblinking, then stood and trotted up the steps and out of sight.

My sweaty hands shook and slipped along the railing as I slowly climbed the steps, avoiding the ones I knew would creak under my weight.

Gibb sat in the second floor hall, beckoning me further into the depths of the house with a flick of his tail and a gleam of those big moon eyes. My heart gave a stammering lurch as he turned his head and stared into the open doorway of Roxus's office. Almost like he could see someone else in there.

Weak light ebbed from inside, probably from a fire in the hearth.

The big cat didn't move as I approached, my heart a cold, frigid stone in my chest. I had no idea what I'd find in there. Roxus's corpse? Whatever the Vindexori had left of him for me to find here?

Maybe it was all a trap.

I held my breath and stepped into the light, turning to face the open doorway.

Roxus stood not five paces away, facing me with a short-sword in his hand, and his entire body bristled for a fight. His powerful shoulders flexed against the fabric of his nightshirt, and his eyes were narrowed, the firelight dancing across them like amber glass.

I froze, gaping up at him.

He stared back.

Little by little, his posture went slack. Relaxing an inch at a time.

Then the sword slipped from his grasp and clattered to the floor.

"Violet." He breathed my name like a prayer of praise.

Of relief.

Tears welled in my eyes.

"I-I ... I'm—"

He rushed me, his powerful arms closing around me as tightly and securely as castle walls. I was immersed in his musky scent, his intense warmth, his complete safety. He gripped me so tight, as though he were afraid I might be nothing but an illusion. Like I might vanish into smoke the instant he touched me.

"You wretched girl," he murmured into my hair. "Do you have any idea how worried I was?"

I cringed as he cupped my face in his hands, gaze traveling all over me to all the tender, swollen places I'd forgotten about until then. I must have looked like walking death, all smeared with black ooze and bruised up like an old banana.

"I'm okay," I assured him.

But his frown of quiet wrath didn't falter as he ran a thumb over the mark around my neck. It stung like fire, and I couldn't hold back a wince of pain.

"We can't do this, not right now," I urged and swatted his hands away. "Mistress Orvana is on her way here right now with Vindexori. They're going to arrest you."

His frown deepened. "Tell me everything," he ordered.

And so I did—as quickly as I could manage.

I couldn't force myself to hold his gaze while I recounted everything that had happened from the time I'd left until now, sparing no detail. I didn't want there to be anything withheld between us. Not anymore.

But I also didn't want to see any traces of doubt creeping over his rugged features. If he didn't believe me, if he questioned the truth of any of it, I wasn't sure what I'd do.

He was all I had in the world now.

"You say he is using magic to disguise himself?" Roxus asked quietly, sinking down into the chair behind his desk as though he were processing it all.

"He's a rajinna, Roxus. Not human. Not elf. I don't know

why he's doing this, or what his goal is. I don't even know what he wants from the vault, but—"

"I do," Roxus murmured. "There are countless valuable wonders in the vault, but only one I can think of that the Tibran Empire might try something this brazen for. Something they might send agents to infiltrate the Zenith's Call for."

I sucked in a sharp breath.

Agents? As in … more than one?

Did he think I was working with Domitri?

Roxus stared back at me, eyes wide but distant, as though his mind had been snatched back to the halls of Arx Eburna, where Domitri was doing gods-only-knew at this very moment.

Then came the rage.

His jawline hardened. His gaze turned to frost-kissed steel. A vein stood out in the side of his neck and along his forearms as he gripped the arms of his chair.

But it was his silence that froze me right where I stood. My heart seemed to stall and stop completely.

Surely he didn't think I was working *with* Domitri?

That realization—that he might think I was trying to lie and manipulate him—ripped the breath from my lungs. Every muscle drew tense, like a bowstring ready to snap.

He … he had to believe me. If he didn't, then … then my fate was sealed.

I would have no choice.

I'd have to run for my life again … from the one person in the world I had thought cared about me.

"We have all been deceived," he growled low, his eyes panning past me to stare into the licking flames as he slowly stood from his chair. "But no more."

I took a faltering step back.

My fate hung in the charged silence that hung in the air like a fine thread ready to snap.

I flinched back as Roxus spat a low, growling curse through his teeth. It was a language I didn't understand, and not one I had ever heard him use before.

I couldn't make a sound as I waited, shivering and watching him lick his teeth behind his lips and look down at his desk. At the object sitting there, exactly where I'd seen it last time. That strange little box.

It was wrapped in a piece of white linen, but I could still see the magical aura glowing through the fabric.

I swallowed hard.

"You have to go to Arx Eburna," he said.

I choked on my breath. "Wh-what?"

"Most of the forces protecting that place are headed right here to find me. That means the vault is vulnerable. It's the perfect time for Domitri to attempt to open it, and this time, he will likely succeed. We are the only ones who know—the only ones who can put a stop to it."

"But I'm not—I-I can't—" I fumbled with my words as he leveled a heavy look on me.

"You're the only one who can, Violet. You can see through whatever disguise he might use."

"But I can't fight him!" I argued. "I don't have magic to counter his! He took me out easily before. What can I possibly do against power like that?"

Roxus's expression never changed as he panned his gaze from me to the pair of gleaming blades that hung above the mantle. The two long, curved silver daggers. I'd seen them the first time I snuck into this place.

I stood perfectly still, my mouth hanging open as he stepped around his desk and marched straight toward them.

CRACK!

He ripped the wooden plaque off the wall, nail and all.

Carrying it over to his desk, he unfastened the two sleek, beautiful daggers from the wooden base and held them to the light. His light brown eyes narrowed, a muscle feathering under the skin of his cheek, as though he were scrutinizing every fine detail.

I stared at them, too.

Each of the thirteen-inch blades was crafted in a sloping, tapered shape with extremely intricate carvings to make them each look like a bird's wing. Something about them sent a shiver up my spine.

They were, by far, the most beautiful daggers I had ever seen. Each one probably worth a hundred times its weight in gold.

And absolutely lethal in the hands of the man who now faced me with an ominous, focused scowl.

I held my breath, waiting for a sudden strike.

Or for him to speak.

I knew he could destroy me either way—with weapons or words—if he really wanted to.

My shoulders drew up, hands balling into fists as I counted my breaths until, at last, he muttered, "A Shield Maiden of Vordega gave these to me many years ago." His tone was low and ominous as he held them up, giving them a test swing.

They hummed a rich, beautiful melody as they swiped through the air.

A feeling somewhere between exhilaration and terror burrowed deep into my gut as he faced me, then.

"They are made with dwarven vidrathian steel," he said. "It absorbs magic and has been used in their great halls to craft runes that would and sing for a thousand years without tending."

My gaze flickered between him and the blades, wondering what that meant for whoever held these weapons. Would they absorb magical attacks and spare their wielder?

I didn't know. But right then, they didn't glow blue. So maybe they had never been used for that purpose.

Or at all, if they'd been mounted to that fancy plaque and left untouched.

"Spelldrinkers," he clarified. "That's what the Ursinaar, the finest and most brutal warriors of Vordega, called them. And believe me when I say, *no one* has spilled more Avoran blood than they have. They carved a vein of fear in the minds and hearts of those ancient elves that their ancestors still remember." Something fond and almost proud winked in his cognac eyes. "There isn't an Avoran breathing now who wouldn't shudder at their name."

"I-I ... I never read anything about that in the divine lore," I admitted.

"And you never will. Vordegans don't keep written records. It's the only way to keep their methods restricted to their own kind." He glanced down at the blades, as though they whispered to him in a way I couldn't detect. "Use them. Draw blood. They'll bond to you and no one else. But it may take time for you to learn to use them to counter powerful magic. Vordegan warriors train their entire lives for it, and some still never fully master it."

Then he held them out to me with an expectant frown.

My heartbeat skipped.

But—but they were real weapons. Not dulled or wooden for practice. Not wooden or clumsy iron. Beautiful, priceless, and devastatingly lethal.

And he really wanted *me* to take them?

My throat went stiff as I reached for them, unable to keep my fingers from trembling. My heart gave a flutter as I took them carefully.

The leather grips fit my hands like they had been crafted especially for me. The flawless dark steel shone as I turned them over, admiring the fine detail of the feathers and runes engraved along the slightly curved blades.

Flawless.

I gave each one a spin over my hands. First one at a time. Then both at once.

Their weight was perfectly balanced.

I couldn't hold back the wicked grin that twisted up my lips.

With these blades in my hands, I wasn't a victim. I could stop Domitri. I could change my fate.

I could make them all see the truth that I was innocent.

But more than that, I was worthy.

Roxus said nothing as I hurried to redress in my dark leathers—the ones he had ordered especially for me. Then he showed me how to buckle on the leather sheaths to each of my thighs, his expression closing into something distant and ominous. Like he knew exactly what kind of storm was coming.

For me ... and for him.

Wrath like cinders crackled over my tongue as I slipped the daggers into their sheaths. Perfect. The last touch was a fistful of soot from the fire pit smeared over my face, right across my eyes, and a single line down the bridge of my nose, over my lips, down to my chin.

A Viperi war blessing.

Domitri had called me a monster before. A beast.

Now I'd show him just how monstrous I could be.

Maybe he had Mistress Orvana and all the other agents fooled, but I could see straight through all his magical disguises. He could use whatever face he wanted, but he couldn't hide from me.

He wanted something in that vault?

Fine.

He'd have to go through *me* to take it.

Thirty-Nine

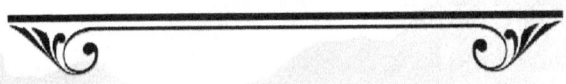

"Y ou can't use the entrance at the temple to get into Arx Eburna," Roxus warned as he hurried me down the stairs.

Time was nearly up. Any second now, Mistress Orvana and her men would arrive. We were already pushing it.

"I don't know any other way in," I reminded him.

"Go to the dockside road and follow it to the north. You'll find a sailor's tavern with a red clay tile roof and an old statue of a siren out front," he muttered as we came to the base of the stairs. We made our way quickly through the dining room and into the larder, where Delthene had all the pantry's inventory neatly organized along rows of wooden shelves.

"I know the place," I recalled. It was a seedy dive where sailors and dockhands liked to gather and fight over card games while chugging mugs of sour ale.

A good place for an urchin to pick a few pockets after the sailors were passed out in their plates.

Roxus stopped at the back of the narrow room, muscling aside one of the still-sealed barrels of flour to reveal a small trap door hidden beneath.

A secret emergency exit?

Roxus opened it, revealing a tunnel with a rickety ladder that led straight down into complete darkness.

I swallowed.

Roxus turned to me then, pulling a coin from his pocket and pressing it into my hand with an earnest intensity in his hard-chiseled features.

But not just any coin. I knew the engravings on it just as I recognized the faint glow of residual magical energy that ebbed off it.

A stemma coin—just like the one Curator Faera had tested me with.

"Go in and show this to the barkeep. He'll send you to the back. You can find your way from there. But keep your head down, understand? Talk to no one," he warned. "At this point … I'm not sure who we can safely trust."

Something akin to regret or even concern twinged in his face, making his expression skew slightly as he motioned for me to go down that ladder. Maybe he wished this had all turned out differently. Or maybe he wished he could go with me.

Could have been a bit of both.

But we didn't have time to start airing those sorts of feelings right now.

"I'll keep them occupied here as long as possible," he said, offering a hand to help as I began to climb down into that pitch black tunnel. "Do what you can, Violet. But … but if it comes down to life and death … "

I hesitated.

His expression went stony, jawline hardening. "You're not Zenith's Call, yet. You haven't sworn the oaths we have. You don't have to give your life for this."

I knew that. I also knew that even if I did all this and

somehow lived—somehow managed to stop Domitri—it still might not be enough. It still might not make me one of them.

But that wasn't why I *needed* to do this. It was for something else, something far greater.

I just didn't know how to put it into words that he might understand.

Viperi didn't teach their children how to talk about things like love. Not even the love a child might have for a parent. The same sort of love I had for him.

I'd have to figure that out later.

"I'll be careful," I promised. It was all I could guarantee him right then.

Roxus nodded.

We both went still as a loud, banging knock echoed through the whole house like the tolling bell of doomsday.

They were here.

I had to run ...

One last time.

FORTY

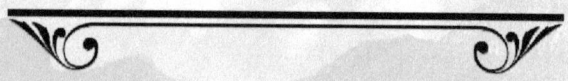

The tavern wasn't hard to find.

Squished between two larger buildings, I could spot that red clay roof even from a street away. But the faster I ran, pumping my legs to their limit, the more it felt like my chest was being ripped in two. Like I'd left half of it tethered there, in Roxus's house, and leaving it was tearing me apart from the inside out.

I couldn't stop my racing thoughts. What if Roxus needed me? What if they beat him? Imprisoned him? Killed him? What about Delthene? I hadn't seen her at all in the house. Had he already sent her away somewhere safe?

I didn't know. And the farther I went, feet numb over the mist-slicked cobblestones and the night wind snagging in the lengths of my cloak, the greater that sense of not knowing became. It burrowed deep into me like the twisting plunge of a dagger, so sharp, it made my breath hitch with every gasp.

Made my eyes want to tear up. Made me hate Domitri even more.

I halted under the eaves of the tavern, noting how the

windows glowed faintly with warmth. Dark figures moved inside, bustling around the tables.

Not as many as the last seedy pirate tavern I'd been in, though.

I chalked that up to the hour—somewhere near dawn if the faint smear of pink on the far horizon was any indication. Most of the patrons would be long past surrendering to the bad ale.

I stepped into the tavern, doing a quick scan around at the few people within. Four men passed out over tables, cups still in their hands. Two buxom barmaids were scrambling to clean, while a minstrel in the far corner packed up his lute and hat filled with a smattering of coins.

None of them so much as glanced my way.

Good.

Pipe smoke still choked the lights in the room like a fog, stinging my eyes and filling my nose with the sharp twinge of tobacco. My boots sloshed in puddles of spilt ale as I made my way to the bar, peering past it to find the owner or barkeep. I was already fidgeting with the stemma coin in my pocket, sweaty fingers sliding over the engravings on the metal.

I jerked back as an old, heavyset man stood suddenly, crouched under the bar where I hadn't noticed him until he moved. He eyed me, gaze lingering on mine before noting the rest of my fitted black leathers. His wooly brows rose and his throat bobbed.

I put the coin on the countertop between us, Zenith's Call symbol facing up, and slid it toward him.

His mouth pinched tightly. He didn't say a word as he tipped his head slightly, gesturing for me to come behind the bar.

A shaky breath leaked through my clenched teeth as I slid the coin back into my pocket and made my way to the far end of the bar. I slipped through the swinging half-door that kept patrons out of the work areas, not daring to meet the barkeep's narrowed gaze again as I strode past him.

"Hatch in the cellar," he murmured quietly.

I nodded, still avoiding eye contact.

Through the back door of the kitchen, I found myself standing in a storage room stocked with bottles of wine, liqueurs, and cooking ingredients. A hatch in the floor revealed the entrance of a cellar down a narrow staircase, just as promised.

The stone steps didn't make a sound under my boots as I descended into the near-dark. The walls were lined with massive wooden casks of ale and wine that nearly reached the ceiling. Each one was stamped with a date and brewer's mark and was so large a small crowd could have piled inside it with room to have a chat.

I stood in the middle of the cramped space, turning slowly to eye each one of the casks. Roxus had said I could figure out my way from here.

But, where was I—?

My heart nearly lurched straight through my ribs when I saw it.

The cask at the farthest corner had a very familiar symbol burned into the front of its wooden spigot.

A crescent moon with a long, slender blade through its center.

The symbol of the Zenith's Call.

I held my breath as I grabbed that spigot and twisted. Something metallic clunked. The whole spigot turned in my hand like a doorhandle, and the front of the cask swung open like a massive round door.

Inside, the thick mineral smell of a cavern rushed out in a gust of bitter cold that made the tip of my nose numb. Another hidden stairwell—this one cut straight into the earth, delved into the total dark.

A smile twisted over my lips. Familiar territory, at least.

I didn't look back as I crawled inside and pulled the door closed behind me. With my heat-vision, I could see the shadowed outlines of the walls and the radiant distant glow of warmth far ahead down those steps.

My pulse boomed like a war drum in my ears, adrenaline tingling through every pore. My breath echoed over the carved walls around me. They reflected and magnified every tiny sound. Every rustle of fabric and scrape of my boots.

The stench of sour ale and pipe smoke gave way to something saccharine and almost floral. Perfume?

I hesitated right in front of an open doorway covered only by hundreds of strings of glass and crystal beads. They sparkled and tinkled softly, catching in the light of colored glass lanterns that hung on either side of the doorway.

But there was no other sound. No music. No voices. Nothing but my frantic pulse still pounding away in my head.

I slid a hand through the bead curtain, parting it enough that I could slip through without too much racket.

I knew what it was the second my feet hit the layers of soft, woven rugs laid out like a patchwork over the floor. The smell of that incense masked something far darker lurking under the faint light ebbing from those glass oil lamps perched on every low table and dangling from the ceiling on gilded chains. Chills swept over me as I tasted it in the air—a heavy metallic flavor.

Blood.

Fresh blood, and lots of it.

But where?

I slid one of the daggers from the sheath at my hip, moving like a phantom down a central aisle made by painted silk screens and hanging tapestries. On either side, those makeshift rooms glowed with the fading light of body heat from figures sprawled over the floor and stains of deep red that soaked through the rugs.

Slaughter.

Vindexori lay with people in much finer clothes—none of them moving or breathing—as the last of their heat-light ebbed away.

My breath rattled recklessly in my chest as I stopped, forcing myself to look. To take in the details.

Most had slash wounds through their flesh, marks left by a sword. But others ... gods, it looked like they'd been crushed. Hit with something forceful that had crushed their bones.

Magic.

A swell of cold chills surged up my spine as I noted one of the Vindexori still lodged in the cracked stone of the wall where he'd been flung with tremendous force.

I only knew one person capable of something like that.

Something crunched to my left.

I whipped into a fighting stance, blade raised, and didn't dare to move.

Breathing scraped, desperate and weak. Then a female voice rasped brokenly, "H-help ... someone ... p-please ..."

Oh, gods, was someone still alive?!

I immediately sheathed my weapon and surged toward the sound.

And I found her.

Half-buried beneath the shredded body of a Vindexori, a woman lay on her back. One of her legs was twisted strangely —wrongly—and a deep wound across her brow bled down her face, neck, and onto her robes. More blood oozed from the corners of her mouth.

She blinked owlishly as I staggered to a halt over her. My mind went blank in shock and horror for a second as we stared at one another, seeming to share that moment of morbid surprise.

Then her name slipped past my lips in a thin, dry gasp. "Curator Faera?"

FORTY-ONE

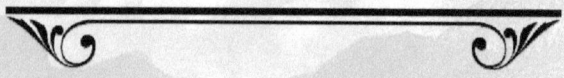

Curator Faera stared up at me, and I knew that look in her eyes immediately.

Desperate. Frantic. Terrified.

As though she could feel the caress of Clysiros's fingertips already on her skin, welcoming her to the silver shores beyond this mortal realm.

It stabbed a brutal memory through my brain before I was ready for it. A flash of the wide desert sun, glaring down over my shoulders and filling my mother's face with hateful heat.

My throat closed. My body went cold.

She was in bad shape—so bad that I was afraid to move or even touch her.

But I couldn't just leave her that way.

Stepping over other crumpled bodies, I heaved the dead Vindexori off her and crouched down to try and assess her injuries. I was no healer, but even I could see that her leg was most definitely broken. She'd taken a blow to the head and, judging by the amount of blood staining the front of her robes, possibly a stab to the abdomen.

But what if there was more damage? Things I couldn't see just by looking at her?

I didn't know—gods, I didn't know! I couldn't help her! I didn't have any potion or tonic, and I had never been taught anything about healing, or—

"I-it was ... Domitri," Faera gasped brokenly. "H-he came i-in ... a-and ..."

"I know," I said gently, my throat still stiff as I watched her struggle for breath. That memory in my chest twisted like a knife. "Try not to move, okay. I'll find help."

The look in her eyes, the solemn understanding that even if I did find someone to help, it would be too late. Not to mention, *I* would likely be the one suspected of this atrocity. It froze me to my very core.

There was no help.

Not this time.

"I have to stop him," I whispered through clenched teeth.

Gods, I didn't even know if I could. One look around this place, at the absolute slaughter, and everything inside me turned to jelly.

What chance did I really stand?

"He's the one who tried breaking into the Vault of Whispers. He's trying it again, right now. I'm going to do everything I can to stop him," I swore. "I need to know where it is. Please, tell me where the vault is."

Her dark eyes welled. Her expression softened, becoming warm as she looked over my face. Then it began to slip—the clarity. I saw her begin to fade.

Panic roared through my veins.

"Tell me! Please! Tell me where the vault is!" I begged.

As her gaze began to grow distant, her lips scarcely moved as she murmured, "Follow the magic." Tears pooled in the corners of her eyes and slid down the sides of her face. "Follow the light."

A thin, rattling breath left her chest, and Curator Faera went still.

My heartbeat stammered.

No.

No, no, no ...

Again. It happened again. Again.

AGAIN!

Agony ripped at my chest like a savage beast, and I covered my mouth as the scream spilled out of me.

She was the only one in this gods forsaken place that had even tried to understand me. To offer me a measure of acceptance not in spite of what I was, but for it. And now she was gone.

My knees shook, threatening to buckle, as I stood slowly.

No, not just my knees.

My whole body quaked, as though something dark and wretched were taking root deep in my soul, breaking apart the fragile bits of good that had been slowly forming over these last few months. I had begun to feel. To trust. To love.

And this is where it had gotten me, on my knees in fresh blood, just like before.

Follow the magic.

Her words still hung in the air like a cool morning mist.

I panned my gaze around the space, scrutinizing every wall, every tapestry, every pile of crumpled bodies, and every lavish cushion and low table. No light. No magic. Nothing that could possibly be—

My breath caught suddenly.

There, in the tangle of the blood-spattered chaos, I saw a faint glow of blue at the far end of the room. Glass crunched under my boots as I made my way toward it, stopping before a long tapestry that covered the wall behind a small dais. The very threads of that fabric, depicting another scene of gods embroiled in battle with angelic Avoran elves, seemed to shine with faint blue light. As though the magic had been sewn into the image stitch by stitch.

But what lay behind it, carved into the wall in thin grooves inlaid with pure silver, was where the light shone brightest.

My whole body seemed to grow cool with focus as I stared at the mark—the crescent moon and sword. It was just like the symbol on the hidden door in the temple. The door Roxus had opened hundreds of times for me.

I knew the words he murmured now. It was an ancient Avoran phrase that granted him passage and was used by every Zenith's Call, but the words alone weren't enough. I understood that now, too.

Because to be oathed in to the order officially also meant bearing their mark on your skin. Every single one of them had it, usually in a place easily hidden by clothing. To the untrained eye, it was just a tattoo. In truth, it was infused with that same ancient elven magic. It wasn't just a branding mark, it was a key burned into their bodies forever that would open secret doors throughout Reatia.

Part of me wondered how Domitri had managed to open it. Had he gotten branded? Or had his mimicry of the brand been enough to fool the magic of the hidden door?

Whatever the case, I still had to find a way through.

But I wasn't a member. I had no mark. No secret key.

I did have a nasty, morbid idea, though.

An extremely Viperi-flavored theory that I knew Roxus and every other civilized surface-dweller would absolutely hate.

And now it was my only option.

Stalking around the fallen corpses of the Vindexori, I used the edge of my blade to cut away bits of their vambraces and gloves, searching their hands and arms for that mark. I didn't see their faces, thanks to the shawls they wore. Part of me was glad for that when I found one with his mark branded on the inside of his forearm.

But another part of me could barely stomach the idea that Varren might be lying somewhere in this room, too.

I didn't know why he'd been dressed like one of them earlier. It was possible he'd already been oathed in and taken on as a Vindexori. Everyone in Arx Eburna had witnessed how much Varren hated me all through our training, so no one would have questioned his loyalty when it came to being involved in my interrogation.

Had he already been oathed in along with the others? Or maybe, once we finished all our trials and assessments, we were taken individually instead of sworn in as part of a whole group?

I didn't know.

I hadn't made it that far, or even thought to ask. I'd been so concerned with survival, with actually making it to the end, that I hadn't considered what might come after if I was successful.

Now, I wished I had.

Just in case, I murmured a quiet apology to the fallen Vindexori as I took my blade and did what only a vile, wicked Viperi would do.

I cut off the dead man's arm, mark and all.

My stomach churned as I carried it over to the door, pressing the palm of it into the mark, and repeated the Avoran phrase I'd heard Roxus use.

On cue, the silver marks of the emblem blazed brighter, glowing to life with vibrant blue light. The stone wall shuddered, lurching an inch, then opening to reveal another cavernous dark passage.

I dropped the severed arm and rushed forward, straight into the tunnel. No looking back. No questioning.

Deeper into the stone. Into the shadows I'd been born in.

I could feel the vibration of the water spilling over the fountain in the walls and floor as I grew closer. Misty light drifted through the tunnel as I drew closer to the end of it. There, a narrow exit emptied right into Krin'Moir through an archway flanked by winged statues.

My gaze panned through the chamber, over the fountain, the glitter of the tiny chips of magically-infused crystals that adorned the ceiling like stars. But instead of the usual strolling figures filling that grand space—murmuring curators discussing texts, patrons and prospects hurrying about their day's business, and Vindexori patrolling the halls—there was only silence.

Not a soul in sight.

An eerie chill swept up my spine like the brush of icy fingertips.

Wrong. It was all wrong.

I prowled onward, drawing both my blades now. My sweaty fingers squeezed against the supple leather hilts. My pulse raced.

Where was everyone?

Why was it so quiet?

I stopped in the middle of the room, right beside the fountain, and eyed every exit point. Every tunnel that led deeper into the complex. Many I'd never dared to explore simply because I was just a prospect. We weren't allowed to go anywhere except the Eternal Hall without a good reason and an escort.

I wasn't even allowed to go there without two chaperones.

Follow the magic. Follow the light.

I searched the room again, but there was so much light. The faux moon. The stars. The braziers. The sconces.

Where should I—?

BOOOOM!

I staggered, almost tripping backward into the fountain as a low, concussive groan made the earth shake under my boots. The stone walls cracked, sending showers of fine dust down from the ceiling. One of the big brass braziers toppled, spilling burning hunks of incense across the marble.

Screams shattered through the cavernous halls, carrying and echoing. Shouts. Clashes of metal.

I gasped, whirling around to face the source of it—one of the big, open doorways leading off to the left.

What, by all the gods, was happening?

No—No time to question.

I ran headlong toward the sound, the earth still rumbling under my feet like a hungry growl.

My teeth chattered, boots skidding over the smooth, polished stone floors as I bolted through the dim hall, passing more toppled braziers and ... bodies. People lying on the ground. Some of them in robes, others in armor. Heavy bronze armor I didn't recognize.

Soldiers?

From where?

The clash of battle hit me like an ocean wave as I rounded a sharp corner, nearly sending me toppling. I skidded to a halt, gaping in awe at the frenzy. Vindexori crossed blades with those bronze-armored soldiers. I ducked as a crossbow bolt whizzed through the air so close I felt the wind on my cheek.

What, by all things divine, was going on?

One of the big, armored men rushed me, charging like a bronze bull straight at me with a longsword raised.

I didn't think. There wasn't time.

I dipped under his strike and tripped him. As he tumbled forward, I sprang at him and drove both my blades into the back of his neck, right where his breastplate ended. He gave a gurgle cry and floundered for a second, but didn't move when I stepped off him.

My chest heaved. My lips twitched as I bared my teeth.

That's when I recognized it—the emblem on the long fluttering red cloak he wore.

The Tibran serpent.

Bile rose in my throat.

Gods and Fates there were *Tibrans* in Arx Eburna?!

FORTY-TWO

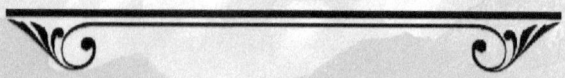

The Vindexori were outnumbered.

Of the twelve still standing, there were at last twice as many Tibran soldiers harrying them with swords, spears, and crossbows.

I could stay. I could fight and probably kill several more Tibran soldiers. But what about Domitri? What about the vault? This was all his doing, wasn't it?

No—I couldn't stay here. Even though that roar of combat heated the flames in my chest, stoking that bloodlust I'd repressed for so long.

Not here. Save it for him.

I whirled through the near dark, ducking and weaving through the battle. Blades hummed and sang through the air, slicing around me as I dodged. Crossbow bolts pinged off the stone walls and floor. Men shouted.

A few of them spat and snarled "Pitathi" at my heels, but in the chaos, I couldn't tell if the insult came from Tibrans or Vindexori.

It didn't matter either way.

One of the bronze-clad soldiers stepped into my path,

sword at the ready. His eyes narrowed through the slit in his helm, and I hesitated.

He was big. Stronger.

But that armor made him slower.

And I'd fought bigger.

I bared my teeth and hissed, showing him my fangs as I spun my blades over my hands. He rushed first, and I feinted, dashing and dipping in a whirling spin to the right. His blade sliced down, and I was already gone—a ghost.

I sidestepped, parried down to keep him from raising that blade again, and drove the end of my other dagger into his side, right where that breastplate buckled. Bone cracked under the steel. He barked a cry of pain that sent a spray of blood across the stone.

Ripping my blade free, I danced back and watched, holding my defense until I saw him start to fall.

Another flash of bronze, a glint of steel, and I whipped into a backbend as another enemy blade swiped down at my neck. I felt the graze of the tip barely kiss my skin, probably leaving a thin red line at the hollow of my throat.

But I came up swinging.

Another quick parry, strike, and cross-parry, and I crushed my knee into the Tibran soldier's groin. He wheezed and faltered, and I went for his throat with the edge of my new daggers.

It was only fair.

His body dropped with a clatter and crunch of armor. But his head rolled a few feet before it scraped to a halt at my feet. I licked my teeth and stepped over it, all my senses alive and crackling like the flames of war. Like the flames that burned molten in my chest and seeped out through every pore.

I lunged for the next nearest Tibran, who had a Vindexori backed in a corner and was raining down blow after blow with his longsword. I caught him on the upswing, twisting my hilt into his and ramming my second dagger into the side of his neck. His blood sprayed my face, warm and thick.

The smell of it ... gods. It kindled that fire. Made it roar from the darkest depths of my soul.

The Vindexori hit the ground on his knees before me, rasping and gripping his side. A fresh split in his armor was all that gave away his injury. Thanks to the black leather and robes, it was impossible to see the blood.

"You're done," I snarled. "Find shelter until it's over."

"Y-you ... saved me," he gasped through the black shawl that covered the lower half of his face. "Why?"

I crouched down, yanking that shawl down so I could see his face, and so he might be able to breathe a little easier.

"Just because you lot hate me doesn't mean it's mutual," I muttered.

"N-no, I mean ... it was you ... before," he wheezed brokenly, sinking lower and finally falling back against the wall. "You came with them. You l-led the siege ... through Krin'Moir and the E-Eternal Hall."

The flames in my chest instantly went out, snuffed as though a winter wind had cut straight through me.

It froze me to the marrow, and all I could do was gape at him.

Me? I had led the charge?

But how was that even—

Domitri.

His name burned like metal pulled fresh from a forge in my mind.

He was doing this—destroying this place—and he was doing it while wearing my face.

Gods curse him straight to the abyss.

"That wasn't me," I whispered, slowly standing and backing away from him. "It wasn't me!"

The Vindexori man stared back at me, his expression every bit as bewildered and terrified as mine probably was.

This couldn't be happening. That fiend, whatever his real name was, had let the Tibrans in here. He'd led a siege of Arx Eburna and used my face to do it.

No.

I had to stop him.

Whatever the cost, I would not let this happen. I would not be remembered as the traitor who helped a foreign tyrant desecrate these sacred halls.

I would end it—even if it ended me.

"Which way did I go?" I demanded with a snarl.

He blinked hard, like I'd slapped him. His brow knitted and he winced, gripping his side and whimpering.

Curse it, I didn't have time for this.

"TELL ME!" I thundered.

"Th-that way." He pointed shakily down the hall.

Good enough.

"Find somewhere safe and stay there!" I yelled as I whirled back to the hall, back toward the clash and rattle of the fight still ringing in the air.

He never answered.

And as I ran headlong into the fray, sprinting as fast as my legs could carry me.

I didn't look back.

FORTY-THREE

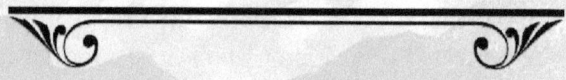

I was cold steel.

I was death, whirling through the air, slicing through enemies, and bringing them down under the bite of my blades. A shadow piercing the light, wavering and flickering. Dancing among golems of bronze with red ribbons of blood trailing the tips of my weapons.

My blood burned like molten metal in my veins. My pulse boomed in hard, heavy thuds. Every sense was keen to the rhythm of the battle, and my mind surrendered to its numb haze. Drinking it in.

Feasting.

I was a shark in my native waters, cruising among the reefs of shadow and death that I'd been made for.

I passed through the battle like a banshee, slaughtering my way to the other side of it and darting away into the dark of the halls beyond.

I couldn't linger. I couldn't help the Vindexori any more than that.

Not with *him* still loose in this place.

I had to stop Domitri first.

One misstep, one mistake, one fumbled strike, and it would all be over. I'd die like a dog on the cold stone floor with everyone in Arx Eburna believing every lie Domitri had ever told about me.

Pumping my legs faster, my brain boiled over with all the lies. The deceptions. The machinations of his grand scheme had been passing right under my nose this entire time. I was too stupid to see it until now.

Domitri had baited me, had used his own prospect, because he needed me on edge—fragile and ready to explode. He needed Mistress Orvana and the other patrons to hate me. He needed the other prospects to reject me so that I had only one person I trusted—the same person he could torment and abuse right in front of me.

Chrysa.

If I was pushed farther and farther away from the rest of the Zenith's Call, they'd never second guess this moment. They'd never doubt that I was the fox in their chicken coop.

Of course I was a Tibran spy.

Of course I had betrayed them, letting Tibran soldiers in here.

Of course I would lead them straight to the vault I'd already failed to break into once.

I was Pitathi—*of course* I was a wicked, traitorous murderer.

My throat burned.

No, no, no! I wasn't!

I'd prove it. I had to. For my sake. For Roxus's.

Skidding to a halt, I faltered in the dark of a large intersection where one grand hallway met another. No sculptures. No torches. No bodies littering the floor, or sounds of combat.

Just a cold, smothering silence like the gloom of a mausoleum.

I glanced to the left and right, studying each path forward.

But one looked exactly like the other. Which way? Where was I supposed to go? The wounded Vindexori man hadn't told me anything. Maybe he hadn't even sent me in the right direction.

I turned in a slow circle, chest heaving with frantic breaths as panic made my mind race and my hands quake.

BOOOM!

Another earthquake shook the world around me, louder and stronger than the first.

I stumbled, but managed to stay on my feet. I dropped into a crouch and covered my head as rubble and dust showered down from the ceiling.

Then the eerie silence swept back in.

I squinted up, wondering if I should be worried about the whole roof caving in on me. I wouldn't be much good to anyone if I got buried alive down here, and—

Light. Soft, ethereal blue light shimmered through the swirling dust in the air.

My breath caught, and I slowly stood.

Ribbons of glittering blue magic shone like veins of precious metal in the stone ceiling overhead, so faint I hadn't even noticed them until now.

"Follow the light," I gasped shakily.

The veins pulsed faintly, growing slightly brighter and then dimming, as though the magical current flowing through them was somehow alive. Ripple after ripple moved along the ceiling, ebbing into the dark hall to my left.

Follow the magic.

Faera's words whispered gently through my mind.

My skin prickled. Those gentle words shone through the haze of bloodlust, clearing the fog like the first rays of morning sunlight. I could feel myself again. I was in control.

This was it. This had to be what she was talking about.

The Vault of Whispers had to be connected to those veins of magic.

I sheathed my blades and followed them.

The rumbling in the stone continued, growling and shuddering the earth under my boots as I moved as quickly as I could track those gently strobing veins of light. Another left. Then down a steep flight of slick stone steps. A right at the next intersection. Deeper down into the earth. Farther from the light.

The air grew colder. But the glow ebbing off those streams of magical energy seemed brighter. The pulsing of the light was faster.

The earth rumbled again, and I felt a sharp jolt under my feet an instant before the earth opened up.

A huge crack split the hall at my heels, and I scrambled, flailing my arms to keep my footing as I ran faster.

Fates, what was happening?

Was it something to do with the vault? Or was Domitri trying to bring down the whole temple?

A massive yawning doorway appeared before me, spanning at least twenty feet to the ceiling. My heart gave a sharp twist of apprehension as I saw that one of the huge black stone doors was already open, and light poured into the hallway from the room beyond.

Blue light.

I shuddered, my pace slowing as I gaped up at the entrance.

The doors and archway were cut straight from the dark stone, but polished and refined until they shone like obsidian glass. The reliefs of vines, roots, and cosmic swirls curled and wove around the images of the sun, moon, stars, strange animals, trees, and three willowy figures. Their bodies were draped in swirling loose robes, their expressionless faces hewn with sharp, peerless beauty. They had wings like the Avoran elves, but I knew better than to mistake them for that.

These were the three Foregods. The makers. The weavers of time.

Itanus, god of All-Past.

Enais, god of All-Present.

And Milontos, god of All-Future.

My mouth went dry.

Whatever lay beyond this door was older than anything else I'd beheld. Older than some of the gods who had sculptures in the temple gardens above.

The three figures were arranged at the very center of the door, arms outstretched to the central shape of an eye.

Not the one of the Viperi, though. No. This one had a slit for a pupil and curled lines around it like a whirlpool.

This was the Eye of Avgior. He was the father of dragons and the sire of the Viepol—beings most just called the Fates, who presided over the realm of the dead and judged souls as either good or evil. He was the keeper of divine secrets. The All-Knowing One.

But that wasn't what made my pulse stir anxiously as I stared up at the doors.

Avgior was one of two gods slain during the War of the Stones, brought down by a mortal's hand. Some texts said it was an arrow that pierced his heart and shattered his very essence. Some said it was a blade. Others described a spear's head. But I'd spent enough time paying attention to Curator Faera's lessons to know that, while the physical weapon varied in the tales, it had to be hewn from an ancient artifact known as the Blade of Souls.

The only weapon capable of felling a god.

My stomach clenched and my insides went watery at the thought that an artifact like that might be hidden just beyond these doors.

Fear gripped me like a hand to the throat.

I didn't want to go in there. I didn't belong in a place like this at all. I doubted any Viperi had ever stood this close to the vault, let alone set foot beyond the threshold in front of me.

But the doors were already open.

Domitri was inside right this second.

And the thought that he might be getting his filthy hands on something like the Blade of Souls sent fear like white fire down to the very marrow of my bones.

There was no one else in sight. No patrons rushing to stop him. No Vindexori with their weapons drawn.

Just me.

I had to stop him, whatever the cost.

I had to save Chrysa. I had to avenge Curator Faera.

I had to protect this place, even if they cursed me for ever being here in the first place.

So I drew my daggers, focusing on the feel of that soft leather under my palms rather than how my knees had begun to shake ...

And I followed the light through the crack in the ancient doors.

FORTY-FOUR

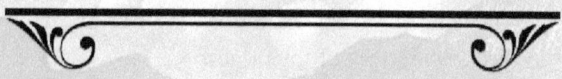

The Vault of Whispers loomed before me like a wall of black, tangled metal.

Bigger than a nightmare, it dominated the entire far side of the chamber, enthroned on a raised dais of polished black stone.

Chills swept through my body, skittering like cold fingertips up and down my spine. My heartbeat slowed, jaw going slack at the sight of it. Massive. Commanding. Complex in a way I could not even begin to comprehend.

Older than the halls I now walked. Maybe as old as time itself.

I couldn't see a handle or latch. No hinges, either. Instead, layers upon layers of metal rings, each one covered in glowing runic marks, were inlaid into its surface. Avoran letters, as though they might spell something out if you found the right arrangement.

Some were only the size of a dinner plate, while others must have been ten or twelve feet across. They spun, sliding like the mechanisms in a clock—some faster, others barely seeming to move at all. But all filled the dim stone chamber with a constant, gritty, grinding noise. Stone rubbing against stone like a miller's wheel.

Or, rather, a hundred of them all at once.

My knees quaked as I took a cautious step forward—closer to it.

How, by all the gods, would anyone think they could crack open a vault like this?

How would one even try?

Then I saw it: a large metal plate set in the floor just before it. No, not a plate.

A plaque.

Engraved into the shining silver surface, lines of more Avoran symbols spelled out sentences:

Brutal master, enthroned within,
Spins tales and visions to twist hearts' whims.
A weight so great, a burden so deep,
A king so cold, few can defeat.
Always feasting, never sated,
Binds with chains their birth created.

I frowned as I read them over and over, worried maybe my new reading skills might be failing me. Was I missing something? Was it a poem? Or a riddle?

I squinted, reading them again. Focusing all my attention there.

A glimmer of silver in the weak light of the chamber was my only warning.

Metal shrieked against metal, clanging as I threw up a frantic cross-parry and managed to twist free. I sprang back, landing in a crouch and gaping at the figure wreathed in eerie blue light as she prowled toward me.

My chest heaved. My teeth ached from the crushing impact of that strike as it still hummed in my bones.

But I couldn't tear my eyes away from her.

Me.

Domitri wearing *my* face.

My mind frazzled at the sight, as though struggling to make sense of it. Bizarre. Seeing myself that way, from the outside, and realizing just how small and thin I looked compared to the other prospects. How that hunger in my blood-red eyes made all my pallid features seem drawn and wild. Unpredictable.

Feral.

Maybe he'd exaggerated a few things, just to paint me more as a villain as he butchered his way through Arx Eburna. But he probably hadn't needed to. Not when the curved scim-itar in my—*his*—hand dripped crimson. More blood spattered his dark clothes, none of it his own.

Curator Faera's face flashed through my mind.

Had that blade been the one to stab her? Had she mistaken this disguise for the real me? Rushed to stop me? To plead with me?

Only to have him ram his weapon through her gut.

Run.

My mother's voice hissed through me like the dry desert wind that had scorched her.

You must run, Visha. Faster than you ever have. They will not spare any mercy on you, my beautiful, wicked daughter.

I choked as bile rose in my throat.

Domitri's cold smile widened, like he could sense my internal frenzy. Wearing that smile—his smile—I truly did look like a wicked creature. One that would never belong with the Zenith's Call.

One that might bring them to their knees instead, and laugh as I danced in the ashes.

That sight hit me like a knee to the gut, knocking the breath from me.

I stared at him—at myself—and snarled.

He bared his teeth back, red eyes glowing like smoldering coals.

"Do you see it now, you little beast? How vile you truly are?" He chuckled, his tone dripping with smug satisfaction. "You think anyone here will ever be able to look past it?"

Rage lit like a furnace's first, fiery gasp in my chest. It sizzled through all my veins, turning my blood molten and singing straight through all my good sense.

I would crush him slowly. A scream for every life he'd taken. Until he begged me to stop.

I threw myself at him, swinging my dual daggers and hailing down three strikes in a manic blur.

He rocked back on his heels, eyes a little wider as he deflected the first two. The third caught him in the arm, and I felt the slice of my blade through his flesh.

Domitri roared and thrust out his free hand, sending a burst of power that filled the chamber with a flash of blue light.

I set my jaw, bracing for it.

WHOOM!

It hit me like a boulder rolling down a mountainside, slamming into my body. I flew back, but managed to drop into a crouch and keep my footing as I skidded across the marble.

My bones creaked. My body trembled.

But I couldn't surrender.

I had to stay focused.

"Try it again," Domitri baited. "Let's see those fangs, Pitathi!"

I clenched my teeth.

No.

He wanted me to break because I was weaker when I lost my grip on those impulses. I couldn't see past them, past the urge to dominate and kill even if it tore me apart. My Viperi instincts were my greatest strength, yes.

But they were also my greatest weakness.

I surged in, my assault purely tactical as I whirled my blades. They hummed a dark melody as they slipped through the air in arcing sterling blurs. He deflected, batting away my assaults as I tested his defenses. Searching for weakness. For a hitch or a falter.

He brought up a hasty parry and tried to sidestep, but I saw it coming.

I ducked under his swing and slammed my pommel into his gut. He coughed and staggered, and I stole another blow to the back of his calf with the cold steel of my daggers.

Domitri let out a sharp bark of pain.

I expected him to stumble. To fall on that now bleeding leg.

But he turned his head, meeting my stare one crimson eye to another.

Domitri's manic smile seemed too wide, his stolen features warping strangely as he gave a flourish with that scimitar. He sent eerie purple flames crackling along the length of the blade an instant before he shot forward, moving as fast as a tongue of lightning.

Heading straight for me.

VOOOM!

It hit like I'd been dipped in a vat of liquid flame. My back arched. My weapons slipped from my hands. My mouth gaped, but I couldn't muster a sound as the force of the blast slammed me against the wall and pinned me there.

Every muscle and nerve screamed, and my vision slipped from color to gray.

Stop—oh, gods, it had to—

I hit the cold of the stone floor in a heap, my entire body shivering as pain still sizzled under my skin. Raw. Sharp.

I screamed.

It was a disgusting, garbled, frantic sound.

Like the bleating of a wounded lamb.

But I couldn't stop it.

"Pathetic," Domitri sneered as he strode closer, still wearing my face, but cringing with every step on that injured leg. His lip curled in disgust, and he used the point of his scimitar to push back some of my hair so he could see my eyes. "All that rage. All that venom. And you're undone with one little spell."

I spat at his feet.

He just smiled behind my disguise again, so wide it revealed the pointed incisors of my teeth.

"Did you really think you could stop me? You may have runesight, but you have no magic. You're decent with a blade, but you're here all on your own." He scoffed. "Where is that large friend you duped into luring me out into the garden, hmm? Or Roxus? You've had him wrapped around your finger for quite some time. Impressive, given his history. To think, he's gone from butchering children to trying to raise one."

My arms shook, pain howling down my back as I fought to push myself back up.

My blades ... I-I had to find them.

Gods, even the inside of my mouth burned.

I sucked in a sharp breath as he put the point of that scimitar right at the base of my throat, letting it spin slightly as he held my gaze.

"Just know that when I cut your head from your shoulders and drop it at Mistress Orvana's feet, they will all praise me for it. They will burn you like the heretics of old and throw your ashes to the pigs," he snickered. "No one mourns a monster."

The ground shuddered suddenly, pitching violently in another earthquake.

It bounced me across the floor and Domitri stumbled. Thankfully, his weapon didn't push into my neck any harder.

Seconds.

I only had seconds.

Curse it, I would *not* die like this.

My hands still shook as I crawled across the marble toward the closest of my daggers. I needed one—just one.

Domitri spat a curse. His footsteps thumped speedily over the ground.

Then another rumble and roar shook the whole chamber. The many dials on the ancient vault gave a unanimous, screeching groan.

Then ... silence.

No more grinding of its many metal wheels and dials. Nothing but my thrashing pulse and scraping breaths.

Domitri stood eerily still, staring up at it with a strange reverence as, one by one, the glowing runes on the dials went dark ... save for four. Four runes. Four Avoran letters that glowed as bright as stars against the dark metal.

S-E-L-F

"Gods," Domitri breathed shakily. "She's done it."

I shoved myself from the floor, grabbing my nearest dagger and forcing my aching fingers to grip it tight as I wobbled.

Wait—*she?*

My vision swerved, still flashing in and out of focus as I looked to the massive vault door. A front portion of it was still moving, mechanisms rearranging and shifting until, at last, a regular sized door unfolded like a paper-crafted star.

It opened with a low boom that echoed to my bones.

And there *she* stood.

Chrysa.

A freshly severed head—an old man with a scraggly gray

beard—dangled from one of her hands. She gripped a bronze-hilted shortsword in the other, still dripping crimson from its slender tip.

With her light, ginger-gold hair pulled up into a high ponytail, the Tibran symbol burned into the side of her neck had never been so visible. Almost like she wore it proudly now. She panned her gaze around the chamber and halted on me, her expression as cool and distant as the surface of a full moon.

Unfeeling. Unmoved.

Unsurprised to see me there, barely on my feet.

Something inside me snapped.

The silvery thread I'd been using to stitch together a patchwork of something good from all my stupid mistakes broke. And in an instant, it all fell apart.

And so did I.

FORTY-FIVE

"CHRYSA!" I hardly knew my voice as I yelled.

But her expression never changed.

She blinked, considering me for a few seconds, before glancing back to Domitri and scoffing. "Really? Were you toying with her again? I told you to take care of this one simple thing, and you can't even manage that."

Domitri cowered like a scolded dog.

His form rippled, shimmering brightly as the disguise of my body and face ebbed away. His horned head dipped low as his mouth twisted into a pleading, desperate grimace. Crazed and frantic, like he would crawl to her and beg her forgiveness if she demanded it.

A blue-skinned rajinna man with brilliant yellow eyes, his too-lean body draped in frayed dark robes. The wound I'd left in his leg bled dark rivulets onto the floor.

"Apologies. I-I was trying to, Knight-Captain," he whined and swished his long, lion-like tail.

"Trying and failing," she deadpanned and tossed the head down from the dais like a rotten melon.

It landed with a squelch right before him, the glazed eyes open and the mouth agape.

Gods—who was that? Another Vindexori? Or someone else?

I'd never seen that man before, but by the look of it, he ... he had already lost his tongue long ago. Now his whole head?

My stomach churned dangerously, threatening to put me back on the ground to vomit.

"You are ever a disappointment. The Emperor will be very displeased that your ego stood in the way of seeing this done." Chrysa strode down slowly, giving a test swing of her blade before she leveled another cold stare upon me. "You should have left the first time they tried to blame you, Violet. All of this could have been avoided. But you're stubborn. And stupidly naive. Though I suppose that will all work out to our advantage now. The gods have smiled upon us."

I tried to swallow, but my throat burned. My stomach twisted. Tears welled in my eyes.

She ... she had done this? Had been the one trying to break into the vault? Had let me believe she was being abused? Had fed me lie after lie so I would only see Domitri?

No. No, it couldn't ... it wasn't ...

"Wh-Why?!" I rasped, my voice breaking.

"Does it truly matter?" Chrysa asked, tilting her head to the side slightly. "What do the Pitathi care about the affairs of kingdoms and crowns?"

My whole body seized. I wanted to crumple. To cave in on myself like a dying star. To scream until I spat blood.

But there was only ... fire.

Cinders in my gut. Ash in my mouth. A hurricane of embers and sparks in my mind.

The fury took hold with blinding speed, and I couldn't stop it. Couldn't fight back the instinct. The rage. The pain.

The need to crush, destroy, and burn. Burn until I was nothing but a pillar of cinder.

And this time, I didn't want to even try resisting.

I would die here. I was outnumbered. Outclassed when it came to magic.

I would be their scapegoat while they slithered away into the shadows again.

But I would not go quietly.

I had taught Chrysa to fight. I could take her down.

"YOU!" I roared as I dove for Chrysa, swinging my blade wide in a reckless strike.

She batted my blade away, moving faster than I'd ever seen her go as she surged for me, chasing down my tactical retreat with brutal precision.

Lies—it had all been LIES!

Her shoddy swordplay. Her meek demeanor. Her friendship.

None of it was real.

I screamed again, the sound welling up from somewhere deep in that internal fire as I dipped and feinted, whirling my dagger and stepping through maneuvers. Strike after strike filled the air with the clang of metal on metal and the scrape and hum of our blades. A sideways roll gave me an opportunity to snatch my other dagger from the floor, but it cost me. Gods, she was fast. *Too* fast.

Standing gave her a chance to rush in, and I barely managed to throw up a frantic block as her sword howled down toward my face.

The impact, her sheer strength, made my brain rattle in my skull.

Her eyes narrowed, frigid and relentless.

Calculating my every move.

I snarled back, unable to keep the hot tears from streaking

down my face as she met each one of my strikes. She matched my speed. My steps. My brutal efficiency.

But I saw her hesitate when I drove in with both my daggers, viciously going for her throat. Her eyes widened, like she hadn't expected me to have the nerve. To really try to kill her.

Her upward block was rushed. Too rushed.

CLANG!

Chrysa let out curse as I slashed one of my daggers down over her shoulder, right at her collarbone. Her footing faltered, and I used that one second to hook a foot around hers and slam the hilt of my other dagger into the side of her face.

Bone and cartilage crunched under the metal of my pommel.

She staggered back, eyes wide and dazed.

I sprang at her, frenzied at the smell of fresh blood. One blow. One slice to that lying throat. Then this would all be—

Pain exploded through my body.

My arms flailed wide, out of my control, and I couldn't hold back a garbled cry of agony. I knew that feeling now. The sizzle of Domitri's vile magic as it surged through me, forcing all my muscles to convulse and spasm while my brain felt like it might burst from the back of my skull.

I fell back onto the floor, back arching as I trembled and fought for control of my body again.

"Stop it," Chrysa barked suddenly, her voice thick with her freshly broken nose pouring blood down her face. She spat a mouthful of it onto the marble as she prowled toward me.

Domitri froze immediately and recoiled, darting back with his yellow eyes wide and confused. He kept his hands raised like he was ready to use that power again at a moment's notice.

"*This* does not concern you," she warned him. "The vault is open. Retrieve the ledger and begone. I will deal with her."

Domitri glanced between us again, his yellow eyes narrowing slightly. Suspiciously. Like he suspected something he didn't dare to speak aloud.

Then he darted for the open door of the vault.

No. No, no, no.

NO!

I screamed the word over and over as my body shook. It took everything I had to keep a grip on my weapons as Chrysa stopped right over me. Her expression stayed so calm, so eerily blank, as she drew back and kicked me in the ribs so hard it sent me rolling.

I stopped on my side, still gripping my weapons. Still fighting to stop that shaking in my body. To force my muscles to obey. Get up.

Curse it—GET UP!

"Get back on your feet," Chrysa spat again. "I know you're not finished."

I snarled a Viperi curse as I glared at her.

I groaned through my clenched teeth as I dragged myself up to my knees, then to my feet. Each movement was agony. My vision spotted with bright streaking stars. My ears rang. My mouth tasted of scorched metal, and I couldn't get my knees to steady.

"It wasn't all a lie, you know," she mused as she stepped around me, circling like a wolf appraising injured prey. "I did like you. I considered carefully if you could be ... recruited. Your skills would certainly be a commodity. But Roxus got to you too early. He'd already turned you soft and useless."

She motioned to me—the way I was still weaving on my feet as I fought to steady my breathing. "Now you see the results. Once, this fight would have been over long ago. You'd have emptied my guts on the floor and walked away clean, even with Kalsin's interference. What a mess Roxus has made you, all for the sake of proving that any beast can be tamed."

My hands squeezed at the hilts of my blades, feeling the give of that leather. Feeling strength and steadiness flood in on a wave of fresh rage. "You ... do *not* ... speak about him ... that way," I seethed hoarsely.

Chrysa paused. Her head tilted to the side slightly, mouth pinching into a tight, thoughtful line. "You care about him, don't you?"

I ground my jaw, testing my weight in my knees. They still wobbled, still shook, but didn't buckle.

Chrysa tsked and shook her head, giving another flourish of her blade. "No wonder your kin banished you to death in the desert. Such sentiment is wasted on a Pitathi. Why even try to love a world that will never love you back?"

I flung myself at her, reckless and enraged.

Our weapons sang a deadly melody, filling the chamber with echoes of steel-on-steel as we dueled. She was fast. But my heart was ablaze with adrenaline and fury that drove me faster. Those instincts my mother had forged burned like hellfire, senses awake and feeling out every move she made.

Every breath.

Every step and swing.

My pulse was thunder in my head.

I locked my hilts with her scimitar and twisted, wrenching her blade downward and out of the way so I could bash my skull against hers just like I had with Declan.

Chrysa's expression blanked, eyes wide and dazed as she stumbled back.

I pounced. Ready to end it. Ready to put my daggers straight through her heart.

"V-Violet!" she whimpered suddenly, her voice tinged with panic as she threw up a hand as though to stop me.

I hesitated.

The fear in her eyes was so primal. So real. It was tinged with something that might have been regret. Or sorrow.

For a single heartbeat, I faltered.

BAM!

She slammed the hilt of her sword across my face.

Instantly, the world went dark.

FORTY-SIX

I knew I was going to die.

Even before Chrysa seized a fistful of my hair and dragged me onto my back. The room spun slowly back into view, nothing but a smear of dark stone and faint glowing blue runes all smudged together like a child's fingerpaints.

I flopped onto the cold stone floor. Useless. Limp.

Where were my blades?

Gods, where was *I*?

My arms wouldn't move. I groaned and tried to blink hard —tried to clear my vision.

I could hardly make out Chrysa's face as she loomed over me, still gripping her blade. Her face was a mask of cold indifference as she studied me. I couldn't tell what she might be thinking.

Trying to decide whether or not to kill me?

"Knight-Captain, I have the ledger," Domitri—or Kalsin, apparently—called out from somewhere nearby. "But, Gods, did you see what else is in there? Should we take anything more?"

"Trinkets for fools," Chrysa snapped. "We were sent to retrieve the ledger for a reason. Do not forget our purpose."

"And what of her?" Kalsin asked, his tone edged with uncomfortable hesitation.

"Even more useless than I suspected," she quipped.

"Then allow me to dispatch her, and let us be off! Quickly! Before the Vindexori arrive!" he urged, tone tight with apprehension.

"You will *not* take my kill, slave," Chrysa commanded.

I groaned through my teeth again as she stepped over me, leaning down so she was mere inches from my face. Her green eyes were so utterly empty. A void of bitter focus like the eye of a winter storm. No feeling. No compassion.

"Remember me," she whispered. "Remember *this* was a mercy."

Pain took me like an iron tide, slamming into my body as she rammed her blade straight down into my abdomen. Her expression twitched, nose wrinkling as she twisted her sword before ripping it free ...

And plunging it in again.

Another twist. My flesh tearing.

I couldn't move. Couldn't scream. Couldn't breathe.

Agony dragged me under like a smothering dark tide. I glared up at her, my tongue writhing at the flavor of blood that filled my mouth.

N-No. It couldn't end. Not like this. Not with me writhing on the floor like a wounded animal.

Not alone.

My vision blurred and tunneled. My pulse thumped wildly. Fast—too fast. I had to calm down. I'd bleed out faster if I didn't get it under control.

"Give me the ledger," Chrysa demanded as she prowled toward Kalsin, sheathing her blade and thrusting a hand out to him expectantly.

He ducked his head low and offered her a thick, black tome bound in dark steel. She swayed slightly under its weight, as though it were a lot heavier than it looked. Her expression softened a bit, the iron-clad focus dissolving to awe as she brushed a hand over its metal cover.

"Lord Argonox will be pleased," she whispered reverently.

"No," a strong male voice cut through the silence, filling the chamber like a clap of thunder. "I don't think he will."

Chrysa tensed and whirled around. Kalsin paled, drawing back behind her and reaching for his scimitar. They gaped in shock toward the room's only exit.

And I saw him there—his tall, wide-shouldered frame standing in the open doorway.

Roxus.

My Roxus.

His gaze held mine for half a second—maybe less.

Then Roxus's whole body began to change. It grew and warped, swelling and filling the room like a monstrous wall of dark, shaggy brown fur.

He hit the ground on four huge, claw-tipped paws and let out a bellowing roar that sent Kalsin and Chrysa stumbling back on their heels.

G-Gods, he … he'd turned into an enormous *bear*.

And he hadn't come alone.

Roxus charged into the room, the ground flinching under his lumbering gait, and a dozen Vindexori followed him. Gods, I could have sworn I saw Mistress Orvana among them, but my vision winked and faltered.

Those dancing bright spots grew, blotting out portions of the room.

My ears rang louder.

Cold. Why was it getting so cold?

N-No. I had to get back up. I had to fight.

Gritting my teeth, I willed myself to roll over onto my side.

There, only a few feet away, one of my blades lay where I'd dropped it.

I crawled for it, leaving a smear of blood on the stone behind me. Just a little farther. Five feet. Then two.

I slapped a hand down over the hilt and squeezed it tight.

I wasn't dead yet. I would fight to the end alongside the one person in the world I knew loved me. The only one who always found me in the darkest corners of my despair.

My friend.

My family.

A hellish cry of rage left my lips as I stood. Pain rocked me to the core. Blood poured from the two stab wounds in my gut. But I didn't stop.

The Vindexori rushed for Chrysa. Roxus barreled toward Kalsin. And I ran like a madwoman to join the fray.

Magic lit up the dim chamber like lightning bolts popping off a thunderstorm. Kalsin slung spell after spell at Roxus, but each one seemed to glance right off his shaggy hide. He didn't so much as flinch as he rose before Kalsin, a wall of fur and muscle. With one mighty swipe of his claws, he sent the rajinna sorcerer sprawling across the room like a ragdoll.

I sprang, pushing away the roar of pain that hummed through my body. Ignoring the way everything seemed to slide sideways every time I took a breath.

I was there when Kalsin stopped sliding and drove my dagger straight down through his chest with a wet *crunch*.

He hissed, baring his fangs as his yellow eyes flashed with feral desperation. His hand came up, ready to hit me point-blank with another blast of his magical power.

Instead, Kalsin's mouth gaped in a ragged shriek of pain as Roxus clamped his massive jaws onto his leg and flung him against the wall.

I started to pursue. To follow up with another attack.

One step—and my legs caved under me.

I crumpled like a marionette cut from its strings.

The stone floor was cool against my cheek as I lay on my side, watching Roxus lumber after Kalsin with blood dripping from his jaws.

Kalsin coiled and cursed like a wounded serpent, staring at Roxus and thrusting out a hand in another reckless magical assault.

The concussive *BOOM* made the whole chamber shudder. It blew me backward, sliding my body across the floor until I rolled to a stop facing the other way. I didn't see it when Roxus ended him. But I heard the garbled scream. The frantic prayer.

And the final crunch of bone under fangs and claws.

Across the room, I only caught glimpses of Chrysa encircled by the Vindexori. They converged like a black leather wave, ensnaring her and pressing in from all sides. She was already injured and now burdened by the weight of that big metal-bound book—the ledger.

It only took seconds for them to bring her down.

She screeched as they tore the book from her hands and pinned her to the ground, shackling her legs, wrists, and neck just like they had mine.

Gods, they had her. They wouldn't let her go.

They wouldn't let her get away with this.

I had to believe that.

With one Vindexori pinning her head to the floor, our gazes locked from across the room. Her soft ivy-green eyes were still wide and crazed. Blood from her broken nose was smeared over her face. But she saw me—and something else filled her expression. It skewed her features with a manic terror I didn't understand.

And it didn't matter right then.

My mind slipped into the haze of pain that seemed to spin the whole room around me like a kaleidoscope. Darkness seeped into the edges of the world, creeping in and spreading before my eyes.

It was so cold.

So final.

I could almost make out someone calling my name.

Roxus?

He was holding me, cradling me against his chest as though I were something precious. Something he valued. Something he loved.

No one had ever held me like that.

"Stay with me, girl," Roxus rasped over me, his rugged features drawn in panicked desperation. "You keep looking at me, you understand? Just keep breathing. Help is coming, you just gotta hang on."

I wanted to.

More than anything, I wanted to stay here. I wanted to keep fighting at his side.

He wasn't my father. He wasn't my brother. But he was more family to me than anyone had been in so long.

He was the only person who'd ever made me feel safe in my own skin.

Something in his expression—the tears pooling in his eyes —made me wonder if he felt that way, too. Like we really were meant to find each other.

But the world was getting dim.

The sound of his voice grew farther and farther away. My arms and legs had gone numb. My heartbeat had gone from thundering madness to a failing whisper.

I was ... leaving him. Slipping into the eternal gray.

And, gods, I was ready to do anything it took to find my way back here. Back to him.

Back to where I had always belonged.

FORTY-SEVEN

I'd never had a home before.

Not the streets of Rienka, where I'd struggled and fought to survive for so many years. Not the empty desert that stretched out with wind-sculpted golden dunes all the way to the towering dark mountains of Nar'Haleen where my mother's bones still lay. Not the deep, endless dark caverns beneath where the Empire of the Viperi had simmered in malice for so many ages.

But before I even opened my eyes, I knew.

I knew the sound of the sea, roaring like it might come surging up to lick at my bare toes. I knew the smell of the salty wind, rushing in through the long drapes over my little balcony. I knew the soft bed and clean sheets, and the faint taste of honey on my tongue leftover from whatever medicines Leruna had been funneling down my throat.

I was home.

Home ... and alive.

Gibb's warm, furry butt was pressed against one of my cheeks. He sat on the pillow next to my head, his deep purr filling my ears like a rumbling lullaby.

I willed my eyes to open and tried to blink away the blurriness—like I'd been lying this way, not quite asleep but not quite awake, for a long time.

Had it been days? Weeks?

Every joint and muscle ached and throbbed as I turned my head to look around the room.

I found Roxus sitting at my bedside, watching my every move in total silence.

Our gazes locked, and I saw it: relief.

It washed over the tense, hard lines of his face. The lengthy stubble he hadn't bothered to shave in a while. The dark circles under his light amber eyes. The deep creases of worry that ran across his forehead and right between his eyebrows.

His thin lips tugged at a half-smile as he murmured, "There you are."

My heart shattered.

A sob I hadn't even sensed was coming rose in my throat as tears filled my eyes.

He was on his knees at the side of my bed in an instant, running his warm, calloused hand through my hair as he whispered gently, "Hey, now. It's okay. It's over now. You're all right."

I wasn't.

Not even a little.

I hadn't seen it. I hadn't even suspected. Chrysa had sat there alongside me, trained with me, taught me to read and write, and I had never once thought she was anything other than what I saw. Another lost girl, trapped in a cage, clawing for a way out of a life she hadn't chosen.

Lies.

I didn't know who she really was. I didn't know how she'd come to the Southern Kingdoms, or what her relationship to that rajinna man truly was.

How had I been so blind? How could I have missed it all this time?

I could still feel the twist of her blade in my flesh. I could still see that strange look on her face as she was being shackled by the Vindexori.

What had happened after that? Had they already executed her? And what would happen to me now? How had Roxus convinced Mistress Orvana he wasn't involved in her schemes? And he'd even gotten her to send Vindexori to the vault? Gods, how? HOW?

I didn't know. I couldn't answer any of the questions that surged through me like Kalsin's wicked magic. Leaving trails of agony behind.

"Easy, easy," Roxus murmured softly. "It's going to be okay. I've got you, Violet. We'll get through it together."

"H-How?" I managed to gasp brokenly.

His hand paused, cradling my cheek tenderly as tension settled over his face like a gray cloud. "The clues were there. Unfortunately, none of us put them together until it was nearly too late."

I let out another shaking breath. "They found Domitri's body under the bed?"

Roxus nodded. "That and a few other things helped to point things in the right direction. Curator Faera had caught on to the type of books Chrysa preferred to check out from the Order's library—texts on particular Avoran enchantments like the ones on the vault. The fact that she was already fluent in the ancient tongues, as practiced as any scholar we'd seen here, tipped her off."

I closed my eyes, letting her name wash over me—through me—like cold rain. Curator Faera had known. Had seen it all. Had seen Chrysa and me for who we really were.

Now she was gone. She'd paid the ultimate price, but not

before setting off the alarm. Not before making sure the right person would be held responsible.

"There was more, like the signet ring you found was made to fit a man's hand, not a tiny Viperi girl's, so it couldn't possibly be yours," he continued, leaning his elbows on the bedside and rubbing at his now heavily stubbled jaw. "But the most damning was Domitri's body. Best we can tell, they killed him months ago. It was a risky, elaborate ruse. But none of us saw it coming."

"What ... did they want?" I asked, voice scraping as I swallowed back my sobs. "That ledger ... what was it?"

His expression hardened, lips thinning as he stared back at me and said nothing for a few long, heavy seconds. As though he were trying to make up his mind on just how much he should tell me right now.

I fully expected him to refuse.

But his voice was deep and riddled with a grim resolve as he said, "The Black Ledger is our most fiercely guarded artifact. It's a book of ancient secrets. Specifically, it contains the locations of many powerful, divine artifacts still hidden throughout the world—artifacts that, in the wrong hands, could be used to catastrophic ends. Its contents are so significant that it warrants its own private guard who has his tongue voluntarily cut out so he can never speak of what is written inside."

The old man's head—the one Chrysa had carried out of the vault—that must have been who he was. She had killed him when he wouldn't tell her the secrets of the book, or had tried defending it.

Those words, and the realization of just how close we had come to losing that ledger to the hands of the Tibran Empire, sent a coldness through me that made my whole body shudder. Gods and Fates. If Roxus and the Vindexori had arrived even a minute later, or if Chrysa had decided to let Kalsin kill me quickly, that book would be on its way to the waiting hands of the tyrant, Lord Argonox.

"The Tibrans want to use them as weapons," I guessed.

"At a minimum," Roxus agreed.

"They'll try to find them anyway," I guessed again.

His shoulders dropped some and he nodded.

"We ... we have to stop them," I realized. "We can't let the Tibrans find one—not a single one."

Roxus's gaze fixed on mine again, and I could sense his thoughts as though our minds had somehow melded in that moment. An understanding that was soul-deep.

We *would* make sure. We'd fight, claw, bleed, and die if that's what it took to keep those artifacts out of Tibran hands.

"Rest," he ordered gently as he began to stand. "Once you've healed, there's quite a lot to do. The work of the Zenith's Call is never finished."

My heartbeat skipped.

Wait—was he really saying ... ?

My lips parted as I stared up at him, words and thoughts all tangling up in my head. "You ... you mean?"

His smile lit his eyes like warm embers, bright and alive. Full of so much promise. "Mistress Orvana has accepted your candidacy. You've proven yourself far beyond the measure of our usual trials and assessments. When you're back on your feet, you'll be oathed officially, if that's still what you want."

It was the only thing in the entire world I wanted.

To keep walking alongside him. To continue honing my skills. To become something more than I'd ever dared to dream of.

"Yes," I managed, my voice a pitiful, croaking squeak of emotion.

His smile widened. "Good. Try to get some sleep. Delthene will bring more healing tonics and something to eat soon. Don't get too excited, though. Leruna has ordered soups and broths only until your abdomen heals fully."

He turned to the door, hands already in his pockets as he crossed the room. As he reached the doorway, however, I saw him tense. He paused, not looking back as he murmured, "You should know she's ... she's not dead."

My heart seemed to jolt in my chest, suddenly far too heavy, as I stared at his broad back.

Chrysa—he was talking about Chrysa.

She was still alive. The Vindexori hadn't killed her.

Gods, I didn't know if I should be furious or relieved. None of the twisted feelings in my head made sense.

"She's been sent to the Necrolis Prison on the island of Kua'Tar." His words cut straight through me, every bit as sharp and cutting as Chrysa's blades had been.

They had sent her to the most notorious prison in the Southern Kingdoms. One guarded by vicious spirits that were trapped there eternally—spirits of past prisoners who would never escape it, even in death.

It was the nearest thing to hell this mortal world could provide. A fate worse than death.

"Remember this was a mercy."

Her words echoed in my mind over and over, endless and leaving scar after scar on my pathetic heart. Had she known that's what might happen to me if I was found alive and blamed?

"Remember this was a mercy."

Gods, it really had been.

I didn't see Roxus leave, although I heard the door shut.

All I could do was stare up at the ceiling with those words repeating in my mind. All I could see was her face in those final moments. Had she known what would happen to her? Or had she expected to be interrogated and executed?

Tears ran down the sides of my face, leaving warm trails

over my skin that cooled quickly in the breeze that ebbed in from my open balcony.

Should I hate her? Gods knew I wanted to.

She was a liar. A traitor.

I should be pleased that she was doomed to rot away in that foul place, far away from me and the Zenith's Call.

So ... why wasn't I?

What did that mean?

I didn't know. But it hurt to think of her. It hurt to think that I'd go back to Arx Eburna to keep practicing and polishing my skills as an official member of the Zenith's Call ... and she wouldn't be there.

I'd sit alone during lectures. I'd train and practice combat on my own. I'd eat by myself in the roof garden of the temple. I'd sit at an empty table in the library to keep studying divine lore.

And for whatever reason—something I couldn't name or even begin to understand—that tore my whole world in two.

FORTY-EIGHT

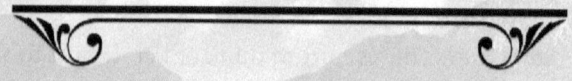

"Wow, you look ... a lot less dead," Declan blurted as soon as he stuck his big, dumb head through my bedroom door.

I'd been ready to climb the walls after the first week. But Leruna had come by the house with more tonics and powerful healing salves, and my ears were still ringing from the lecture she'd given me about letting my injuries fully heal. No heavy lifting. No heavy foods.

And absolutely *no* combat training.

Delthene teased me that no one had ever died of boredom, but I was willing to bet I had come close.

Four excruciating weeks of reading, brooding, pacing, and sulking later, I'd finally gotten the okay to leave the house. My wounds were healing nicely. I wasn't supposed to spar just yet, but I could eat solid food and go on walks again.

Walks—outside—with an escort.

And that's exactly why Declan had come here today.

"You're sure about this?" he asked, shifting uncomfortably as he lingered in the doorway.

I hurried through tying the laces on my boots. "Yes. Gods, you have no idea how sure. This place feels like an asylum."

He chuckled, running a hand through his lengthy hair down to the back of his neck. "Fine, fine."

I bounced to my feet and muscled my way around his large form, squirming my way into the hall. I pretended not to notice the fresh bruises on his face, or the way his lip was split again. Another round in the pit. Another beating.

It made my stomach sour at the thought.

"Roxus told me what happened," he said as he followed me down the stairs. "I guess that means you finally saw his, uh, *other* side."

My hands clenched as my mind seized around the memory of what had happened in the vault chamber. Of Roxus transforming into that beast—a bear far too big to be anything natural.

Well, now I understood why Roxus could give someone like Declan reason to pause. He might have seemed smaller and slighter by comparison, but he harbored a very dangerous secret.

I'd spent some of my bountiful free time combing through whatever books I could find in his office that might reveal the reason he could take on that form. There was no mention of bear-shifting humans in any of the texts on ancient divine lore, though. Not even a hint of it in any of the Avoran texts, either.

At least, none that he kept here.

And I was too much of a coward to ask him outright.

"We haven't discussed it," I admitted once Declan and I were out the front door.

The warm evening air filled my lungs like a breath of new life. The salty brine and faint hint of fish drew me farther away from the house, luring me along the sidewalks toward the dockside markets.

"Why not?" Declan seemed genuinely surprised. "I didn't

think it was a big secret. Everyone around here knows he's an Ursinaar. That's why you won't find a petty thief or bandit on this island brave enough to try to pick his pocket."

My mind seized that new word—Ursinaar—like a trap snapping closed on an unsuspecting mouse.

Only ... it wasn't completely new, was it? I'd heard it before. Roxus had mentioned Ursinaar when he talked about the origins of the daggers. He'd said they were brutal warriors from Vordega, which was a kingdom I knew next to nothing about. Well, apart from the fact that it had warred against the Avoran Empire centuries ago, and had been quite good at cutting down the angelic elves. Better than most, he'd claimed.

Now I had to wonder if that had something to do with the Ursinaar, like Roxus.

"Is that also why Mistress Orvana is willing to put up with him challenging her on things?" I wondered aloud.

Declan's grin was smug and wolfish. "Probably. She'd be hard-pressed to replace him if he did decide to leave the order."

Hmmm.

"So, why haven't you asked him about it?" Declan put his hands behind his head, making a big show of avoiding eye contact as we strolled the steadily sloping sidewalk that led into the harbor.

"I will, just ... not yet," I answered pathetically. I really didn't have an excuse except that it felt like a very invasive thing to question him about.

Especially since he hadn't volunteered that information about himself already. There must have been a reason he hadn't wanted me to know. Had that reason changed now that I was going to be Zenith's Call?

Or was this much more personal?

"What do you know about him?" I dared to ask, and slid Declan a sideways glance just to see how he reacted.

His jawline tensed, and he angled his face away like he

could sense my probing stare. "Not much more than you, apparently."

I frowned. "But people talk."

"Yes, they do." He sighed.

"And drunk people talk even more. How convenient that you work around those kinds of people every night, hmm?"

His brow furrowed, and he scrunched his mouth to one side. "Look, I really don't know all that much. Yes, people talk. But it's not people who actually know him. He's Ursinaar, so he comes from Vordega. No one seems to know how or when he arrived here, but I've heard stories that he showed up on a slaver's vessel, beaten within an inch of his life, and it was the Zenith's Call that bought him out of it."

I couldn't hold back my shock as a cold chill tingled up my spine, spreading shivers over my skin. He'd been a slave? How? He was so strong and ... and surely Vordega prized fighters with skills and abilities like his. Right?

It didn't make any sense.

But I was suddenly very glad I hadn't worked up the nerve to ask him about it yet.

That was bound to be a very sensitive topic—and certainly one I should wait for him to bring up on his own when he was ready.

"Don't overthink it," Declan added quickly and gave my head a rough pat. "I don't even know if that story's true."

"Right." I sighed.

We walked on. I caught myself stealing more glances up at him. The wind tousled his brownish-gold hair, and the tattoos on his neck and throat were all too visible over the collar of his tunic. I wondered when he'd gotten them, and if they meant anything specific.

"Hey, um, I wanted to thank you," I remembered suddenly.

He turned a puzzled frown down to me. "For what?"

"For what you did at the temple," I said. "Causing a distraction."

His face skewed with discomfort. "Oh. Right. That."

"If you hadn't bought me that chance, I wouldn't have found the body of the real Domitri. Without that evidence ... " I shuddered. It was possible that, if I had never found it, Mistress Orvana wouldn't have been convinced to look into what was really happening at the vault.

"You're, uh, you're welcome," he stammered as he scratched at his chin.

"Did they arrest you for causing a scene?" After I'd slipped into the apartment building, I really had no idea what had happened to him. Gods, I hoped I hadn't landed him in jail for a night.

Declan wafted a hand. "Nah, nothing like that. They tossed me out on my rear and told me to go home and sober up. No big deal."

I puffed a breath of relief. I slumped some, my thoughts drifting to that night before I could stop them. To being under that bed, lying in a puddle of old blood. To finding Domitri's corpse. And then being faced with—

Declan's big hand bumped mine. Not on accident. Like he wanted me to know that he was there, right beside me. Within reach, if I needed.

I didn't dare look up as my heartbeat raced. My hand drifted toward his, as though pulled by some invisible force. I wondered what it might feel like to take his and entwine our fingers.

But I didn't dare try it.

"I'm ... I'm sorry. You know, about ... her." He stumbled over his words again.

My steps slowed as my heart seemed to plunge from my chest down to the soles of my boots. "Me too," I admitted quietly.

"It's not supposed to be like that. You're supposed to be able to trust people. I hope you know that," he said, his tone tight with earnest.

All I could do was nod a little. Not convincing, probably.

We walked on in silence for a few minutes, but I couldn't shake the pull of that memory. I had done everything I possibly could to not think about that—about her—for four weeks. Now, all those memories were roaring through my head like a surging river.

"I keep looking for her," I said, my own voice shocking me into stopping mid-step. I stood on the sidewalk with him, head bowed, and the weight of that confession settling over my shoulders.

"Yeah?" he coaxed, like he wanted me to go on. Like he actually wanted to know how I felt.

So I told him.

"It's stupid, I know. And I know she's not coming back. But I just ... can't help it. Every time I go back into Arx Eburna. Every time I pass the Eternal Hall. I keep expecting to see her walk in. Part of me wants her to *so badly*. I know it's wrong, but I—"

"It's not wrong," he interrupted, his voice deepening with resolve. "You hear me, Violet? It's not wrong. Not even a little. She was your friend. She was someone you cared for. Someone you trusted. And she betrayed you. You're allowed to feel however you need to about it—sad, angry, confused—whatever you need."

Suddenly, I couldn't breathe. Everything seemed to slip into a strange, too quiet fog around me as the memories replayed. Her lying on the floor. Her words still repeating in my head.

Remember ... Remember ...

I would. Forever.

Warm fingers brushed my chin, slowly tilting my head back until I stared up into Declan's worried gaze. "Violet?"

I blinked hard, and everything seemed to snap back into clarity.

But I couldn't look away from him.

He wouldn't betray me like that ... would he?

The thought crushed down through my body, and I flinched hard. Oh, gods, if he did. If he turned on me like that. If I lost him the way I'd lost Chrysa.

I immediately pulled back from that touch.

His expression fell some, dark brows crinkling as he slowly dropped his hand back to his side.

A long, excruciatingly awkward minute passed before I finally dared to start walking again. He hesitated for a second, then started following along beside me, and I noticed he was keeping a little more distance between us.

For some reason, that made my heart ache like someone had reached down into my chest and was twisting it.

I just didn't understand why.

"So, about your oathing ceremony," he said after we'd strolled a while, very obviously trying to change the subject. "That's coming up, right?"

"In three days," I confirmed.

"Nervous?"

I shook my head.

"Picked out a spot for your oath mark yet?" He sounded genuinely curious about that, at least.

I tapped my right upper forearm, just below my elbow.

He made an approving grunting sound. "Easy to conceal."

"Hopefully."

"And what happens after that, eh? You start running around doing secret Zenith's Call missions with Roxus and never spar with me again?"

I could spot that ridiculous ploy a mile away. "Yes, I will still spar with you, you overgrown manchild."

His mouth bent in a real smile that put a dimple in one cheek and made his earthy-green eyes sparkle. I realized too late he was ... handsome.

Very handsome.

And big—so big he made me look like a child toddling along next to him. Every part of his brawny form seemed to be made for war.

Something about it made my pulse skip erratically, and I had to look away.

Gods, why was my face so hot?

"What?" he asked when he noticed me staring down at the sidewalk like I'd found the meaning of life there.

"Nothing," I answered quickly—too quickly.

He noticed that, too. "We don't have to keep sparring if you don't want to. Honestly, at this point, there's not much more I can teach you. It's just nice to have someone to practice with who's on a similar level skill-wise."

"*Similar* level?" I scoffed, baiting him. "Don't insult me."

I could hear the mischief drenching his tone without ever having to meet his gaze. "Oh yeah? Let's see who can do the most sit-ups. Or maybe we can go on another nice jog to the beach?"

I stuck my tongue out at him, determined not to let him see how much I would have loved another jog to the beach. "I'm injured. It doesn't count."

He laughed and tilted his face back to the warmth of the morning sun. "Fine. I'll give you a few more days to heal. Then, we'll settle this the old-fashioned way: with too much ale and feats of strength."

I couldn't hold back a laugh of my own. "It's a deal."

FORTY-NINE

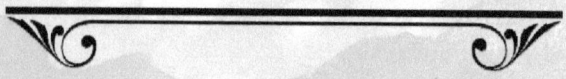

Three days might as well have been an eternity.

But my time in medical confinement was over. I could return to Arx Eburna. I could take my oath and become what I had been trained to be ...

As soon as Roxus returned from his morning meeting.

Uggh.

From where I sat under a shady potted palm at the edge of the grand temple courtyard, I could see Arx Eburna's newest arrival towering over a crowd of young female prospects who gawked and giggled like he was some sort of street performer.

He might as well have been, for all those showy, wide smiles. He was the most obnoxious idiot I'd ever seen. Not what I'd call Zenith's Call material by a long shot. But Mistress Orvana probably hadn't been left with much of a choice when it came to bringing in fresh talent to replenish the ranks here.

The mess with Chrysa and Kalsin had left deep scars in Arx Eburna. A significant portion of the Vindexori had been either killed outright or gravely injured in the final attack on the vault. Their ranks had never been thinner, and so Mistress

Orvana had called upon most of the newly-oathed prospects to join them immediately.

Only one was omitted from that path, actually—myself.

I was still set to become a field agent. Or, rather, a dextrum, as they called it. I'd be working with Roxus on missions as his tandem partner. That, I could only guess, was my reward for nearly dying to defend this place.

I'd taken it straight away.

And now, today, my oath would be finalized. Set in ink upon my skin forever.

Gods, I'd never been so ready for anything in my life.

So where the heck was—

"Let's go," Roxus grumbled, appearing over me suddenly with his arms crossed.

I didn't look away from the spectacle of a guy who was lavishing friendly greetings on each and every one of his admirers. "Who is that?"

He followed my glare to the young man and arched an eyebrow. "Hmm. Well, we had to bring in a few agents from Esfolar, including an old acquaintance of mine," Roxus said. "I believe that is her new tandem partner. He's fresh out of his own trials, just like you. I don't know his name, though."

I curled my lip. I could think of a few for him all right.

That flashy smile with too-perfect teeth was nauseating. His golden tanned skin shone like bronze in the sunlight, and his shoulder-length hair was as black as raven feathers. High cheekbones, sharply angled jawline, and pointed ears. A half-elf? Probably.

I rolled my eyes.

If vanity had a face ...

"Glad to see you're already making new friends," Roxus snorted and nudged me with the toe of his boot. "Come on, my little sour grape. It's time."

Right. I had far more important things to do with my time.

I loosed a breath and hopped to my feet, falling in step next to Roxus. We walked the temple grounds and took the hidden entrance in the archives. My heart pumped more fiercely with each step down into the sacred caverns, feeling the weight of that familiar chill like a yoke around my neck as we made our way to the base of the massive central fountain.

There, Mistress Orvana was already waiting with a company of four Vindexori. Two stood on each side of her, so eerily still I could have mistaken them for statues.

Well, save for one.

Varren stood on her right, arms at his sides and shoulders back at attention. He wore the same black covering over his nose and mouth, but I knew his eyes all too well. He really was a Vindexori, after all. And he'd risked that for my sake when he set me free from the jail.

Knowing that put a strange twinge of emotion in my chest as I prowled past him.

"Pitathi," he muttered with a nod.

I smirked and nodded back. "Idiot. Your breastplate's crooked."

I heard him hiss a curse under his breath.

Mistress Orvana arched a brow at me as I came to stand before her, Roxus close behind. Her eyes scanned me from head to toe, as though silently taking measure of my new black fighting leathers and the fine daggers belted to my thighs. Delthene had wound my pale hair into a plaited braid, and I'd dared to buckle Orvana's own black leather whip to my belt— just to remind her of that day.

My first day here.

"You seem well," she said coolly. "I trust that, after this rite is complete, you will be able to conduct your duties promptly?"

I fought back the smugness that threatened to leak into my words. "I'm fully recovered and more than able to take on any request you might have of me, Mistress."

Her eyes narrowed ever so slightly. "We shall soon see, won't we?"

Roxus cleared his throat, as though trying to diffuse the growing tension in the air somehow.

Guilty or not, I was not stupid enough to think for even one second that Mistress Orvana trusted me—let alone approved of my presence. I was still Viperi. But she was all out of excuses to keep me from joining.

For now, anyway.

"Make no mistake," Mistress Orvana added swiftly, her glare as relentless as ever. "You will still be carefully monitored as you continue your apprenticeship with Roxus."

Of course. Because almost dying to protect their precious artifacts wasn't proof enough of my loyalty. Not that I expected anything less from her, but it still made me scowl.

I had to look away, tasting every bitter word I wanted to hiss back at her.

Control, control. Breathe.

"What happened was despicable, and had we not been so preoccupied dealing with you, our agents might have caught on to Domitri's machinations far sooner," she scolded.

Roxus took a step closer, moving right beside me with an eyebrow arched, as though silently inviting her to choose her words more carefully.

She smoldered in silence for a few seconds, seeming to consider that, and finally turned away, giving us her back. A gesture of dismissive defiance.

She took a large, silver goblet from one of the waiting Vindexori beside her and bent to hold it under the pouring water of the fountain behind her. Then, she turned and handed it to Roxus, her expression more composed ... but no less frosty around the eyes.

"You were, in this case, merely the lesser of two evils, girl," Orvana muttered as Roxus took the cup. "See that you tread lightly; these walls have eyes that see far more than your Pitathi ones can."

Roxus let out a low, rumbling growl that thrummed in the stones beneath my feet.

The Vindexori shifted uncomfortably, but did not yet daring to touch their weapons.

Because none of them wanted to fight an Ursinaar.

I couldn't hold back a smirk.

"Of course, Mistress. I live to serve the order as you see fit," I murmured back and dipped into a low bow as she began striding away, her guards close behind.

It made her pause and glance back, her glare scorching. "You have my blessing to be oathed. But you have my assurance that I will be watching."

I did smirk then. Chalk it up to my Viperi pride, but I couldn't hold it back for one second longer.

Mistress Orvana strode away, head held high and shoulders thrown back in proud dignity as she disappeared into the hall that led back to her chambers.

She wanted to keep playing these games? Fine.

I'd master them, just as I'd master the rest of the knowledge the Zenith's Call had to offer. And someday ... I'd make her eat those words.

I would prove myself to this order beyond the shadow of any doubt, no matter the cost.

FIFTY

It would hurt.

I knew that even before I crossed the threshold into the Oathing Chamber.

Chills climbed my body like I was easing into freezing water, inch by inch, until I could hardly breathe. My heart beat wildly and my fingers tingled. But I wouldn't let it show.

Not now. Not when I knew this was the moment my whole life would change.

My gaze drew up to the domed glass ceiling more than twenty feet overhead, marking how the black obsidian glass was cut in silhouettes to give the shapes of the crescent moon and constellations. It painted eerie shadow patterns across the onyx and alabaster floor all around the circular room.

Statues of the gods stood evenly spaced all around the perimeter, as though silently bearing witness over the rite. Candles wavered and danced, encircling each statue and bathing them in wavering golden light.

Beautiful. Serene. Mysterious in a way that made the flames of my soul flicker and shudder. Everything about the place commanded a quiet reverence more deep and profound than any place I'd ever been.

But the chair drew all my focus.

Positioned in the very center of the room, a lavish chair of silver-inlaid wood crouched on clawed feet, its arms wide and mimicking the wings of a bird with engraved feathers set off with silver whorls. The black leather back and seat were stitched with millions of tiny marks in shining silver thread, all coalescing into the shape of a crescent moon with a sword straight through its center.

The same mark that would soon be inked into my skin.

I recognized the healer, Kaedan, in the same sweeping silver and green robes from my time in the infirmary. He stood alongside two temple priestesses, their heads bowed and hands clasped, and smiled as he motioned for me to come closer.

"Well, well. If it isn't my favorite troublesome patient. What an honor it is to be the one to give you your oathmark," he said with a smile, his eyes glinting with a mixture of mischief and approval. "Please, have a seat and get comfortable."

Roxus followed me to the chair, then handed off that fine silver goblet filled with water from the fountain to Kaedan. My heart pumped like mad as I sank into the soft leather seat, feeling it give slightly under my weight. I stared, struggling to control my breathing, as Roxus stepped back and assumed the same reverent pose as the two priestesses.

Kaedan swirled the water in the goblet, then turned to where he had a small rolling table already set up with a variety of tools.

Or, rather, torture devices.

That's how it looked from where I was sitting, anyway.

He had an array of needles in all different sizes, folded pieces of gauze, and fine, tiny blades so sharp they could split a hair down the center—all spread out on clean black velvet.

I let out a slow, shaking breath.

"Try to relax, Violet," Kaedan said with another gentle, knowing smile as he held the cup aloft, raising it over me and muttering a prayer in Avoran.

The words seemed to spill over me like the water pouring from that fountain, tumbling down and making every tiny hair on my body prickle. Then he handed the chalice off to one of the priestesses, took a small, slender blade from the table, and reached for my hand.

It took everything I had not to jerk away as he pricked the end of my finger and let three drops of my blood drip into the water. It swirled and spread like crimson smoke as he continued his prayer. Then he stopped, fixing me with an expectant look.

"Repeat after me, and take your oath. Walk among us. Bleed with us. Die with us. For ours is an eternal charge not to king, crown, or earth, but to the threads of the universe woven at the dawn of time. Accept our charge and assume the mantle of our sacred duty: to stand guard over the divine secrets entrusted to us, that they might not be lost to time or foul hands."

I repeated the oath, word for word, forcing my voice to stay steady. Sure. Resolved, even if Avoran was still a difficult language for me. I named each of the gods and begged their blessing. Their oversight. Their mercy.

Their acceptance of my blood.

My breath caught as the blood swirling in that clear, crystalline water slowly began to spin. It became darker and darker.

As black as ink.

Lowering the cup, he gave Roxus a confirming nod. "Her oath is accepted."

I could have sworn I saw Roxus's chest heave and his

shoulders drop, as though he'd been holding his breath this entire time. Wondering. Unsure.

After all, I had no idea if the gods even heard the prayers of the Viperi—a race made to spite and destroy them.

But today, apparently, they had.

"Have you chosen a location?" Kaedan asked without looking up as he carefully placed the goblet on the table.

I swallowed hard as I unbuckled my right vambrace and rolled up my sleeve past my elbow, then presented my arm. I motioned to the spot right below my elbow, on the inside of my upper forearm.

Kaedan nodded.

He showed me how to sit, relaxed with my elbow on the broad arm of the chair. He gave me a sip of strong wine that immediately made my head go warm and fuzzy. My whole body relaxed into the embrace of the chair, my gaze drawn up to the ceiling overhead. To the stars. To the stare of that silver glass moon.

And while I felt the sharp pain and burning discomfort as Kaedan marked me with the blessed ink forged from my blood, I didn't think about it. My thoughts roamed that night sky, wandering back to the halls of my father. To the cold bitter stone walls where he likely still sat, enshrined in ruins I was now sworn to defend.

And the irony made me smile.

He had been right all along. I had turned out to be quite the vicious little heretic. I'd defied him by escaping those halls and living. I'd defied the Tibrans by thwarting their mission to steal the Black Ledger. Now, I was defying every generation of my bloodline by oathing myself to the service of the very gods we had been created to war against.

It would not get easier. I knew that. My war with a world that despised me had only just begun. Fates only knew what new manner of trouble a rogue Viperi could stir up in an empire of blades.

And I was just getting started.

EPILOGUE

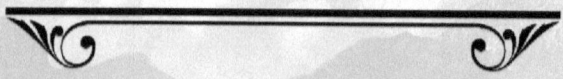

The smiling idiot was back—the tall, half-elven boy who'd been brought in from Esfolar as a new agent.

He had a name, probably. But I hadn't bothered to learn it. Not while he swaggered around every room in Arx Eburna like he owned it.

This time, he filled the sparring chamber with his flock of admirers, all pleading for a chance to talk with him. Some wanted to spar and train with him. Others, it seemed, just liked admiring him up close.

Yuck.

Not if he was the last breathing person on the planet.

Now that the trials were officially over, those of us who were new to the order were permitted to roam the grounds more freely. We could use the other sparring areas, which were much larger and provided finer materials than the one reserved for the prospects.

The dulled practice weapons were much more realistic in terms of weight and balance, and the obstacle courses were far more complex. Ropes hung from the ceiling for climbing, and weighted packs were stacked in a corner. You could put on one to simulate running or doing obstacles with a pack of gear.

That had been my focus for the past several days.

Endurance.

Strength.

Mine were comically poor, according to Declan. The jerk. He didn't mince words.

The only downside to the new training facility was the lack of decorum by everyone else who used it like a social parlor half the time. Or, at least they did now that we had so many new faces bobbing around.

Including *his*.

The half-elven young man had elected to do push-ups right in the middle of the room ... with only a sleeveless white linen tunic on. His deeply tanned skin, glistening with sweat and hard with lean muscle that showed through that thin fabric, had immediately drawn the eyes of every female with a pulse in the room—including mine.

Unfortunately, the rest of them didn't share my disgust.

Instead, they found excuses to move closer and closer to where he was working his way through some sort of training regimen. What kind, I couldn't tell. I'd yet to see him even pick up a weapon.

He pounded out sets of a hundred push-ups, veins standing out along his powerfully corded arms. I might have been impressed, if he hadn't paused at the end to flash a wide, roguish grin to his captive audience.

I curled my lip. Pathetic.

When he finally stopped, he sat back on the floor, laughing merrily with another young human man who had been following him around like a fly pursuing a dung wagon. A would-be lackey.

I slid them both a sideways glare as I prowled away from the obstacles, slinging the now sweaty weight pack off my shoulders and tossing it to a pile with the others. My shoulders ached, and my sweat-drenched hair stuck to my neck and forehead.

Gods, I needed a bath.

But not yet. I still had training to do. Declan had gone to the trouble of writing me out a full routine to continue growing my skills, and I didn't intend to waste a second.

When I turned back, I caught the half-elven boy staring straight at me. His keen eyes narrowed slightly in spite of the smile that still curved his lips. Blue eyes, too bright to be normal, studied me with the same intensity as an eagle surveying a mouse.

Interesting.

Good thing I wasn't a mouse.

I immediately looked away as I went to snatch a practice scimitar off the weaponry rack, giving it a few test swings before I started for one of the sparring circles. I'd work on refining my parries and balance, and then I'd—

"Need a partner?"

I froze.

Curse it all.

Turning slowly, I lifted my gaze to find the half-elven boy standing right behind me, hands on his hips and that coy, vulpine grin aimed right down at me. He, like almost everyone else, stood far taller, so that my head nearly came to his shoulder.

I had to wonder if that was why his grin widened as he tilted his head to the side slightly, waiting for me to answer.

I scowled. "No."

"You always practice alone," he pointed out. "Are you sure you wouldn't like an opponent for once?"

I glanced to the crowd of other young, fresh-faced agents standing around the room. Other dextrum, like me, eager to prove themselves. His many admirers.

They didn't even try to disguise their morbid curiosity and disgust at why he was talking to me—the pitathi. Oh, yes, I knew that look all too well.

"Do you know what I am?" I asked him outright. It wasn't a real question because, *of course,* he did. He'd been here a few weeks now and had undoubtedly seen me in passing. There was absolutely no possible way his many admirers hadn't filled him in on who I was and what had happened right before his arrival.

He blinked, probably doing what he thought was a good job of feigning shock. "I ... assumed you were also an agent of the Zenith's Call," he stammered at last.

Wow. What a performance.

Perhaps I should have clapped.

"Don't patronize me," I growled instead, swinging my scimitar in a blur over my hand. A demonstration. A threat. "I'm not something for you to toy with. There's plenty of other willing insects here for you to pick apart."

His brows went up, expression seeming genuinely blank in surprise for an instant.

"Not very friendly, are you?" he said, his tone deep, smooth, and faintly touched with an accent I couldn't place.

Not Damarian or Rienkan. Not Nar'Haleenan, either. Hmmm.

"Friendly is for healers and barmaids," I quipped and turned my back to him.

"It can also be convenient if you find yourself in need of help," he countered. "Everyone needs a friend sometimes."

The word stung at my heart, and I flinched.

Friend.

I bit down hard, hating the rising tide of pain that twisted around in my chest like a serpent. I'd tried that. I wouldn't make that mistake again—not here.

Here, I would keep my walls up and fully reinforced.

"Don't talk to me again," I warned and started walking away, suddenly finding another empty sparring circle on the *other* side of the sparring room much more attractive.

Fortunately, he didn't follow.

And I didn't dare look back to see if he was staring after me or not.

It didn't matter. He was *not* a friend.

I had Roxus, Declan, and Delthene. I didn't want or need anyone else.

I poured all my thought, all my focus, into running drills of parries and strikes. I worked until my body burned with exhaustion, every muscle quivering with fatigue. My head throbbed and sweat drizzled down the sides of my face and soaked through my clothes.

At last, I threw myself down on the floor in the middle of the circle and fought for breath.

Silence. My head—my stupid brain—was finally quiet.

"Impressive." Roxus's voice spoke over me so suddenly, I nearly fell backward.

He laughed as I sprang to my feet, my head burning with embarrassment. Gods, how long had he been standing there watching? Why hadn't he said anything?

"You're looking better," he said, tipping his chin to the scimitar in my hand. "Trying out something more substantial?"

"I need to build strength," I said. "Declan suggested using heavier weapons for training."

He nodded. "Very well, then. Come on. I don't know about you, but I'm ready for dinner."

I *almost* missed it.

The glint in his smile made me pause. I studied him, finally spotting the folded piece of parchment he was holding with a very specific silver wax seal on it.

Holy gods. That ... that was a mission signet, wasn't it?

Mistress Orvana only used those seals when she handed down official Zenith's Call orders!

"Have you read it?" I blurted, pointing to the paper in his hand as I chased him across the sparring room.

Roxus chuckled and waved it proudly. "No. I just received it. I figured I'd wait to open it until—"

"NO!" I hissed and tried to snatch it away, but he held it out of my reach. "Read it! It's a mission for us, isn't it? Open it! Right now!"

Roxus laughed, his shaggy hair sweeping his brow as he shook his head. "All right, all right. Calm down. It's probably something like a security escort. Nothing to get worked up about."

My pulse thrilled and I couldn't pry my eyes off him as he opened the seal and read the paper, his expression never betraying a thing.

Curse it—how could he not at least give me a hint? The tiniest smile or frown?

"Hmmm," he groaned cryptically.

Augh! I couldn't take this anymore.

I tried standing on my toes to peek over the edge of the letter. "What? What is it?"

"Ahh. Interesting. It indeed seems to be a mission for the two of us," he purred, putting a hand on top of my head and shoving me back down as I tried standing on my toes to read over his shoulder.

I growled at him, and he just laughed louder.

"Fine, fine, fine. Here." He surrendered and handed me the letter so I could read it myself.

I hurried along after him as Roxus sauntered away, reading the letter as fast as I could.

He wasn't lying!

It really was a mission request—our very first mission together.

"Looks like you've reason to polish and clean those daggers properly," he said as he pushed the sparring room door open with a shoulder and held it ajar for me.

I couldn't pry my nose away from the paper, though. Every line was delicious. A pure delight.

A purpose.

"Will it be dangerous?" I looked up, finally realizing what he'd said. "I've never been to Banaris." Gods, I'd never been to any of the other islands in Rienka. At least, not since I'd first arrived here, all those years ago.

He just shrugged and shuffled along beside me, hands buried deep in the pockets of that long brown coat. "Could be. Always better to be prepared."

A wild, probably manic-looking grin spread over my face as I practically skipped beside him. "And you're really letting me go along with you? This isn't a trick? You're not teasing me, are you?"

He better not be.

Roxus slid me a broad, knowing smirk that made his light brown eyes shine like fire-lit amber. "I wouldn't dream of it."

He totally would.

"Come on, my dear apprentice," he said, giving me a playful nudge with his elbow on our way out into the Eternal Hall. "The day is fleeting, and now we've got work to do."

And he was right. I had a purpose.

A path ahead, and a mission to accomplish.

I just had to survive it.

⟶⊹⟨⟩∗⟨⟨⟩⊹⟵

GLOSSARY
OF TERMS

ADIANA – Goddess (or godling, specifically) of the Moon. She is considered a young goddess and is highly revered by the Lunostri elves. Symbolized by the panther.

ARX EBURNA – A prominent stronghold of the Zenith's Call located on the island of Sol'Karr in the small kingdom of Rienka, where the Mistress of the Call resides.

AVORA – Once a powerful empire of divinely-touched elves that stretched over the majority of Reatia. Their beauty and magical power was considered unrivaled, and they were the children of Enais. They fell from power after the War of Falling Stars, and now has limited territory in the north that is strictly guarded from outsiders.

CLYSIROS – Goddess of Death. She is revered as the guardian over the realm of the dead, judge of souls, and the prison of stars. Symbolized by the jackal.

CURATOR – Zenith's Call agents who specialize in dealing with ancient artifacts and texts.

DAMARIA – A vast human kingdom that specializes in agriculture and mining of precious gems. It was once a part of Nar'Haleen, but was divided and developed into a separate kingdom at the behest of Emperor Tashaar to appease his twin sons who did not want to share the throne upon his death. Since that time, Damaria has been fiercely independent and refuses to merge with Nar'Haleen once again. This refusal sparked the War of the Stones, which saw Nar'Haleen mount massive military efforts and enlist several of the gods to try to reclaim the land.

DEXTRUM – Active Zenith's Call agents who are sent out on missions, usually with a combat threat. They must be skilled in all areas, but may choose a specialization that makes them better suited for certain missions.

ENAIS – Foregod of Present. Symbolized by a golden three-pointed star.

ETERNAL HALL – A specialized area of Arx Eburna reserved for training and testing new prospects for the Zenith's Call.

HOLVRADIX – A race of hardy, war-like elves from the north known for their immense stature and physical strength. They have long warred against the Avoran elves, and care little for the world beyond their icy homeland.
ITANUS – Foregod of Past. Symbolized by a right hand.

KRIN'MOIR – The main hall of Arx Eburna. It features a

large ancient fountain depicting the two Fates, or Viepol. The waters of this fountain are considered highly sacred.

LUNOSTRI – A race of elves from Nar'Haleen who roam the vast desert in nomadic tribes. They are considered fierce warriors and keepers of ancient religious rites and knowledge that predate the War of the Stones.

MAGISTER – A senior agent of the Zenith's Call with greater than twenty years of experience.

MILONTOS – Foregod of Future. Symbolized by a golden eye.

MISTRESS (OR MASTER) OF THE CALL – The elected leader of the Zenith's Call who makes all major decisions regarding the order. He or she rules with the help of a council of six elder magisters from strongholds throughout the world.

NAI'POL – A large joint-temple complex on the island of Sol'Karr that houses prominent priests and priestesses and is dedicated to the entire pantheon of Reatia.

NAR'HALEEN – A vast kingdom to the east that once spanned the entirety of the southern region and was rivaled only by the Avoran Empire. It was divided into two halves (Damaria and Nar'Haleen) by former Emperor Tashaar to appease his twin sons. It remains the prominent power in the south, boasting military might and a rich mining industry of precious metals, but continues seeking to regain its lost territories through brute force.

PALIGNO – God of Life. He is known as a benevolent but

mysterious god, who first seeded life upon Reatia and often referred to as the shepherd of the wild. Symbolized by the stag.

PATRON – Dextrum agents of the Zenith's Call who are actively training new recruits, referred to as prospects, and overseeing their education.

PITATHI – A slur word used to refer to Viperi. In Nar'Haleenan, it translates literally as "dirty snake."

PROLEUS – God of War. He is a stern but fair god who values justice, mental and physical fortitude, and honor. He is often referred to as the father of humankind. Symbolized by the wolf.

PROSPECTS – New recruits still going through their training and trials to join the Zenith's Call. These may be children or young adults, but seldom are older than eighteen years of age.

RAJINNA – An ancient humanoid race highly gifted in magic. They are said to have been the first children of the goddess Astaris, making them one of the five peoples first created by the gods. Their skin colors are diverse, but all have shared features of horns, fang-like incisors, and tails. Their lifespan is far longer than the average human, ranging between 1,000 to 3,000 years.

REATIA – The known world (see map at the beginning of this book).

RIENKA – A small, newly-formed kingdom that has declared its independence from Damaria. Ruled over by five merchant lords who call themselves the Trader's Guild, it is known for its many islands, rich trade ports, and vibrant tapestry of cultures from throughout the world.

Sivanth – A magical boundary wall created after the War of the Stones by the gods to separate the divine and mortal realms.

STEMMA – Ancient Avoran currency touched with magic. They are frequently used by the Zenith's Call as calling cards or identification markers.

SUROTRIX – The "Keeper of Whispers" that resides in the Vault of Whispers at Arx Eburna, overseeing the most volatile and secret archived documents and items for the Zenith's Call. This is considered a high honor that demands a lifetime of loyalty, and chosen candidates must have their tongues removed.

TANDEM – Pairs or partners of dextrum agents within the Zenith's Call that work side-by-side on missions.

UNDAE – Goddess of the Sea. Often referred to as the great mother, she is known for her changeable moods, love for adventurous souls, and beauty. Symbolized by the hippocampus.

URSINAAR – Bloodline of ancient Vordegan warriors who have the inborn magical ability to transform into a large bear. They are considered the most powerful and brutal of all Vordegan fighters.

VESCOR – God of the Void. Symbolized by a black spiral.

VIDRATHIAN STEEL – A prized and rare metal mined by

the dwarves of the Whitecrown Mountains and forged by the
Vordegans into weapons. The metal has the unique ability to
absorb magical energy, sparing the user from its effects if
wielded in the right way. Vordegan warriors train their entire
lives with these mystical weapons, learning to deflect or even
redirect magical assaults with them.

VIEPOL – A pair of powerful god-like beings said to embody
fragments of Avgior's shattered essence. They guard the
boundary of the Sivanth, judge the souls of the mortal world,
and take on the appearance of dragons. They are also known
as the Fates.

VINDEXORI – Agents of the Zenith's Call who specialize in
combat and are used as guardians or foot soldiers to protect
certain sites, temples, or artifacts.

VIPERI – The ill-regarded offspring of Vescor. They are an
ancient humanoid race that dwells in the caverns, cave systems,
and long-forgotten ruins of ancient cities far below the surface
world. They are vicious, highly skilled fighters and have no
love for anything outside their subterranean realm. They are
known to have pallid complexions, pale hair, red eyes, and
fang-like incisors.

VORDEGA – A small, isolated kingdom to the west that is
ruled by brutal, warlike tribes of humans said to be gifted at
thwarting magic. They were known as the most efficient forces
against the Avoran elves during the War of Falling Stars, but
rarely deal with other kingdoms.

WAR OF FALLING STARS – An ancient war between the
Avoran elves and the human kingdoms of Tibrus, Vordega,
and Nar'Haleen. As the Avoran Empire expanded across

Reatia, it absorbed and enslaved a great many other kingdoms, showing particular hatred and disgust for humans. The human kingdoms allied against them, resulting in a brutal conflict that lasted nearly 800 years. The human kingdoms managed to drive back the Avoran Empire in a costly victory that left both nations forever diminished and broken.

WAR OF THE STONES – An ancient war between Nar'Haleen and Damaria that became interwoven with the affairs of the gods thanks to Emperor Zarexius's blood pact with Vescor. Many of the gods chose sides, and the result was catastrophic. The war left the landscape eternally scarred, many races of peoples nearly extinct, and two of the gods themselves were destroyed. To see that no such war ever took place again, the gods all made a pact to seal their power behind a mystical barrier called the Sivanth. Their influence would be tempered through sacred stones with a mortal individual acting as their mouthpiece.

ZAREXIUS – Emperor of Damaria during the War of the Stones who made a deal with Vescor, the God of the Void. He is also known as the father of the Viperi, as he was given leadership over them after the fall of Vescor.

ZENITH'S CALL – A secret society of scholars, assassins, mercenaries, historians, and priests that formed after the War of the Stones. They are sworn to protect the secrets and artifacts of the gods and those who worship them.

A Special Thanks To ...

My wonderful husband, Keith, who continues to support me every day. You are my person, my always, my forever, my knight in shining armor. You are the person I can't wait to be standing beside for all our days to come. I love you with all my heart!

Samantha, Ashley, Juliana, and Kristin. I couldn't ask for better friends. Ya'll are my ride-or-die!

My OUTSTANDING Beta team!!! You guys continue to blow me away with your enthusiasm for these books. Thank you so much!

Jennifer E, Jennifer B, Julie R, Melanie M, and Shaila P — my rock since I first started this crazy journey. Thank you so much for being the hive mind of wisdom!

Philippians 4:13

BOOKS FROM
NICOLE CONWAY

MAD MAGIC
Mad Magic
Vicious Vows
Wicked Ways

SPIRITS OF CHAOS
Scales
Wings
Hearts

EMPIRE OF BLADES
Born of Shadow
Oath of Moonlight
Cage of Secrets
Curse of Thorns